Grant waited patiently to see if she would help him remove his boots. Eleanora tilted her head. "Did you forget to bring your bootjack? What a shame if you had to sleep in them."

"It was you I was thinking of. I'm a restless sleeper."

Fuming at his comment, she moved to the foot of the bed, and lifted his foot. It struck her as she held the boot in her hand that it was a fine weapon. A speculative gleam came into her eye.

"I wouldn't," he drawled, divining her temptation.

Eleanora nodded. "No, it's not nearly lethal enough."

He smiled and stretched hugely, raised his arms above his head. Lowering them, he began to unbutton his tunic.

Then he was behind her, his hands on her shoulders, drawing her back against him. His touch was firm, yet gentle on her warm flesh.

He kissed her deeply, and the lingering, spiced-wine freshness of bay rum invaded her senses. Unconsciously she moved closer. Awareness receded. Suddenly she felt that she was being consumed, losing herself in the overwhelming heat of his need. . . .

THE
NOTORIOUS
ANGEL

Patricia Maxwell

A FAWCETT GOLD MEDAL BOOK

Fawcett Publications, Inc., Greenwich, Connecticut

For Sue Lynn Anderson—
and for all other women
who have wished, even halfheartedly,
that something would happen.

THE NOTORIOUS ANGEL

ISBN 0–449–13825–9

Printed in the United States of America

10 9 8 7 6 5 4 3 2 1

PART ONE

One

The noise echoing under the colonnade of the French Market was deafening. Vendors cried their wares, children chased by harried nurses ran up and down the long length, horses and carriages clattered past along the cobbled street outside, women followed by basket-carrying servants called and laughed and bargained, parrots squawked from bamboo-cane cages, monkeys chattered; trussed geese hissed, ducks quacked and chickens cackled nervously, not without reason. New Orleans was in fine form, preparing for one of its greatest pleasures, the evening meal.

The chill wind of late November swirling through the arcade seemed not to bother the men and women who poked at the fishmonger's and butcher's stocks, smelled the pears for ripeness, or hefted pumpkins and potatoes for weight. But Eleanora Colette Villars shivered into her threadbare cloak, wishing for the warmth of the padding of a horsehair crinoline beneath her unfashionably narrow skirts. Standing was not warm work; still she could do nothing else. She could not afford to set her boardinghouse table with the best. It was necessary to wait until everything had been picked over and the merchants were tired of haggling. Then a piteous expression in her gold-flecked green eyes might bring her not only more value for her picayunes but an extra generous lagniappe.

"Mademoiselle! Mademoiselle Eleanora!"

At the sound of her name Eleanora turned to see a young man coming toward her. He held his silk top hat clapped firmly on his head, his black silk cravat was askew, and the full tails of his frockcoat flapped as he dodged around an Indian woman stolidly weaving baskets to sell. He kicked a pottery bowl, bowed, apologized, then came on, his face red.

The delicately molded lines of Eleanora's mouth tightened. Her chin lifted a fraction. The man was a friend

6

of her younger brother's, though she could not for the moment recall his name. Jean-Paul's friends came and went on the way to cock fights, gaming hells, and bear-baitings. Embarrassed by her unmarried state, the condition to which she had lowered the once-proud name of Villars, and their inability to help her, they seldom lingered in her bedraggled salon. She had learned to avoid the furtive admiration and hurtful pity hidden behind their air of dashing nonchalance.

As she realized how unusual it was for any of these young blades to allow themselves a show of agitation, pain closed around her heart. "What is it?" she called sharply. "Is anything wrong?"

"Forgive me if I startled you, mademoiselle," the dark-haired young blade said, snatching off his hat, thrusting his malacca under his arm, and inclining his upper body in a swift gesture of respect. "I've been looking for you everywhere. It is Jean-Paul—no, not hurt. He is at Bank's Arcade talking to one of Walker's agents. If someone doesn't stop him the addle-pated halfwit—beg pardon— is going to commit himself as a filibuster!"

Eleanora's relief that Jean-Paul was not lying dead in the sawdust of a barroom floor or on the dueling field beneath the moss-hung oaks outside the city, was short-lived. A filibuster. At eighteen, two years her junior, her brother was too young to be a soldier. It was the enthusiasm in the city for the exploits of William Walker in Central America, the fervent sympathy for the oppressed people of those countries, and the blazing advertisements in the news sheets for soldier-colonists that had turned him in that direction. How she despised these men who played on the emotions of sensitive boys, promising them fortune and adventure for their own gain.

"I've got to stop him," she said, almost to herself.

"My thought exactly. He'll listen to you. But we'll have to hurry before he puts his name to anything." The young man reached to take her shopping basket from her unresisting fingers. "Where is your maid?"

Despite herself Eleanora felt a faint flush rise to her cheekbones. "She is laid down upon her bed with a rheum.

7

I had to slip out of the house without her. This wind would have given her pneumonia."

He looked nonplussed, then with a movement of his shoulders, he set the basket down among the shallots in a nearby bin. "Never mind. Let us go."

Zébe, that was his given name, though she could not call him by that, of course. "It is good of you to be concerned, m'sieur."

He waited until a carriage rattled past before taking her elbow to help her across the street. "Must help old Jean-Paul. *Mon père* says the men who flock to Nicaragua just because Walker took a city like Granada are most likely to wind up before a firing squad. Jean-Paul don't have a father to set him straight."

No, nor a mother. Until two years before there had been their grand-mère Villars. Pampering Jean-Paul, indulging him as the perfect embodiment of a Creole gentleman such as her son had been, she had not been the best person to tell him how to go on. Still, they had been comfortable, she and Jean-Paul, entertaining all the usual expectations of young people of their class and family distinction in New Orleans. Then Grand-mère had died. It was discovered that they had been living for years on the rents brought in by a small property adjoining their house on Royal Street. Other relatives, in particular an uncle by marriage and his son, had demanded their rightful share of the succession, and the property had to be sold. The portion of the sale which fell to Eleanora and her brother was hardly enough to keep them six months.

Eleanora, with a marriage arranged by her grandmother before her, had thought a home for Jean-Paul securely in her grasp. Then, discovering there would be no *dot*, her fiancé had found it convenient to remember the mésalliance of her father with the daughter of a Scotch-Irish laborer. He made disparaging remarks about her family and her person, in particular the, to him, embarrassingly fiery brilliance of her red hair. He deplored her grandmother's lack of business acumen on every occasion, and hinted there was something unbalanced in her father, a gentleman, becoming a doctor and working among the degenerate and diseased immigrants from Erie living in shacks on the outskirts of the city. From somewhere he conceived the idea that her father's and mother's early demise from cholera, contracted during their work, was a judgment upon them for deserting their class. Long before the period of mourning for her grandmother was over, Eleanora had broken the engagement.

She had had reason to regret her temper since. It was not easy seeing boarders in the salon and the halls where once only family and invited guests entered. A brother-in-law might have been able to point out the error of his thinking to Jean-Paul. Now there was only herself to do so, and how could he be expected to listen to a sister who had become a drudge and an ill-tempered shrew?

Eleanora and Zébe passed a *vendeuse* in white apron and tignon crying hot, parched peanuts. Their rich smell lingered in the air, mingling with the smells of coffee coming from the open doors of the coffeehouses, and horse dung and sewage from open gutters that lined the streets. This sewage stench was more pervasive this afternoon since the gutters were being cleaned by a crew of convicts. Moving around the detail of men, chained wrist to ankle, and their armed guards, Eleanora averted her eyes. It was a gesture made not to avoid their degradation but to avoid adding to it by her recognition of their plight.

Bank's Arcade was located on Magazine Street near Gravier. A meeting place for business and professional men as well as filibusters, it boasted three stories, one of the longest bars in the city in its barroom, the most popular auction mart, and the only glass-roofed courtyard. Much of the plotting for the War for Texas Independence, the Mexican War, and Lopez's abortive filibuster expeditions into Cuba was done in its upstairs rooms. Mass meetings held in the auction room usually spilled over into the patio. Many a bargain had been struck and secret passed over the beer and whiskey-soaked tables in the barroom. Now, with this new rev-

9

olutionary spirit in the city, there was a constant stream of men in and out.

Eleanora could not enter. Only a certain class of woman could do so with impunity, and they were not welcome in this establishment devoted primarily to business.

"I won't be long." The young man known to his friends by the nickname Zébe frowned, pausing with one hand on the barroom door. "It's awkward for you without a maid, but you should be all right. If I might make a suggestion—your hair, it would be better to cover it."

In their hasty progress the hood of Eleanora's cloak had fallen back. The wind had disturbed the smoothness of her severe, center-parted style. Gold-red wisps had escaped from the plaited chignon low on her nape to curl about her temples. With a nod she accepted the advice, drawing her hood up and stepping back against the plastered brick wall.

The light was growing dimmer. Across the street the uppermost fronds of a banana tree, just visible over a courtyard wall, thrashed in the increasing wind. Dirt blew along the wooden banquette, or sidewalk, on which she stood, stinging her ankles as her skirts billowed about her. It looked like rain might set in, in which case more of her boarders would stay in to dinner. She would have to add to the rice pot.

Through the door as it opened and closed she caught snatches of conversation. Slavery, states' rights, secession. Men talked of little else these days. There seemed to be something in the air that encouraged strife. She did not understand the undercurrent of anger she heard everywhere, possibly because she had no time to concern herself with it. If slavery were abolished she would suffer no great loss. The Villars slaves had been sold to satisfy the succession laws and reimburse their other relatives so that she and Jean-Paul could keep the house on Royal Street. Their sole remaining slave was the woman who had nursed both their father and themselves. They loved her dearly, but her only value was as a *dueña* for Eleanora. She was too ancient, too weak to do more. In truth, she was an added responsibility on Eleanora's shoulders, another person to look after, another mouth to feed.

10

She straightened as Zébe left the barroom and strode toward her.

"I'm sorry, mademoiselle. I seem to have disturbed you for nothing. Jean-Paul refuses to see you."

"Refuses?"

"It touches on his pride, I think. There was no way I could speak privately to him, and he would not have those around him think he is at your beck and call."

"Tell him—tell him the matter is urgent. I need his advice."

"Your pardon, mademoiselle. It's more than my life's worth. Jean-Paul—he is not himself."

"You mean he is in his cups?"

"No, no. Only a trifle *piqué*."

Her dark, winged brows drew together in a frown, then she gave a nod. "I see. He threatened you."

"Jean-Paul has a good eye. I'd have no desire to face him on a dueling field even if he wasn't my friend."

"A churlish return for your efforts to help him, was it not?" She pushed her arms through the slits in her cloak and clasped her hands together. "I doubt he will offer me a challenge."

"You can't mean to go in there?"

"Can't I?" she asked, stepping past him.

"It might be best if you went home, as Jean-Paul said."

"Oh? You seem to have lost your zeal for saving my brother from himself very quickly."

"You don't understand—"

"Nor do you," Eleanora said, anger coloring her tone. "My brother may not be at my beck and call, but neither am I at his!"

The blue smoke of fine cigars draped the ceiling beams. It swirled and eddied about her as she made her way through the tables to a long trestle in the corner. Papers were spread out upon the mahogany surface. Scattered among them was an assortment of pewter steins, and shot glasses with a single drunken fly buzzing their contents.

Five men were at the table. One had been pointed out to her before as Walker's agent in New Orleans, Thomas Fisher. One was her brother. The others wore uniforms,

11

blood-red jackets trimmed in gold, white doeskin breeches, and black cavalry boots.

Eleanora expected them to rise at her approach. The lack of this token of respect, coupled with their cool appraisal, was disconcerting.

Jean-Paul made a movement, then was still as no one followed suit. His wavy brown hair was ruffled into soft curls, as if he had been running his hands through it. Annoyance increased the naturally high color on his cheeks and darkened his brown eyes to black. Under Eleanora's accusing stare defiance compressed his mouth into a thin line.

Fisher was a nondescript man made noticeable only by the fanatic light burning in the depths of his eyes. Beside him lounged one of Walker's men, a battle-scarred veteran with his left arm in a sling. In his right he held a glass of beer, which he used to push his campaign hat to the back of his head, the better to see. On his left, at the end, sat a sandy-haired, broad-shouldered man, his chair tipped back on two legs against the wall and a panatela glowing red-tipped between his fingers. The third soldier stood at the opposite end of the table with the flat of one hand resting upon it. Like the others, he was tall and wide of shoulder, but there was a different stamp to his features. With his copper-bronzed skin and straight black hair, Eleanora put him down as a mercenary of some foreign nationality. Her summation was hasty, but it seemed they were young to be carrying the epaulettes of such high rank on their shoulders.

"Forgive this intrusion—gentlemen," Eleanora said tightly, "but I crave a word with my brother outside."

"I have nothing to say," Jean-Paul muttered.

"I have a great deal, and I do not intend to go away until I have been heard, Jean-Paul."

When her brother looked away without answering, Fisher cleared his throat. "We were discussing a matter of business—"

"I know what business you were discussing." It was warm in the room. She threw back the hood of her cloak with an impatient movement of her head. The lamp, lit against the gathering gloom, slid over her hair with

12

the glint of bright flame as unexpected as a sulfur match struck in the darkness.

"Then it looks as though you must hold your brother excused until it is completed."

"I think not," she replied evenly, though her eyes flashed emerald green at the attempt to dismiss her. "Jean-Paul," she said, turning to her brother. "This is no way to repair our fortunes. You are not a soldier."

"I have faced the muzzles of guns on the field of honor!"

"Yes, boys of your own age and station who know the rules, who know there is to be a little pain, a little blood, but not much chance of killing or being killed. This will be different."

"I'm not a fool, Eleanora," he said with dignity.

"Then don't act like one! Think. What is it you hope to gain?"

"There is land to be had. Recruits are promised two hundred and fifty acres just for entering the country as a colonist. There will be more, much more, to be had once Walker has consolidated his position. Whole estates will change hands—"

"And they will be fought over by all the rest of the paid killers. What chance do you think you will have against the rogues, thieves, and murderers, the scum of the world that is flocking to Nicaragua?"

"Take care, Eleanora," her brother warned.

She flicked a glance around the table, scarcely seeing the stiff faces before her. "Why? It cannot matter to them what I think."

"It matters to me," Jean-Paul said quietly. "They are Falangistas, three of the fifty-six 'Immortals' who sailed with Walker in May of this year. They risked their lives to free the oppressed peons of Nicaragua in the name of democracy. I will not have them insulted."

"Democracy? For glory more likely, glory for themselves and William Walker!"

The man standing at the end of the table straightened to attention, his startlingly blue eyes hard in the darkness of his face. "Are your motives any less selfish?" he demanded. There was an edge in his voice, but the cadence,

13

the accent, was indisputably American. "Tell us why you are so determined to keep your brother tied to you. Maybe you see your security slipping away from you? Maybe you're afraid he'll discover he can do very well without you?"

Eleanora stared at the hard-bronzed soldier. "Sir—" she began, at a loss. His estimation was far off the truth, but she could not set him right without embarrassing her brother.

"Colonel—Colonel Farrell," he supplied, the name definitely not a foreign one.

"Colonel, you have no personal knowledge of my brother. He is not a soldier, his nature is far too sensitive."

"Soldiers are not born, they are made," he answered curtly, "as are men."

"Forged in the crucible of war?" She quoted the bit of rhetoric with irony. "First you must have the right metal."

Jean-Paul came to his feet, pushing his chair back so hard it bounced off the wall. "Enough. Give me the pen and paper. We will see if I am inferior metal!"

"I did not say inferior, Jean-Paul!" Eleanora protested, "Only too fine." He was not listening. He slashed his signature across the enlistment agreement in a splatter of ink and took up his beer stein.

Fisher picked up the page, waving it in the air to dry it. "Drinks around," he called, his smile as it rested on Eleanora unpleasant. "Drinks around for everybody!"

The impulse was too strong to deny. Eleanora reached out and snatched the paper from his hand.

Quickly as a striking snake her wrist was caught, imprisoned in a strong grip. Her breath trapped in a startled gasp, she stared into the blue eyes of the colonel, vibrant with anger, as he leaned across the table.

"The paper you hold belongs to the American Phalanx in Nicaragua. Drop it!"

The fingers biting into her arm were dark against the paleness of her skin. Their strength was cruel and utterly unrelenting. From the corner of her eye Eleanora saw her brother move uneasily, as though he would come to her aid despite his irritation with her. A glance at the

14

set bronze mask of the man who would be his superior deterred him.

Eleanora would not willingly capitulate, but it was not a question of will. Her hand grew numb, feeling left her fingertips. The foolscap slipped from her grasp, settling to the table, where Fisher pounced upon it.

"Someone should teach you not to meddle in the affairs of men," he said testily.

The moment she released the paper, the colonel dropped her wrist and stepped back, his gaze resting in a grim and derisive amusement on her white face.

Her wrist throbbed, her hand tingled, but Eleanora refused to allow them to see her discomfort. With a supreme effort she steadied her voice. "I have no interest in your warmongering or your search for glory. I was concerned only for my brother's welfare, something I considered very much my affair. It seems I was mistaken. I will bid you good day."

Blindly she turned away, making her way through the tables more by instinct than sight. She heard behind her the thud of chair legs hitting the floor but the sound held no meaning. A man with a silly grin on his face and a whiskey glass in his fist put out a hand to stop her. She brushed past him, her mind refusing to assimilate the crude suggestion he mouthed.

The door was her goal. Just as she reached it, it swung open and a man entered in a rush of wind-driven rain.

They collided, and for an instant she was swung off her feet, held tightly to a red uniform jacket. At the flash of that hated color, she pushed violently against the embrace, which automatically tightened.

"Ah, what have we here? A small, flame-haired *puta,* one of the devil's favorite handmaidens, of a certainty."

The lilt of the Spanish was softly Castilian. The face, dark and mustachioed, was alight with exultant laughter.

"No—" Eleanora began.

A voice, cutting despite its drawl, came firm behind her.

"I hate to blight your hopes, Luis, but the woman in your arms is, despite appearances, a lady."

15

"Es verdad?" the Spaniard asked, one brow lifted as he gazed down at her.

Eleanora nodded. Instantly she was released.

"My most humble apologies—and regrets." His bow was a model of grace despite the guitar slung across his back. "An introduction is permitted?"

As he spoke he looked beyond Eleanora. Turning, she recognized the sandy-haired giant who had been sitting against the wall. His insignia was not like that of Colonel Farrell.

"There is no need to apply to me," the man said. "I have not the pleasure of the lady's acquaintance."

"I find your attitude bewildering then, Major. Who appointed you the lady's protector?"

The undercurrent of friction did not escape Eleanora's notice. These men might both wear the same uniform but they were not friends.

"I find myself in sympathy with all who run afoul of the temper of Colonel Farrell."

"Especially if they are female, eh?"

"Please," Eleanora said. "Let me pass."

"You will be soaked if you go out there," the major objected. "Perhaps you would care to wait in the courtyard. The glass roof leaks like a sieve but it should be an improvement over the streets."

"Thank you, no."

"Then permit me to offer you my escort."

"I—couldn't—"

"Because I am a stranger? Major Neville Crawford, at your service, mademoiselle."

"And I, Lieutenant Colonel Luis Andres Charles Emmanuel de Laredo y Pacquero."

"You are most kind," Eleanora said, her hands clasped tightly before her, "however—"

"You cannot go alone," the Spaniard insisted.

From vagueness Eleanora's senses sharpened to a painful perception. There were spatters of rain like dark blood on the red jacket of the lieutenant colonel. The lamp nearest them flared in the wind from the open door. In the humid atmosphere the reek of spirits was

16

strong. At the trestle table in the corner there was a shift of men as the colonel started toward them.

Panic scoured Eleanora's mind. "You—you must excuse me," she said in a parody of good manners, and slipped past the Spaniard out the door.

Cold rain directly in her face took her breath. She could not go back, however. Ducking her head, she hurried along the banquette already slick and shining with wet. She could hear someone calling after her, but she paid no heed. Only the dark form of a carriage looming up beside her caught her attention.

"Mademoiselle Eleanora!"

It was Zébe, holding the door of a hired hackney wide. "Get in. Get in, quickly."

The carriage lurched away down the street, sending geysers spouting as its wheels spun through the gathering puddles. Eleanora leaned back on the dingy upholstery. Taking a deep breath, she forced herself to calm. It was good to be away. She did not care if she never saw that place where she had been so humiliated and insulted again. Her life in the past years had been far from easy. Still, never had she been treated in such a manner. And, as bad as it had been, why did she have the feeling that she had escaped lightly, that it could have been far worse?

"You were too late?" Zébe said at last.

"I—yes. Jean-Paul has signed." How could she explain what had happened when she wished above all to stop thinking of it?

"No doubt he—wished to celebrate?"

Eleanora inclined her head in a weary nod.

"Under no circumstances would I have let you enter that place alone if I had not been certain that Jean-Paul would feel himself obliged to escort you from the premises himself at once. I feel I have failed you."

"Jean-Paul was not pleased to see me. There is no harm done. Let us forget it."

"But your good name? What of that?"

"It scarcely matters, though it is good of you to be concerned."

17

"If I may be allowed to make reparation—"

"You are not going to do anything foolish such as make me an offer, are you?" Eleanora asked, striving for a light note to relieve the gloom.

"I would be most honored—"

"No, no, really, m'sieur. I spoke in jest only. Forgive me if I sounded facetious, I did not mean to be. All I want is to return home and try to think what I am to do. Believe me, you owe me nothing."

Nor, it seemed, did Jean-Paul; not even loyalty.

It was a great pity that she could not think well of the dead, but Eleanora placed her brother's defection squarely at her grandmother's door. The three years they had lived with her had been more than enough to spoil his character. Their father's mother—she had cosseted Jean-Paul, indulging his every whim. He was her husband and her son come back to life, especially the latter, and there was no red-haired Irish woman sprung from the world of work gangs, shanties, filth, and disease to wrest his love from her this time. At thirteen Jean-Paul was impressionable. He had accepted his grand-mère's evaluation of his own worth and the overweening importance of his desires. Sometimes it troubled him to see his sister pushed into the background, ignored because she reminded the old woman of the daughter-in-law she had despised, and because she did not fit the image of raven-haired beauty then in vogue. To have the taint of Irish blood, only a little more acceptable than a touch of café au lait, was bad enough; to look it was a disgrace. Jean-Paul was too young, at first, to make his displeasure felt, and with time the discrimination ceased to be remarkable.

Not that Eleanora was mistreated; far from it. She was fed and clothed and, at the proper time, introduced to society with due ceremony at the St. Charles theatre. Grand-mère would have scorned to allow New Orleans to see that she considered her granddaughter in the light of a penance upon her old age. Still, Eleanora felt it, and learned early to depend upon her own devices.

It was natural for her brother to be more affected by the death of the old woman. There was not only a vast

18

change in his style of living, there was no longer anyone to bolster his ego or approve his every action. He could not quite reconcile himself to giving up the image of himself given to him by his grandmother, that of a fêted young rake, welcome wherever he chose to go because of his birth and position. He loved his sister, but her warnings and strictures carried no weight with him. He obeyed no will other than his own.

Dinner was late. Because the roux was not simmered long enough the gumbo was thin. There had been no time to heat the bread, and the custard did not set properly. These defects were pointed out in minute detail by the pair of maiden aunts who hired the bedchamber which had been used by her mother and father in happier years. The retired army captain from Kentucky, a veteran of the Seminole Indian War, made no complaint, eating everything set before him. He slept downstairs in the room which had been her father's surgery because of difficulty negotiating the stairs with his wooden leg. He never complained of it either.

In order to head off the recitation of the unfailing success of the aunt's various methods with custards, Eleanora turned the conversation to William Walker.

"Knew the man well," the captain said, leaning back in his chair. "One of those damned—forgive me, ladies—liberals. Never quite came out antislavery in his paper, the *New Orleans Crescent*, but had some hard words to say about it. 'Twas a much better doctor than he was a newspaper editor, in my opinion. Looked at this leg—forgive me, ladies, appendage—of mine once, seven or eight years ago. Gave me a salve for the—ahem, well, we won't go into that, not at the dinner table. Odd little man. Remember he went around summer and winter in a black hat and overcoat. Constant mourning for his sweetheart, some said, a New Orleans beauty who died of yellow fever. You remember him, don't you, Miss Eleanora? He used to drop in on your father right there in that room of mine. They both studied at some university in Germany, had a lot in common. I used to see you in there helping your father before he died. Just a little thing you were, but not afraid of blood or hard work, no, sir, not like a lot of these

19

fine ladies you see today. Why, I bet you teethed on a mortar and pestle!"

The captain's conversation had a tendency to be colorful and rambling, but he had spent most of the last twenty years since he lost his leg sitting about the city, watching people go by. He had a son with political ambitions back East who had married into the Tidewater gentry in Virginia. The son sent him a monthly stipend to live on but never a steamboat ticket. In the last years of her grandmother's life the captain had been an admirer of hers in a gallant, unassuming fashion.

"I seem to remember a man like that, though he couldn't have been much older than I am now."

"Twenty-three, twenty-four."

"That would make him barely over thirty now."

"It takes a young man to have the nerve to set out to conquer the world—and old men to stop him."

"What do you think of his campaign in Central America?"

"All this big talk about relieving the downtrodden and establishing democracy? I've been around long enough to be suspicious as H-Hades—beg pardon, ladies—when men start such talk. There's always money involved somewhere, you mark my word. War and money go together."

If Jean-Paul had been present at the dinner table that statement would, doubtless, not have gone unchallenged. He was not. It was long after their elderly boarders had straggled off to bed that he put in an appearance.

Eleanora sat in the salon, trying to concentrate on a piece of Berlin work by the light of a single candle, when he let himself into the house. He strolled into the room where she was, sailed his top hat onto the settee and dropped down into the chair across the table from her.

Eleanora did not greet him. A long silence descended, punctuated by the soft rasp of her needle moving in and out of her canvas.

He ventured, "I see you returned safely."

"Yes."

"If you had not it would have been your own fault. You should never have come."

Eleanora did not answer.

20

Jean-Paul picked at a spot of mud on his breeches with his thumbnail. "Oh, very well. I know I should have looked after you. I'm sorry. But you know it was a stupid thing to have done, coming into the Arcade barroom—let alone without a chaperone. You must admit that?"

"Freely."

"I hope you don't intend to go on in that way while I'm gone."

"I see little likelihood of it," she said, looking up to meet his gaze squarely. They both knew she had done so only out of concern for him.

"Yes. Well, I'm sure Cousin Bernard and Uncle Narciso will take better care of you."

Eleanora's needle was still. "Cousin Bernard?"

"You must have realized you couldn't stay on here alone. Cousin Bernard has kindly repeated the offer to have you make your home with him that he made when Grand-mère died. And so you need not feel that you impose. You can make yourself useful in the nursery he and his rich wife will be setting up any day now."

"You—must have been busy since I left you to have made these arrangements for me."

"I do have some sense of responsibility," he said, his deep brown eyes not quite meeting hers.

"I fear you have put yourself to a deal of needless trouble. I have no intention of leaving this house."

"No, and you won't have to. Cousin Bernard—and everyone—will be coming here."

Eleanora got to her feet abruptly, the Berlin work falling unheeded to the floor. "What have you done?"

"Don't upset yourself, Eleanora. There was no other way. I could not pass up such an opportunity."

In his harassment he ran his hand over his hair, a gesture that reminded Eleanora poignantly of their father. Looking away, she demanded, "Tell me."

"The estates of the *hidalgos* are being confiscated. Some have been given to the Immortals. Others are available for purchase, but at much less than their worth since Walker needs money. For the price of this house I can buy a *finca* of more than a thousand acres. We will be land-owners again, and from the land comes wealth!"

"You sold the house?"

"You know Cousin Bernard has always wanted it."

"You sold it, without discussing it, without asking me what my wishes were—"

"I am a man. It is my place to make these decisions."

"But it is my life you are deciding too. Doesn't that matter?"

"You will be much better off with Bernard. You will have a place in society again. You won't have to work so hard. He has servants—"

"And I will be one of them! You are a fool, Jean-Paul, if you think it is that easy to regain the ground lost when we decided to take in borders."

"Then if you feel like that, why did you ever do it? Why didn't you just go to Uncle Narciso and Bernard in the beginning?"

"If you will recall, it had something to do with your dislike for the prospect of becoming a scribe on a stool in the office of Cousin Bernard's shipping company."

The sudden silence told her Jean-Paul remembered. Carefully she went on. "I'm not saying I regret not going to Bernard. What I am saying is, I don't want to go now. It would make all the work, the—the sacrifice, if you will, worthless."

Turning away, she walked to the table at the end of the settee. Automatically her hands went out to straighten the bouquet of ribbon-trimmed palmetto fans standing in a vase upon it. Jean-Paul, leaving his chair, came to stand beside her. "It won't be for long, just until the government has stabilized in Nicaragua. Then I will be able to leave the army and concentrate on making the estate pay. When it is ready I will send for you. We'll be a family again. Please, Eleanora. This wasn't an easy decision. Don't make it more difficult for me."

A brittle laugh was forced from her throat. "No, of course not. Your peace of mind is the first consideration. Never mind my comfort, my convenience."

"Sarcasm will not help, let me tell you," he told her, his own temper flashing up like powder in a pan. "I have the money here, in my pocket. It is all arranged. I have only to turn the money over to the land agent in the morning.

He sails next day, the twenty-sixth, on the *Prometheus*. By the time I arrive three weeks later he will be ready to present the deed on the property he has purchased."

"Where did you meet this land agent? What guarantee have you that he is who and what he says he is?"

"Must you question everything? Don't you have any respect for my judgment?"

A truthful answer would not do. Or would it?

"Trust?" she said softly. "Shall I prove my trust, Jean-Paul?"

A wary look invaded his features with their vulnerable look of youth. "What do you mean?"

"This money, you meant to use a portion of it to reach Nicaragua?"

"The fare has been lowered substantially by the steamship line for Walker's colonist—but yes, I suppose my expenses will have to come from the proceeds of the sale."

"And as your sister, half of it is mine since we inherited jointly?"

"Legally, yes, but as head of the household—"

"Never mind. I believe it only fair that my fare be paid from it also."

"Your fare? Where are you going?"

"To Nicaragua. Where else?"

Two

The ocean steamer *Daniel Webster* left New Orleans on December 11, 1855. Under a fitful sun she steamed slowly down the Mississippi and out into the Gulf.

Eleanora stood at the rail, watching as the water turned from a muddy brown to a deep, saltwater blue. The wind was fresh, only slightly tainted with the smell of coal smoke from the huge smokestack forward. She faced into it, consciously putting New Orleans and everything known and familiar behind her. She had not watched the city out of sight, though not out of any sense of pain. It was just that she had no time for regret or self-pity. She had spent the hours putting away her things in her cabin and making herself familiar with her cabin and the ship.

As a "colonist" for Nicaragua Jean-Paul could have traveled steerage for only twenty dollars, while her fare would have been no more than fifty. First-class cabin passage was a hundred and seventy-five dollars, second class a hundred and twenty-five. After due consideration it had seemed best to pay for better accommodation. In steerage there would be no outside light or air, no privacy, no segregation of the sexes. For over two hundred people, sleeping, eating, relaxing would all have to be accomplished in one large room. The berths, built in tiers of three, three berths wide, were without curtains, without bedding. Passengers provided their own. They also provided their eating utensils. To be served, they were expected to line up at the galley door, after the first- and second-class passengers had finished, naturally.

Second class was better. Cabins in this section held no more than fifty, the sleeping cubicles were curtained, and passengers had the privilege of the dining saloon. Jean-Paul reserved space for himself in this section, but such a thing was not possible for Eleanora. Ordinarily second-class cabins were divided along sex lines, but at this time they were given over entirely to men. Because of the recent fighting in Nicaragua few women were willing to travel either to that country or across it, along the transit route to California. Those who decided to brave it were, for the most part, traveling first class with their husbands so they need not be separated. A first-class ticket had to be purchased for Eleanora.

In this class the stateroom doors opened directly out of the dining saloon, providing cross ventilation with the porthole, an important point as they steamed southward into warmer weather. The floors were carpeted, a mirror and washstand, water bottle and glasses were provided. In Eleanora's cabin there were two curtained berths with space beneath for storing luggage. She had met her cabin-mate briefly though they had exchanged nothing beyond a civil greeting. They might have managed more if Eleanora had not been so taken aback by the woman's traveling costume

24

of gold velvet the exact shade of her elaborately dressed hair. The skirt had been supported by a hoop so large it seemed to fill the cabin. Epaulettes dripping gold fringe had decked the shoulders, and military buttons had fastened her corsage—up to a point. A deep vee had been left open, exposing the soft, white curves of her breasts. On her head she wore a milliner's version of a compaign hat in gold felt with one side pinned to the crown by a diamond-studded hatpin and the brim edged with gold fringe. Her name she gave as Mazie Brentwood. It seemed, in a way Eleanora could not quite comprehend, to fit her.

"Hello!"

At the hail Eleanora turned to see her cabin-mate making her way toward her against the wind. Her skirts were fluttering like sheets on a clothesline, exposing without hindrance a generous froth of lace-edged petticoats and a pair of nicely turned ankles as high as the calf.

With one hand the woman clung to her hat while she grabbed for the rail with the other. "I begin to see why most of the passengers are congregated in the dining saloon," she said by way of a greeting.

"The breeze is a bit stiff," Eleanora agreed, firmly suppressing a smile at the sight of the destruction of such expensive elegance. She had no cause to worry. Her gown, far from new, was a serviceable broadcloth in fawn with blue piping. Her bonnet was of straw with blue ribbons which she had tied together and looped over her arm rather than have the wind take it off her head.

"You seem to have found the best spot on the ship. The starboard side is wet with spray from the paddlewheel, and at the bow in front of the deckhouse the ship's officers are constantly tripping over you."

"Join me then, by all means," Eleanora invited.

Mazie Brentwood directed a shrewd look at her from tip-tilted hazel eyes. "You are sure you don't mind?"

"Not at all. Why should I?"

The smile that moved across her wide mouth was wry. "You don't look like a complete innocent."

"I—beg your pardon?"

"You are obliged to share a cabin with me because we are the only two unattached women on the ship. You are not obliged to be seen in public with me. And if that is not a sufficient hint I will tell you, before someone else does, that women who dress in the restrained fashion you represent seldom associate with women of my—profession."

There was no anger, no belligerence in Mazie Brentwood's voice, only a dispassionate statement of fact. That, more than anything else, helped to subdue Eleanora's flush of embarrassment. There was little doubt in her mind of Mazie's meaning. The two old maids who had lived upstairs had had a passion for scandal and were often forgetful of her comparative inexperience. In addition, sight of the women known as "ladies of the night" was not too uncommon along the poorly lighted thoroughfares of New Orleans after dark. They had not appeared to be in quite the same style as Mazie; still by all the rules she had been taught, she should have turned on her heelless kid slipper and walked away. That she didn't had something to do with the upheaval of her life. Nothing seemed to matter as much as it once had.

Lifting her chin she said, "Why, I wonder?"

"We are thought to spread corruption and immorality."

"For the sake of my character then? I don't believe I am so easily influenced. And if for the sake of my good name, I have little to protect."

"That sounds interesting. I warn you, I am insatiably curious."

A slow smile lit the gold flecks in the depths of Eleanora's green eyes. "So am I," she replied.

They watched a whirl of sea gulls give up following the ship and head back toward land. The green and brown shoreline receded at a slow but steady pace. The blue smoke hovering above Balize at the mouth of the river became no more than a smudge on the horizon. Beneath their feet the movement of the deck was a novel sensation. From their place at the rail they could see the spreading foam of their progress, hear the rush of the waves as they cut through the water. The churning waterfall sound of the paddlewheel came from behind them, a pervasive noise that, after a time, they ceased to notice. They carried no sail on the masts that towered fore and aft, but the wind hummed through the rigging and snapped the banners that flew from the top-mast spars, and the stars and stripes displayed at the stern.

Mazie, tiring of holding her hat, unpinned it and tucked it under her arm. The wind immediately began to tear at her elaborate mass of gold waves and curls, but she ignored it. "So," she said, turning to Eleanora. "Why are you on the *Daniel Webster?*"

"My brother signed on as a colonist with William Walker. We have arranged to purchase an estate also, and I am going to see after it until Jean-Paul has honored his commitment."

The other woman waited a fraction too long to comment.

"What is it?" Eleanora asked, all her misgivings reviving to sharpen her voice.

Mazie shook her head. "I wish you luck. The *aristocráticos* around Granada haven't held onto their estates nearly three hundred years by giving up easily."

"You sound as if you have some knowledge of the situation."

"This will be my third crossing along the transit line. I went to California in '53 and only returned to settle a matter of business last spring. There isn't much to do on these trips except talk. You can learn a lot, if you have a knack for listening to men."

"You have seen Nicaragua? This is marvelous. You can tell me all about it."

"What do you want to know?"

"Everything!" Eleanora said, smiling.

"To begin with, it's hot, tropical in fact. A big part of the country is covered in jungle. There are also mountains, however, and volcanoes, and a pair of large lakes."

"What is this, a geography lesson?"

The voice was lazy, and tantalizingly familiar. Even before she turned, Eleanora remembered the tall blond man who strolled up to them, and, taking his welcome for granted, stopped to lean with one elbow on the railing.

"Neville!" Mazie greeted him. "Neville Crawford, you scoundrel, I didn't know you were aboard."

"A man would have to be blind to miss you, Mazie," he answered, his smile quizzical.

"Flatterer. Let me make you known to my cabin-mate, Eleanora Villars. Eleanora—"

"We have met. I almost didn't recognize you out of uniform, Major Crawford."

"I am crushed, mademoiselle. I knew you at once. One remembers ladies who remain elusive."

"I resent the implication," Mazie said in mock affront, but her eyes, as she glanced from one to the other, held a question.

"My apologies. Your charm, of course, is your openness, Mazie."

"Not, I hope, my only one?"

"Stop angling for compliments you don't need, and tell me why you are here."

"I had a notion to see if some of the money changing hands in Nicaragua could not be diverted to mine. But what is this about a uniform? Surely you haven't succumbed to the trappings of war?"

"My reasons, my dear, are every bit as mercenary as yours. In addition I find the uniform has a beneficial effect on females."

"A hired killer, Neville? That doesn't sound like you either."

"Thank you, Mazie. I'm glad I have some character left in your eyes. Tell me, mademoiselle, how is your brother?"

"Well enough. He is aboard also."

The major heaved a sigh. "I was afraid of that."

"Eleanora was asking about Nicaragua. Perhaps you would like to instruct her?"

"Very much," he agreed, a light glowing brightly for an instant in his eyes the pale blue of a robin's egg.

"I meant concerning the countryside," Mazie admonished.

An expression of suitable gravity descended over his face. "Oh, the countryside. Well. We land at San Juan del Norte, the first stop on the Atlantic side of the transit line."

"You will think me ignorant, but I don't fully understand what you are talking about when you mention the transit," Eleanora interrupted.

28

"No? The Accessory Transit Company was begun five years ago by the millionaire, Cornelius Vanderbilt. The idea was to take advantage of the California gold rush; half the world was anxious to get to California by the quickest route possible. There was already a passage through Panama, but Vanderbilt figured to put it out of business by saving prospective passengers better than seven hundred miles of travel using the natural waterways of Nicaragua to cut across to the Pacific. The route laid out by Vanderbilt begins at Point Arenas, where passengers begin their journey up the San Juan River to San Carlos at the entrance to Lake Nicaragua. There they take a lake steamer to Virgin Bay. Then a twelve-mile carriage ride brings them to San Juan del Sur on the Pacific coast, where they connect with a ship bound for San Francisco."

"This route is still open, despite the war?" Eleanora inquired.

"It was when I left for New Orleans."

"When I first went over the route, transport overland from Virgin's Bay to San Juan del Sur was by mule," Mazie said. "It was the rainy season and the mud was belly deep. How I made it I'll never know. Nor will I ever forget it!"

"You probably had to walk around the river rapids at Machuca, Castillo Viejo, and El Toro, too. The new steamers make the trip over the rapids during the wet. If we're lucky we can arrive in comfort at Granada."

"I believe that is Walker's headquarters."

"That's right."

"Is it a large town?" Eleanora persevered.

"Not large, about ten thousand people, but important. Until we captured it two months ago it was the stronghold of the landed gentry, the Legitimistas, as the conservative party is known."

"The rich are always conservative," Mazie commented. "The haves are always anxious to keep things as they are, to prevent the have-nots from crowding in. I take it William Walker is allied with the have-nots in this instance?"

"The Democráticos, yes. So far he's done a fair job of

29

parceling out the wealth, though not as thorough as some would like."

"Then there is some left, that's what I wanted to hear." Mazie's tone was enthusiastic.

"If you were half as greedy as you pretend," Major Crawford teased, "you would be a rich woman in your own right."

"Who says I'm not?"

"You wouldn't be here if you were."

"Don't you know there is no such thing as enough money?"

"You and Vanderbilt would make a good pair."

Mazie touched a beautifully shaped nail to her lips. "You think so? That idea will require some thought. I understood, however, that Commodore Vanderbilt resigned as head of the Accessory Transit Company. That, because of stock manipulation and in-fighting among the directors, he has set himself up in competition by establishing a new line, the Independent Opposition Line using the Panama route."

Slowly the major shook his head. "You always leave me wondering about your sources of information, Mazie."

"So long as that isn't all you wonder about."

The provocative answer. Watching her, Eleanora thought the response was automatic, having little to do with what the other woman was actually thinking. Clearing her throat a little, she said, "Walker must consider himself securely in command at Granada to send so many of his officers out recruiting."

"Recruiting—you mean at the Arcade? It was Fisher doing the recruiting. Colonel Farrell was there to arrange for the cost of transporting them. Colonel Henry was recuperating from battle wounds and had nothing better to do. Luis—Lieutenant Colonel Laredo—and I were along for the spree. Farrell and Henry returned two weeks ago on the *Prometheus*."

"And the lieutenant colonel?"

"I hoped you wouldn't ask. He's below in his berth as drunk as a *conde*. Ever so often he tries to pickle the past in alcohol. He succeeds to a point, like preserving a corpse in brandy, or so he says. But then, like the corpse, he must carry it with him until he finds the proper place of burial."

Mazie shuddered. "What a charming fellow this Luis must be."

"Most of the time," the major agreed. "At others he is hopelessly Spanish."

"His right, surely," Eleanora protested. "Nicaragua is a Spanish country."

"Spanish speaking. Officially it is the República de Nicaragua, and those who live there are, of course, Nicaraguan—including your brother now, and Luis also, though he was born in the Guadalquivir Valley of Andalusia, near Córdoba, Spain. If you will take my advice though, you won't ask him about it unless he's drunk."

Major Crawford broke off, his attention going beyond Mazie's shoulder. Following his gaze Eleanora saw Jean-Paul rounding the corner of the deckhouse from the stern. A frown drew his thick brows together and his eyes were narrowed, though that might have been the effect of the coal smoke swirling around him in a sudden down draft.

"Could I speak to you, Eleanora?" he said as he approached.

"Certainly, but first let me present my friends."

His bow was perfunctory, his face did not relax into the slightest vestige of a smile as he acknowledged the introductions. Taking Eleanora's elbow he said, "I'm sure you will excuse my sister?"

"By all means," Mazie replied, her eyes bright. "Don't let us keep you from what is obviously a grave matter."

Color stained Jean-Paul's cheeks but he inclined his head. Without another word he led Eleanora away, moving so swiftly that she had to lengthen her stride to prevent it appearing that she was being dragged.

The long length of the dining saloon held only a pair of domino players and a man reading one of the pile of newspapers before him. The smell of cooking wafted from the galley, though the dinner bell was not due to ring for some time. In a deserted corner of the dining saloon, Jean-Paul pulled out a chair for her. Holding her full skirts with both hands so she could slip into it, Eleanora demanded, "What is it? What is wrong?"

31

Her brother seated himself across from her. "Have you any idea what kind of woman you were chortling with out there as if you were bosom companions?"

Eleanora, smoothing her hair, went still. "I feel sure you are going to tell me."

"She is not a suitable acquaintance for you."

"No? I found her amusing."

"Did you indeed," he said grimly. "*Mon Dieu*, Eleanora. I gave you credit for more discernment. She is little better than a streetwalker. Let me tell you—"

"No! Let me tell you, younger brother. I am well aware of who and what Mazie Brentwood is; she told me herself. But at this particular juncture I scarcely see that it matters. Moreover, no one, Jean-Paul, gave you the right to choose my friends or to embarrass me in front of them."

"It is my responsibility as the man of the family."

"It has taken you long enough to come to it, then."

It was dim in the dining saloon. The only illumination came from skylights set into the deckhouse above. Even so, she could see the blood receding from her brother's face. It was a moment before he could speak, then his voice was quieter, more reasonable.

"Don't you realize where friends like that woman can lead? Right or wrong, we are judged by the company we keep. Nicaragua may not be New Orleans, but it is a civilized country and the conventions still stand."

"I am more than a little weary of the conventions."

"Nevertheless—"

"Besides, who am I to talk to? The few other women on this ship are preoccupied with their husbands, their fears, and with how they will live when they get to California—those who are not too seasick already to care. I'm sure you wouldn't approve of me talking to strange men—"

"You can talk to me."

"Yes. Where have you been for the last hours? In the deckhouse having a drink and a game of cards with the officers in their quarters, and spying out the windows! You see, I am not quite as ignorant as you imagine."

Quarreling. Again. It seemed that was all they had

done since that afternoon at Bank's Arcade. When Jean-Paul had been convinced, after bitter disagreement, that she intended to come he had argued that she ought to wait at least a month until he had looked over the situation and made arrangements for her. A month with the condescension of Cousin Bernard was not to be borne. Too, she was afraid there would be excuse after excuse to delay her until she gave up her determination to go. They had quarreled over the necessity of asking their lodgers to move. Jean-Paul was for the clean-cut, she for a more gradual transition after she had found other places for them where she knew they would be comfortable. Since all the trouble would be hers, she had won that set-to. She had not fared so well over the baggage they would carry. Two trunks plus a Gladstone bag for Jean-Paul contained all their belongings. Many small things, heirlooms, mementos, had to be left behind in the dubious care of Uncle Narciso and Cousin Bernard and the supercilious creature who was his wife.

On the table before her was a much-thumbed copy of *El Nicaraguense*. Several weeks old, the lead story told of the death by firing squad of one Mateo Mayorga on the orders of William Walker. An elderly man, his only crime seemed to have been that he was an aristocrat. Looking away, Eleanora felt the vibration of tension along her nerves. What were they getting into? What were they doing? It was this uncertainty which caused her temper to flare. Perhaps it was the same with Jean-Paul.

Her brother reached out, touching her hand where it lay on the table. "I don't think you are ignorant, only inexperienced, which is as it should be, ordinarily. It's just that I worry about you. If anything unpleasant— happens to you it will be my fault."

"I would never blame you," she answered, touched by the concern in his soft brown eyes.

"But I would blame myself."

They reached the dark green coastline that curved into the Bay of San Juan de Nicaragua in a streaming rain. The group of transit company buildings huddled beneath

33

thrashing palm trees at Point Arenas looked far from pre-possessing in the gloomy light. Across the bay the rubble of what had been Greytown before the bombardment in July of the year before had a forsaken look, as if at any moment it would melt into the brown sand of the beach-front or the dark green vegetation of the encroaching jungle would reclaim it. Some rebuilding was in progress, a two-story frame structure labeling itself a hotel and what looked like a docking pier. A sign proclaimed it to be the site of a new city to be known henceforth as San Juan del Norte.

The destruction of Greytown by the United States sloop-of-war *Cyane,* though instigated by the transit company after a dispute over port dues, had had nothing to do with William Walker. It was, however, an indication of the temper of the times, the political importance of the transit route across Nicaragua, and the license claimed by some representatives of the United States.

The riverboat *Colorado* waited with steam up to take the passengers aboard. There seemed no reason to linger in that drenched port at the mouth of the San Juan River. The transfer was made, the gangplank pulled in, and churning the cocoa-brown water into a froth, they proceeded upstream on the ninety twisting miles to the head of the Rio San Juan.

The river ran high in its banks joined by a thousand trickling runnels pouring out of the steaming jungle. There was the musty reek of decaying vegetation, overladen by the pervasive perfume of flowers. Trees made a bower over the river, their branches festooned with hanging creepers flowering orange and yellow, white and red. Thick-leaved vines, their juicy stems as large as a man's wrist, strangled the trunks of mahogany and avocado trees. Thick clusters of plants with hanging aerial roots nestled in the crotches of their limbs. Palm trees waved split fronds and tree ferns pushed their lush greenery toward the wet gray sky.

Here and there they saw the brilliant flash of color as parrots and macaws took wing. Once, as the boat passed under an overhanging branch, a snake colored a bright yellow-green thudded to the deck. It was dealt with

34

swiftly, unemotionally, by the Indian deckhands, as if it were an everyday occurrence.

The stone bastion of Castillo Viejo, rising high on its steep, clifflike hill, was nearly obscured by rain as they passed it in the afternoon. Gray, deserted, it had an air of ancient, crumbling mystery. The pole-and-thatch houses hunched head to head at the foot of the hill had a mildewed look after the long rainy season. The Castillo Rapides were crossed without slowing. A few miles further upstream, however, the *Colorado* developed a steering problem. The boat sidled into the port of San Carlos at half speed.

There were supplies to be unloaded for the dingy little town on the shore of Lake Nicaragua. With the repairs there would be a delay of several hours.

For the convenience of the passengers who wanted to go ashore, dinner was served early. The rain stopped halfway through the first sitting and the clouds cleared in the west. Resting low on the horizon, the sun burned orange, sending long wavering shafts through the white streamers of lake mists. Its light touched the waves of the "Gran Lago" with gold, and on the opposite shore, tipped the distant blue cones of the volcanoes Orosi, Madeira, and Ometepe with copper.

The mist lent a spurious enchantment to the scabious thatch-roofed houses of the town, reaching as high as the gates of Fort San Carlos, which guarded the meeting of the river with the lake. The streets, however, ran with water in which refuse floated. There was nothing to be seen but mud and squalor. Returning to the ship from a short exploration, Eleanora and Mazie, escorted by Jean-Paul and the major, were halted by the sound of gunfire. It came from down the lake. Major Crawford dropped his air of relaxed companionship like the devil shedding a cassock. Bearing alert, he herded the women back to the steamer. Wading back through the cluster of vendors at the foot of the gangplank, the major set off in the direction of the sound.

The alarm was unnecessary. The shots had been fired by a group of men from the steamer who had taken advantage of the halt and the lull in the rain to practice

35

their marksmanship on some of the alligators they had been seeing off and on all day. To make amends to the ladies for rushing them, Major Crawford bought small, red finger bananas, coconuts and pineapples from the Indian vendors in their costumes dyed in deep primary colors, and presented them. They were welcome tokens of their first day in the tropics.

After being cooped up so long, Eleanora would have liked to stay on deck. Despite the effluvia of the jungle and primitive sanitation, there was a heady quality in the air, the exotic essence of a strange and new country. She was denied the pleasure by the cloud of mosquitoes, enormous and black, which descended as night fell. As she went below, the deck vibrated into life once more beneath her feet. They were underway again.

In their stateroom, designed on this smaller river steamer to hold four women, Eleanora found Mazie stripped to stays and petticoat. She was brushing her hair with a furious impatience, her face shining with the goose grease she had applied against wrinkles.

As Eleanora came through the door, she tossed the silver-back brush onto the berth she had chosen and put her hands on her hips. "Bad news, honey. The best I can tell, your trunks are missing." She nodded at the baggage that littered the floor, her own trunks, bags and boxes plus those of the two other women who must share with them while their husbands repaired to the one large men's cabin. "I've been through these things a dozen times but I can't find hide nor hair of them—nor of the hat box with my three best hats in it I bought from Madame Helene in New Orleans for ten dollars a piece!"

"You must be mistaken," Eleanora said, starting forward.

Mazie gave a shake of her head, her mouth grim. "Gone."

"But—how?"

"Stolen during the transfer from the *Daniel Webster* to the *Colorado*, most likely. What official in this God-forsaken country is going to stand around in the rain to watch that every piece is put aboard? It's an old story on this run. I've heard in the early days, when there were so many transfers plus the mule trip, it was a lucky group that got through in either direction with more than half the luggage they had when they started out."

"Can't it be recovered?"

"I've already lodged a complaint with the captain for both of us, but there's not much chance. It's probably well on its way into the jungle by now, and back in there are still places no white man has ever seen. No, before long some Indian's wife is going to be picking beans in a hat worth more than her whole village!"

Eleanora sank down on the edge of a berth. "They won't have much when they open my trunks, but everything I had to wear was in there. All I carried off the ocean steamer with me was an extra chemise, a handkerchief, and a few toiletries. What am I to do?"

"Granada isn't the end of the world. It does have seamstresses."

"Even if I make it myself I can't afford a new wardrobe."

"You still have what you have on. Surely you can afford just one or two more gowns, something cooler."

Doubtfully Eleanora surveyed the gown of brown velvet she had donned that morning. She had made it over from a riding habit worn by her mother. It was rather masculine in appearance with long, tight-fitting sleeves and a high neck. The day had been cool due to the rain, but already she had regretted her choice. What would it be like when the sun came out? Moreover, after their excursion about San Carlos the hem was caked with mud. Knowing it was unlikely that she would ever be able to wear it again in this tropical climate, she had been careless about soiling. It was doubtful the skirt could ever be cleaned.

Eleanora raised bleak eyes to the other woman. Mazie chewed on her full lower lip. "Well, I don't like that gown on you anyway. It's too drab, too old-womanish. And the rest of your clothes were the same. I think it's just as well you have to start over."

"But I tell you I can't."

"Nonsense. There are always ways and means. Let

37

me see, something light and airy, something in green—or pink—"

"I've always tried to wear subdued colors. My hair—"

"Your hair is glorious!"

"My grandmother—"

"Your grandmother may have been a lady, but she sounds like a jealous old witch to me, jealous of your mother, jealous of you. You are a beautiful woman, face a perfect oval, fascinating green eyes, those dark lashes and brows and ivory skin inherited from the Creole French side—all crowned by that flaming Irish head. I call it a terrible waste to see you try to deny the way you look, subdue yourself into invisibility."

"I don't want to attract unwelcome attention," Eleanora tried to explain.

"Something else your grandmother warned you against, I don't doubt. Oh, I know you don't want to dress quite like me, and I don't mean that you should, but there's nothing wrong with making the most of what you have. You'll never find a man otherwise."

Eleanora tilted her head, a militant look rising in her eyes. "It may surprise you to learn I don't want a man."

"You may think you don't, but unfortunately a man is a woman's only security."

"I had a fiancé once. I seemed to lose my attractiveness for him when I lost my dowry."

"He was a fool. You are better off without him."

"That may be, but I prefer to place my trust in Jean-Paul—and myself—from now on."

"Wonderful! Except that brothers have a way of marrying and putting their wives first. Then where will you be? You need a husband, a life of your own."

"You seem to have done well enough without one."

Mazie stiffened, then relaxed slowly. "I had a husband once, and a child—a son."

"I'm sorry—"

"No, let me tell you. We had a place in the hills of Georgia. One winter night the house caught fire, a spark from the chimney on the wooden shingles. I was out in the separate kitchen-cabin setting bread, my husband was dozing before the fireplace. Half the roof was

38

ablaze before it was discovered. I ran into the smoke-filled bedroom where my son slept. He was small, not quite two years old. Since it was cold I rolled him in the bedclothes and picked him up. My husband told me to carry him outside and stay out while he tried to save a few things. I did as he said, though I couldn't help looking back, thinking of everything I was losing. And then I began to unwrap the bundle in my arms. I had picked up not my son, but a stuffed toy I had made for him. I screamed to my husband and he went back after him. A moment later, the roof-tree fell in."

Her voice died away in a husky whisper. "Mazie . . ." Eleanora stretched out her hand to the other woman, unable to find the words to express her sympathy.

"I am thirty-three," Mazie went on. "I've spent over ten years trying to forget, trying to find some way of relieving the torment of self-blame. Nothing ever works—quite. And yet I've learned a few things. I've learned that men and women need each other. That the closeness of men and women, the fusing of their bodies in a passion of caring, is one of the few things that makes life bearable."

"And yet," Eleanora said, looking away, "you speak of—what you do as your profession."

"So it is, except that I am more selective." She smiled. "A conceit, I expect, but I prefer to call myself a courtesan. The difference is, I restrict myself to one man at the time. But come, I have shocked you enough for one night. We were speaking of clothes. I have one or two things cluttering my trunks you can take off my hands. I let a dressmaker in Saratoga last summer convince me that a pretense to delicacy would be beneficial. I've decided since that it just isn't my style. I'm a bit rounder in places than you, but I still have a sewing kit somewhere among my things, and that can be remedied."

"I appreciate the gesture, but I couldn't take them, you know," Eleanora said.

"Why not? You are one of the most sensible young women I've seen in some time. Surely you can see the necessity. I think you can understand, too, that I will be hurt, and insulted, if you refuse."

"You make it impossible to hold out against you," Eleanora said wryly.

"Good," Mazie answered, turning to her trunks. "That was exactly what I intended.

The dock at Granada swarmed with people. Men with handcarts pushed and shoved, raising a cloud of dust in their efforts to secure a place near where the gangplank would be let down. *"Carreton de mano! Carreton de mano!"* they cried, using sign language to show their willingness to carry baggage. Women with dark curling hair hanging down their backs adjusted trays of fruit and pork, older women and boys gathered up their offerings of conch shells and woven palm-fiber hats, leather goods and curiosities made of cow horns.

Soldiers, Falangistas in red shirts, their wide-brimmed, red-banded hats pulled low against the bright afternoon sun, leaned against the deckside buildings. Most were American or European in appearance, a few were Spanish. All shared a lean, hard-bitten look that contrasted sharply with the men crowding the rail of the steamer.

It had been an uneventful trip across the lake. They had gone first to Virgin Bay, where the passengers for California had disembarked. The carriages to take them to San Juan del Sur had been waiting, their side panels painted with scenes of California and Nicaragua, their wide blue-and-white and red-and-white stripes glistening in the sun. At the sight of them a cheer had been raised, a spontaneous reaction to reaching this next-to-last stage in the long transit crossing.

The only other event of note was the sighting of a shark in the lake. "But yes," one of the steamer's officers had explained when some of the passengers scoffed. "The shark, he has always been in the "Gran Lago," and very tasty he is, too."

The first priority was a hotel. There were, not surprisingly, a number to choose from near the lake shore, the best of which appeared to be the Alhambra. Following their handcart, taken because of the elaborateness of the design painted in green, red, yellow, white, pink and black on its solid wheels, they created quite a stir. Mazie, in honor of the occasion, had chosen a gown of heavenly blue tarlatan trimmed with miles of grosgrain ribbon. Her hat, which she wore tilted forward upon her piled golden curls, was a ribbon confection topped by an enormous Democrático cockade. In her gloved hand she carried a parasol of white lace. Eleanora had no need of such protection. Her hat was a cartwheel in the leghorn style made of several layers of white muslin through which the sun cast pleasing shadows upon her face. The pink ribbon that circled the crown was echoed in the pink cabbage roses strewn across the white foulard silk of the gown Mazie had pressed upon her. Though the two women were near the same height, in their alterations they had forgotten the extra length in the skirt allowed to cover Mazie's fashionably large hoop. At the last moment Mazie had pressed her extra crinoline, a lightweight collapsible Thompson hoop, upon Eleanora. As a result the gown stood out like the petals around the heart of a flower. The round, scooped-out décolletage was cool compared to her brown velvet, but its lowness brought more than a little warmth to her cheeks. Jean-Paul's air of smoldering disapproval she found excessive, however, and to spite him she took the major's arm, entering into a spirited conversation which consisted largely of parrying his gallantries and nodding as he pointed out the features of Granada.

The town was a vast improvement over the others they had seen. It was built in the Spanish style around a series of squares or plazas. The buildings were of warm golden stone or whitewashed plaster roofed with red tiles. Cool courtyards, known here as patios, were incorporated within the walls of the houses. From them waved the shining green of orange trees and magenta masses of bougainvillea. The bell towers of churches reared above the rooftops, and the figures of sandaled priests in cowled robes moved among the throng crowding the streets.

The major left them at the hotel steps. Jean-Paul took

a room for only one night since he must report to his barracks the first thing in the morning. For convenience Eleanora and Mazie took a room together next door. That she would not have been able to afford so fine a hotel, or choice a room, if she had been alone was a sore point with Eleanora, but she insisted on paying her share.

Anxious to remove his sister from her present company as soon as possible, Jean-Paul went off at once to discover the whereabouts of the land-purchasing agent's office as given on a card left in his possession. After looking over the room and ridding themselves of the dust of the streets, the two women waited some time for Eleanora's brother to return. When it grew too dark in the room to see each other's features, they descended to the dining room alone.

In the doorway they encountered a man just leaving. He drew back with a muttered apology and a stiff inclination of his dark head to give their wide skirts room through the opening. The lamplight glittered on the gold fringe of his epaulettes. Eleanora, flinging him a glance through her lashes, recognized Colonel Farrell, the man at whose hands she had suffered humiliation and defeat in New Orleans.

She looked away at once, moving past him with her face averted. Still, she could not forget the sapphire-hard indifference of his eyes as they raked over her, or the sardonic quirk of lips as he inhaled the violence of Mazie's amber scent.

They ate slowly, savoring the strange, highly spiced dishes set before them; Jean-Paul had still not joined them when they were done. It did not seem prudent to remain downstairs. Taking up one of the bed candles left conveniently at the foot of the stairs, they returned to their room.

The night grew later, the streets quieted. Once they heard the distant clanging of church bells for a fire. That provided conversation for a time, though nothing came of it that they could see from their window. After a time they dressed for bed and blew out the candle.

Mazie, lying in the darkness, tried to console her. "He

42

probably rode out of town to see this estate; you know how enthusiastic he is. Or he may have had to report tonight and go straight to the barracks without being able to send a message. I've heard Walker insists on a strict regimen for his men."

"Yes," Eleanora answered. It was also possible he had decided to celebrate his last night of freedom with some of the recruits of a similar mind. She had waited for him too many nights to be seriously concerned. However, despite the comfort of a bed wider than her shoulders that did not rock, she could not drift into sleep. She was lying, staring wide-eyed into the dark, when she heard the shuffle of footsteps in the hall.

Plainly through the thin walls she could hear the rattling of a key and a muffled curse as someone tried to fit a key into a lock. At the familiar timbre of the voice, Eleanora threw back the covers.

Barefooted, she crossed the gritty floor to the door and turning the key, drew it open a crack. "Jean-Paul?" she whispered.

Mazie, waking, sat up in bed. "Eleanora, what are you doing?" she asked in what was, for her, a sharp tone.

"It's Jean-Paul," Eleanora explained over her shoulder.

The voices attracted her brother's attention, and he stumbled into view, putting out one hand to the door to catch himself. He half staggered, half fell into the room. Eleanora clutched at his arm to keep him from landing flat on his face.

"Eleanora," he said, the tone in which he spoke his slurred words bordering on desperation. "I've got to tell you something."

"Yes, but come and sit down first."

"No," he said with the obstinate will of the truly drunken. "I've got to tell you now."

Mazie, her ripe charms more revealed than concealed by her nightgown, slid from the bed and touched a sulfur match to what was left of the candle beside the bed.

"All right," Eleanora agreed, her gaze going to the

43

other woman as she moved to stand on Jean-Paul's other side.

"I couldn't find the land agent. No such street—no such house as on the card. Nobody ever heard of him. I saw Colonel Farrell. He said it was all a cheat. The man was a crook. There was never án estate, no house, no land. He said we'll never see the money again. Never. It's gone, Eleanora. It's gone, and we have nothing."

Shock loosened Eleanora's grip on her brother's arm. It was Mazie who lowered him to the floor and rolled him to his back with a kind of efficient pity.

In grim silence they stood staring down at him, staring at the splotches of food and drink that stained his shirt front and waistcoat, at the rip in his waistcoat pocket where someone had stolen his watch and fobs—and the tracks of tears in the dust and perspiration grime of his near-beardless face.

Three

Money. Everything seemed to come to that essential. Eleanora could not return home, there was no money. She could not stay at the hotel, there was no money. She could not hire a house or engage the companion who would convey respectability upon her singular existence without funds. She could not, in good conscience, accept Mazie's charity and remain in the hotel at her expense. The other woman refused to understand her scruples, taking Eleanora's refusal as a personal affront. The rift between them had not been bridged when Eleanora packed her few belongings into a bundle and moved out. Mazie's sole acknowledgment was to send the things she had given her after her with a curt note saying if she did not feel comfortable wearing them she could consign them to the nearest trash heap—or sell them for what she could get out of them.

There had not been much time to look for lodgings. Jean-Paul could not really spare the morning he spent at the task. It would, no doubt, be held against him that he had not reported at the earliest possible moment. He supposed, with the typical Creole attitude toward the importance of family, that the welfare of a sister would be understood to take precedence. Eleanora was not so confident. If Walker, the civilian who had made himself chief commander of the Nicaraguan army, was a disciplinarian, that facet must necessarily be reflected in his officers.

The room taken for her was on a side street off the Central Plaza, behind the Cathedral of San Francisco. It was, appropriately enough, in the home of a widow, an ancient crone of a woman with a bent back and an endless supply of shapeless black dresses, all just alike. There would be no sympathy, no companionship, and little protection from that quarter. The old woman was almost completely deaf, and from her silent void, she looked out upon the world with a suspicious and bitter scorn. She had taken the centavo she demanded in payment and clamped toothless gums upon it, more as an insult than a precaution. That done, she had gone into her portion of the house and slammed the door.

A further drawback was the situation of the widow's house. It shared a common wall with a cantina enormously popular with the soldiers and the young men in the vicinity. Eleanora's room was, of course, next to it. Every night the irrepressible din of guitars, zithers, and concertinas competing with raised male voices disturbed her slumbers. To pass the place after noon was to invite insult, she discovered, and more than once she was followed to the door of her room. One gallant even camped outside her door for several hours, until the widow, coming out to do her marketing, stumbled over him and sent him on his way in a barrage of shrill and extremely idiomatic Spanish.

In self-defense, Eleanora began to wake early, with the silver voice of the cathedral bell calling the early risers to mass, and make her way to the well at the end of the street for water, and to the market for the little food she could afford. She discovered an intense enjoyment of that

45

time of morning. It was cooler, with fewer people about to interfere as she took her exercise, staring at the walls of the central plaza with their pockmarks caused by bullets during the taking of the town by Walker and the Falangistas, the towering front, arched doors and series of rose windows of the cathedral, and the arabesque portal flanked by guards of the Government House where General Walker had made his headquarters. She enjoyed the flaming brilliance of the poinsettias, the waxy whiteness and fragrance of the wild gardenias, and the small sunflowers and ferns that seemed to grow in every crack and cranny. There were fewer people at that hour to bargain with Indian and meztizo—Indian with a Spanish admixture—women for their eggs and stone-baked cakes, their tropical fruits and slivers of meat, which they sold every morning in the open-air market on one side of the plaza.

Day by day the aimless routine she was following grew less endurable. There was a limit to how long the few dollars she possessed would last, even in a country where a filling, if frugal, breakfast could be had for three cents. She must find something to do, a way to keep herself.

The possibilities were few. She might be able to teach English. Surely in a country dominated at present by English-speaking foreigners there must be people anxious to learn the language? She was not proficient in Spanish, but there had been enough spoken in New Orleans, a city that had once been an outpost of the Spanish empire, to enable her to make herself understood. If the parents were not interested perhaps they would like to look to the future and have their children taught. Failing that, she might use some of the skills with a needle she had learned at convent school to make articles of clothing to sell in the market. If she were successful she might set herself up as a modiste. Or as a last resort she might become a laundress, joining the other women pounding clothes on the shore of the lake. Soldiers were always in need of laundresses, having little time and less inclination to keep their clothing fresh. Never mind that the position was looked on as only a little higher than that of a camp follower.

She had been in isolation with the widow six days. She

was lying on her bed, trying to do sums in her head despite a Spanish arrangement of "O' Susannah" coming through the wall, when a knock fell on the door. She waited before moving to be certain it wasn't coming from the cantina or from the door of the widow.

"Eleanora?"

At the sound of her brother's voice, she swung from the bed to lift the heavy bar and draw the panel inward.

"Jean-Paul, where—" she began, then stopped as Mazie sailed into the room in a gown of muslin printed with improbable blue poppies. A bunch of scarlet poinsettias filled her décolletage for an effect that was, at the very least, eye-catching.

"Merry Christmas," Mazie exclaimed, sweeping Eleanora into an amber-scented embrace that was as forgiving as it was encompassing.

It was Christmas Eve. Somehow Eleanora had managed to forget the date. That Mazie had remembered, and chosen to remember her, brought a tightness to her throat.

The other woman, pulling off her lace mitts, fanned herself with them. "It's as hot as an oven in here. It has to be going to storm again. People who are saying the rainy season is over are out of their heads. How you can stand—but never mind. I have come with a warning, Eleanora, my pet, as well as the greetings of the holiday. Single women, I fear, are not wanted in Granada."

Jean-Paul, after only a week as a soldier, seemed leaner than he had been, Eleanora thought as she greeted him with a swift hug. The change was not an improvement.

"Not wanted?" she asked distractedly, looking around for a place for them to sit. There was only one chair in the small room, an article which looked like an unsuccessful experiment in the art of furniture making. Its rawhide seat had stretched, sinking deep in the middle, its frame had warped so one leg on each side was shorter, and the top two rungs of the back were missing.

Mazie solved the problem in the same manner Eleanora usually did, by sitting on the bed. "Single, unattached women, that is. I had a visit from your Colonel Farrell. He is everything you said he was, arrogant, dictatorial, unreasonable—and more. He explained that he is provost

47

marshal for the town, and in that capacity, advised me to leave as soon as possible!"

Outrage throbbed in Mazie's voice. Staring at her, Eleanora frowned. "Can he do that?"

"As the town is under military rule and he is head of the military police, I suppose he can. But you will never believe why he is doing it. General Walker, if you please, has set himself up as the moral, as well as military, leader of the country. He refuses to have his men consorting with camp followers or the low women of the town. It encourages vice, disease, and disorder. Colonel Farrell actually said that—to me!"

"If you think that is bad, you should hear the general's strictures against drinking," Jean-Paul said, propping his shoulders clad in the red shirt of the Democráticos against the wall. "A soldier caught under the influence gets ten days in the guardhouse to sober up. The second time around he is forced to drink an emetic, then jailed, and the third time it's the emetic, twenty-four hours lashed to a cartwheel, and jail. A civilian selling liquor to a member of La Falange Americana must pay an arbitrary fine of two hundred dollars, American."

Mazie ignored Jean-Paul. "I tried to explain that I am not a common whore, but it made no impression on Colonel Farrell. He seemed to think a woman who saved her favors for one man was, somehow, more dangerous, since she contributes directly to the practice of dueling among the men while she is making up her mind. He contends that women like me grow odious with conceit, having so many men vying for them, and actually encourage the men to compete among themselves out of vanity. Walker is determined not to lose his men to such senseless killing. Never have I been so insulted!"

"Now, he's right about the dueling, though maybe not the cause," Jean-Paul said. "Yesterday two men met, a Frenchman and a Prussian, because they could not agree on whether the Seine or the Rhine River was the prettiest. They were bored. They came to fight, to win honors and booty, and all they get is regulations and drills, a constant harping on duty and discipline. It seems the war was over in two battles, won by fifty-six men."

48

"Tired already of being a *soldado* for Nicaragua?"

He looked away with a shrug from Mazie's too-knowing hazel eyes. Eleanora, with a glance at her brother's drawn face, stepped into the breach. "What are you going to do, Mazie?"

"The question is what are *we* going to do? I was told in no uncertain terms to inform any of my friends of a similar mode of living of the new regulations. I very nearly asked him if Walker considered himself above other men, since it is well known that he has taken one of the aristocratic Nicaraguan women into his bed, and it was her influence that brought about the coalition government with the Legitimistas. They even say President Rivas, the man named as head of government, is a distant cousin of hers."

"An interesting form of nepotism," Jean-Paul commented.

Eleanora shook her head impatiently. "Are you leaving Granada?" she insisted.

"I don't know. I'm tempted to stay here just to see what the colonel will do about it. Or perhaps President Rivas has a weakness for blondes? I would give a great deal to prove to Colonel Farrell that I have absolutely no interest in causing quarrels among enlisted men."

"You don't, by chance, suppose his reaction would be to put you on a boat back to New Orleans?"

"Not if he suspected that is where I had rather go, I'm sure."

"I'd join you in tweaking the lion's beard if I thought he would."

"Eleanora," Jean-Paul began, then subsided as she shook her head at him with a smile.

"There is always California," Mazie reminded her. "I'd be glad to pay your way for the sake of the company."

"And then?" Eleanora asked softly.

"I don't know," Mazie admitted. "I just don't know."

Mazie insisted on sending Jean-Paul next door to the cantina for a crude meal of chili con carne and meat-filled maize cakes washed down with sour red wine. Afterward, they sat talking well into the night. With Jean-Paul to act as escort, Eleanora attended the midnight mass in celebration of Christmas in the cathedral. Mazie accompanied her out of curiosity. When they returned Jean-Paul insisted on carrying the celebration further by ordering two more bottles of wine, the majority of which he drank himself. By the time Mazie was ready to leave, he was pleasantly relaxed, but by no means as drunk as he was capable of becoming.

Eleanora saw them to the door. Mazie turned back, letting Jean-Paul go ahead. After a long searching look, she reached out to tap Eleanora on the cheek. "You are too pale, and your eyes have such lavender shadows under them you look positively dissipated. You can't go on like this. Something must be done, even if Jean-Paul has to go to the colonel and explain."

"I want no favors from that man. If it weren't for him we wouldn't be in this mess."

Mazie's face took on a grim cast. "That's easy to say."

"It's true!"

"Even so. There is such a thing, honey, as too much pride."

Because of her late night, and the long hours before dawn lying wide-eyed wondering what she was to do, Eleanora overslept. When she awoke the heat was already overpowering in the small, windowless room. She dressed hurriedly in the lightweight gown of white with pink roses. She was not particularly hungry at the moment, but her water olla of red clay was empty and she had contributed the slim supply of food that was to have been her midday meal to the feast the night before.

In the market she bought tortillas wrapped in corn husks and a bunch of finger bananas. Coming back through the square with her purchases in a string bag, she spared no more than a glance for the serenity of the cathedral or the Government House with Walker's flag, a vibrant red star of five points on a white ground, hanging limp above it. In an effort to save time she dove down a side street, a wide, quiet thoroughfare which had impressed her before as having a private air. Many of the more impressive homes of the Granadan aristocrats fronted upon it.

50

She was passing a palacio of small size but beautiful proportions, with Roman columns of stone and a soft gold coloring applied to its plaster over adobe bricks, when a movement caught her eye. A man walked out onto the upper galería and stood at the railing with a cup of coffee in his hand, staring out over the rooftops in the direction of the lake and the distant volcanic peaks. It took her a moment to recognize him without his uniform coat, but the bleak eyes, the uncompromising chin were the same. It was Colonel Farrell.

The sound of her footsteps alerted him to her presence. The brightness of derision untempered by amusement leaped into his face. It was as if he suspected her of just wending her way homeward after a night of debauchery.

Eleanora knew a perverse impulse to put a provocative swing into her walk, to make the bell of her skirts sway to a seductive tempo. It was what he expected of her, wasn't it? But why should he always get what he expected? With the cool lift of a dark eyebrow, she moved on, treating him as the insensitive boor he undoubtedly was. It was obvious, from the things he had said to Mazie, that the colonel had an exaggerated sense of importance. How nice it would be if someone deflated it!

Depositing her purchases in her room, Eleanora took up her olla and walked to the well at the end of the street. The water was clear and fresh, fed by an underground spring. As was the custom, she drew, hand over hand, a full bucket for herself and one for the stone animal troughs that abutted the well curb. When she had filled her olla, she carried it back balanced on her hip, her thumb in one of its earlike handles.

In front of the cantina a trio of men lounged against the wall. She saw them from a distance but kept her eyes downcast, pretending to be watching her step in the dried, rutted mud and animal dung of the street.

As she drew nearer she heard a softly murmured phrase. *"Muy bruja rojo."*

The red witch. The bewitching redhead? Either way, she did not see it as a great compliment. Feigning deafness, she started past them.

Her way was blocked by a young Nicaraguan with the

self-assurance of a *conquistador* and the soulful eyes of a poet. He was, she thought, the young man who had been sent away from outside her door earlier in the week.

"Señorita," he said, taking her arm, moving in close against her. "I am crazy with love for you. You drive me wild. Say I may hope, say you will be mine."

"Please let me pass," Eleanora said, keeping her voice level with an effort. She, as a child of New Orleans, had some inkling of the mind of the Latin male. Observation in the last few days had taught her more. He was much concerned with his *dignidad de la persona* and his masculinity, the *machismo*. Both must be guarded and treated with due respect. A direct refusal from her would be seen as a challenge to his manhood, a curt dismissal as an affront to his dignity.

"No! No, *cara*. You may pass only into my heart's keeping."

There was about him the cloying smell of vanilla scent on a hot day. The three men had been joined by others attracted by the commotion, a number in uniform. They exchanged glances, laughing and talking under their breath. The drift of their remarks was vulgar. With determination she closed her ears to them.

"I am sorry," she said lifting her chin, slipping insensibly into his dramatic manner of speaking. "My heart is dead. Once a man betrayed me and I have sworn never to trust another."

"Such a man should be shot before the wall, señorita. But you are wrong to withhold your trust. All men are not such as he. You only need to be brought back to life by the caress of one who loves you."

"Forgive me, but I prefer my heart unawakened. It is less painful that way."

"For you, but what of me?" he cried. His hand tightened, drawing her nearer. His arm swept around her waist, dislodging her water olla so that it crashed to the ground, breaking into a dozen pieces. The water wet her slippers and mired the hem of her skirt as she struggled to keep the Nicaraguan gallant from possessing her mouth. His breath on her cheek was hot, smelling faintly of garlic,

52

and she dragged her head back frantically, pushing against his chest.

"Enough! Let her go!"

The command cut sharply across the confused babble of encouragement and advice from the onlookers. The arms about Eleanora fell away. Her assailant stepped back, making the smallest of bows to a higher authority. With a sense of shock, Eleanora was left to face Colonel Farrell under the barrage of stares from the growing crowd.

"So, it's you," the colonel grated. "I might have guessed. You can go. I will deal with you later."

Eleanora stood her ground. "What—are you going to do?"

"That need not concern you."

The heat, the worries, her precarious position, her moment of fright, combined with the threat the colonel had implied and the contempt in his voice, rushed to Eleanora's head. She lashed out, "Of course it concerns me, much more than it does you!"

"Maybe I misunderstood. Maybe you weren't objecting to the attention you were getting?"

"Naturally I was, but—"

"Then," he interrupted, "it is my duty to come to your defense, no more than that." He looked away, letting his hard sapphire eyes roam over the onlookers, resting finally on the young Nicaraguan. "It is also my duty to inform these men that the penalty for forcing a woman against her will is death from now on in Granada—for civilians as well as the military. Be warned. You must either pay or use cajolery to get what you want."

The young man shifted uneasily. "This one, she has no *dueña*, no man to protect her. I offer myself. My family is a rich one, and ancient. My word is my bond. I will keep her well."

"And you turned down such a proposition?" the colonel asked, turning a sardonic gaze upon Eleanora.

"I have no need of a protector," she said, temper scalding her cheeks, touching sparks from the gold flecks in her eyes. "I'm not a child or an imbecile that I need someone to lead me about."

53

"Nor are you a man. You are likely to be found in an alley with your throat cut if you go on as you have been."

"That need not trouble you."

"Unfortunately, as provost marshal, I would be put to the inconvenience of finding your killer for the sake of order."

"I will try to save you that chore."

There was a ripple of amusement through the crowd, which the colonel ignored. "Thank you," he said with cool sarcasm. "Now if you will allow me I will take this man to the Government House for questioning."

"No! You can't do that. He had no real intention of assaulting me, not in broad daylight."

In the crowd a man spoke. "Thees colonel, if he can't bring thees one small red-haired woman to order, how can we expect heem to keep order in the town, *hein?* Tell me that?" The ripple of laughter that followed was louder than before.

Colonel Farrell's face hardened. "Mademoiselle, you will stand aside or accept the consequences."

She did not move. What could he do to her? She was the injured party, he could not arrest her without making himself ridiculous. She did not think, given the mood of those gathered around, that she need fear physical violence. It was good to feel for a change that she held the advantage over this man who was the cause of her present situation. It would not hurt him to suffer a little.

His next move was so unexpected she had no time to avoid it. He reached out, catching her forearm in a bruising grip, and dragged her against him. His mouth, cruel and grim, descended upon hers. Lips parted in surprise, she could not withstand his sudden invasion, could not move in the steel bands of his embrace. A torrent of anger, buoyed by an odd exhilaration, rushed along her nerves, and for an instant she was aware of a red haze of disbelief behind her eyelids.

A roar of approval went up from the onlookers. This they understood. It made some sense of the quarrel over the unchaperoned red-haired woman who lived with the widow. Now all would be well, the unpleasantness done

54

with. In the future Carlos must be more careful of whose woman he honored with his attention.

As she was released Eleanora stumbled back. Before she could catch her breath she was lifted, swept high against a muscular chest in a froth of skirts and lace-edged petticoats.

"No!" she cried, but struggling only caused her hoop to billow, exposing her knee-length pantaloons to the lascivious gaze of the men who crowded close. It did not affect her captor. His grip tightened until she could hardly move or breathe.

When she subsided the colonel swung to the young man they had called Carlos. "The lady has spoken on your behalf. A swift end will be made of this if you will give your word to present yourself for a report at the Government House this afternoon."

"Very well, you have it," the young man agreed, bowing.

A curt nod and Colonel Farrell strode away back in the direction he had come.

When they were out of sight Eleanora swallowed the tears of helpless frustration that rose in her throat. "You can put me down now."

He did not answer, nor did he slow his firm, even pace. Slanting a quick glance at his face, so near, Eleanora saw that his jaw was rigid with anger. A frown of fierce concentration chiseled twin lines between his dark brows, and behind the thick screen of his lashes, his eyes glittered deep indigo.

The beginnings of a nebulous fear stirred inside her. Perhaps he had something more in mind than merely demonstrating his authority? What? Where was he taking her? Was there some unknown law she had trespassed by disobeying his requests? Unconsciously she had considered Walker and his takeover of Nicaragua as an *opéra bouffe* lacking in force. At the moment, as she realized the ability of the colonel to dispose of her as he pleased, the force was all too apparent.

The Calle Santa Celia, the street which led to the central plaza, and on which the palacio of the colonel stood, stretched quiet and empty before them. The sound

55

of his boots was loud on the stone banquette fronting the houses. A few trees, oaks and mahoganies, shaded this avenue and as they passed under the cool dimness, Eleanora grew aware of the perspiration that sheened the colonel's face and the dampness of her clothing where their bodies touched.

And then it was no longer necessary to wonder where he was taking her. The heavy, nail-studded wooden door of the palacio loomed before them. It swung open at their approach, and a tall, thin woman dressed in rusty, unrelieved black held it while the colonel shouldered through with his burden.

He did not stop, but continued along an entrance hall floored with cool, dark-green tiles which terminated in a large interior patio. An upper gallery, its railing painted dark green, a foil to walls of soft ocher, ran around the patio like the boxes at a theater. From the exposed crossbeams of the lower gallery hung ollas of water in rope slings cooling by condensation. Terra-cotta pots stood everywhere, filled with vines and spiny cactus and bright flowering plants. In the still air the smell of orange blossoms, from the trees which shaded one end, was overpowering.

Eleanora was allowed no more than a glance. With the black-clad woman trailing blankly behind, Colonel Farrell turned toward a raised staircase that rose to the right. Mounting it, he strode along the upper gallery to the door which stood open halfway down the wall.

Inside was a small bedroom. The walls were whitewashed, the polished floor strewn with Indian rugs in vivid colors, red, blue, and yellow, and also more somber black, beige, terra cotta, and white. The furnishings were few, a four-poster bed of dark carved wood with plain white bedclothes and hangings, a tall armoire, a washstand with utilitarian pitcher and bowl, and in one corner the inevitable *cuadro,* the painting of a saint, in this case La Virgen del Perpetuo Socorro, with beneath it a narrow shelf holding slim yellow-white candles and a wilting bouquet of some strange lavender flowers.

Eleanora was set upon her feet. The colonel turned away as if some galling task had been satisfactorily completed. At the door he held the panel open while the thin woman passed back out, then he shut it with a decisive click. A moment later there came the sound of a key turning in the lock.

The bed was directly behind her. Eleanora sat down upon it suddenly, her breath leaving her lungs in a slow, shaky sound of mingled wrath and relief. Before she could collect her wits a noise came from behind her. Through thin white curtains over a set of French doors she could see the colonel on the galeria that fronted the palacio. He was fitting a grille of wrought iron into place over the doors and locking it into place.

Locked in. As quiet descended the enormity of what had happened to her settled upon her like a crushing weight. She jumped up, shivering in spite of the heat, hands clasping her forearms. The hem of her skirts left muddy streaks on the polished floor as she paced. There was a weakness in her limbs that came from emptiness, though she could not have eaten a bite.

He could not do this. He could not. But wait. What, precisely, had he done? Kissed her, taken her against her will to his home, locked her in a bedroom. All that. Yet, his attitude held nothing carnal. It could be that he only intended a final end to the disagreement she had provoked plus, possibly, a mild punishment for defying him. This afternoon, when his temper had cooled, if she could bring herself to appear chastened, he might let her go.

And if he did not? There must be someone to whom she could appeal. It was not possible that he could keep her here, his personal prisoner.

As the hours went by heat began to build in the closed room. She could have opened the doors to the front gallery, letting in air through the grille, but anyone passing could look in upon her. It was too much like being caged.

For a similar reason she kept her gown on. Without it she would have been too vulnerable. It would, in addition, have been too much like giving up, resigning herself to whatever came to her. This she refused to do.

She did wet a linen cloth in the water in the pitcher on the washstand and bathe her face and neck. When the hem of her skirts dried in the hot still air, she lay down upon the coverlet of the bed. The house was still. The air inside the room was faintly musty, as if, despite the flowers upon the small altar, it was not often used. Who had owned the house before Walker came and Colonel Farrell took it? Who was the woman in black? One of the former owners? A housekeeper? A relative of the colonel's perhaps. No, not that. Colonel Farrell had a solitary look, as if he had never had relatives, never needed them. Never needed anyone.

She did not intend to sleep. It was bewildering then to come abruptly awake to a loud knocking in a darkened room that was unfamiliar. Her lips were dry. She moistened them with her tongue before she answered.

"Yes?"

The voice which replied was thin and reedy, a fair copy of the woman who owned it. "The colonel has returned. He asks that you make yourself ready to have dinner with him."

Dinner? Was it so late? If the colonel had returned, where had he been? At the Government House, dealing with the weighty problem of Carlos, no doubt.

Her first impulse was to refuse, to say she was not hungry. That would be foolish, however, as well as a lie. Her position was too precarious to risk antagonizing this man. It would also be too easy to starve her into submission, if he wished. No, far better to go with head high and some semblance of grace.

"Yes, thank you," Eleanora replied. There was one other thing. If escape should prove necessary, she would have a much better chance of effecting it from another room.

Make herself ready? Charming. She had no hairbrush, no comb, no change of clothing. Her gown was soiled and crumpled, and it was, in any case, too dark in the room to see in the tiny mirror of distorted glass which hung above the washstand. She could wash her hands and smooth her hair by touch, no more. The colonel would have to be satisfied.

At a tap on the door she moved toward it, expecting to be freed. Instead it swung open to admit a small procession. Two men, Nicaraguan soldiers in red shirts, came

58

first, bearing a small but heavy table. The colonel came next with a pair of chairs, while following him was the black-clad woman and a plump, aproned female, both carrying trays of food and drink. Last was a small girl, of seven or eight, the daughter, from her scolding, of the woman who appeared to be the cook. The child held a wooden candelabra of upright design with three lighted candles. With glassy eyes and a painful care, she set the candelabra in the center of the table, then dropped a bobbing curtsy before, smiling her relief, she skipped out the door.

Pushed to one side, Eleanora watched as the chairs were placed, the table laid, the food set out. The final ritual was the pouring of the wine in delicate Venetian goblets before the thin woman followed the others from the room. Eleanora was left alone with Colonel Farrell.

Disappointment that she was not to leave her room gathered in a hard knot at the base of Eleanora's throat. With an effort of will she kept it from her face as she met the intent, considering gaze of the colonel. He had shaved in honor of the occasion but had not donned full uniform. With his breeches he wore only a white lawn shirt open at the neck against the heat. The copper-bronze of his skin was in sharp contrast to the white, an impression intensified by the wavering candlelight. The flames cast odd angles and planes across his face, making a curving beak of his nose and cliffs of his cheekbones so that, for an instant, Eleanora caught the impression of something savage, ancient, in his features. He moved and the impression was gone. Still she stood straining after the image as he stepped to the French doors and threw them wide.

The coolness of the night crept into the room with the warm fragrance of orange blossoms and wild gardenia. The man at the window put a hand on the iron grille with its curling arabesque design and gave it a small shake. The chain and padlocks held it firm, clanking with a cold metallic sound.

At his air of satisfaction Eleanora felt her fingers clench. With an abrupt movement she thrust the betraying hand among the folds of her skirts. He turned, instantly alert, but seeing her standing still where she had been

59

before, he relaxed and moved to draw her chair out. A mirthless smile indented one corner of his strongly molded mouth. As she took her place, Eleanora flicked a glance at him under her lashes. How old was he? Thirty? Thirty-five? There were fine lines radiating from his eyes, and a deep gash on each side of his mouth. Combined with the harsh aspect of his features, they denied him the conventional idea of handsomeness. And yet it was an infinitely memorable face—and a compelling one.

The food was plain but well cooked, a variation of the omnipresent beans, spiced meat, and corncakes. The wine was red with the warm, dry taste of Spain. Dessert was a salad of chopped fresh fruit served with cream and followed by a cheese tray.

Once or twice during the silent meal Eleanora knew an impulse to introduce some topic of conversation. She quelled it firmly. The colonel was host. The responsibility was his. Why should she help? But if he felt any such constraint, any need to fill the void between them with talk, he gave no sign. Once she caught him watching her, his eyes narrowed in speculation. He held her regard for long, tense moments, his eyes dark, measuring, unreadable. She found she could not look away until, with abrupt decision he let his eyelids fall, and lifting the glass in his hand, drained the wine it held to the dregs.

He set the glass on the table and leaned back. "I believe you will be happy to know that the man, Carlos, who accosted you this morning has been released with a reprimand."

"I—yes, thank you."

"Why are you thanking me? I assure you, if he had deserved to be shot he would have been."

"Probably. But I have been given no reason to believe in your sense of justice," Eleanora replied, carefully refraining from indicating the room that, for no more than his whim, had become her prison.

Amazingly, a smile curved his mouth then was gone. He let the comment pass.

Emboldened by his lack of censure, Eleanora asked, "Then, if you are satisfied with the outcome, may I return to my own lodging?"

"No."

"But—why? I don't understand."

"Don't—or won't?" he asked coldly. "This is your room. I have sent for your things and left word with your landlady that you will not be returning."

"You can't do that," Eleanora protested, her face as blank as her mind.

"I can. I have."

No. No. No. The negative screamed inside her brain, but with an effort of will she held it back. She could not decide, somehow, whether the colonel was acting as the provost marshal or as a man. If the first, she had few resources with which to defend herself. If the last, then she need feel no compunction about the methods she used to defeat him.

"I understand," he said slowly, as if feeling his way, "that you have a brother."

She agreed tentatively.

"His commanding officer tells me that you are stranded here, penniless, because of a land deal that fell through."

Eleanora stared at him doubtfully. "That is correct."

"I have been empowered to offer you, Eleanora Villars, passage to New Orleans and General Walker's regrets for your misfortune. That is the reason I followed you this morning."

"Oh," Eleanora said, at a loss. It was the last thing she had expected to hear.

He went on without pause. "I have decided, on second thought, to withdraw the offer."

"You—" Eleanora's thoughts were too confused, too heated to put into words. Her fingers were trembling. She laid down her spoon with care and dropped her hands into her lap, clasping them together until the knuckles whitened.

"Don't you want to know why?"

"Of course," she answered briefly, resisting the urge to sarcasm.

"Because Uncle Billy has taken unto himself a mistress."

Her incomprehension was obvious.

"Uncle Billy—William Walker. It is a name given to

61

him by his men. We all have our nicknames, a sign of the bond among the men who came here with him."

"The Immortals," she said.

"That bit of mythology began in Rivas, started by the Costa Ricans—or maybe it began in Sonora. It's hard to tell now."

The reflective tone of his voice was an encouragement. "And you, Colonel? Do you have a nickname?"

He stood up, his manner abrupt as he crossed to the window to lean his arm upon the grille, staring out into the night. "None that would interest you. My name is Grant. You had better get used to calling me that."

"Had I?" Dryness edged her tone. Quiet self-control had its purposes, but it was beginning to appear that it would avail her nothing. "You were, I think, going to explain."

"The woman the general has taken under his protection is an aristocrat, a *criolla*, born of wealthy parents of Spanish descent here in Nicaragua. Her parents, now dead, were Legitimistas, as was her husband, an elderly man who wasted her inheritance trying to return to Spain as a grandee. He died there without ever sending for his Nicaraguan wife, Niña Maria. Despite the present cooperative government with the Legitimista president at the head, the aristocrats have no love for Walker. They resent Niña Maria's association with him, and they have most successfully ostracized her." He turned to face Eleanora. "Do you begin to see?"

She had no intention of helping him. She shook her head.

"Walker has arranged a reception tonight for the American minister, John Wheeler. The men of the town will come; the execution of Mayorga had that much influence. But their stiff-necked wives have sent their excuses. A plague of indispositions seems to have struck the women of Granada. Walker has sent out an S.O.S. to his officers. Bring women. He does not intend for his Niña Maria to be more uncomfortable than he can help. There are not that many women who, even under the circumstances, will make a respectable addition to the company. Something about you reminds me of Niña Maria Irisarri, a look as though if life had treated you differently you might have been a lady. You will attend the general's reception with me—as my mistress."

The blood drained from Eleanora's face, then rushed back with a suffocating heat. "No," she said. Rising to her feet, she repeated louder, "No, I will not! You must be mad to suggest such a thing. I would rather die than be paraded before the world as your woman. I hate you! Because of you I have lost my country, my home, and security, my clothes, the mementos and keepsakes of my family. Because of you I have been reduced to poverty and squalor in a country I had hardly heard of a month ago, a country that is breaking my brother's heart and spirit. In spite of all that, Colonel, I am a lady. You can insult me, but you cannot take that from me, I won't let you. And I advise you to think twice before using force to get what you want. I have nothing to lose in making you the laughingstock of Granada at this reception!"

That reminder of the events of the morning touched him on the raw. He moved closer as he spoke. "It's easy to see you know nothing of force. I could make you much sorrier than you realize. It will not be necessary to demonstrate, I think. There is a detail you do not know. Have you any idea where your brother is, now, at this moment?"

"What do you mean?" she asked, anxiety sharpening her voice.

"I thought not. There is a Jean-Paul Villars at present in the guardhouse on charges of drunkenness and resisting the military police. And there he will stay until I free him. I may be wrong, *cara*," he said, injecting a sarcastic amusement into the endearment, "but I believe your brother will serve as a hostage for your good conduct. He will serve his ten-day sentence, but whether he gets out at the end of it will depend on you, and how you—please—me."

Four

Eleanora stared at him. She wanted to defend her brother, to deny the accusation, but it seemed all too probable the colonel was telling the truth. "You—you wouldn't take such a base advantage?"

"No? Who will stop me? You asked for the name given to me by the men. I'm called—and it's no compliment—the Iron Warrior because I always do what must be done. I am the man who commands the firing squad, the man who orders the whippings and brandings of the men in the ranks. I have been told to bring a woman tonight, and I will, whatever the cost."

"It's very well for you to talk of cost," she told him bitterly. "You won't be paying it."

"That is a matter of opinion." His mouth grim, he strode to the door and flung it open. "Señora!" he shouted, and stood in the doorway with his hands on his hips until the thin Spanish woman arrived, her wrinkled-crepe cheeks flushed with hurrying.

"Señora Paredes, the young lady has decided to attend the reception. You will help her dress."

"I do not need help," Eleanora declared. Neither of the other two paid the least attention to her.

"Her things have come. She hasn't a great many gowns to choose from," the señora said.

"There must be something else besides what she has on," the colonel answered impatiently.

"One other."

"Then bring it."

Her lips tight, the woman did as she was bid, returning with Eleanora's belongings packed tidily in a palm-fiber basket.

"I have taken the liberty of ordering a bath," she said.

Eleanora found herself watching Colonel Farrell as anxiously as the señora. On the ship the only facilities for bathing had utilized seawater, and at the Hotel Alhambra, she and Mazie had indulged in a long, leisurely soak to remove the salt from their pores. There had, however, been no facilities whatever at the widow's house.

Looking from one to the other, the colonel gave an abrupt nod. "Keep in mind that the reception begins in less than an hour and a half. The general does not like to be kept waiting, nor do I."

When the footsteps had receded the short distance down the inner galería to his bedchamber, Eleanora turned to the older woman. "You need not stay," she said. "I can manage quite well by myself."

The señora looked away. "I have my instructions."

"I see. You mean you have been set to guard me. Doesn't it bother you that I am being kept here against my will?"

"I know nothing of the circumstances, and I don't want to know," the woman answered in a colorless tone. "I do not interfere with the colonel."

"Are you so afraid of him, then?"

"He has been good to me, allowing me to stay here in my home."

"Allowing you to be his servant?" Eleanora suggested.

"I serve as his housekeeper, yes, in return for my food. It is better than begging in the streets, the fate which could have been mine, that will still be mine if I displease him."

"The man is despicable, a barbarian," Eleanora raged, turning with a violent switch of her skirts to walk to the open floor-to-ceiling window.

"He is always just."

"How can you defend him?"

The older woman moved past her to close the pair of French doors. "It is easy. First of all, it is true, and second, I have no wish to offend him by discussing him behind his back, especially when he may hear from his bedchamber next door." The look the woman flung her over her shoulder sent a tremor of apprehension through Eleanora. Then she straightened her shoulders. What did she care what he felt? He had not troubled to hide his opinion of her.

Lying back in the warm, violet-scented, soapy water, Eleanora closed her eyes. The tin tub was small, she sat with her knees practically under her chin, but it was deep. Best of all, there was no one waiting to use it. Odd that she could enjoy anything so much with such an ordeal looming before her, and this terrible uncertainty in her mind.

When the reception was over, what then? Would her usefulness be over also? Would she be allowed to leave, steamship ticket in hand? She had no reason to think otherwise, and yet her lips were tender from the kiss Colonel Farrell had taken, and there were faint blue shadows where his fingers had dug into her arms. She could not delude herself that she held no attraction for him; she obviously did. The weakness, then, of her position brought a sick feeling to the pit of her stomach.

She stood in stays and petticoats before the mirror, her arms raised to secure her coronet of braids, when the colonel entered the room once more. Swinging around, she dropped her arms, crossing them over her breasts covered only by the thin lawn of her chemise. "I'm not dressed," she protested.

He did not retreat. "So I see," he replied. "You should have been quicker."

His uniform was immaculate, the crimson jacket adorned by a number of ribboned medals, the white doeskin breeches neatly fastened under his boots. Noticing her gown laid out upon the bed, he placed his hat under his arm and moved to investigate it.

Señora Paredes stood aside. "I have pressed it with a warm flatiron."

"You have my sympathy," he replied.

The task had indeed been a formidable one. The gown of pale-green muslin was made of tier upon tier of flounces edged with delicate white embroidery. Even the wide neckline, designed to display white shoulders, was encircled by a bertha flounce which, falling to the elbows, formed the gown's only pretense to a sleeve.

"It is satisfactory?" the señora asked.

He nodded slowly. "I trust your taste."

"Thank you," the woman returned with grave courtesy,

and catching up her limp black skirts, hurried from the room.

Colonel Farrell turned his attention to Eleanora, ignoring the sparkle of temper in her eyes. "Do you always wear your hair like that?"

"Always," she said briefly, tossing her long, thick braid back over her shoulder.

"I don't like it."

A scathing retort hovered on her lips, then she saw the expectant look hidden behind his lashes. "How would you like me to wear it?" she asked with dulcet sweetness.

"Something softer, with a few curls."

"I'm sorry. I have no idea how to go about it." Her gaze was limpid, her smile smooth.

Tossing his hat onto the bed, he moved toward her. "You begin by loosening the plait."

Eleanora backed away, but not quickly enough. With a quick grip on her elbow, he spun her around and catching her braid, began to undo it. Freed, her hair spread like a fiery mantle over her shoulders, falling well below her hips. Behind her the colonel went still, his hands lax upon her warm tresses.

With a sudden movement, Eleanora twisted away, aware of an overwhelming need to put herself out of his reach. His reflexes were like lightning. One of his hands fastened in her hair, the other caught the wide, ecru ribbon strap of her chemise. There was a rending sound as the age-fragile lawn parted from the ribbon. Slowly, inexorably, she was drawn back against him. Bending his head, he pressed firm, warm lips to the soft curve of her neck.

"Don't," she said with a catch in her voice.

"Please?" he suggested.

"Please."

"Grant?"

She hesitated a long moment, then with tears of pain and chagrin starting in her eyes, she repeated obediently, "Please, Grant." Still, it was not the pressure he exerted that forced the words from her lips; it was the peculiar tension that stretched taut and vibrating between them.

The señora appeared in the doorway, a cluster of milk-white flowers in her hand. "Two of these in the hair, the others at the bodice—" She trailed off in confusion as she beheld the tableau before her.

Without haste, Grant Farrell released Eleanora. Stepping to the bed, he picked up his hat. "Good. I will wait downstairs. Eleanora will tell you what is to be done with her hair."

The easy assurance that rode his shoulders as he moved toward the door set Eleanora's teeth on edge. Without conscious thought her hand went out to her pin-box, a small painted tin which had held almond *dragées*. In a rain of steel pins, she sent it hurtling at his head.

Her aim was not true, the box sailed over the galería railing, landing with a tinkling crash on the stones of the patio below. Señora Paredes gasped, her cheeks as waxen as the wild gardenias she held. The colonel halted. He turned with slow, deliberate restraint, his eyes blank and cold. And then the familiar derision sprang mocking into his eyes. "Next time," he said softly, "aim for the heart, and choose a more lethal weapon."

Eleanora did not answer, neither did she drop her gaze. His was the last word, but she had had the satisfaction of seeing the Iron Warrior flinch.

The fragrant, still air of the patio rose like a warm breath to greet her as she paused at the head of the stair. Seeing the colonel waiting among the lamp-lit shadows of the orange trees below, she lifted the front edge of her hoop and descended with conscious grace and the gentle fluttering of gossamer thin flounces.

"*Bella*—a dream of radiance."

The low voice came from the tiled patio entrance. A man stepped from the dark doorway and moved to the foot of the stairs where he stood waiting in the flickering glow of a lamp on an iron bracket. Dark, softly curling hair, audacious eyes, neat Spanish mustache, Nicaraguan dress uniform, it was Lieutenant Colonel Luis de Laredo, the man she had met in Bank's Arcade in New Orleans.

As she reached the last step, he made her a deep obeisance. "I know now why the moon has hidden her face behind the clouds tonight. She is jealous of you."

To smile and give him her hand in appreciation of the compliment seemed a natural thing. "Thank you," she said softly, though her nerves tingled with the awareness of Colonel Farrell's silent approach.

"Why, it is the lady from New Orleans who would not give her name," the officer continued. "I should have known there could not be two such. I think, perhaps, it is destiny that we should meet again."

"We might have met sooner," Eleanora told him, gently withdrawing her hand, "if you had not kept to your cabin for the entire voyage to Granada."

"You were on the ship? My accursed sickness of the sea! A horse I can ride for days without end, but the very sight of a ship—" He shrugged. "You appear to have survived in good frame, except I think you are thinner than when I last—held you in my arms."

If he meant to make her blush, he succeeded, and it did not help to recognize the cynicism with which the colonel surveyed her heated condition. Had he missed, then, that moment when she had collided with the lieutenant colonel in the barroom?

"Good evening, Luis. I see you are already acquainted with Mademoiselle Eleanora Villars."

"In a manner of speaking, amigo."

The colonel did not respond to the teasingly significant tone. Reaching out, he placed a hand beneath Eleanora's elbow in a gesture that in any other man might have been called possessive. "Then let's go."

Luis stood still, making no attempt to follow them. Looking back, Eleanora thought there was a sallow hue to his features. Sensing her hesitation, the colonel looked back. "Coming?" he asked impatiently.

"I—just thought of something I must do," Luis replied, his face unreadable as he moved out of the circle of lamplight. "I will see you at the reception."

"Don't be long," the colonel said dryly. "You'll miss the grand entrance."

"Now that would be a shame—" Luis agreed, but his mood was distracted.

Niña Maria Irisarri. She swept into the long, mahogany-paneled reception room on the arm of William Walker, a magnificent creature in stiff, gold brocade. Her raven hair, drawn back from a center part, was worn in massed ringlets over her ears and covered by a starched black mantilla. Despite the heat, black velvet had been used to construct the bodice of her gown which narrowed to a point at the waist and over each shoulder. From beneath the shoulder points fell cascades of deep lace ruffles which served as sleeves. Behind the woman walked a pair of identical Indian boys wearing their native costumes of unbleached cotton, full-sleeved shirt, and multihued trousers reaching just past the knee. Upon the shoulders of each boy perched a brilliant green-and-yellow parrot. Following the boys came a tiny girl carrying a fan of yellow feathers so large she was nearly hidden by it.

As Niña Maria passed near where Eleanora stood beside Colonel Farrell, Eleanora saw that she was not as young as she had first thought. Her face was not lined, but she had the self-assurance and lack of freshness that indicated a woman nearing her thirtieth year.

Walker, surveying the predominantly male gathering with displeasure he did not trouble to hide, caught the colonel's eye. He gave a slight nod before moving on to settle his mistress into a high-backed chair at the far end of the narrow room. The chair was not canopied, but with her honor guard of parrot-boys and her fan-bearer, Niña Maria gave the appearance of something perilously near a queen. General Walker leaned to speak to her, then straightened and began to make his way back toward the colonel.

He was not a large man, standing nearly a head shorter than Grant Farrell. Built on slender lines, he had small hands and feet. Hair the color of unbleached flax lay soft and flat across his skull, and freckles from exposure to a too-hot sun meshed in a near-solid cover over his skin. His mouth was wide with an unexpected quirk of humor at one corner. The nose was straight, patrician, but it was his eyes, deep-set behind prominent cheekbones, that snared the attention. From beneath heavy brows they burned a clear and determined gray that was hypnotic in its intensity.

"Colonel," General Walker said in greeting, then turned to Eleanora, patiently waiting to be introduced.

"May I present Eleanora Villars, recently come to Nicaragua, General Walker?" The colonel actually smiled as he spoke, his voice holding a nice blend of pride and affection. More disturbing, he moved nearer, putting his arm around her, resting a hand lightly at the smallness of her waist.

Did one curtsy to a general? It might, under the circumstances, be in her best interests. The light of the hundreds of candles in the overhead chandelier shimmering on the curls massed at the crown of her head, Eleanora gave the general her hand, murmuring, "How do you do?"

General Walker smiled, his gaze minutely appraising, but he skipped the social banalities, swinging back to the colonel. "There is a man waiting in my office whom I would like you to interrogate. He was caught climbing the stairs to my private apartments this evening. Fellow claims to be a nephew of Niña Maria's maid, but the maid is old, with failing eyesight. She has a relative of that name, but she can't be sure this is the man. It strikes me as odd that a nephew would come visiting with a gun hidden under his shirt."

"An assassination attempt?"

"That's one of the things I want you to find out."

"There are others who are better at prying information out of unexpected visitors."

The general nodded his comprehension. "I would prefer not to turn him over to the Nicaraguans unless I have to. I will abide by your decision."

"Very well."

Walker smiled. "I understand your reluctance to leave such a charming lady. However, I will try to keep the wolves at bay for you until you return."

Grimly amused, Eleanora watched the colonel's departure. If he was reluctant to leave her it was more likely to be because Walker was beside her. He could not know how she would behave without his threatening supervision. Perhaps Grant Farrell did not quite realize what a potent weapon he held in her brother?

71

"Tell me, General," she said in a brittle voice, "do you really fear for your life?"

"Let us say instead that I fear betrayal of some kind."

"You mean—spying?"

"Such a thing is not without precedent. I'm beginning to think there is no loyalty or honor in this country. Betrayal seems almost a way of life—but that can't interest you. So you have recently come to Nicaragua? That, I suppose, is true of all of us. How do you like what you have seen so far?"

"It's a beautiful country. I could, I think, learn to love it."

"You say that as if you mean it. I find that most women think of it as overhot, pestilential, and infested with sinister and frightening creatures."

A laugh lit Eleanora's green eyes at his droll tone. "How very unappreciative of them, after you took so much trouble to win it. But I come from Louisiana. I love hot countries."

"Ah, I thought so. Your voice, the way you speak, reminds me of a girl I knew once, a Creole girl from New Orleans."

The gray of his eyes had darkened with the distant remembrance of pain. Was it true, then, that he had loved a girl who died of fever?

"I believe, General," Eleanora said diffidently, "that you may have known my father, Doctor Etienne Villars?"

"Villars? Dr. Villars who treated patients from his house on the Rue Royale? Yes, he was a good friend to a young man just arrived in your city."

"Friend—and colleague?"

Walker grimaced. "At the time I fancied myself a doctor. Then I discovered I could do absolutely nothing to save the people I loved most from pain and death. I watched my mother, for one, die by crippling degrees of rheumatism. All my father's prayers and my expensive skill could not save her."

"I'm sorry," Eleanora said.

"So was your father. He thought reading law and scribbling with a pen for the *Crescent* a terrible waste of my time—and he was right. It was nearly, though not quite, as wasteful as studying for the ministry at my father's knee."

The ministry. That made excellent sense as applied to this man's ban on women and drink for his men. "You have been many things in many places, General, but surely they all helped to prepare you for your present position?"

"As a politician?"

Eleanora smiled, as she was meant to. "As a leader."

"You flatter me, Eleanora, and I have had enough, lately, to feed my conceit. You heard of the visit from the Indians?"

"No, I don't think so."

"They came nearly four weeks ago, a delegation of Toacas and Cookra Indians from the unexplored regions northeast of here. They are extremely primitive people, almost never seen near a town. According to one of their ancient legends, there would come to Nicaragua a gray-eyed man who would deliver them from the oppression of the Spanish. They stood about in the plaza outside for three days watching me come and go, then they asked for an audience. They had decided I was the gray-eyed man destined to fulfill their legend. In recognition, they presented me with offerings of fruits and vegetables."

"It must have been—"

"—Embarrassing? Yes, it was."

"I was going to say moving."

"It was that too, I must admit. The editor of *El Nicaraguense* has gone to excessive lengths to give the story circulation, which—lessens its effect, to my way of thinking. And yet, what happened has reinforced my own feelings about why I am here. Manifest destiny, or my own personal predestination, there is, to me, a fine rightness in being where I am."

It was only as the general finished speaking that Eleanora realized someone was standing at her elbow, waiting to attract her attention. She turned reluctantly, and then her polite smile widened. "Mazie! And Major Crawford. How nice to see someone I know."

William Walker acknowledged the major's bow, but he did not seem particularly pleased to be presented to

73

Mazie. He barely touched her hand before turning to Eleanora. "If you will excuse me, I will leave you to your friends then, mademoiselle. I believe the American minister is finally arriving and the reception line beginning to form."

"Certainly."

"Perhaps we can reminisce about New Orleans another time."

Her reply, if she could have found one, would have been made to his retreating back.

"I think," Mazie said quizzically, "that it was not Minister Wheeler, but the beauteous Niña Maria who required his presence. She has been casting Spanish daggers at you with her eyes this past ten minutes, dear Eleanora. What can you possibly have been talking about with the general to fascinate him so?"

"Don't be ridiculous. He was only being attentive to a guest."

"Yes, well, you will forgive me, won't you," Mazie said archly, "if I point out that I was not singled out for such a signal honor?"

Though she could not say so, Eleanora suspected Mazie's gown of a blatantly Democrático red was a part of the reason. Its skirt was looped and poufed over its enormous girth with clutches of scarlet rosebuds nestled in blonde lace. The low neckline was edged in the same lace in a style known in New Orleans as the *tatez-y,* meaning "touch here." It was not precisely the toilette to appeal to the son of a Protestant clergyman.

His eyes on the new, softer lines of her hairstyle, the major said, "You make a welcome and charming addition to our company tonight, Eleanora. I suppose someone told you of Walker's decree to his officers to bring women?"

"Now, Neville," Mazie protested, unfolding a fan of red silk and ivory and plying it against the heat directly beneath the chandelier. "That isn't very flattering to either of us."

"It's true, nevertheless," Eleanora said, a trace of bravado in her lifted chin. "I came with Colonel Farrell."

Mazie stared at her, a frown beginning in her hazel eyes. "Farrell? But why? You hate the man."

"I had no choice. Jean-Paul—"

"Jean-Paul wanted his sister to plead his case with the general. He's in the guardhouse, you see. I tried to convince Eleanora that Walker wouldn't listen, but she will do anything for her brother."

At the sound of Grant Farrell's voice, hard and even, so close behind her, Eleanora controlled a start, a *frisson* of something like panic running along the surface of her skin. He had not reentered the room by the same door from which he had left it. To be forced to endure his fingers on her arm, pressing into her skin, and his subtle threat, nearly destroyed her composure.

The remainder of the evening passed in a strained haze of stilted conversation and restricted movement under the watchful eye of Colonel Farrell. She remembered moving in the line past President and Madame Rivas, the American minister, John Wheeler, and her host. She could recall when Major Crawford and Mazie left them for more congenial company. Still, her greatest awareness was concentrated on the increasingly proprietorial attitude the colonel adopted toward her. He wasted no opportunity to touch her, guiding her, directing her attention, helping her with her voluminous skirts. Standing before the refreshment table he took her glass from her hand, and turning it, deliberately drank from the side her lips had touched, a look of such obvious anticipation in his eyes that she longed either to slap him or to run. That is, she did until she realized his act was for the sole purpose of annoying her.

"You look besotted," she told him in a fierce undertone.

"Maybe I am," he replied.

"Yes, and maybe mules fly like Pegasus," she scoffed.

"You underestimate your attractiveness."

"And you my intelligence. You have no use for me or the kind of woman you think I am. Why pretend?"

"No use?" he queried with the lift of a dark brow. "I can think of at least one—other than distracting notice from Uncle Billy and his paramour."

Eleanora followed his sardonic gaze to the end of the

75

room where William Walker leaned attentively over Niña Maria. "You are hypocrites, both of you."

"Explain." His voice was terse, his eyes hard.

"You do remember inviting Mazie Brentwood to leave Granada, don't you? That's hardly just, since apparently neither you nor the general leads the life of a monk." It was irritation that carried her through that difficult speech. Why had she embarked on such an awkward subject? She did not know, but pride would not let her abandon it.

"The general objects, first of all, to camp followers in the line of march because they make the column un-wieldy, take the minds of the men off their job, and increase the possibility of the enemy being informed of our movements. He recognizes that during the lull in fighting they have their uses, and though the last objection still holds, he is willing to overlook them. Your friend Mazie now," he went on, nodding to where the woman, changing partners, was taking the floor in a waltz with Colonel Thomas Henry, another of the officers Eleanora had seen at Bank's Arcade in New Orleans—though he had discarded the sling he had worn then. "She is a different breed. She is here to sell her favors to the highest bidder, and it makes no difference to her how the price is settled. The phalanx has too few good officers to lose any of them on the dueling field over the disposition of a hundred-dollar whore."

"You—"

"And if you see a warning for yourself in that, you can take it exactly as it sounds."

"Mazie is an American citizen. You can't order her around."

"This is Nicaragua, not the United States, and a military government. I can, and I will, do whatever is necessary to keep the men of the phalanx from killing each other."

"The Iron Warrior," Eleanora said, in driest accents, lifting her head. "Take care. At this moment you look more as if you are threatening than seducing me."

"We are making progress then," he replied, his smile without warmth as he set down the punch cup and drew her to his side, "for that is exactly what I am doing."

It was, perhaps, unwise to provoke him, but she could not be silent. She let her hand lie flaccid in the crook of his arm, asking in a bored drawl, "Again?"

His grip as he covered her fingers with his was not gentle. He was prevented from answering only by the appearance of Lieutenant Colonel de Laredo at his side.

"You see before you a desolate, a ruined, man," the Spaniard said with a tragic gesture.

A wary look came into Colonel Farrell's eyes. "How is that?"

"I have searched high and low through the *calles* of Granada and could find no woman who held the least attraction. Only fair women can now arouse my ardor, and here I find Colonel Henry, he of the hundred battle scars, in possession of one of the two such women in the city, and you, amigo, in possession of the other!"

"You do have a problem."

"Yes, and it is this, the gun or the knife?"

"Am I supposed to ask you why?" the colonel inquired with a lift of his brow.

"But yes, amigo. This problem, he concerns you greatly. Colonel Henry is one formidable hombre, the most immortal of the Immortals. He would be hard to kill even with his arm in a sling, and the plump blonde woman, this Mazie, it would not be so rewarding to fight for her as for the woman on your arm, the woman they are calling in the plazas the red-haired witch."

How much of what Luis said was banter, how much serious, Eleanora could not tell. She only knew that his words, coming so close upon Grant Farrell's explanation, gave her a feeling curiously like guilt. She could not help the color of her hair or the fact that her fairness was a rarity here in this country of dark-skinned, dark-haired people. She only knew with a fearful sureness that she should never have come.

"You think," Colonel Farrell asked, "that I would be easier to kill?"

"No, no, my friend, only a little less willing to kill me."

"Forgive me, gentlemen," Eleanora said, "but I think I ought to warn you that I do not automatically go to the victor."

"No, Eleanora, don't say so. You take the challenge from life," Luis said mournfully.

"Good," was her heartless reply. "I believe—Grant, the general is trying to get your attention."

President Rivas had left the reception early, almost immediately following the ordeal of the receiving line. The next to go was Minister Wheeler. Finally it was Walker's turn, the signal that the reception was over and all could retire in order.

Taking his leave of the colonel and Eleanora, the general had been a most gracious host, presenting Niña Maria and insisting that Eleanora and Colonel Farrell join them in their private apartment for dinner some evening. What could Eleanora do but express her delight at the prospect? At the same time, she was aware of a growing sense of unreality. The events of this day, this night, could not be happening to her. She was desperately tired, her sensibilities bludgeoned into apathy, and yet her nerves felt flayed, quivering with the anticipation of yet another blow. What she would do when it came she did not know.

Five

There were no street lamps in Granada. The open expanse of the central plaza was dark except for the faint glimmer of a lighted window here and there and the firefly flicker of linkboys lighting the way of the guests home with their lanterns of pierced tin. The colonel threw a coin to one of the waiting boys, and with a softly murmured *gracias* he started off, silent in his bare feet, looking back often to be certain they were following.

It was slightly cooler outside than in, but the air was heavy, with a sulfurous smell. Low on the horizon to the southeast there was the shimmer of heat lightning, a steady pulsation that seemed to intensify the darkness around them. As they passed the rear of the cathedral they heard the disturbed murmur of pigeons from the cote kept by the holy fathers and the croak of a tree frog, a monotonous sound from a tree in the garden.

A torch burned brightly on either side of the palacio doorway, illuminating the street for some distance and picking out the intricate iron grilles that covered all the windows along the front of the house. The sight was a reminder of Eleanora's close confinement in the upstairs bedroom. Setting her lips, she preceded the colonel into the entrance corridor. She could not, she would not, be locked in again.

A single lantern, hanging from a crossbeam at the foot of the stairs, illuminated the patio. Eleanora stopped beneath it and turned. "Colonel Farrell—"

The commanding lift of his head stopped her, and then she grew angry with herself for being intimidated. "Why must I call you Grant? The masquerade is done, over."

"Is it?"

"Of course it is. I have done what you wanted. Now you must let me go."

"Go? Where? To what?"

The sneer in his voice was all too apparent. Eleanora stiffened. "I don't see that it concerns you. I have resources—"

"I'm sure. You can just as easily put them to use here."

As the probable meaning of his words penetrated, Eleanora flushed. "You don't understand. I can't stay here with you, I can't."

"Because you don't particularly like me? You should have considered that before you made yourself so pleasant to the general, and before you tried to promote a feud between Luis and me. Both maneuvers only served to make it necessary to keep you close to me. Uncle Billy wants to see you again. That is, in effect, a royal command, since whether you realize it or not, he is head of the government here. Add to that, Luis is one of my best officers. I will not have you playing him off against all comers."

79

"I did no such thing!" Eleanora exclaimed in indignation when she could catch her breath. "Lieutenant Colonel de Laredo spoke only in jest."

"Not a healthy thing to do in Granada. Why would he speak at all unless you encouraged him?"

"If you have such a low opinion of me I'm surprised you can tolerate my presence!"

His smile was grim as he moved in closer. "You do very well, as long as your mouth is shut."

She stepped backward, but the newel of the stair was behind her and she was brought up short against it. The metals on his chest cut into her shoulder as she was dragged against him long length. His fingers sank into the soft curls at the back of her head, tightening, holding her motionless for the warm descent of his lips, firm, consuming, destroying thought or resistance. She could not move under the controlled savagery of his passion, and for her involuntary quiescence she was rewarded by a lethal tenderness. His grip loosened, his mouth moved to the quivering corner of hers. A bell pealed, and startled into awareness by its reverberations, she tore her mouth away, twisting out of his arms, half-falling as his boot trod upon the edge of her dipping hoop skirt. He caught her arm, but in the instant of balance she wrenched free, plunging for the dark tunnel of the entranceway.

Once more the bell clanged. It was the pull-bell hanging beside the great front door. That portal had not been barred. Eleanora grasped the handle and pulled it open, then checked, panting, as she saw the uniformed man who stood before her. That instant of hesitation was enough. The colonel was beside her, his fingers closing like a vise about her wrist.

"Yes?" he rapped.

With an obvious effort, the soldier on the threshold conquered his curiosity, schooling his face to impassivity. "Beg pardon, sir. The general requests your presence at the Government House at once. Urgent business."

"Urgent?"

"It's the prisoner, Colonel, the man caught sneaking into General Walker's quarters. He's dead."

"Under questioning?" the colonel asked, his voice sharp.

"No, sir. The Nicaraguans never got a thing out of him. Looks like he was killed to keep him from talking."

"Inform the general I will be with him shortly."

Without waiting for a reply, Colonel Farrell closed the door in the man's face. His voice rasped across the dark space between them with a harsh impatience. "You can walk to your room, or you can go over my shoulder like a sack of horse rations. Take your pick."

Principle should prevent her from cooperating even to that extent, but what did principle matter compared to the prospect of indignity? There was always the hope, however frail, that he would be satisfied with baiting her, with presenting the outward appearance of possession.

"Well?"

"I prefer to walk," she replied in a stifled tone that turned abruptly vicious, "if I must go."

"You must," he said, and it was not only the hollow echo of the stone passageway that gave his words the timbre of grim disappointment.

The heat was a fierce presence in the closed room, an enemy that drew the smell of dust and ancient mildew from the dry and creaking walls and scorched the breath in Eleanora's nostrils. A slow dew of perspiration formed upon her face, trickling into her hair. Stripped to chemise and one petticoat, discarding even her ankle-length pantalettes, she lay upon the bed, listlessly fanning with her handkerchief, thinking with longing of her grandmother's evening fan of pleated lace with mother-of-pearl sticks which had been in her trunk. Gone. Irretrievable, like so much else.

She would not think of that. Try as she might, she could change nothing. Explain? Plead? How? How was she to find the words to make the essential truth plain? And having found them, how could she hope to have the colonel believe her against the evidence of his own eyes? And yet, she must try. She was not a fool. She knew it was imperative that she try.

In agitation she swung her feet off the bed and stood up. There was water in the pitcher on the washstand beside the bed. By touch in the night-black room she wet her handkerchief and held it to her flushed face. With her hand trailing upon the high mattress for guidance, she moved about the room. Now and then from beyond the curtained French doors came the glimmer of distant lightning. Perhaps Mazie had been right, perhaps the rainy season was not over.

Lifting the heavy weight of her loosened hair, she pressed the damp cloth to the back of her neck. The beginning of a headache was forming between her temples. It was the oppressive atmosphere in the tightly shut room. She needed air. It was ridiculous to cower here in misery. There was no safety behind those shut doors when the key to the grille beyond was not in her possession. And what good did it do to protect even her modesty when Grant Farrell could come striding into her room at any time he chose?

The table had been shoved out of the way against the wall. Pushing aside the thin muslin curtain, she released the latch and threw the double frames wide. The night air crept around her, not perceptibly cooler but charged with an ozone freshness that was a great improvement. She stood for a time clinging to the cool metal of the grille, watching the heat flashes light the lower edge of the black night sky to gray-blue. Tiredness trembled along her nerves, but she could not compose her mind to sleep. When would Colonel Farrell return, and in what mood?

After a time the trembling communicated itself to her fingers. Relaxing their cramped hold, she turned away. Her petticoat dragged at her waist, a constricting weight that flopped limply around her ankles as she walked. In sudden annoyance she jerked the bow in the tapes undone and stepped out of it, flinging it at the bed.

It was much cooler in her thigh-length chemise. The torn ribbon strap allowed the neckline to gape, showing the soft fullness of one breast nearly to the pink aureole, but it could not be helped. She had nothing with which to make repairs, and nothing else to use for a nightgown.

If only the bed was in front of the window. She might be able to sleep in that slight draft. The whole room might have been pleasant enough if she could have opened the door to the inner galería for cross ventilation. That was denied to her, of course. The next best thing then was to place a pallet on the floor, something she had often done as a child in New Orleans. It was cooler at that lower level, cooler without the smothering softness of a mattress. A sheet spread over one of the rugs strewn over the floor would make an acceptable substitute.

She had not been stretched out upon the floor long before the silent current of a breeze stirred her hair. Sighing, she turned on her side, moving her hair from under her face, spreading it out around her with a sweep of her arm. She closed her eyes.

Alarm, insistent, jangling, woke her. Wind, chilling in its rush, swirled over her. It had torn the curtains from where she had draped them, billowing the gauzy material toward the ceiling. Outside, it scoured the stone face of the palacio with a whining rush, rattling the grilles beneath the overhang of the galerías, and, in the distance, setting the cathedral bell to swinging so that it announced the storm with a mournful and discordant chime.

Eleanora sat up, hugging her arms, her gaze going automatically to the window opening. Lightning streaked molten silver across the blue-velvet night sky. It was followed by the rumbling roar of thunder, but she did not hear it. Her concentration was focused on the man who stood on the galería outside her window. The wind tore at his dark hair but had no other visible effect on the bare-chested figure planted with his back to the railing, the bronze muscles of his shoulders and forearms etched in silver fire against the skyline.

It was Grant Farrell, his eyes unreadable and his teeth bared in a ferocious smile as he stared at her. How long had he been there, how long had he watched, gloating, over her near-nakedness?

Scrambling to her feet, Eleanora ducked under the blowing curtain, reaching for the leaves of the French doors. With an almost casual movement, the colonel reached out and stripped the chain, already unlocked, from the grille. The wrought-iron barrier creaked open, he shouldered through, and with upraised palms blocked the closing doors. Eleanora braced, straining, against them,

83

but she was no match for either the colonel or his battering ally, the wind.

The doors gave way, crashing against the wall. Eleanora stumbled back, then kept retreating, watching with exaggerated care the lithe and sure advance of the man silhouetted now in darkness.

"Wait," she said breathlessly, one hand going out in an unconsciously supplicating gesture.

"Wait for what? You knew it would come to this in the end." His voice was soft, not gloating, not coaxing, just quietly unrelenting.

"No," she denied, her voice strained. "If you do this— I will never forgive you."

"I have no use for forgiveness."

It was useless. Words could not reach him, still she had to try. "You will regret this. I am not—"

"Regret it?" he cut across her faltering attempt at an explanation. "Are you threatening me? Fair enough. I never mind paying for what I want."

The shock of anger rippled through Eleanora. In a flash of blue-white lightning she saw the cynical twist of his lips and, without conscious intent, struck out at him. Her wrist was captured, twisted, pinned behind her back. She was dragged against him, her breasts pressed to the board hardness of his naked chest. Eleanora gasped as the breath left her lungs, but she brought her free hand up, clawing instinctively for his eyes. He snapped his head back, letting her rake his neck before he wrenched that arm down and behind her also. Her hands were numb, her shoulders straining in their sockets as he lifted her, still she jerked her head forward. With satisfaction she felt his lip split against his teeth, heard his muffled oath. And then she was swung violently, dizzily so that for a panic-stricken instant she was still, accepting the iron-bound circle of his arms.

They landed on the bed with a force that jarred it against the wall and set the rope supports to jouncing. Her knee came up, and in burning determination, she thrust herself away from him, arching her back. With a surge of triumph she felt the grip of his fingers loosen and break on her left wrist, and setting her teeth, she redoubled her efforts. But using his free hand he gripped the lawn of

84

her chemise between her heaving breasts and pulled, rending it from neckline to hem. The blood rushed to Eleanora's head. She stiffened. And then as she felt his warm hand cup the soft ripeness of her breast, she brought the heel of her hand up, flailing at him with frantic strength, wriggling, sliding, letting her weight drag her over the side of the bed. What was left of the chemise rode up about her shoulders baring her lower body, but she did not care. Nothing mattered except escaping Grant Farrell's merciless embrace.

She could not. The ends of her hair were caught under his elbow. The bones of her right wrist ground together as he retained that hold. He reached for her, his hand sliding over her bare hip before catching the back of her thighs and heaving her upward. He rolled upon her, clamping her arms to her sides, pushing his knee between her legs. Lightning crackled. Panting, they stared into each other's eyes, she with a wild despair, he with baffled ardor. Slowly he lowered his blood-stained mouth to her trembling lips. Long and deep he kissed her, taking full advantage of her exhaustion. Tears of pain and frustration rose, overflowing in wet tracks across her temples, running into her hair. Outside the first shafts of rain struck the house, blowing onto the floor of the galería with the wet splutter of ridiculing laughter.

He explored the moist corners of her eyelids, the curve of her cheek, and the line of her jaw where it merged with the tender curve of her neck. His quickening breath seared her skin, touching off a prickling reaction of gooseflesh that became an uncontrollable shudder as his lips trailed fiery kisses to the valley between the white globes of her breasts. As he chose one of them for closer attention she felt an explosion of such helpless wrath that she lunged under him, hands spread, braced on the mattress, every muscle straining to throw him off. The effort served only to whet his desire. He shifted, divesting himself of his breeches in a few swift movements before she could renew the attack. And then he was upon her once more, his hardness, the ridged muscles of his legs, pressing into her thighs. He possessed her mouth, his hands ravaging her flesh with an intimacy she could not prevent. From

85

deep inside she felt the acid spread of a growing weakness, a primitive impulse toward surrender that had nothing to do with her will. She fought it, moving her head in a faint negation, but the heat of his body, his every touch added to the destruction of her defenses. The vulnerability of her loins became an ache needful of assuagement. Still she resisted that final pillage—resisted, and her writhing helped his implacable, burning entry. Her indrawn breath was trapped, bursting, in her chest while her every muscle and nerve tensed in rejection. He released her hands as he changed position, and immediately she clutched his shoulders, digging her nails into the skin in a mindless effort to communicate her extremity to him. His lips caressed the taut skin of her neck below her ear. His whisper was a soft rustle of reassurance. Slowly, insidiously, her distress was soothed; she began to relax. Then came the tumult of his pleasure. She could only cling to him, accommodating him in his passion as he wished, because it was less hurtful, until it was over.

He withdrew from her abruptly to lie, raised on one elbow, staring in her direction through the dark. Gradually her breathing slowed. She could hear the rain, drumming on the roof. Turning her head, she could just make out the muslin curtain flapping wetly in the mist-laden wind.

The bed creaked as Grant Farrell swung off the side. There was the scratch of a sulfur match, and light bloomed atop the candle on the washstand. She made a swift attempt to cover her nakedness, pulling at the rag of her chemise, her eyes wide and deep, dark green. Shaking out the match, he tossed it to the washstand, then like the release of a tightly wound spring he reached for her, dragging her from the bed to stand beside him. Together they stared at the red stain smeared on the sheets. His hands tightening on her arms, he swung her to face him.

"Why?" he demanded, a shadow that might have been bewilderment clouding his eyes.

The coldness of angry pride invaded her face, smoothing her features to a bitter contempt. Slowly, almost gently, she removed herself from his grasp. Shrugging out of her torn garment, she let it fall to the floor, then took up her petticoat that had fallen over the foot of the bed. Its wide width wrapped about her like a cloak, she moved to the window, and stepping around the wet floor and sodden curtain, stood leaning against the frame, staring out over the red roofs of the town, glistening under the last fitful flares of lightning, toward the cloud-shrouded cones of Ometepe.

"You sound," she said at last, "as if I am to be the accused."

He stepped to the foot of the bed, his hand resting on one of the upright posts. "I don't rape virgins," he said grimly.

"Don't you? Well, no, perhaps not, not the ones who are properly guarded. Those who aren't must, of course, be fair game."

"You have a tongue in your head, you could have told me."

"Yes, and I might have if I had realized it would make a difference. You could have made certain before mistaking me for a—a woman of the streets."

"There was ample reason to take that for granted," he grated.

"Indeed? But then, it doesn't matter, does it? I have your word for it that a woman, any woman, may not be forced, in Nicaragua, that she must be paid or cajoled." Slowly she turned to face him. "For what you have done, Colonel Grant Farrell, the penalty is death."

No flicker of expression crossed his face for a long moment, then a wolfish light blazed in his eyes. He advanced upon her, and bending, scooped her high into his arms. His gaze raked her stiff face and the soft swell of her breasts where she held the material across them.

"Then," he said, his voice holding a rough edge in its softness, "I will have something more to make it worth presenting my back to a firing squad."

Fists, pounding on a door, jerked Eleanora from the deep sleep of exhaustion. She was instantly aware of many things, the flood of sunlight in the room, her nakedness under a thin sheet, the warm abrasiveness of a man's body against her, soreness, the wild tangle of her hair, and a deep mental malaise.

The knocking was coming from the door to her room which overlooked the patio. Above the noise came the sound of women's voices raised in altercation. The colonel lay still beside her, but he was not asleep. She could feel the tension of alertness in his muscles. The knob of the door was shaken viciously, and then the voices began to fade.

Throwing back the sheet, Colonel Farrell sat up and, from the sound, began to pull on his breeches. Eleanora closed her eyes, a slow flush moving painfully to her hairline. Perhaps he would leave without speaking. She had nothing to say to him, no wish to look into his face ever again. His easy mastery of the responses of her body was like a canker hidden deep inside her. She thought she had kept the full knowledge of it from him under the mantle of darkness, but she was not certain her powers of dissembling would be proof against the bright glare of morning.

In the next room a door opened. Footsteps crossed the board floor and clattered nearer along the galería. They could hear the voice of Señora Paredes in unusual agitation, coming nearer. "Wait, Juanita! No! This is stupid, a madness."

Suddenly the muslin curtain, dried in the morning breeze from the lake, was swept aside. A woman, dark, Spanish, stepped into the room. Her face was aristocratic with thin, arching brows and an imperious nose, the thin nostrils flaring with anger. Her sherry-colored eyes narrowed as she surveyed Eleanora in her tangle of sheets, and she tossed back the mane of dark hair that hung between her shoulder blades. Beneath the low neck of the thin white blouse, such as the peasant women wore, her honey-colored breasts rose and fell with the swiftness of her breathing. Her feet were bare and spattered with mud from the street. She wore no petticoat under her tiered skirt of red and blue and green, for the sun shown through it, outlining her sturdy limbs.

"Your pardon, Colonel," Señora Paredes said from the doorway. "I could not stop her."

88

"That's all right. You can go." His voice was curt. He did not take his eyes from the woman called Juanita.

The señora effaced herself at once. Juanita took a step forward, her hands on her hips. "So. I heard it in the plaza, but I did not believe it. The iron *soledad* has taken a woman, a *norteamericana,* into his house to warm his bed. Why, *amor mio?* Did you grow tired of coming to me? I would have come to you. You had only to ask."

"But I did not ask, did I?"

His distaste for the scene she was enacting was plain in the deadly quiet comment. In Juanita's place, Eleanora thought, she would have been too mortified to continue, even if she could have brought herself to descend to such self-abasement in the first place. Feeling at a disadvantage, she struggled to a sitting position, hugging the sheet to her chest, her gaze on Juanita.

The Spanish girl flushed a dusky carmine. Her eyes began to glitter. "Do you think I am some side-street *puta* to be cast aside when you are done? I am Juanita! Half the Falangistas are wild for me."

"Then go to them."

"You—you are a devil, Grant," the girl said, changing her tactics abruptly. "Why? Why do you do this to me? Why have you replaced me with this pasty-faced weakling with no blood in her veins? She is a frail reed, she will break in your arms. You will have to take your pleasure, for she can give you none."

Eleanora stirred restively. Glancing at her, Grant smiled for the first time. "You're wrong," he told the other girl.

Juanita controlled her temper with an effort. Her hands dropped to her sides, the fingers curling into claws. "Then I am to be nothing to you, to have nothing."

An added hardness crept into Grant's face at that last mercenary suggestion. "What did you expect?"

"Something more than to be left for such a one as this—this shadow of a woman. See her sitting there? She cares not what you do. She has no feelings for you or she would curse me, she would fight me for you."

"Maybe she knows there is no need."

That remark struck Eleanora as exquisitely humorous

under the circumstances. She tried to keep from smiling, but she could not.

"Hah! You dare to laugh at me," Juanita screamed. "I'll scratch your grinning face to ribbons, you thieving she-dog!" Her teeth bared, she threw herself across the bed at Eleanora, tearing at the sheet, reaching for her hair with talonlike fingers. Eleanora evaded her by reflex alone, flinging out a warding hand that caught Juanita full across the bridge of her nose. The other girl's nails raked down the inside of her forearm in long, bloody stripes while she mouthed curses through tears of pain.

An instant later, it was over. Grant dragged Juanita shrieking from the bed with an arm about her waist. His clasp none too gentle, he carried her out onto the galería. As he hoisted the girl over the railing, Juanita's screams of anger turned to pleas for mercy and she twisted against him, clinging with both arms around his neck. Alarmed, Eleanora left the bed in time to see him drop the woman's legs, and reaching up, pry her hands loose. Holding her wrists, he let her hang, dangling at arm's length, for a long moment, then he let her go.

She fell with an ear-splitting cry, landing with a thud in the muddy street below. A flood of shrill invective proclaimed her unhurt. Within seconds she appeared in the middle of the street, her skirt plastered with mud, and her dirt-streaked face contorted with rage. "You will pay for this, Colonel Farrell, you and your red-haired bitch! You will pay!"

Without answering Grant turned and stepped back into the room. He paused as he saw Eleanora standing just inside, her green-gold eyes wide in her pale face, sheet gripped in her hand as if for protection, then he pushed past her. Moving to the armoire, he opened the door and took from it her three dresses, her petticoats and panta-lettes, and the collapsed cage of the hoop Mazie had given her. With these under his arm, he stepped from the room, clanged the iron grille shut, and locked it. He stared at her through the arabesque intricacies of its design, as if waiting for her protest. When she made none, he swung on his heel and walked away.

Breakfast of hot coffee, fruit, and a pastry much like a French *beignet* though made of corn meal was brought to her with a bath and a change of linens. With each trip Señora Paredes carefully unlocked the door and locked it again behind her. Since the woman did nothing without consulting the colonel, Eleanora supposed she had him to thank for the attention to her comfort. The thought did not incline her to charity toward him. Nothing could do that.

The hot meal cakes were fried light and crisp, the coffee, diluted with warm milk, was fragrant. Eleanora had little appetite, but it would be ridiculous to starve herself for the sake of her vanished chastity. Who would know, or care? Later, as she lay in the tin tub with her hair draped over the side to keep it dry, she had to admit to a certain sense of well-being. If she was not being kept a prisoner she thought, idly squeezing water from her bathcloth over her knees, she might have felt well indeed.

The sound of a key in the lock roused her. She turned her head, expecting to see the señora once more. It was Grant Farrell, militarily correct in his uniform, who entered. In his hand he carried a small box of polished wood which he opened and placed upon the bed. The interior was lined with maroon velvet and divided into compartments. From one of these he took a small glass bottle and a square of cloth. Holding these in his hand he straightened and issued a one-word command. "Out."

"What is it?" she asked without troubling to hide her suspicion.

"Carbolic for your scratches," he answered, moving closer.

"Leave it and I'll attend to them."

He stared at her a considering moment before shaking his head. "I want to know it's done. Scratches can lead to blood poisoning in this climate. Are you coming out, or will this have to be the hard way too?"

"If you try it," Eleanora said, tilting her head, "you are going to get wet."

He did not smile, but in some peculiar way his face lightened. "If I do you won't enjoy it. I'll have to take off

91

my uniform, and while it dries I will be in need of—entertainment."

Eleanora was the first to look away. "How can you—when you know how much I dislike this, and you?"

"Dislike? That's an improvement. Yesterday you hated me. Who knows how you will feel a week from now?"

She glared at him before asking, "Will you hand me the towel?"

"With pleasure," he replied, and tucking the carbolic and cloth under his arm, picked up the linen cloth from the end of the bed and held it wide, inviting her to be wrapped in its softness.

Holding out her hand for it did no good; Eleanora let it fall. She sat biting the inside of her lip, then with the dignity of an ancient princess passing into the hands of her menials, she rose and stepped from the tub. He enfolded her, his hands moving over the curves of her body. She tried to move away, but he would not release her until she stood still within the circle of his arms.

"My scratches?" she reminded him, her color high and a trace of sarcasm in her tone as she gained possession of the towel.

"Scratches. Yes."

He removed the stopper from the glass bottle and poured the pungent solution on the cloth. Taking her arm, he swabbed the long, raw stripes with swift efficiency, paying no heed to her involuntary wince of stinging pain. From under her lashes, Eleanora watched his frown of concentration. She could see the bluish bruise on his bottom lip and the small cut where she had struck him. The sight was most satisfactory, yet at the same time, it made her feel a little ill. Her fingers curling, she remembered the feel of her own nails tearing his flesh. There was, above the collar of his tunic, an abrasion of the skin. Was that her doing? Had he put anything on it, she wondered, but would not ask.

He put the disinfectant away and fastened the box. Flicking a glance up at her, he said, "You haven't asked why I took your clothes."

"I doubt I will like the answer. I am more interested in when you intend to bring them back."

92

"You'll get them back when I'm ready to let you go."

"I am to be your—guest—indefinitely, then?"

"Exactly." Inclining his head, he picked up the medicine chest and started toward the door.

"You can't leave me here again with nothing to do," Eleanora said. "I'll—I'll go mad."

He paused, looking back at the appealing picture she made clothed in the satin mantle of her russet tresses and the linen cloth that barely came to the tops of her thighs. "What did you have in mind?"

"I don't know. Sewing. Books, newspapers."

"Don't tell me you mean to accept your prison?"

"What choice have I?"

His blue gaze turned disconcertingly intent. "None," he said shortly.

She let him get as far as the door before she spoke again. "Grant?"

He swung back, waiting.

"Is my brother all right? Does he need anything? Food? Clothing?"

"Nothing you can give him," he answered, and let himself out the door, locking it behind him.

The smell of carbolic lingered on the air, a potent reminder of their exchange. To escape it, Eleanora picked up her hairbrush from the washstand and moved to stand in the shadows to one side of the window, staring out.

Men with pushcarts cried their wares up and down the streets. Servants carrying market baskets moved toward the plaza. From the direction of the cathedral came a widow from early mass, her mantilla dripping with black jet tears of mourning. Behind her moved two government clerks in yellowing white jackets. A nun, shepherding several pigtailed girls with gold earrings flashing in their ears, passed. The *religieuse* looked incredibly hot in her black habit even though she, like the rest, kept to the shady side of the street opposite.

Eleanora's throat ached with the need to call out to the people moving past for help. But what was the use? They would not dare defy the authority of the head of the military police. And if they did, then what? Even if she had a place to go and work to sustain herself, she could not leave Jean-Paul to the dubious mercy of Colonel Farrell.

Ruined. Her mind rejected both the thought and her position. Still, in the bright light of morning, she realized how useless was her implied threat to see Grant Farrell pay for what he had done. Who would believe it, and if they did, who would arrest him? General Walker? Hardly, when she had allowed herself to be presented to him in the role, if not in fact, of the colonel's mistress.

Beneath her window a door slammed. Grant Farrell moved from under the overhang of the galería. He stood for an instant placing his hat on his head, then strode purposefully away, heading up the street to the plaza.

Eleanora watched his receding back out of sight. Her hand on the door frame trembled faintly, and doubling it into a fist, she pressed it to her mouth. The numbness of disbelief lingered at the back of her mind. This could not be happening. It could not.

Swinging from the window, she stared about the small room that was her prison. In the corner between the bed and the French doors was the *cuadro*. The sun illuminated the dark colors of the painting. Crudely done, there was still a feeling of compassion in the bowed head and tear-stained cheek depicted on the canvas. Eleanora would not cry, but moving carefully in her towel wrap, she struck a match and held it to one of the candles beneath the likeness of Our Lady of Perpetual Sorrow.

Six

The morning crept by with infinite slowness. Only two events provided diversion. Shortly after the colonel left Juanita returned and was admitted. Eleanora expected the woman to come to her room, perhaps to resume her taunts or her attack, but she did not. Once she heard the sound of breathing outside her door and the rustle of clothing as someone stooped to the keyhole, but they went away when a handkerchief was stuffed into the slot. The bell rang again later. The second visitor was not allowed to enter, however, and Eleanora moved to the window in time to see Mazie retreating, her skirts held high as she crossed the muddy thoroughfare below on pattens. She called after her, but a mule-drawn cart with a furiously screeching wheel intervened and Mazie did not hear.

Colonel Farrell failed to return for the midday meal as Eleanora had half expected. A bowl of chili con carne, corncakes covered with melted goat's cheese, and fruit was served to her through the grille. When she had finished, she pushed the dishes back out onto the galería for the señora to collect, but they sat there through the afternoon, attracting a buzzing horde of flies. Heat-drugged, they flew into the room, bumbling about between the walls and ceiling with a maddening sound that destroyed sleep. For a time Eleanora closed the French doors against them, but the airless heat was worse than the flies. She was forced to open them again.

Sometime after three o'clock the clang of the bell resounded through the house once more. Eleanora lay still. She had realized finally that the señora had orders to turn away visitors. On consideration it was not surprising. Even if the colonel did not fear reprisal, it could not add to his credit to have it known that he had to use force to keep a woman.

She had nearly forgotten the visitor when a thumping noise came from the far end of the galería. A board creaked under the weight of a tread. Beyond the iron grille loomed a shadow form, and then as Eleanora raised on one elbow, a man peered into the room.

"Ah, Eleanora, I have found you in spite of that dragon's handmaiden below."

"Luis—Lieutenant de Laredo; how—what are you doing here?"

"I wanted to see you. There was a bougainvillea growing at the end of the house. The thing arranges itself. I have only to brave the thorns." He looked ruefully at his palms covered with bleeding lacerations.

"Well you will have to brave them again. You can't stay."

"Eleanora, you could not be so cruel. I have come to entertain you. See?"

She barely glanced at the guitar he brought from where it was slung on his back by a cord. "To entertain me?"

"But yes, *querida*." His voice was softly beguiling, his smile, below the dark line of his mustache, caressing.

"Has it occurred to you that you are braving more than thorns?"

"You mean the colonel? He is a busy man, busy counting the new arrivals, issuing weapons, planning this, planning that with the general. And this morning the man who killed the traitor was discovered. No one will be allowed to give to him the mercy of a bullet to prevent him from telling all he knows. Today he will be—encouraged—to explain his actions and those of his compatriot, and tomorrow they will shoot him."

"The firing squad?"

"The fate of traitors."

Eleanora resisted the impulse to question him further. "It doesn't matter why you came. You can't stay."

"Tell me why, *querida*," he said, resting his shoulder against the grille the better to see in.

"Because—Grant will not like it, and—and I am not dressed."

"My amigo knows we have the same taste in women," he said, his eyes on the length of her legs and her bare shoulders not covered by the towel she still wore wrapped about her. "As for dressing, I like you as you are, but if you insist on it, I will wait."

"You don't understand."

"No?" He lifted a droll brow, making a joke of his desire. "Reveal all to me."

"I have no clothes. Your friend took them."

His face went blank, and then a delighted grin spread across his face in a flash of white teeth. "I never suspected my amigo of such impatience."

"It was not impatience," Eleanora snapped, her anger and sense of ill-usage getting the better of her discretion. "He took them to keep me here."

Stillness sat upon his features. "You wish to go?"

96

"Why else do you think I am locked in with a guard over me?"

He straightened, frowning. "This is bad. That he holds few tender feelings toward women I knew, but I have never known him to use them with cruelty."

"Then you should have been here this morning when he threw Juanita from the galería."

"Yes? I would like to have seen this. Juanita—"

"Yes, I remember, you have the same taste in women," she said as he paused, searching for a way to indicate his knowledge of the Spanish girl.

"There are some women, *querida,* that it is unwise to treat with too much kindness."

"Perhaps I am one of them?" she suggested tartly.

"No, no. There is no comparison, believe me. I don't understand my friend Grant. I don't understand at all. To seduce a lady is one thing, to hold her against her will is another. I think—yes, I think I will have to talk to him."

Eleanora's brows drew together. "That might be dangerous."

"You begin to understand this man then, my Eleanora. But I, too, am dangerous." Without looking at her, he unslung his guitar, and propping against the door once more, began to play a soft and melancholy tune.

She stared at nothing, her green eyes unfocused. How nice it would be to have someone fight her battles for her, remove her from the colonel's sphere of influence, and yet, it would not work. There was always Jean-Paul. She knew also that she had not been strictly honest, and she could not allow Luis to become embroiled in her affairs for the sake of a false premise. She lifted her gaze to that slender figure, narrow-hipped in breeches of cordobán brown leather, his wide shoulders covered by a red shirt with full sleeves, the glint of a gold chain at his neck. Grace, gallantry, and humor—Luis was everything Grant was not. It was a thousand pities he was not the provost marshal.

"Luis?"

"Yes, *querida?*" he answered, his fingers moving on the strings.

"You may understand Grant better if I tell you he did not realize I was—an innocent. He thought I was something very different, as you did in New Orleans."

"And now he knows better?" he asked without looking at her.

She agreed.

"Then you are most generous."

"No," she refused the compliment. "I am only trying to be fair."

"For whose sake, mine or his?" When she did not answer at once, he turned his head. "What I mean is, are you sure you want to leave?"

Eleanora shook her head unhappily. "I want to, yes, but I can't."

"Locks can be broken."

"But not the ties of the heart."

"I see."

"No, you don't. I didn't mean it like that," she began, but already he was moving away. Slinging his guitar over his back, he stepped over the railing, hung for a moment by his hands, then dropped out of sight. In a moment he reappeared down the street, following a dark-haired feminine figure with a seductive swing to her skirt of red and green and blue. It was Juanita, moving away from the house as if she had only just left it. From her vantage point beside the window Eleanora watched as Luis caught up with her, and gripping her arm, swung her to face him. The Spanish girl laughed up at him with a quick greeting that included a kiss on each cheek. Winding her hand inside his arm, she pressed herself against him. Luis, leaning to catch what Juanita was saying, walked away with her without looking back.

The sun went down in a rust-red haze that put a soft edge on objects in the ambient light. Colors were muted, the gold of the stone buildings in the street outside blending with the blue evening shadows. Eleanora seemed powerless to stop herself from watching down that darkening *calle* for the colonel's return. In self-defense she told herself it was better to be forewarned. What good was a pretense to indifference if it left you vulnerable to surprise? She was ready to admit, in any case, that she was not indifferent. Rancor, fueled by a long night of apprehension and a long day of close confinement, burned with a cold fire in the back of her mind. She wanted to make him feel some degree of her helpless humiliation at his hands. She wanted the satisfaction of seeing him called to the account that she had been forced to deny herself earlier in the afternoon. In short, and as far as she was able to accomplish it without endangering her brother, she wanted revenge. For this his presence was necessary.

It was possible that she was not the only one with ideas of revenge. Juanita had been enraged with her dismissal, enraged and hurt, if she was to be believed. It would not be astonishing if, after her degrading expulsion from the house, she felt some desire toward vengeance. Did that, perhaps, explain her visit to Señora Paredes? Was the señora her ally? Wearily Eleanora shook back the warm red mane of her hair. If Juanita was plotting to regain the colonel's affection, then she wished her good fortune. It was a shame they could not scheme together for his downfall.

Night had long fallen and Eleanora was beginning to fear a design to starve her when she heard the rattle of a key in the lock. She lay in darkness upon the bed, completely, and wryly, conscious of the forlorn picture she presented. The colonel's form was outlined for an instant by the gray light of the courtyard, then he stepped into the room, closing the door behind him. She knew he moved, but his footsteps made no sound. Her searching eyes could not penetrate black space around her. He is looking for a light, she told herself. Still her scalp prickled. Abruptly the bed sagged beside her, and long arms reached, dragging her to a hard chest. She felt the imprint of metal buttons and the rasp of beard stubble, and then his lips captured her in careless plunder. For an instant she allowed herself to respond, pressing the open palm of her hand to the muscles of his back. His arms tightened. With an in-drawn breath that verged on alarm she went stiff.

He raised his head without releasing her. "Did you think," he asked softly, "that it was Luis, returned to save you?"

It was an instant before she could find breath to answer. "If I did, I must be disappointed."

"You have a tongue like a viper."

"It is the last form of protection left to me, one I may stand in need of if you are going to set informers around me."

Without warning he let her go. She fell back against the pillows, then reached for her towel, drawing it more securely about her as she heard the striking of a match.

His face had a shuttered look in the yellow glow of the candle. Though he did not glance in her direction, Eleanora was under no illusion; she knew he was aware of her every movement. "Señora Paredes," he began deliberately, "is not an informer. She knows, however, that I am interested in your visitors."

"And what of hers? Did she tell you Juanita was here for the best part of the day?"

"Did she trouble you?"

Eleanora shook her head, her gaze going for an instant to the key still in the door. "I had a certain amount of protection."

"Too bad the same thing kept Luis at bay. When can I expect to receive a challenge from him?"

"I—don't believe you have to worry about that."

"You mean you were able to keep yourself from pouring out your sad story?"

The sarcasm in his voice was an unbearable irritant. "I mean I was able to keep you from sounding the beast you really are. I have no more desire to have blood spilled for my sake than you have to spill it!"

He surveyed her from behind the screen of his lashes, the blue glitter of his eyes grimly assessing. "Noble of you."

"I thought so, considering the possibilities."

This was not what she had intended. Animosity, however much provoked, would get her nowhere. Still, there was no power on earth that could make her take back what she had said. It might even be a good thing, this quarrel. Too much compliance too quickly might make him suspicious.

"Possibilities?" he queried.

She lifted her chin. "You might have been killed."

"I might," he agreed, "then again, I might not. It was smart of you to consider that last possibility the longest."

After that exchange, dinner was a silent meal. The moment it was over, the señora cleared the table, retrieved the dishes from the outer galería, and bade them good night. From his room next door, the colonel brought a sheaf of papers, spreading them out over the table in the light of a candle covered against moths by a hurricane globe.

The moths came anyway, of course, attracted by the light. They swooped about the room, huge winged creatures in gray and soft yellow and green. They seemed to have nearly as great an affinity for Eleanora's hair as for the candle. One, a luna moth, crawled from a russet strand to her bare shoulder where it sat, gently fluttering, a living ornament, for ten long minutes. When it took wing again she followed its flight, watching in concern as it swung in delirious circles about the opening of the hurricane globe. She got to her feet when it perched on the rim, one wing directly over the rising heat. Moving stealthily, she cupped her two hands about it, and carrying it to the grille, pushed her hands through and wafted it up, free, into the night.

She turned back into the room to find Grant watching her, an odd expression hovering at the back of his eyes. Nervously, she adjusted her towel, tucking the ends in place between her breasts for the thousandth time.

Grant's mouth firmed in a thin line. Pushing back his chair, he left the room, returning in a few minutes with what appeared to be a dressing gown swinging from his hand. He tossed it to her without a word, then resumed his seat, bending over his work.

Eleanora shook out the garment. Glancing from the man's dressing gown, or robe, of blue brocaded satin to Grant Farrell, she could not feature him ever wearing it. Where had it come from? The state of warfare between them prevented her from asking. It did not prevent her from accepting it, or from thanking him in subdued sincerity. If he heard he gave no indication.

Before the candle had sunk an inch she was given an

opportunity to show her gratitude, however. Looking up, Grant asked, "You write—and read?"

"Yes."

He indicated the chair across from him. When she had seated herself in it, he pushed a bound book in front of her and handed her a pen. "Copy the name and particulars of these new recruits in the roster," he said, touching a stack of enlistment papers in front of him.

Eleanora flicked her eyes down the page of those already entered. It looked straightforward enough. She nodded and dipped her pen in the ink stand between them.

The only sound was the scratch of pen nibs across paper and the soft rustle of blotting. Now and then as she reached for another paper, Eleanora saw Grant's hand slashing over the page, listing what appeared to be horses and mules and shipments of supplies; food, canvas tents, blankets, saddles, horse blankets, feed bags, grain; and kegs, barrels, and boxes of items with the sound of munitions. At his elbow was a journal identified on the cover as a guard book.

A hundred, a hundred and fifty, two hundred men were recorded as soldiers for William Walker's American Phalanx, with still more to go. Grant had finished the table of supplies and guard book, and was working with a map and several sheets of closely written notes. Flexing cramped fingers, Eleanora asked, "Don't you have a clerk to handle some of this?"

He almost smiled. "The men who came down here with Uncle Billy came to fight, not to count horses."

"You must have come for the same reason."

"Yes, but as military second-in-command this is my responsibility. I don't delegate it because I like to keep the information—close to hand."

Odd. She had thought he was going to say he liked to keep the information to himself. She supposed an interested person could tell a great deal about the strength of the phalanx by looking at the papers scattered around them. And what was it Luis had said? That Grant and Walker were always plotting? There might also be some hint to be found of the general's plans for the future.

102

Yet, what did it matter? As far as she knew Walker was secure in Nicaragua, the two political factions were no longer at war. No, she must have imagined the hesitation. If there was the least danger of the colonel revealing anything of importance, he would never have allowed her near the papers.

The call to filibustering must be a strong one, she thought as she took up her pen once more. If the influx of "soldier-colonists" continued at the same pace for the month of January as for December, there would be more than twelve hundred men under Walker by the end of it. If he had taken Nicaragua with only fifty-eight men, he should be ready to conquer the rest of Central America with that force behind him. She looked up to communicate the humor of that observation to the colonel, but his face was closed, uncompromising.

The night drew in. The moon rose, a pale, cool-looking disk, above the roofs of the town. The satin dressing gown grew overwarm and Eleanora pushed the sleeves above her elbows and eased the heavy shawl collar away from her neck, sweeping the weight of her hair to one side. The action drew the colonel's attention. With her head bent, she was aware of his gaze on the moist skin of her temples, moving lower to where the dressing gown closed in a deep vee. Tossing his pen down, he leaned back, stretching, then with a shake of his head, he reached for it again. The pen skittered across the table and rolled over the edge, falling with a clatter to the floor. He grabbed for it, missed, then dived after it. The thing seemed to elude him with a life of its own. He was so long in returning to an upright position, that Eleanora moved restively, conscious of her bare legs beneath the table and the way she had let the dressing gown fall apart over them for coolness.

The pen had fallen on its point, ruining the nib. The colonel threw it down in disgust and began picking up the books and papers, piling them one on top of the other with a fine disregard for order. He strode from the room with them in his arms, slamming the door behind him. Eleanora could hear moving about in the next room. After a time she dared to hope that he intended to leave her to sleep alone, and began to ready herself for bed.

Her hopes were rudely deflated when Grant Farrell entered the room once more. In his arms he carried his guns, a pair of pearl-handled revolvers, his shaving kit, two silver-backed military brushes, three red shirts with the insignia of his rank on the collars, an extra pair of breeches, and an assortment of other odds and ends. The toiletries and guns he dropped on the washstand, the clothes he threw into the armoire, slamming the door upon them and resting his hand upon it, watching her frown with sardonic amusement.

His purpose was obvious. Still Eleanora could not prevent herself from asking, "What are you doing?"

"I am tired of traipsing back and forth. It seemed more—convenient—to move in with you."

"I suppose I should be flattered," she said tartly.

Moving to the bed, he lay down, stretching out with his hands behind his head, staring up at the drawn muslin that lined the half-tester. "Why?" he asked.

"You prefer to—to have me at arm's length instead of keeping me in some cheap lodging on the other side of the city."

His voice when he spoke was deliberate. "I don't know that I prefer arm's length. And Juanita's lodging, cheap or not, was her own affair. I didn't provide it."

"But you took advantage of it, and her?"

He lowered his gaze. "There are some women who ask to be taken advantage of, and some who resist. Those who ask usually want something."

"Something you don't have to give?" she asked, her face flaming. "Shouldn't you be careful? If you show me too much partiality I might begin to cling."

Even harkening back to their first crossing of swords failed to anger him, or to move him. "I'll chance it," he replied, his tone dry. "Right now I need you to cling to the heel of this boot."

He lifted his leg, waiting patiently to see if she would help him remove his boots. Eleanora tilted her head. "Did you forget to bring your bootjack? What a shame if you had to sleep in them."

"I've done it before, I can do it again," he replied

carelessly. "It was you I was thinking of. I'm a restless sleeper."

She could not resist. "I wouldn't know. I don't remember you sleeping at all last night."

"That," he said gently, "was your fault."

"*My* fault?"

"You shouldn't tempt me. Well, is it to be with, or without?"

It was a task she had performed for Jean-Paul many times when he had come home so deep in his cups he could not make it up the stairs. Fuming at his suggestion, she moved to the foot of the bed. She was so incensed she hardly realized she was complying with his request in a manner that showed acceptance of his presence. It struck her as she held the boot in her hand, and she weighed the heavy cavalry footwear, a speculative gleam in her eye.

"I wouldn't," he drawled, divining her temptation.

After a brief struggle with herself, she nodded, dropping it, reaching for the other. "No, it's not nearly lethal enough."

He smiled and stretched hugely, raised his arms above his head. Lowering them, he began to unbutton his tunic.

Eleanora set the other boot on the floor, lining it up beside the first with care. On the floor, half-hidden beneath the bed, she found a gardenia. Brown, crushed, it was one of those which she had taken from her hair the night before. Her fingers curled around it as she straightened and turned blindly away. With her back to him, she began to shred the flower, filling the room with its decaying fragrance.

His tunic fell to the floor, followed by his breeches. The bed ropes creaked a protest, then he was behind her, his hands on her shoulders, drawing her back against him. Under his fingers the knot of the dressing gown's belt slipped away, the edges fell open. His touch was firm, yet gentle, on her warm flesh.

Her inarticulate murmur of protest was smothered by his lips as he easily quelled her abortive attempt to free herself, turning her to face him. The dressing gown fell away as his arms crossed behind her back. She was pressed

105

to him along the entire length of her body, her breasts flattened against his chest, every sensitive plane and hollow crushed to the mahogany hardness of his frame.

His kiss deepened. A jolting quiver ran along her nerves. Her lips softened, parting beneath his with confiding sweetness. The torn gardenia fell from her fingers unnoticed as she slid her hands along his shoulders, clasping them behind his neck. The lingering, spiced-wine freshness of bay rum invaded her senses. Unconsciously she moved closer. Awareness receded. She felt that she was being consumed, losing herself in the overwhelming heat of his need.

Abruptly she tensed. It would not work, that tenuous plan to make him desire her so that he would be bereft when she disappeared the instant Jean-Paul was released. A pitfall she had not perceived while the colonel was absent was made plain to her. Responding to him could be a major mistake. If she lowered the barrier of her resistance at all, he might enter and take what he pleased. He had the use of her body. He must have nothing more.

Stiff, silent, she lay as he placed her on the bed. She clenched her teeth, straining away as she felt his lips at the base of her throat, half-expecting the tantalizing slide to the mounds of her breasts with their nipples contracted in what must surely be revulsion.

Suddenly he raised his head. "If that's the way you want it," he said, his voice rasping harsh with frustrated disappointment in the darkness.

Grasping her wrists, he wrenched them above her head, holding both in the grip of one strong hand. His mouth forced her lips open in a savage exploration that tasted of blood as he reopened his old cut. His free hand searched her body with a thoroughness that made her gasp and writhe under it. He pushed her thighs apart, turning her to him, fitting their bodies together in an inescapable bond.

In a suffocating upheaval of the senses, Eleanora endured his domination. And when he was done with his ruthless use of her, she twisted away from his slackened

106

hold and lay on her side, chest bursting as she fought the tears that gathered like acid behind her eyes.

She might have won had he left her alone. Instead, he reached across the width between them, and twining his hand in her hair, drew her inexorably closer to lie with her back to him and his body curled about her. This final imposition of his will destroyed her strained defenses. The silent, difficult tears streamed as his hands moved over her, caressing the soft, resilient skin of her waist and belly. Slowly she recognized that the brush of his fingers had grown more questing, his breath on her neck warmer, quicker. With the suddenness of shock her crying ended as she realized that his cure for her sorrowing self-pity was going to be the same as the cause.

Eleanora awoke to a soundless dawn. No wind stirred, the muslin curtains hung limp and straight. The growing light was clear, heralding another fair day, and yet there was a gray threat in the air that seemed to stem from the quiet.

Lying still, she listened. There was no noise of people on the streets, no carts or wagons moving. The house, the room around her was deathly still. No one breathed beside her.

Turning, spreading her arm over the bed, she found what she expected. Grant was gone, as was his uniform. Where he had lain was cold. All that remained was the indentation of his head in the pillow.

She sat up. Something nagged at the back of her mind, something infinitely disturbing. She should be able to remember, but she could not, quite. It was something told to her. Luis—

In that instant of remembrance, the heavy air of the morning was torn by the roaring explosion of a rifle volley. Immediately afterward came the whir of pigeon's wings in startled flight, then a single shot, dull with finality.

The firing squad. The man who had murdered the traitor was to die with the dawn. The bed beside her was empty. It was no accident. The man who had held her in his arms in the night was also the man who commanded the firing squad.

Seven

"They brought the traitor-killer out from the side door of the Government House, through a double rank of Falangistas, the escort party, into the plaza. Eight men waited at attention, weapons at their sides, one containing the squib."

"Squib?" Eleanora questioned Luis. The Spaniard perched upon the railing, his fingers drawing a wandering tune in a minor key from his guitar as he described the public execution in the central plaza only a few hours earlier.

"The blank, the conscience round, sometimes loaded so that each man may tell himself his was not the fatal shot. A useless device. The recoil is different. A good rifleman always knows."

Eleanora nodded in comprehension. Luis continued, his eyes dark and unseeing.

"At ten paces the escort stopped. The priest came forward. The old women began to tell their beads. When the holy cross was kissed, the priest stepped back, the blindfold was tied in place. The man was turned with his back to the rifles and forced to his knees in the dust. The colonel drew his sword, gave the order to present arms—aim—fire. The sword fell. Eight shots rang out as one just as the first rays of the sun struck across the plaza."

"And it was over."

"Not quite. The seven shots did not kill. My amigo must needs examine the fallen man, and finding him living still, administer the *coup de grace,* a bullet from his revolver in the ear."

"Dear God," Eleanora breathed.

"It is a terrible responsibility, but someone must do it. Still, if the colonel is silent this evening, you will know what preys upon his mind."

"I—can't believe it will trouble him overmuch."

Luis looked up, his gaze keen. "Then you do not know Grant."

It was a subject Eleanora had no wish to pursue. She let it pass. After a moment of watching Luis's nimble fingers upon the guitar strings, she observed, "It seems a groveling way to die."

"It is the Spanish way. It is not intended to be a proud death."

Was there a rebuke in his grave tone? She did not think so, and yet, she could not be sure. He was not an easy man to understand. His moods changed so easily from the gay to the somber, from passion to remote friendship. Yesterday he had left her in what she had thought to be the anger of disillusion. Today he had returned without explanation, disarming the bougainvillea at the end of the galería with an incongruously large bowie knife, and herself with music and a report of what was happening beyond the palacio.

Looking up, he caught her gaze upon him, and his lips moved in a slow smile that gave a glimpse of the whiteness of his teeth against his teak-dark skin. "Don't be sad, *pequeña*. To die is no great thing. It is living that requires courage."

"That's easy for you to say," she replied, with a lifted brow. "You are one of the Immortals."

His smile fading, he inclined his head in acknowledgment of the shot.

"The name fascinates me. Grant did not want to discuss it—and Major Neville Crawford, when I asked him on the ship coming here, treated the whole idea as a joke."

"Grant has not the gift—as I have—of explaining the beginning of a legend in which he plays an heroic part without embarrassment, and so he will say nothing. Major Crawford makes light of the Immortals because he has no claim to the title. It began in Sonora nearly three years ago with the general's attempt to take Lower California. Major Crawford joined us in New Orleans just before we sailed for Nicaragua this past May."

"Tell me about Sonora."

"That was a madness, an act of chivalry, a noble crusade. The general was plain William Walker then,

109

doctor, journalist, but not a soldier. In the name of the "manifest destiny" of the United States of America to extend democracy to other lands, he marched into Baja California with forty-four men behind him and proclaimed it a free republic with himself as president." He shook his head. "Madness indeed."

"He failed?"

"Nobly. When reinforcement arrived, he moved to annex Sonora. He wanted to free the people of the country from the oppressive yoke of Spain, and make the frontier settlements between it and the United States safe from attack by marauding bands of Apache Indians. This ambitious and idealistic plan had only one flaw. The Mexican government had no wish to give up these lands rich in gold and silver. Walker expected support from the American government for his action, and when it was not forthcoming he was forced to retreat."

He paused a moment, his eyes narrowing. When he spoke again his voice was low. "Have you ever been to Baja? There is nothing there that welcomes man. In the heat and sand, rocks and cactus, even the snakes and lizards must scrabble to stay alive. From La Paz we marched over five hundred desert miles to the Colorado River. The horses died and were eaten. Our shoes wore out and we marched barefoot over the scorching rocks and cactus like needles. The yellow sand grew red with our blood. We ate prairie dogs and rattlesnakes and gila lizards and the pulp of the organ cactus. We even ate buzzards. Our lips parched, our brains baked, and our skins burned and cracked open like meat oozing fat on a spit. The wounded, the weak, the stupid, and the squeamish died first. Fever, more deadly than any enemy, attacked us when we had no strength to fight it. Even now the trail from La Paz to the border below Tia Juana can be traced by the sun-bleached bones of the men we left behind."

His face was so bleak, his voice so softly portentous that Eleanora stood unmoving, waiting for him to go on. The words of sympathy that hovered on the back of her tongue were useless, she knew. They remained unspoken.

Luis's fingers upon the strings of the guitar stilled their

110

melody. He stared down at their slender length and the signet ring on his smallest finger as if he had never seen them before. "There was a mountain pass three miles from the California border. From that height we could see the flag of the United States waving above the military post north of the dirty little town of Tia Juana. It represented safety, food, medicine, all the things we so sorely needed. And then we were stopped. The pass was in the possession of bandido-soldiers in the pay of Mexico, and their Indian allies. The man in command, Colonel Melendrez, sent his Indians under a flag of truce with an offer of his kind permission to leave his country if we would lay down our weapons. It was a base trick, of course. We were to surrender our arms so they could murder us at their leisure. We sent back this reply: If Colonel Melendrez wanted our guns he would have to come and get them! And he came, oh, yes, he came, riding hard and fast. The men who met his charge ran before him in what looked like a panic-stricken retreat, but led him straight into our ambush. Our first volley emptied a dozen saddles, and then we waded into them, revolvers blazing, with hate in our hearts and the desperation of men who have counted themselves dead in the sunsets of countless days. The bandidos and their Indian friends fled in terror. Thirty minutes later we reached the American post and surrended ourselves to the officer on duty. The date, we discovered, was May 8, 1854, General Walker's birthday. He was thirty years old."

"But you survived—you, and Grant."

"Yes, and Colonel Henry, and thirty others. We had looked into the grinning face of death and smiled back. We were the "Immortals." People love heroes, and even in defeat, that is what we were to the hero-hungry press. Without that, without Sonora, Walker would never have raised the money for this venture in Nicaragua, and without Grant and his Apache blood, death would have won in the desert. That is why your *amante* sits on Uncle Billy's right hand."

"His—Apache blood?"

"But yes, Eleanora. You are shocked, appalled? No

111

matter. This is something you must know if you are to understand Grant."

It would be foolish to pretend disinterest. She would even admit to a certain amount of shock, though she refused to own herself appalled. With startled clarity she recognized the origin of the blue-black straightness of Grant's hair, the copper tinge of his skin; recognized, and in the same instant, accepted them. The blue of his eyes was unaccounted for, however.

She gave a shake of her head, frowning. "He is not full-blooded."

"No. Half."

"You know how it came about?"

"I know," Luis agreed. "On long marches men draw close together, and, sometimes, they talk."

A challenging light in her green eyes, Eleanora asked, "Do you intend to tell me what was said?"

"I think yes," he said, his smile flashing.

"Why?"

He shrugged. "Who can say? Not I. Perhaps for you, perhaps for him, perhaps only to meddle."

"Or to make trouble?"

"Or to make trouble," he repeated, his gaze level, though a trace of rich red lay beneath the surface of his skin.

"You have the advantage of honesty," she said, smiling to take the sting from her words.

"And audacity," he added, tilting his head to catch the soft tune he had begun to pluck from the guitar once more. He became absorbed in the sound, his fingers moving with blinding precision, the tempo quickening, hovering on the edge of frenzy.

Watching him, Eleanora felt an odd constriction in her throat. She should be thankful that he took the time to visit her. He did not have to. Certainly he had nothing to gain by it. It was ungrateful of her to accuse him of treachery to Grant. It might be that she, too, was beginning to lose faith in integrity.

"I'm sorry, Luis," she said when the music had slowed once more.

He did not acknowledge the apology or give any sign he

had heard, but after a moment, he began to speak. "Grant's mother was from Virginia, a lady of angelic charm, golden hair, and eyes bluer than the sky. She was gentle, soft, used to comfort, even luxury. She met Thomas Farrell when he came to buy horses from her father for the land he had bought in what was then the section of northern Mexico called Texas. The attraction was strong. This horse-buying trip stretched into a visit of a month. The pair were married. For a few days they were happy. Then they quarreled. There had been a great misunderstanding. Farrell had taken it for granted his new wife would return to Texas with him; she had been just as certain he would stay and help run her father's holdings. If he loved her, she thought, he would not ask her to endure such hardships as this new land promised. If she loved him, he insisted, she would be eager to share his future. Neither would try to understand the other. Both were stubborn. Thomas Farrell was a good man, but hard. He threatened to ride away, leaving his bride behind. As is always the way, the bride gave in. Still, Thomas Farrell did not get off without payment. His Amelia complained and found fault over every bump of the whole weary journey, waxing tearful at every opportunity. Texas, when they arrived, was hot and dusty and windy. The house he built for her was little more than a sty for pigs. Her husband left her alone with only a Spanish maid and a crippled *vaquero* far too often and for too long a time. Hearing this day after day, it was natural for Farrell to leave her alone more often still, and for longer. That is the way of it, no?"

Tiring of standing, Eleanora had settled herself to the floor. Leaning against the doorjamb, she curled her feet under her, drawing the blue brocade of the dressing gown over her knees. "I suppose," she agreed.

Nodding, he went on. "Raiding parties of Apaches were known to enter the area from time to time. They were a nomad tribe. They thought it their ancient right to plunder whatever fell in their path. One day, while Thomas Farrell was absent, it was the Farrell ranch. They took horses, food, blankets, and Amelia Farrell. A golden-haired squaw, a great prize, one to be savored.

113

The band moved too slowly. At the end of the fourth day, Farrell and a half-dozen of his neighbors caught up with them. The leader, a tall, straight Indian with long black hair called Black Eagle, offered either to return the horses if he could keep the woman—a magnificent offer from an Apache—or to fight for her in mortal combat. Thomas Farrell shot him where he stood, then they gunned down the others. After that, they had no use for the white flag they carried. They threw it down among the bodies."

"And what of Grant's mother?" Eleanora asked when he fell silent.

"They took her home. For a week she lay in delirium, rambling, her words half-crazed, though the name of Black Eagle was often on her lips. She grew better finally, but she never left her bed. She lay there, pale and silent, growing thinner in the face as her belly grew larger. Her husband would not leave her now, but when she looked at him there was nothing in her hollow eyes except accusation. Nine months later her child was born. He was christened Grant Farrell."

"The son of the Apache, Black Eagle?"

"Without doubt."

"Of what was she accusing her husband, of leaving her, or killing the Apache?"

"She never said, and that was his punishment. But, on the other hand, she could not bear the sight of her son. When he was brought to her, she went into hysteria. Grant was given into the care of a Mexican nurse. His first words were in her tongue. Thomas saw that Grant was fed and clothed, but most of all, he attended to his discipline. He was determined to crush any appearance of wildness before it began. When Grant was eight years old, they sent him away to an Eastern military school, but with so many people able to guess at his origins, it was inevitable that his story would catch up with him. At sixteen he returned to Texas looking much as he does now, tall, straight, with Indian-black hair and hard blue eyes. He had been suspended from school for trying to kill a boy who called him a half-breed. Thomas Farrell decided the punishment had not been severe enough. He took a whip to him. His mistake was getting half-drunk first. Grant jerked the whip out of his hand, flung it in his face, and rode away. His mother had grown old, a white-haired, gray-faced invalid. She had made no move to protect him, had not even said good-bye. Grant, abandoning her in his heart as she had turned from him at his birth, went to join the people of his father."

"He found them?" Eleanora asked.

"They allowed him to do so, when they wanted to be found."

"Then?"

"Then why didn't he stay? He did, for four years. Long enough to learn how to survive in a barren land, long enough to earn his Indian name, Warrior of Iron, and take pride in it, and long enough to discover that blood alone was not enough to make him an Indian. Too civilized to be a savage, too savage to be a civilian, all that was left to him was soldiering, the craft for which he was trained. He was lucky. Mexico declared war. He joined the army of the United States."

"A curious way to look at a war, as a lucky chance," she commented.

"Nonetheless, the military became his vocation."

"No doubt it was fortunate William Walker came along then, when peace was won in Mexico."

"For those of us who needed a war to fight, yes."

"You—count yourself among such men? Why?"

"That is another tale, one that cannot interest you."

"Why not?" she inquired. But he refused to be drawn into it or to turn his eyes in her direction. "Listen," he said, and began to sing a soft and lilting madrigal, a song of love with a hauntingly sad counterpoint.

When the last entrancing note had died away Eleanora was not certain whether he had wanted merely to distract her, or to make some message known that he would not speak.

The shadow of the roof slowly pushed the sun back over the edge of the galería floor. The blue of the sky faded in the heat of noon; still Luis did not leave. He talked, rambling entertainingly from one subject to the next, from the problem of the camp cook supplied by the

115

Nicaraguan Indians who had peculiar ideas about what was edible, to Walker's growing preoccupation with Niña Maria and its interference with his command.

They fell silent, staring, only at the rattle of a key in the door. The panel swung open. Grant stepped through, then stopped, his head up as if the scent of danger was in his nostrils.

His uniform was correct, his brass buttons, and his boots highly polished, his breeches well creased. The line was ruined, however, by the pearl-handled revolver strapped about his waist. For a moment Eleanora could not drag her eyes from it, thinking of that final, echoing shot in the plaza, then she lifted her gaze to his gray-tinged face. His mouth was set in a straight line, and his eyes were dark and empty beneath the jutting bone of his brow. The impression lasted no more than an instant before the swift light of anger lit his face. He shut the door behind him and sauntered slowly into the room.

Eleanora resisted the impulse to scramble to her feet. It was unpleasant to have him towering above her, but there was no need for panic. She was doing nothing wrong by her own standards; she refused to be bound by the colonel's. It would have been more reasonable, of course, if she could have managed not to feel just a little guilty.

"Here again, Luis?" Grant said with controlled sarcasm. "I didn't know you were so bored. I'll have to see if the general can't find a little action for you."

"That is most kind of you, my friend. Still, I couldn't let you put yourself to the trouble for nothing. It is not boredom which brings me here, but fascination. Captive maidens, you know, always attract rescuers."

"Chivalry, Luis? I thought you were forsworn."

"You doubt my word? But of course you do. So would I, in your place. I could, I suppose, bare my breast for your examination, but I give you my word you will not find the imprint of this very pretty iron grille upon it. Neither will you find it upon Eleanora, though I would be most happy to help you look—"

Flushing, Eleanora watched as the two men exchanged a long look charged with something more in unanswered questions than the obvious one. Luis had come slowly

116

to his feet, his guitar resting on end on the floor beside him, his fingers just touching the neck. His face was set in proud Castilian lines, but in his eyes lay a rueful acceptance.

Abruptly Grant smiled. Brushing aside his tunic, he fished the key to the lock and chain that secured the grille from his watch pocket and handed it through to Luis. "Here, let yourself in. Señora Paredes is a good cook. You may as well eat with us."

"I accept your gracious invitation." Stepping forward, Luis fitted the key in place.

Grant turned, extending a hard brown hand to Eleanora. The last vestiges of humor lingered about his eyes. His grip was warm, a firm support that drew her effortlessly to her feet and held her close against his side.

With two men to satisfy, the señora put her best effort into the meal. Though unimaginative, she was, as Grant had said, a good cook. The dishes she presented were well seasoned, the meat tender, the sauces thick and rich. Fresh fruit was the invariable dessert. On this day it was oranges, the golden-red globes piled high in a wooden bowl with a fruit knife thrust among them.

Taking the knife and an orange, Grant leaned back. "When I reached the palacio just now I had to identify myself to a pair of guards at the door before I could get into my own house. Your bodyguards, Luis?"

Luis stared at the wine glass in his hand before looking up. "Yours, amigo."

"Mine? Why?"

"There are those who are jealous of you, jealous of the trust the general gives you, those who find the authority you hold inconvenient to their schemes. If an assassin can reach the stairs of Walker's apartments, why not yours?"

"In the past I have always been judged able to take care of myself without nursemaiding," Grant observed mildly.

"You will forgive me if I point out that you are no longer alone?"

"I see," Grant said. "In other words, your concern is not entirely for me."

117

Luis inclined his head. "As you say, you can look out for yourself; Eleanora obviously cannot."

Studying the orange he was peeling, Grant did not reply at once. Halving the fruit, he laid a portion on Eleanora's plate, retaining possession of the knife with an unsmiling deliberateness that was, nevertheless, provocative. He held her irritated stare while he tore his own half apart, then glanced at Luis. "All right. Leave them, if you are quite sure they can be trusted."

"They are my men, from my own regiment," Luis answered sharply.

"I'm sure they are loyal to you, but they will be guarding me—and mine."

When the meal was over, Grant returned to the Government House, taking Luis with him. Eleanora stacked the dishes and pushed them onto the galería, discovering in the process that the grille had been left unlocked. It did not matter, of course. She was not going anywhere as long as Jean-Paul's fate rested in Grant's hands, and she certainly had no desire to parade the galería, much less the street, in a man's dressing gown.

She napped through the heat of the afternoon, waking feeling drugged and heavy, her skin veiled in perspiration, to the tapping of the señora on the door. She sat up, pushing her damp hair to the side off her neck. "Yes?"

"A note, señorita, from Colonel Farrell."

At the scrape of the key, Eleanora sat up, drawing the dressing gown, which she had allowed to slip for coolness, about her. The older woman entered, extending a folded square of paper. While Eleanora read it she pretended disinterest, fastening the door key to her chatelaine before looking up.

"It's General Walker. He has planned a private dinner party and has commanded the colonel to bring me."

"I have had a message also. I am to assist you in whatever way pleases you," the señora said.

"My clothes?"

"They are in the colonel's room. I will bring whichever gown you choose."

"You are too kind," Eleanora said, exactly matching

118

her formal tone. "I would like water, then, to wash my hair."

"It would be easier under the pump in the patio—"

There was an odd tone in Señora Paredes's voice. Was the suggestion she had made as helpful as it appeared? It might be an attempt to avoid the labor of climbing the stairs with heavy cans of water, or it might be in the nature of a test. The woman could be giving her the opportunity to venture out of her room under the cloak of the colonel's permission. If the prisoner used the extended freedom to escape, the señora could not be blamed entirely, could she? Eleanora had not forgotten Juanita's lengthy visit. It might suit the Nicaraguan girl for Eleanora to be gone. It was difficult, however, to pass up the chance to be free of both her room and Grant's supervision at the same time.

Eleanora bathed inside and soaped her hair in the tub, but for the rinsing she descended to the patio. Afterward she sat under the orange trees, watching an iridescent green hummingbird, letting the faint breeze that stirred the heady fragrance of their blossoms dry her long, flowing tresses. She did no more than glance toward the entranceway, even when Señora Paredes went out into the street to buy a string of peppers from a vendor, and left the front door standing wide behind her.

Between the rose print and the green gown, she chose to wear the green again. It seemed odd to be confined once more in stays and a crinoline after two days of going without them. With silk stockings and kid slippers she felt overdressed, and at the same time, armored to well-nigh invincibility.

From a center part she drew her hair back into a low chignon in the shape of a figure eight. Then, for no reason she cared to examine, she took it down. The second time, she let it fall in deep, loose waves on each temple, then drew it high and secured it to the crown of her head. It draped down her back in soft curls that gleamed with the look of burnished copper in the candlelight.

The señora offered to bring fresh wild gardenias to dress it with again, but Eleanora refused. Their smell had become faintly sickening to her. Instead, she accepted the

119

offer of a long length of jade-green ribbon which she divided in two pieces. One section she tied about her waist, fastening it to the side so that the ends streamed from a spray of vivid magenta bougainvillea broken from the woody vine at the end of the galería. The other was reserved for her hair where it fell from another cluster of papery bougainvillea to twine among her curls.

Halfway through her toilette she heard Grant return. A little later the señora came and wrestled the empty tin bathtub out of her room and into the one next door.

Ready, Eleanora sat in one of the straight-back chairs, waiting. A cool breath of air from the lake found its way across the rooftops and through the unlocked grille. It was so fresh after the stifling room that she got up and stepped outside onto the galería, pursuing it.

Night was creeping in purple stealthiness among the cube-shape houses. A flight of pigeons circled, then inclined toward the cathedral, where the notes of the angelus bell were dying away. The pale ghost of a moon was riding three-quarters' full. Dark specks of high-flying bats swooped, their eerie screeching a lonely sound above the soft notes of distant music and laughter from a cantina in the next plaza.

Eleanora breathed deeply of the flower- and dust-scented air. A strange peace enveloped her. Some of the resentment which lay like a twisted knot in the pit of her stomach began to dissolve. She let her thoughts wander to the tale Luis had unfolded for her. How beguilingly innocent and easy her life seemed in contrast to that Grant had led. Thinking of his mother, she could begin to see how he had come to have so little regard for women. It was not every woman who had the strength and will to brave the dangers of the frontier, and certainly what had happened to his mother must have been a terrifying experience, but that did not excuse her aversion to her child or her callousness toward him. He was, after all, of her blood also, and free of guilt.

In the room behind her the door opened. She glanced up to see Grant enter, a linen towel slung about his neck. His chest was bare above his breeches, and his dark hair shone wet and tousled from washing.

120

He paused on the threshold, searching the room with his eyes before staring fixedly at the open grille. His face grew rigid, the muscles tight. He exhaled slowly, and moving to the bed, reached out to touch the dressing gown Eleanora had thrown across the footboard. His fingers closed upon the brocade, then loosened. A smile twisting the corner of his mouth, he separated from the embroidery of the brocade a single russet hair, the long length of which he curled with care about the end of his forefinger.

A frown flicked across Eleanora's brow. Then, without conscious thought she moved, sighing, allowing the wide width of her skirt to enter the range of the light flooding across the galería floor. The iron grille squeaked as she passed through it. When she looked up as she entered the room, Grant was standing with his back to her before the washstand, searching his kit for his razor.

Eight

"The mind is a powerful instrument. We haven't yet begun to understand its strengths and how they are brought to bear, and yet, it is true that some men are capable of controlling other people, that they can inspire them, lead them to anger or to tears. In Europe I studied mesmerism, the science of animal magnetism discovered by the Austrian physician, Franz Mesmer. He was undoubtedly something of a mystic, perhaps even a charleton, but he was also a man of vision. He sought to use what he felt to be true about the power of the mind for good, and he was successful in the field of medicine. There are documented case histories of remarkable cures using nothing more than the natural ability of the body to heal itself—plus Mesmer's psychic control of his patient. He made great strides in the relief of pain without—"

"William, if you please?"

William Walker, holding forth with animation at the

121

head of the table, paused in mid-sentence. Niña Maria's lips curved into a smiling pout. "As interesting as this subject is to you, I'm sure Eleanora finds it as fatiguing as I."

"Not at all," Eleanora disclaimed politely. "My father was an admirer of Mesmer also. He used some form of hypnotism advocated by him to relieve my mother's birth pains when my brother and I were born."

"Indeed?" Niña Maria said in chill tones, the yellow-green moire-silk of her gown shimmering as she drew in her breath in distaste. The low, square neck revealed the curves of her breasts and the huge topaz which hung on a fine gold chain between them. Earrings of topaz flashed in her ears and on the brooch made of plaited hair which held her headdress of yellow-green egret tips in place. Behind her, at the foot of the table, stood the bright-eyed Indian girl holding the same fan of canary feathers she had carried at the reception. She had slowed in plying it, her eyes shielded by thick lashes, watching as her mistress reached for one of the pastel-colored bonbons piled in compotes at either end of the table.

Eleanora, ignoring the displeasure of Walker's mistress as she had learned to ignore her gibes and pettish curiosity during the interminable meal, felt sorry for the child having to stand waving the heavy fan for so long a time. In sudden compassion, she reached for a pink bonbon and handed to her.

The girl's face lit up. She snatched the candy and without pausing for appreciation, popped it into her mouth.

"Señorita Villars," the Spanish woman said, "I must ask you not to feed my fan girl. She must not be spoiled into begging for scraps from the table."

"She looked tired, and hungry."

"She will be fed at the proper time, when she is through with her duties."

"But she's only a child! You mean she hasn't eaten at all?"

"You needn't disturb your sympathies. She is an Indian, an animal with a name. They are used to making do with much less than I give this creature, I assure you."

She spoke with the disdain of the aristocrat for the lower orders, and yet she was supposed to be dedicated to the democratic cause which espoused the freedom of the common people. As a guest, both in the general's quarters and in Nicaragua, Eleanora felt it was not her place to point out the error of the woman's thinking to her, but her expression was censorious before she turned back to the men.

"You approve of my choice of Fayssoux as commander of the *Granada,* then?" Walker was saying.

"He's a good officer," Grant agreed. "Arrogant, but that's not a bad thing in a man who has to protect the waters of Nicaragua with a single schooner-of-war."

"People can laugh if they like at our one-ship navy, but we'll see who laughs last."

"I don't like them laughing," Niña Maria interrupted, her voice clear and cutting. "What was it that American newspaper called you, the Don Quixote of Central America? This I do not understand."

Walker's mouth twisted in a smile. "Who can say what they mean? It may be they see me as an idealist tilting at the windmills of oppression. The only one who can truly free a people is the people themselves, or so the conservatives of the world insist. They don't believe in the efficacy of the helping hand. But I have been counted among the liberals since I took my stand in the *Crescent* and later in the *Daily Herald* against slavery, and for free trade, women's suffrage, and the right of divorce."

"Most young men are liberals," Niña Maria said with a fond, if superior, smile. "When they grow older they learn the hard lessons of responsibility—and expediency."

Walker turned his gray gaze to his mistress. "Such a cold philosophy, as most are when they are formulated to serve a purpose."

"Really, William," she began, uneasiness creeping over her face.

"Yes?" His voice was gentle, though a clear fire seemed to flare in the depths of his eyes.

As the woman let her eyelids fall, retreating into a sullen silence, he turned to Grant. "Niña Maria, you see, despite the fact that slavery was abolished in 1824 by the Confederated Congress of Central America, proposes to revive the institution."

Grant asked after a long moment, "You mean reinstate slavery in Nicaragua?"

"Precisely."

"Why?"

"Why?" Niña Maria demanded, flinging her head up. "We are an agricultural country. To grow we must export foodstuffs, to export we must utilize the land, and that takes organization and cheap labor—or slaves."

"You would run the risk of alienating both the government of the United States and our other possible ally, Great Britain," Grant told her.

"What guarantee have you the American government will ever recognize us, much less help us? We fête Minister Wheeler and he does nothing. On the other hand, the Southern States will surely be in sympathy with us. If they secede over this question, as they have been threatening, we will most assuredly have their support as well."

"If—" Grant said succinctly.

Niña Maria leaned back, the flush of anger staining her cheeks. "Very well. Counsel prudence then. But strength is what is needed, and quickly. We must consolidate our position before the Legitimistas have a chance to recover. If we do not, Nicaragua will have another change of government, the sixteenth in less than six years. Events will not move in our direction without encouragement. It is necessary to act."

"Not just for the sake of acting, not without careful consideration."

The woman made no answer. A small silence descended. Walker turned to Eleanora. "And you, mademoiselle, have you no opinion to offer on this weighty problem?"

"I haven't been here long enough to form one. In any case, I somehow doubt it would influence you."

From the sudden glint in his eyes she thought General Walker appreciated the diplomacy of her answer, though he made no direct reply. With a gesture of one slim, freckled hand, he said, "Grant is right. A move to revive slavery would be premature at this time, though I, personally, find the attitude of the United States government hypocritical, since slavery is at present still legal in the District of Columbia. There is, however, as Niña Maria has indicated, an urgent need to fill the treasury. I have been studying the records of the Transit Line. It appears that the company is in debt to the government of Nicaragua for a considerable sum due by contract for the charter which allows them to transport passengers across the country. The amount agreed upon was $10,000 per year plus ten per cent of the net profits for the operation. The $10,000 was paid for the years from 1849 to 1852, but despite annual reports published in New York of profits in excess of two million dollars over this period, Nicaragua has never received more than the base amount, and this has not been paid for the past three years."

"What of the $20,000 advanced by Garrison?" Grant asked. "I was under the impression that it was pledged against monies due the government."

Walker shook his head. "That was a personal loan made to me last fall in order to help me consolidate my position here. Garrison learned Vanderbilt and his relatives were buying up stock in the line once more. He was afraid that, should I be ousted, the Legitimista party would favor Vanderbilt in any future negotiations over the charter. It was, you might say, in the nature of insurance for Garrison and Morgan. In any case, the amount was only a fraction of what is owed."

"It was a bribe," Niña Maria said scornfully. "If they are fools enough to offer their money, they deserve to have it, and everything else they own, taken from them."

"Meaning?" Grant asked, his eyes narrowing as he stared at Walker rather than the woman.

The corner of Walker's mouth twitched in a movement that was not quite a smile. "I think you are beginning to see. It is more than likely that Vanderbilt will be able to have Morgan removed as president of the board of the Transit Company and himself reinstated as manager. Vanderbilt, maybe because he is reluctant to see a leader of strength who cannot be ignored or manipulated emerge in Central America, is against me. It is much easier to take advantage of a country or a nation that is in a state of constant chaos. He would see me shot if he could. For this reason I cannot allow the Transit Line to become his tool again."

"What do you propose to do about it?"

"Annul the present charter," Walker said quietly.

Grant leaned back. "The government hasn't the means to run the line alone."

"But Garrison and Morgan, rich men in their own right, do. If they are pushed out of the present company I believe they will jump at the chance to form a new line. Their feud with Vanderbilt goes too deep to pass up the opportunity, in addition to the profit motive."

"You propose to use the nonpayment of past revenues as a reason to annul the present charter and award a new one to Garrison and Morgan?"

"The reason is entirely valid, but yes, that is the gist of it. We will, of course, charge the new line a premium. We mustn't forget the empty coffers."

"You realize it will make Vanderbilt your bitter enemy?" Grant warned.

"He is that already." His gray eyes hooded, Walker picked up his water glass. It was a clear indication that the debate was ended.

Since Walker neither smoked nor drank the men did not linger behind the women at the table but moved with them to the *sala* for coffee in the Continental fashion. The effect was not markedly different even so, for in that room, heavy with paneling and red damask, they withdrew into a corner, leaving the two women to make conversation between themselves. It was not easy. When compliments had been exchanged over the dinner, the decor of the apartments, and their respective toilettes, and the weather and the climate thoroughly examined, Eleanora searched her brain for some further meeting ground. In the ensuing quiet she caught a snatch of the men's topic of discussion and immediately made use of it.

"It must have been frightening, having your rooms invaded by the Legitimista. I expect you were happy to see the man brought to justice?"

Niña Maria looked at Eleanora, her gaze sharp and yet unfocused, as if she were looking through her. "Yes, nat-

126

urally," she said. In sudden annoyance she turned on her fan bearer. Snatching the fan from the little girl, she sent her to the kitchen. When she had closed the door behind her, the woman sat fanning herself with the quick movements of either irritation or agitation. Then without a word she snapped the fan shut and tossed it from her onto the spindle-legged table that sat beside the damask-covered settee. She stared for several seconds at Walker, but when he did not glance in her direction the Spanish woman sprang up and walked to a Pleyel piano with its yellowed ivory keys. Seating herself, she began to play a Strauss waltz. Though technically correct, her touch was heavy, lacking in delicacy of feeling. She was, in fact, cow-handed with nerves. Mulling over this fact, Eleanora did not see Grant approaching until he was at her side.

"I believe this waltz is mine," he said, bowing as gracefully as a revolver worn at his belt would allow.

With Walker watching as fatuously as a father from the window embrasure, she could not refuse. She gave Grant her hand, letting him draw her to her feet. The action reminded her of the afternoon and of the feel of his hand upon hers, and she went into his arms with an awkward stiffness, determined to limit her response to his touch.

Gently they whirled. At some time Grant had had expert tutoring in the art of the waltz. His steps were sure, the hand at her waist correctly placed, the distance between them well judged and circumspect enough for the most straitlaced gathering of sour-faced chaperones. Without being aware of it, Eleanora relaxed, following his lead, growing unmindful of anything except the music and the firm strength of his arms. She felt his gaze upon her cheeks and slowly raised her dark lashes to meet it. The expression she saw hidden in the blue depths of his eyes brought the blood to her head, where it pulsed with a feathery flutter against her eardrums. She was certain the music had come to an end only when the general began to walk toward them, applauding softly.

"Very nice," he said. "A fine show, one I find most satisfactory, Mademoiselle Eleanora. I had a visit this afternoon from a Miss Mazie Brentwood. She insisted that you were being held prisoner by Grant in his quarters. From what I have just seen, I am more inclined to believe he is all too willing to be yours."

There was an instant of time when she might have blurted out her predicament, might have enlisted the general's aid. It was gone before she could bring herself to grasp it. She had smiled and turned away as at some light compliment, but she was left feeling confused and foolish, haunted by the thought that she had failed Jean-Paul. It did not clarify her thinking to have Grant follow her into the room they shared at the palacio, throw his hat down on the table, and with his hands on his hips demand, "Why?"

"Why what?" she fenced. She was tired. It did not take much to turn her pretense of a sleepy yawn into a real one.

"Why didn't you explain to Uncle Billy?"

"It—it would have been useless."

"Maybe, maybe not. You couldn't know unless you tried."

Eleanora stared at him. "Did you want me to tell him?"

"Uncle Billy is not unreasonable; I would have had the chance to present my side. That isn't the point."

"You mean—you wouldn't have had to face disciplinary action?"

"I doubt it. It would be much too disruptive at this time, even if I deserved it. Are you trying to say the thought weighed with you enough to hold you silent?"

"I have no wish to have a man's death or dishonor on my hands."

His eyes narrowed. He drew a deep breath, then let it out slowly. "I thought I understood you, but I don't."

"That isn't surprising," she replied, her voice muffled as she bent her head to disentangle the flowers and ribbon at her waist. "Anyway, I don't see that it's necessary for your purpose."

"And just what is that?"

At the anger in his tone she looked up. His brows were drawn together in a frown that was not entirely directed at her. His question vibrated in the air, but the

128

answer was so obvious Eleanora saw no need to put it into comfortless words, even if she could have found them.

The bougainvillea under her fingers shattered, cascading to the floor. Turning away, she plucked at the knot once more, and as it yielded, jerked the ribbon free and tossed it to the washstand. It hung on the edge, then slithered to the floor like a green snake.

"Is it because of your brother? Uncle Billy could have ordered him freed if he thought it the best course."

"I—suspected he might," Eleanora said. "Still, I never supposed that you put Jean-Paul in the guardhouse simply to suit your convenience."

"No?" he asked in disbelief.

"No. You said he had been drinking, and I believed you. As much as I would like to see him released, it is right that he should pay the price for breaking the rules."

"Generous of you."

"Only just," she said.

"But unexpected, all the same."

"Fair play is not restricted to men."

"Apparently not," he answered in such a thoughtful tone she glanced at him in the mirror before her. "Tell me," he continued, "do you plan to even your own scores, or do you prefer coals of fire?"

Eleanora drew in her breath. "Must it be one or the other?"

"In my experience, yes. You see," he said with a grim smile, "I have reason to absolve you of enjoying my company."

She would liked to have thrown his conclusion back in his teeth, but she was by no means certain he was mistaken. "It would be wrong," she replied, "to warn you, either way."

It was galling, after that trading of hostilities, to have to stand and let Grant help her out of her gown and petticoats. She might have managed the row of minute buttons down her back, but Señora Paredes had tied the laces of her stays into a hard knot that defeated her most determined efforts. Grant, for once, did not take advantage of the situation. He left her alone to finish undressing while he disrobed in a brooding silence.

Removing her last petticoat, Eleanora slid quickly beneath the covers. Grant blew out the candle and lay down beside her, leaving a careful distance between them.

For a long time Eleanora lay rigid, staring wide-eyed into the darkness. The tension that stretched taut over them convinced Eleanora that Grant was not asleep. Still, he made no move toward her. She was glad, of course, but she did not pretend to understand it. She could not imagine that his strange reaction to her reluctance to expose their relationship to the general would prevent him from taking her if he so desired. No, certainly not. He must not want her then—not that it mattered. It was not very flattering that his interest had waned in so short a time, but she would not let it affect her. With this vow, she turned on her side with her back to him. He appeared not to notice the movement. Indifference was a game two could play. Closing her eyes, she breathed deeply, then settled into an even, regular rhythm. In time the feigned sleep slid unrecognized into reality. Grant did not move, nor did he give any sign he knew she was there.

Such an unnatural estrangement could not endure between a man and a woman living in close quarters. On the morning of the fourth day Grant sat over his breakfast coffee, watching without seeming to as she stood in the early-morning sunlight pouring through the grille, trying to bring some kind of order to her wayward hair without resorting to the despised braids. The sleeves of the dressing gown fell away, revealing the soft roundness of her arms, their transparent ivory skin tinted pink with the warmth of her coursing blood. Her neck curved as she worked with the heavy hair, and her movements caused the too-large neckline to gape with an innocent, unknowing enticement. As if impelled, he set down his cup and got to his feet.

Eleanora looked around in startled inquiry as he neared her. She flinched slightly as he reached out and picked up a strand of her hair, letting it drift slowly from his fingers, watching the iridescent slide of sunlight along the individual hairs like ultra-fine copper wires. Her eyes darkened to emerald as his fingers touched the silken softness of her cheek, then slid, lingering, to the tender

130

curve of her mouth. There was about him the fresh smell of shaving soap and the aroma of warm linen and cotton cloth. The rich taste of coffee was on his lips, and then as she was drawn close against him, awareness grew dim, washed away by the swift race of the blood through her veins.

They were still in bed when an orderly was sent to inquire after him hours later.

Laughter bubbling in her throat, Eleanora watched Grant's hurried efforts to find enough of his uniform to make himself presentable while receiving the man. When he had gone the smile hovered for the length of time it took for her to stretch, smothering a yawn. Slowly, it disappeared. The room grew quiet and hollow with emptiness. With an abrupt movement, Eleanora flung her forearm up over her eyes. Tearless she lay, feeling the monotonous rise and fall of her breathing, refusing to remember, refusing to hope, hiding from herself. It was a futile exercise, as futile as denying her unaccountable attraction for Colonel Grant Farrell.

Nine

The new year came and went. The days ran, molten with heat, into each other. There was a passive sameness about them, a deadly dullness, that made an event, by comparison, of Grant's twice-daily return. At least, that was the way Eleanora tried to explain her anticipation of his homecoming to herself.

It was unbelievable to her how quickly they settled into a routine. They might have been the most stolid of wedded couples, eating together, bathing, sleeping, poring over his paperwork together. He found for her a sewing kit, and she spent a number of hours during the day tightening the buttons on his shirts, mending a few tears and parted seams. Once, in an idle hour, she carefully sewed the front of the dressing gown she wore together, using

131

blind stitching, with herself inside it. She had no real thought of thwarting Grant; she only wanted to see the expression on his face when he found himself balked, and see what he would do. It *was* comical. She lay biting her lower lip, her eyes shining with barely suppressed merriment—until he drew out a pocket knife and flicked it open. The rush of panic was momentary, though it did make it harder to restrain the somewhat hazardous laughter that shook her as with owl-solemn concentration he leaned over her, cutting each tiny stitch from bottom to top.

The only other relief from monotony was Luis's visits. They continued as before, though at irregular intervals. He was prone to making her small gifts, flowers, delicacies of fruit and candy from the market, soap scented with attar of roses, a small basket of nuts gleaned from heaven knows where, a French novel falling apart with damp and mildew and old age, but still readable. His most impressive gifts, however, were a blouse of unbleached cotton with a drawstring neck and wide, puffed sleeves, and a skirt of several widths of gathers in Democrático red. It was the costume of the peasant women, cool, practical, and more welcome than the finest silk gown, primarily because Grant made no objection to her wearing it. Why, she could not quite decide, unless he felt it was unlikely she would wish to appear in public in such an ensemble. If so, he misjudged her. After the costume she had been wearing, she felt marvelously well dressed in the skirt and blouse; she would have thought little of moving about the streets in them. In any event, she did not get the chance. Grant, despite her gradual acceptance of her confinement, always locked the door behind him.

The morning of the fourth of January dawned cloudy and mercifully cool. Grant rose early, removing the warm weight of his arm from across her waist, leaving the bed with an abrupt roll. He slipped into his breeches and went to stand, staring out over the rooftops. His fingertips where they gripped the facing were colorless, but there was a determined set to his shoulders.

Eleanora stirred and sat up. Sensitive to the sound, Grant spoke over his shoulder. "Your brother will be released this morning. He will have to return to his barracks, but he will be free this evening, if you want to see him."

"Yes. Certainly," she answered.

It was a moment before he spoke again, then his voice was hard. "What will you do now?"

Was this her dismissal then? Her mind was curiously blank. A frown of pain flickered between her brows to be replaced by a saving anger as he swung to face her.

"I asked what you are going to do, where you intend to go?"

"I'm not sure. Mazie mentioned California. Maybe I'll go with her."

"The ticket to New Orleans is still available."

"That's very kind of you," she said steadily, "but I feel a craving for independence now."

"Independence isn't an easy thing for a woman without money."

"I will manage, no doubt. You needn't let me weigh on your conscience."

"Don't think you will," he said too definitely. "You brought what happened on yourself."

"Did I indeed?" She sat up straighter, unaware of the soft, alluring gleam of her unclothed body in the dim room.

"Your clothes, your company, led me to believe you were not inexperienced."

"I could not help that—not that it matters. You don't have to make excuses to me!"

"I'm not making excuses," he said, lowering his voice as she raised hers.

"No, of course not, and you're not blaming me for the pass your arrogance and conceit have brought us to either, I suppose?"

He stared at her a long moment before looking away. "All right," he agreed wearily. "The fault is mine. What more do you want? Apologies?"

"No—no," she said, unable to take her gaze from the gray shadow that lay beneath the bronze surface of his skin. "We can agree, if you will, that we were both at fault."

"Eleanora—" He stepped to the end of the bed, bracing his arms on the footboard.

She waited, her nerves coiled as tightly as a carriage spring. The timbre of his voice sounded low and strained to her ears. He seemed, for the first time in her knowledge of him, vulnerable.

The impression was a fleeting one. As a knock sounded on the door, he straightened, the mask of hardness descending over his face.

"Yes?" he snapped.

"Pardon Señor Colonel." The quavering tones belonged to Señora Paredes. "I thought I—that is—I heard voices. As long as you are awake, I thought you might be ready for breakfast."

Had the woman been listening? She could not have chosen a more inopportune moment to interrupt. Grant appeared to find nothing unusual in it. Without looking at Eleanora he replied, "Breakfast for the señorita only. Just coffee for me— on the patio."

"*Sí,* Señor Colonel," the woman said, and her footsteps faded along the inside galería.

His movements swift and economical, Grant dressed without bothering to shave. Strapping on his revolver, he took up his campaign hat and stood turning it in his hand an instant before placing it on his head. He crossed to the door and pulled it open. Face shaded by his hat brim, he looked back. His eyes rested on the softness of her mouth, then fell to the smooth curve of her neck and the gentle fullness of her breasts veiled by the gossamer curtains of her hair, moving slightly with her breathing. A muscle in his jaw corded, then with a decisive step, he passed through the door and shut it firmly behind him.

Eleanora strained, listening for the sound of the key in the lock. It did not come.

Standing before the house pointed out to her as belonging to the English actor John Barclay, Eleanora frowned. It was an odd structure, wide, high, and almost featureless. It was not at all impossible that it had served as a barn at one time, for the front boasted a pass door set into a heavy panel large enough to admit a carriage.

Plastered clay color, it did not, despite the information she had been given at the Hotel Alhambra, bear any resemblance to an abode which she thought Mazie Brentwood might consider occupying. Nevertheless, she shifted the bundle she carried onto her hip and raised her hand to the wrought-iron knocker.

"Eleanora!" Mazie cried, swinging the pass door wide. "What a surprise. Come in this minute. I have been so worried, you can't imagine."

"How are you, Mazie?" Eleanora asked, smiling.

"Never better, but we can't talk out here. Come in, do."

"I don't want to impose," Eleanora said.

"Nonsense," Mazie declared, nearly dragging her over the threshold, her eyes, sharp for all their guileless hazel color, taking in the bundle which represented Eleanora's total possessions. "One more won't matter a whit. John will be glad to have you. Tell me, how do you like our place?"

There was no entrance hall, nor orderly placement of rooms, only a vast, open area supported by square, wooden columns with a set of utilitarian stairs leading up on one side to an unpartitioned loft. A floor of polished wood had been laid over the beaten earth, and the loft had been curtained off into cubicles, but there the improvements to what had most certainly once been a stable, if not a barn, ended.

"It's—nice," Eleanora said, the back of her nose stinging from the fresh lime smell of the whitewash used on the walls.

Mazie gave her rich laugh. "Yes—well, it's nice for a makeshift theater, I must say. John and I are living here now, along with the rest of the troupe, while we get it fixed up. But it won't be permanent."

"The troupe? A troupe of actors?"

"That's right—come from England by way of Boston, St. Louis, and San Francisco to bring entertainment and culture to the masses of Nicaragua and the bored soldiery of William Walker. If you are wondering at the quiet, they are out now scouring the countryside for props for our opening production. They are a grand lot, you'll enjoy meeting them."

"I know I will," Eleanora replied, "but tell me how you came to be mixed up with them?"

"I will," Mazie promised, leading the way up the stairs and through a set of rust-red muslin curtains into a comfortable area furnished with a number of low, couchlike settees. The couches, covered with fringed India shawls, piled high with jewel-colored cushions in brocade and velvet hung with cords and tassels, were obviously used as beds. A low table held a steaming coffee pot and a tray of paper-thin china cups and saucers. Dropping down behind it, Mazie went on, "First I want to hear how the terrible colonel persuaded you to live with him. Come now. Don't spare my blushes. Tell me everything."

Mazie was nothing if not understanding. Still, it was not easy to tell her what had taken place. It was necessary to backtrack, to explain in detail, without becoming too personal, in order to be sure she grasped the exact nature of what had occurred and the reasons behind it. Why it should be so important that Mazie understand the reasons she did not consider, nor did she want to.

"I was right then, you were a prisoner. I think, under the circumstances, that you must be a most forgiving woman," Mazie commented.

"No." Eleanora's response was immediate.

"No? You haven't forgiven him then?"

"It isn't a question of forgiveness."

"What then? Revenge? I think that would be my reaction—to have his hide, no matter what the cost."

Looking beyond her, Eleanora smiled. "You would have no use for coals of fire then?"

"A dangerous business," the other woman answered. "You can get badly burned yourself."

Eleanora's smile faded. "You were going to tell me about this acting business. Have you taken to the stage?"

"Not really. I was given my warning, if you will remember? I saw at the reception we both attended that Walker was one of those men who never retract an order. The country is small, the party in power has more control of the people, and little concept of laws as we know them.

I was afraid I might find myself kicking my heels in the guardhouse too if I didn't find a niche for myself fast. I've never fancied working the cribs—too far down the ladder for comfort—and I'm too lazy to start a cat house —brothel to you, honey—on my own. My only course was some form of respectable alliance. Setting up with an actor was as close as I cared to come to that. The rest of the troupe, this theater, came with John Barclay."

"You don't feel anything for him?"

"Did you feel anything for the colonel?" she returned, then as Eleanora lowered her lashes without replying, she said, "You see? There are some questions it is better not to ask. The answer is too distressing, either way."

"If you think I'm in love with Grant Farrell—"

"Did I say that? To hate a man is more upsetting than loving him, if you must live with him regardless." With perfect nonchalance she passed on to another subject. "I haven't asked about Jean-Paul. How is he? I was never more shocked than when I heard he was in the guardhouse. He must have been arrested not long after he left me at the hotel."

"He will be released today."

"As you were. I wonder if such a coincidence will escape General Walker's notice?"

"I hope so."

Mazie looked at her oddly, but made no comment. "You left a message telling your brother where you would be, I suppose? No? Never mind. We'll send one of the boys with a note to the barracks after awhile. There are three boys in the troupe—young men, really. One of them is semi-betrothed to one of the three girls. We number eight in all, counting John and myself."

She prattled on about their arrangement of duties, the play, *The School for Scandal,* they were to present in two weeks' time, and the roles each would play. Eleanora, involved with her own thoughts, was glad to be spared the necessity of answering too often. As she considered Jean-Paul, his hot temper, and Mazie's ability to piece together the facts of the case, fear like a numbing poison began a slow invasion of her mind. With plenty of time to think and, she was sure, plenty of people to keep him

137

informed of what was happening to his sister, Jean-Paul might also exercise his mind by searching out the facts.

With chilled fingers she set her cup and saucer upon the table. The half inch of cold coffee sloshed dangerously and the cup rocked before settling.

"Are you all right?" Mazie asked. "What is it?"

"Nothing," Eleanora answered, producing a valiant smile. "It may be nothing."

The day wore on with a sullen and murky light like the effect of smoke passing before the sun. The troupe returned, a boisterous crowd, affectionate among themselves, casual; they accepted Eleanora in her peasant blouse and skirt as easily as they expected her to accept them. Of the three men, one was elderly with a mane of white hair and a habit of sprinkling his conversation with Shakespearian allusions, one was a hulking giant with few mental powers but great good nature, and the last was a young Adonis only too obviously smitten by the youngest and freshest of the female members, a blonde and sweetly perfect ingenue. The other two women were attractive in a hard fashion, though their cynical smiles seemed to hint at more experience than they could have attained on the boards of a stage. Meeting them, Eleanora wondered for an instant if she, too, had that air of bitter assent. She thought not, on consideration. It was, more than anything else, an attitude of mind.

John Barclay was a surprise. He had no single outstanding feature, an asset, he explained, in an actor. He was of average height, with nondescript-colored hair somewhere between sandy and brown, a neatly trimmed beard and mustache, and a personality that came alive only when he assumed a part.

A meal was cooked and served finally, even though it was more toward the middle of the afternoon than at luncheon time. While the others cleared away the dishes, the two youngest troupe members, the betrothed pair, were sent with the message for Jean-Paul. Scripts were broken out along with half-made costumes and unfinished scenery. Soon the place was strewn with pins and snippets of material, and reeking with the fumes of linseed oil and turpentine.

138

Eleanora sat industriously basting a seam on a gown to be worn by Lady Teazle in the second act. While she worked, she watched with enjoyment while one of the actresses declaimed her lines wearing a sheet draped over a set of makeshift panniers. She had almost finished the costume before the young couple returned from the barracks.

"Ah, methinks you have been dawdling by the wayside, sighing and seeking the remedy," the Shakespearian gibed.

Mazie was less subtle. "Where have you been?" she demanded.

"Trying to find out what all the excitement is about in the plaza. We were sure you'd want to know," the young Adonis said, clearing off a couch by pushing the materials it held to the floor.

"Excitement? What excitement? We haven't heard anything."

"It all started at the Government House. Seems Jean-Paul Villars, this gent you sent us to find, marched into the office of Adjutant Colonel Farrell this morning and gave him the glove, so to speak."

"He—challenged him?" Eleanora said faintly.

"That's the story. They say at first the colonel refused, superior rank and all that, but this Louisiana Creole made him a long speech about some stain on the family honor. I guess he convinced Farrell he had reason, because he agreed to meet him."

Mazie reached out and caught Eleanora's arm as she started to her feet. "Wait a minute, honey."

"I've got to see Jean-Paul. I've got to stop him. He'll be murdered."

The young man shook his head. "Too late. They met this afternoon at five o'clock in the garden behind the cathedral."

"You mean—it's over?"

"Yep."

"Yes, that's right," the ingenue added softly.

"And Jean-Paul?" Eleanora breathed, going still. Mazie's grip tightened, as if in anticipation of the worst.

"Fit as a fiddle. The colonel's the one who caught it. Your brother shot him just below the collarbone, Miss

139

Villars. It's my opinion he intended a heart shot, but when Farrell deloped it shook him, spoiled his aim."

"Deloped, did he?" the Shakespearian asked with an air of professional interest.

"Shot straight up at the sky. Gave the pigeons a fit, I can tell you."

"Why? Why would he do that?" Mazie queried, voicing the bewilderment Eleanora felt.

"Two thoughts on that, as far as I could tell. First says he was following General Walker's example. The general makes a habit of deloping since he's against the practice of dueling but refuses to be called a coward." The young man cocked a curious glance in Eleanora's direction. "The other says it was the colonel's way of admitting he was in the wrong."

"Are you saying he stood there and let my brother shoot him?" Eleanora whispered.

"That's about it."

She shook her head. "I can't believe it."

"God's truth."

"But why?"

"Who knows what men take into their heads?" Mazie said, getting briskly to her feet. "It makes no difference. The colonel is no longer your problem."

"No," Eleanora agreed, "unless—there was nothing said about disciplinary action against Jean-Paul, was there?"

The young man looked at the girl beside him, who shook her head. "Nothing we heard," he said.

"John?" Mazie said, applying to the actor.

"So far as I know there's no law against dueling in Nicaragua, just a general feeling that Walker disapproves, mainly on practical grounds. He can't be too specific. There was his famous duel in San Francisco with a man named Hicks, friend of a district judge Walker had raked over in the *Herald*. It puts me in mind of this one we've been talking about. Walker deloped as usual. The proper thing to have done was follow suit, delope also, but Hicks leveled his pistol and shot him in the arm, just missed the bone That made Walker mad. He ignored his wound and called for a second shot with murder in his eyes, and he'd have killed him, too, if the seconds hadn't intervened and stopped the fight." Slanting a glance at Eleanora's blank face, he shook his head. "But you're not interested in that. Like I said, I don't expect much in the way of repercussions. There may be an inquiry, seeing who was involved. Still, if they put everybody in jail who fought in a duel they'd have half the army in the guardhouse."

Despite the actor's attempt to reassure her, Eleanora could not be satisfied until she had seen her brother for herself. That indulgence was accorded to her that evening. It was late, near ten o'clock when he presented himself. The inconvenience was slight. The troupe, after a couple of hours of rehearsal, was just beginning to think of their dinner.

Relief flooding over her, Eleanora embraced Jean-Paul where he stood upon the doorstep. He was thinner, and pale, except for spots of color high on his cheekbones. The red of his uniform did not become him. In some manner it emphasized his youth rather than his manliness. He returned her quick, affectionate hug without enthusiasm, averting his eyes from the sight of her uncorseted figure in her informal peasant's costume.

"Hello, Eleanora," he said awkwardly, then stood staring past her until she drew him into the room.

Introductions to the others were noisy and exuberantly confusing. She could not entirely blame Jean-Paul for the stiffness of his bow. He remembered Mazie, naturally, but his greeting was so brief, so ungracious, that his sister flushed, though more in irritation for his lack of manners than in embarrassment.

"Could I—would it be possible to speak to you privately?" Jean-Paul asked.

"I'm sure it can be managed," Eleanora replied with emphasis, "if my friends will excuse us."

As soon as she led him into the curtained cubicle she was to share with the blonde ingenue, Jean-Paul swung on her. "What have you gotten yourself into this time? These people look like gypsies."

"Keep your voice down," Eleanora told him in a fierce undertone. "They are actors, and they have been most helpful and kind to me."

141

"Actors? Halfwits, whores, and pimps would be more like it."

"Jean-Paul!" she exclaimed involuntarily.

"Don't be coy, Eleanora. After the way you have spent the past ten days, you needn't pretend you aren't familiar with the terms."

"I never thought to hear you use them."

"And I never thought to see you in a situation where it would be warranted. You were a lady, Eleanora."

Eleanora's face went smooth with shock. "I still am."

"Don't try to cozen me. You were the colonel's mistress."

"So I was. And you must have had some inkling of the reason for it, since you challenged him. Or did you do that, Jean-Paul, not for my honor, but for your own?"

"For the family name," he grated, the light in his cinnamon brown eyes burning with a feverish brightness.

"You will forgive me, but I don't believe even Uncle Narciso, libertine that he is, would approve of avenging the family honor by callously shooting a man who has deloped."

"I didn't—that is, I was so astounded I couldn't hold my fire, and I had no time to pull up completely."

"You should not have issued a cartel without first speaking to me."

"Why? Every loafer in the city knows the colonel picked you up in the streets and carried you into his quarters like a common trull."

"He had some reason to believe that was what I was," she said with a weary gesture.

"Because of that woman in there, that Mazie."

"I suppose, though she meant only the best."

He stared at her then looked away, running one hand over the rough curls of his hair. "I'm sorry. I shouldn't have spoken to you like that. It's just that I—I feel such guilt. As long as you are being forbearing, perhaps you will forgive me, Eleanora, for bringing you here, to this God forsaken country."

Reaching out, she placed a hand on his arm. "Don't torture yourself, Jean-Paul. I didn't have to come. Some things just happen; they are accidents of nature for which no guilt can, or should, be assigned."

"You can't ignore cause and effect."

"No, nor do I have to be crippled by them."

"That's not a comforting philosophy. It does away with God as a crutch."

"And leaves Him for more important things."

It was not possible to persuade Jean-Paul to stay for the late supper. He could not be easy with the group of actors and actresses, and would not pretend otherwise. He made no suggestion, however, that Eleanora leave them. He was too well aware she had no place safer to go.

Marketing, housekeeping, sewing, were her skills. With these she began to try to pay for her keep in the following days. With the amiable giant, or John Barclay, at her side to carry her basket and act as protective escort, she took over the buying of the food, and eventually, its regular preparation. She was often in the central plaza then, since there were few facilities at the made-over theater for the storing of food. Mornings, and again in the afternoon, she would stroll past the palacio. When the large man was at her side, she would send him to inquire of the guards still posted before the doors how the colonel fared. Never did she speak of him as Grant. It was a polite fiction, this pretense of distant acquaintance, one in which they all participated.

Bit by bit she was able to piece together a picture of what was occurring within the palacio, regardless of how little she liked it. Grant was not in danger, but his wound was fevered. The field surgeon with Walker, Dr. Jones, had removed the lead slug and left him in the care of an orderly, a Nicaraguan as broad as he was tall. The man was deathly afraid of the colonel, and irritated him by showing it. Señor Paredes also exacerbated his temper with her fluttering ways and her dependence on the orders of the surgeon, rather than his personal wishes. He refused to stay in bed, preferring to move during the day to a chair at the table where he worked as hard as he would at his desk at the Government House. His visitors with problems were as many, his hours as long. Though he never complained, he used his left arm no more than was necessary; in the opinion of the orderly—as given to the guards—he used it less every day.

Some of her information on Grant's progress came from Luis. He was coming from the Government House as she crossed the plaza on her second shopping excursion for the troupe.

"*Chiquita!* How I have missed seeing you. I have promised myself each morning that today I will come to visit you. Grant would not tell me where you had gone, but I have my ways of finding out these things. I know now where you stay. Still, this business of Grant has me working like a hundred horses. I am Walker's right hand while Grant is not able, and I am telling you I am amazed at my amigo's strength of body and will. I say to myself a dozen times already this morning, I will work myself into the grave for this man, my general—or else I will cut his throat!"

He walked with her as far as the cathedral, where she was to take a cross street away from the Calle Celia. There they stopped beneath a mass of white jasmine hanging over a patio wall. The petals littered the ground as thick as snow, as if trying to cover the refuse lying in the open gutter beneath their feet. Looking up abruptly, Luis said, "I am worried about Grant. This médico, Jones, is good enough of his kind, but he has seen many wounds in the last months. If a hole does not spout blood and show bone, he feels no challenge to his skill; it is a small thing which any Falangista can heal by himself, alone. He forgets the dangers of the climate, makes no allowances for a man who will not lie down and let his body do its work."

There was nothing Eleanora could do, a fact he accepted, finally, before he let her go. Even so, Luis's misgivings could not help but affect her. She stared long and hard at the palacio the next morning as she moved slowly past. It was quiet, still somnolent in the early-morning sun. That did not allay her anxiety. What if Grant died? The general might have Jean-Paul shot if he lost his

144

second-in-command. Walker, in effect, was judge, jury, and executioner for Nicaragua. He did very much as he pleased.

The door leading out onto the galería from the bedroom she and Grant had shared stood open. As she watched through her lashes she thought she saw a flash of movement in the dimness beyond, though the shadow beneath the overhanging roof was too deep to be easily penetrated, and she would not stare. Head high, she moved on; she even managed a smile and a comment for John Barclay strolling beside her.

They were returning across the sun-burned earth of the market place on the far side of the plaza when they saw Grant's orderly running toward the Government House. His round face ashen, he called out to the guards as he neared them, *"Hola!* Send at once—*pronto!*—for the médico. Colonel Farrell has fell himself down—and he will not wake up!"

His message given, the man spun around and panted back toward the palacio. Eleanora picked up her skirts without thinking and hurried after him. From a distance she could see the black shape of Señora Paredes crouched on the galería. She hovered over Grant, trying to shade his head from the hot sun creeping inward over the floor toward the wall.

The guards passed Eleanora without question. John Barclay was detained the length of time it took for her to turn back and vouch for him. That done, the two of them followed the orderly up the stairs to the room she had left in such furious haste so short, and yet so long, a time before.

The orderly, realizing he had been followed inside, looked disturbed, but his relief at being no longer alone with the responsibility for the colonel's life overcame his scruples. The four of them, with a sheet for a makeshift litter, managed to get Grant back inside and on the bed. He lay unmoving, the blue shadow of his beard making him look gaunt and unkempt.

Bending, the orderly removed his boots. Fighting against a wave of sickness mingled with the salt ache of unshed tears, Eleanora reached to adjust his arm, which

145

seemed to be lying too high upon his chest in its sling. The movement dislodged the triangle of black cotton, exposing the bulky bandaging beneath his shirt. Then, as she traced the outline of the bandage with her eyes, the red of his shirt over the shoulder began to darken.

John Barclay drew in his breath. "He's bleeding. His fall must have reopened his wound."

Ten

Dr. Jones was brisk and efficient, a man nearing middle age with center-parted, pomaded, gray hair, steel-framed spectacles, and wearing a long surgeon's coat of white cotton shadowed in splotches by ancient, irremovable blood stains. He cut the bandage away from the still-unconscious man, viewing the suppurating wound with its swollen proud flesh with detachment. At the unmistakable stench of putrescence, he did frown slightly, waving forward the orderly holding the bottle of diluted carbolic acid.

Eleanora winced as she watched his thorough cleaning of the mangled hole. In her concern for the neglected state of Grant's injury, the welling blood no longer affected her. Her fingers tingled with the need to take the pad from the surgeon and finish the task with more care.

The reek of carbolic cleansed the air, and then the doctor began to bandage the wound again. At a barked order, the orderly, panting still from his search for the doctor, leaped to lift and turn the inert man, and to hold the thick pad of cloth over the wound while it was bound in place.

As the flat knot was tied, the surgeon stepped back. "Now I want to know how Colonel Farrell came to fall while he was in your care?" he said to the perspiring Nicaraguan.

"I do not know, sir. He complained of a fever. I

146

brought the cool water to bathe him with as I was shown, but he would not let me. He said to take it away. He was not himself, I could tell by his eyes, but what else could I do? He is the colonel. I took it. I heard him cry out, as to someone in the street, and when I entered the room, I saw him on the floor. Is he in extremity, sir? Will he die?"

"Not that bad," the surgeon said. "He's got a lump the size of a goose egg on his head. With that, and being as weak as he is, it may be a while before he comes around. You can count yourself lucky he didn't take a fall over the railing in his state. If you can't take care of your patient you'll have to go back to the field hospital."

"I will do better, Señor Médico, sir, I promise. But you must tell the colonel to allow me to tend him."

"It's your job to persuade him."

"I know, sir, but who persuades the Iron Warrior to do what is against his will, even if it is best for him?" The man shrugged, a hopeless gesture.

Eleanora raised her eyes from the hollows beneath Grant's high cheekbones. "I could try."

The doctor swung on her as if seeing her for the first time. "And who are you?"

"I—I am the colonel's mistress," she said.

"I see," he told her, nodding his head with narrowed eyes. "The woman who caused all this?"

Eleanora did not reply. The surgeon studied her proud chin, the firm mouth, and steady gaze of her green eyes. Abruptly he nodded. "All right. He's yours if you want him. The orderly will come in handy for the heavy work, but if you'd rather not have him around just say so."

"I'm sure I will need him."

"Good. Then I will leave Colonel Farrell in your hands. God knows you have to be better than Pedro here."

His instructions were brief and concise. These given, he did not linger, but picked up his leather case and strode out the door, his white coat flapping about his knees.

John Barclay touched Eleanora's shoulder. "You're sure you want to do this?"

147

"I have to," she replied. "But you needn't stay. The troupe will want their breakfast."

"Yes," he agreed with a rueful glance at the basket he had set down out of the way in the corner near the door. "I hate to leave you."

"I'll be fine. It's not as if I were alone."

"No, but I have to answer to Mazie, you know," he said, his mouth curving beneath his mustache with gentle humor. "She will probably be around to talk you out of this."

"You can tell her she won't succeed," she warned.

"With Mazie, I don't think that will make any difference. She's a lot like you that way; she has to try." Putting a finger under her chin, John Barclay leaned to brush her cheek with a kiss. Turning, he picked up the woven basket and let himself out of the room.

The click of the door latch was loud in the silence. Eleanora took a deep breath, giving herself a mental shake. The orderly was watching her with patient eyes. She smiled at him. "I think, Pedro, that first we will try bathing him with that cool water again."

Though it lowered his fever, the sponge bath did not revive Grant, nor did shaving him, though it did make him look more alive. When smelling salts held beneath his nose had no effect, Eleanora abandoned the effort. Sending the orderly from the room, she drew a straight chair to the side of the bed and sat down. She was still there when Señora Paredes brought her noon meal to her on a tray.

The woman set her burden upon the table before she looked directly at Eleanora, and then her glance was veiled. Clasping her hands in front of her, she said, "I made the colonel some broth, good broth with the strength of beef."

"I will see he eats it if he regains consciousness."

"Is he bad?"

"The doctor doesn't seem to think so, but his idea of bad may be different from ours."

"That Pedro is filling his belly in my kitchen. Do you need him?"

148

"Not just now."

"I will not let him leave. If you will step outside and call from the galería I will send him to you."

"Thank you," Eleanora said in some surprise.

The woman left without answering.

As the afternoon wore on Grant's fever began to climb again. By nightfall he was growing restless, plucking at the sheet and pressing his hand to his shoulder. Loosening the bandage seemed to help for awhile, but he was soon turning his head on the pillow and pushing at the sheets as if fighting the restraints, like trailing ropes, that held him to unconsciousness.

Beyond bathing him again, there was little that could be done. Eleanora could only sit, watching him, thinking. What had she done? It was stupid to come back here, a foolish sentimentality to indulge in simply because she suspected that Grant had been calling after her when he fell. Perhaps it was more of a wish than a suspicion? Ridiculous. Or was it? She had not hesitated when a chance arose to return. Was duty, then, only an excuse? Certainly not. She felt a very real obligation. Grant would be unharmed except for her. Anyone could be moved to compassion by the sight of a strong man reduced to such helplessness. Just because she was affected to the point of tears did not mean she loved him, did it? It would be different when he was himself again, awake, rational, on his feet. He would have no need of her then. She would like to be gone before that time came.

On four separate occasions a courier from the Government House came to the door asking to see her patient. Each time Eleanora told him the colonel could not be disturbed. The fourth time, when the knocking roused Grant from what had appeared to be the beginning of natural sleep, Eleanora lost her temper. "Inform General Walker that Colonel Farrell is unconscious, that he is unable to answer questions or prepare reports, or to be useful to him in any capacity, and if he ever expects him to return to duty he would do well to leave him alone!"

"And who am I supposed to say the message is from?" the soldier had asked, grinning.

149

"Eleanora Villars, his mistress!"

Once again she had proclaimed it. When the man had gone and she had resumed her post beside the bed, Eleanora sat with her hand over her mouth, staring at the harsh face of the man who lay there. Within her chest her heart beat with the painful heaviness of a leaden weight. Slowly, then with growing violence, her head throbbed in time with its beat. For someone of her upbringing, the desire to own herself the mistress of any man came perilously close to love. When that man had taken her by force, kept her prisoner, and, tiring of her, sent her from him, and she still could not deny him, must that love not be a proven fact?

Grant stirred. Reaching out, she smoothed his dark hair back, laying her cool hand across his burning forehead. He muttered something under his breath, a whisper of sound. Eleanora leaned to catch it, but, lying quiet, a long shape under the sheet, he did not speak again. When she moved her hand, however, he grew restless once more, and so she stayed with her arm outstretched until the muscles of her back became hard with cramp and the orderly entered the darkened room bearing a lighted candle to relieve her while she ate her evening meal.

The night passed with aching slowness. Hourly Grant grew worse. Tossing in delirium, he seemed to be reliving the march from Sonora. The thought of water preyed upon his mind, but though Eleanora and the orderly moistened his lips and allowed drops to trickle down his throat time after time, he was never satisfied. At first her touch served to soothe his movements, but toward dawn that failed and he had to be restrained from leaving the bed and reeling across the room. The bandages they had loosened earlier had tightened once more as his shoulder swelled. Red streaks ran down his arm and in radiating lines across his chest.

Drawing the nightshirt back to look at them, Eleanora bit her lip. Something had to be done, and quickly, or he would die. Despite Luis's words, or perhaps because of them, she placed little confidence in Dr. Jones's readiness to recognize the necessity. His attitude was much too

150

casual to inspire faith. Her father had not been casual. A slow and meticulous attention to his work had been his hallmark—that, and a fanatical addiction to cleanliness.

As memory shifted inside her brain, Eleanora looked up at the orderly lolling half-asleep in a chair by the open windows. "Pedro," she called, "put some water on to boil. Find the colonel's razor and drop it in the pot then add salt, a double handful. When the water starts to roll, bring it all up here."

"Señorita, I—I could not touch the colonel, if that is what you are thinking of."

"*I* don't intend for you to do it."

"Then you—but, señorita, you have not the skill. You will kill him."

"I promise you I will not, but if I should, I also promise I will explain to Dr. Jones, and even to William Walker, himself, if need be."

He would have liked, she thought, to run straight to Dr. Jones. Eleanora did not try to prevent him, a fact that seemed to cause him worry. He was caught squarely on the horns, afraid to stay and assist her, afraid to leave and be accused of deserting his patient again. In spite of her reassurances, only the threat of making her own preparations and attending Grant alone caused the orderly to cease his objections and obey her.

With the scissors that had been a part of the sewing kit Grant had found for her, she cut the bandage away. The ragged hole gaped more purple and yellow than the day before, and just as smelly, despite the surgeon's swabbing. Using the blade of her scissors, Eleanora picked up a compress of cream-colored linen and dipped it into the steaming salt water. She pressed it against the side of the pot to remove some of the excess water, held it a moment to cool slightly, then laid the steaming cloth upon the wound.

Grant's arm twitched, a shudder ran over his frame, but he lay still. Slowly the orderly relaxed his hold on his other arm. Again and again she repeated the operation, each time discarding the linen as her father had shown her. The process was his. In his travels, including his tour

151

of the great hospitals of Europe as a young man, her father had noticed that wounds healed faster with fewer problems on board ships. Sea air was noted for the promotion of good health, regardless of the geographical location of the seaport. The one factor in common was salt. Brine was used for the preservation of meat. It must, then, have some property that helped to prevent decay. Why not apply the principle to living flesh, he reasoned. Boiling the water helped to dissolve the salt and to remove the traces of soap from the razor. Her father had maintained that it helped in other ways in the healing process, though his theory was laughed at by his colleagues, since he could not explain how it worked.

The moribund flesh at the mouth of the wound turned white under her treatment. Clenching her teeth, Eleanora put down her scissors and took up the razor. With her left hand she stretched the skin of his shoulder taut, and carefully lowered the blade. Suddenly Grant moved, his right hand coming up to fasten with paralyzing force about her wrist.

He had been insensible so long Eleanora had come to think of him as immune to pain, uncaring of what was done to him. Now she stared into his eyes, bright blue and heavy with fever, in a kind of numb disbelief. His gaze moved from the razor in her hand, traveling up her arm to her face above him. A frown of intense concentration puckered the skin under his eyes. By slow degrees his grip lost its strength, grew slack, fell away. His face smoothed. His eyelids fluttered down.

Eleanora stood still, watching the red marks on her wrist fade. The razor in her hand trembled with the jerking of her nerves. Had he lost consciousness again? Had he, in that brief moment, been trying to tell her not to touch him?

Her doubts were answered as he spoke, his voice a soft rustle in the strained quiet. "What are you waiting for?"

An instant longer she stood, weighing the razor in her hand. Then, with a silent prayer, she blanked out what had happened, concentrating on the job before her, deciding how it must look when she was done. With quick, sure strokes she trimmed away the whitened, nerveless skin, clearing the opening with as much precision as she had ever used on eyelet-lace cut-work. That done, she laid the razor aside and placed her fingers firmly on either side of the wound, exerting a gentle, but steadily increasing, pressure. Bloodstained pus welled, but in it was something she had more than half-expected to see, tattered bits of red cloth. It was tiny pieces of Grant's red shirt, driven into the wound by her brother's bullet. The larger sections the surgeon had removed, no doubt, but these smaller bits had been so nearly invisible in the fresh, bleeding wound they could not be found.

"Pedro," Eleanora said, nodding at the linen square laid ready. Carefully, he wiped the accumulated matter away. Twice, three, four times they flushed the bullet hole, continuing until Eleanora was satisfied nothing remained inside that should not be there. A final application of carbolic, the dressing, and they were done. Grant was pale, with a white line about his mouth, but his pulse was firm and even. With the orderly holding his head up, he was able to drink a little water colored with a few drops of the tincture of opium she had found in a small vial in his medical kit.

Waving Pedro out with the soiled cloth and the pot of water, in a silent order that would not disturb Grant, Eleanora picked up the carbolic and the razor and started to move away. She had taken only a step or two when she realized she was caught. She stopped, glancing down. Grant's left hand, lying on the edge of the bed where she had leaned over him, had become entwined in her skirts. She was held fast.

Her fingers turning numb on the things she held, she stood barely breathing. This gesture hurt her as nothing had ever done. The ache burgeoned within her, pushing past her defenses, liquefying them, assaulting her heart with the flow of acid tears. She did not move until the opium had taken effect and his fingers grew lax with sleep.

It was late afternoon, the breeze from the lake was beginning to blow cool across the water and the blue shadows, when Dr. Jones visited the palacio once more. He stopped in the doorway, his eyebrows arching above the rims of his spectacles. "What is this?" he growled without heat, his gaze going from Eleanora, sitting on the edge of the bed with a bowl of the señora's beef broth in her hand, to Grant, propped high upon a mound of pillows.

It was Luis who answered from his perch on the table. "It is a demonstration of raw courage. My amigo is as out of temper as a rattlesnake with two tails, both sore, and Eleanora is attempting to feed him. It would be dangerous indeed, except he is too weak to do more than shake his rattles."

"I can well believe it," the surgeon said, advancing to the bed. " 'Evening, Colonel, I didn't expect to see you so fit. You restore my faith in miracles."

Grant looked at him, then at the merriment dancing in Luis's brown eyes. " 'Evening," he said with a marked lack of grace.

"You will have to forgive the colonel," Luis said on a laugh. "We were just discussing the angelic nature of Eleanora's healing power, but since she spent the morning cutting on Grant, he is in no mood to appreciate it."

"Cutting?" the surgeon demanded. "Let's have a look at this."

Eleanora spoke quickly. "I would prefer that he finishes this broth before he is disturbed. It's the first thing he has eaten in two days."

Dr. Jones stopped, his bristling gaze clashing with the clear, green reason in Eleanora's eyes. He gave an abrupt nod, and looking around, found a chair for himself and sat down to wait.

"A remarkable job of débridement," he said a little later as he fastened the bandaging back into place. He had not troubled to completely remove Eleanora's handiwork after one swift glance at the wound.

In answer to the expectant tone in the surgeon's voice, Eleanora told him of her father.

"I'll repeat what I said yesterday. Colonel Farrell is a lucky man. I should have done what you did yester-

154

day morning, but I had two amputations and a broken leg waiting on me at the hospital. Then, there was a report of a skirmish on the Costa Rican border. The casualties got in late last night, eight men in all, five of them bad."

"I thought we were at peace," Eleanora exclaimed.

"We are," Dr. Jones replied with irony, "but the patrols along both borders, Honduran as well as Costa Rican, can't resist taking potshots at each other. Now and then a patrol is discovered across the line and all hell breaks out. That's when we get our wounded. God knows what the casualties would be like if there was another major battle. Do you know these so-called Immortals averaged sixty wounds for the fifty-six of them in this last little set-to? The results of Walker's tactics, the charge with revolvers blazing, that he's so fond of. Brave and romantic, and in its place, effective—but it can be dangerous when the enemy doesn't get too rattled to shoot straight."

"You dare to criticize the military genius of our general?" Luis asked in mock ferocity.

Dr. Jones shrugged. "I can't quarrel with success, but I'd be better satisfied if he had more care for his men."

"It isn't that he doesn't care," Grant said, entering the conversation. "It's just that he rates some things higher than human life."

"Idealists are fine in their place," the surgeon grunted. "Their place is just not in a position where they control the lives of human beings."

"I think you must be something of an idealist yourself, Dr. Jones, or you would not be here in Nicaragua," Eleanora said.

"What I am is a damn fool," he answered.

When the surgeon took his leave, Eleanora saw him to the door, and then, obedient to his signal, walked with him along the galería to the head of the stairs.

"Keeping the colonel quiet is the right thing, certainly it's more than I ever managed. Fluids, he needs those. Solid food when he asks for it, which will be soon, if I'm any judge." He went on in this vein, though Eleanora

155

thought his mind was not on what he was saying. At the stairs he came to a halt.

"I meant what I said about coming to the hospital. Our orderlies are like Pedro, recruited from the natives here. They are fine, but they're untrained for the most part, and language is still a problem. I'm worried about the increase in casualties lately. I see a trend, a build-up in the resistance to Walker and the Demócraticos, and in the fighting. I'm not sure it's accidental any more, these border clashes—not that Walker listens to me. He wants the peace to last so he can entrench himself here. He won't listen to anything he doesn't want to hear. Never mind that. The point is, I'd be grateful for your help if you can see your way to giving it. Yours, and any other woman who can speak English. Anybody can point out the hospital to you. Just ask for me."

Eleanora could promise to do no more than think about it. Dr. Jones had to be satisfied with that. Watching him clump down the stairs after a last round of compliments, she did not think he would let it end there, however. The idea had its appeal, but she had other duties to attend to first. Dismissing the doctor and his request in an instant, she turned back toward the sickroom.

Grant's improvement was steady. He slept much of the time at first. When he was awake his mood varied from temperamental to a docility that was infinitely more distressing. He would lie, watching her every movement until she grew clumsy with embarrassment. Sometimes at night she would leave her bed in the room next door, his old room, and pad through the darkness along the galería to assure herself he was all right. She often thought, standing beside his bed, that quiet as she tried to be, her presence wakened him. She could never be certain; she had no more desire to call his attention to her vigil than she thought he had to acknowledge it.

Luis was the only visitor admitted. Gradually the emissaries from the Government House stopped coming, sending their most urgent requests through the lieutenant colonel. In time, Eleanora learned to trust his judgment of how much or how little to ask of Grant on a given occasion. The Spaniard had an innate courtesy, based on a well-hidden sensitivity, that prevented him from over-tiring his friend. By degrees the two men moved their work from the bed to the table once more. As long as Luis was with Grant, Eleanora could relax, seeing to the small things she had neglected, such as keeping up her scanty wardrobe, washing her hair, and marketing for special foods she wanted prepared.

Meeting Mazie in the plaza on one such shopping excursion, she brought her back to the house for coffee. As they settled down in the patio with their cups, Eleanora inquired after the troupe.

"Doing fine," Mazie nodded. "Excited just now about the new play. It opens the day after tomorrow, you know. If Grant is well enough the two of you will have to come and see it before the run is over. And if you see the general, you might put in a good word for us. The rest of the bunch would be thrilled if he came, and I don't imagine it could hurt the box office, either."

"I'll try," Eleanora said ruefully. "I don't think the general is too pleased with me at the moment, since I denied him access to his favorite officer."

"How you dared I can't imagine. The man frightens me to death."

"I doubt I could have in person, but then, I don't imagine it would have been necessary. The general may be self-centered, but he isn't unreasonable. If he had realized how ill Grant was he would not have troubled him anyway."

"You sound as if you like him."

"I do."

"Such a cold fish?"

"How can you say that of a man whom the men under him call "Uncle Billy"? A man who keeps a mistress—and such a pretentious shrew of a woman—against his own principles?"

"Men follow other men, and men have been known to take mistresses, for a number of other reasons besides a warm nature."

"I suppose," Eleanora agreed, running her finger around the rim of her coffee cup. "But I still like him. He's charming and audacious; he has character and courage. You can't say as much about most men."

"Dear Eleanora, don't turn cynical on me at this stage. Believe me, it's fatal. Women without expectations attract men they can expect nothing from."

"Marvelous," Eleanora teased, "and what do you expect from John Barclay?"

"A ring," Mazie said, and leaned back, waiting for the reaction.

"You mean—marriage?"

"Why not?"

"No reason—I'm just surprised. He doesn't seem the type of man I would—you would—"

"Because he isn't rich? Money matters only when something else is missing."

"Such as—"

"Respect, affection, common interests."

They had both carefully avoided the word love. Eleanora left it unspoken. "You think you will be happy?"

"As happy as I have any right to expect to be. Why not? I will have John, the troupe for a family, and a quasi-respectability. I may even have a career as an actress."

"Here, in Nicaragua?"

"Or in New Orleans, San Francisco, Mobile, Charleston, even Boston or New York. All that's needed is a little push to turn the troupe from a collection of players into a successful theater company."

"I'm sure you can do it, if anybody can."

Mazie laughed and they were quiet a moment, looking out into the sun-soaked center of the patio where a cloud of sulfur-yellow butterflies moved from pot to terra-cotta pot of the señora's flowers. When they rose from the mauve blossoms of a creeping plant up and out of the confining walls like a yellow cloud, Eleanora spoke again.

"I had the offer of a new pastime several days ago."

"What was that?" Mazie stretched, narrowing her eyes to slits like a large tiger cat.

"Hospital work."

The other woman froze. "You didn't accept?"

"I couldn't, not just now."

"You realize what it means?"

"It means they need help, I would imagine," Eleanora said, nettled by Mazie's portentous air.

"No, my pet. Doctors only ask women of a certain class to work in hospitals. It is assumed that we, having seen the seamier side of life, will not be shocked at anything we may encounter—and, of course, the sight of naked males is presumed to be no novelty."

"My mother worked with the sick—" she protested.

"Women and children, I'm sure, and with her husband close to hand. What you are being offered is dark, dirty rooms full of sick and maimed men, lousy, bedbug ridden, fly-blown, wallowing in their own filth."

"You have seen the inside of the hospital?" Eleanora asked, the skin of her scalp tight with horror at the picture Mazie evoked. "You have seen it, and didn't try to help?"

"Help? Have you any idea of the back-breaking labor involved? One person couldn't make a dent in it, even if they could stand the horrible sights and smells."

"That's not true. The papers were full of tales a few months ago of an Englishwoman who went into the military hospitals in the Crimea to nurse the soldiers. I've forgotten her name, but she was a lady, certainly not a prostitute."

"Nightingale was her name, so theatrical, I remember thinking. The 'Lady with the Lamp.' Touching, but that was in Russia. The woman would faint dead away at the sight of a military infirmary in this tropical climate. The wounds have maggots, Eleanora. Arms and legs swell in the heat. Open, running sores, fevers that rage so high they can kill overnight. It is truly unbelievable."

"And yet, sick men are supposed to live and get well under such conditions. No wonder those who can, stay away from the hospital."

"Hospitals are always like that in warm places."

"Not my father's; and summer in New Orleans has been likened to Hades."

159

"That was for the upper class, I would imagine, for patients who could afford the best—and who had their own servants to wait on them."

Eleanora frowned. What Mazie said was true, but instead of discouraging her, it served to increase her interest. She had not dreamed, despite the words Dr. Jones had used to couch his request, that the need was so great.

Their cups were empty. Leaning forward, Eleanora refilled them, then settled back. "You haven't seen anything of Jean-Paul, have you?" she asked with a casual air that, she was sure, fooled Mazie not at all.

Mazie's lashes, tipped with gold dust, fell. "I was hoping you wouldn't ask."

"He—isn't in trouble again?"

"Not officially, for which you can thank your Spanish friend upstairs. I've seen men from the Laredo regiment leading him to his lodgings a half-dozen times."

"Lodgings?" Eleanora inquired without looking directly at the woman across from her.

"He's left the barracks to make way for new recruits. As long as he performs his duties it doesn't matter where he bunks—or with whom."

"Meaning?"

"I thought you couldn't know," Mazie said, sighing. "I hate bearing tales."

"Please don't feel that way. I have no other means of knowing, if someone doesn't tell me. It was too much, I suppose, to expect Jean-Paul to understand why I had to come back here, but I haven't seen him since that night at the theater."

The other woman nodded. "Your brother found himself something of a celebrity after his meeting with the colonel. Every man in command makes enemies, people who are happy to see him hurt, brought down. These people fastened on Jean-Paul, making over him until he's got to the point he's proud of what he did. The most influential of them is a woman, a dark-haired Nicaraguan vixen—who seems to hate Walker, the colonel—everybody except Jean-Paul. Her name—"

160

"—Her name," Eleanora said, speaking with slow and absolute certainty, "is Juanita."

Eleven

Juanita, the woman who had aspired to be Grant's mistress, the woman who had given Eleanora the scratch marks finally fading from her wrist, the woman Grant had dropped from the galería: it was not surprising that she held a grudge. It was unusual, however, for someone of her volatile temper to take such an indirect means of revenge. Still, what else could it be? The chance of her pairing with Jean-Paul by coincidence was much too slim.

After Mazie had gone, Eleanora made a slow circuit of the patio, mulling over the problem. Her conclusion was no different. Juanita had to have a reason for what she was doing. The tiles of the patio were littered with the spent blooms of an orange trumpet-shaped flower. She had stooped to pick them up when she heard the slamming of a door above. She straightened to see Luis moving quickly along the galería. It took only a step or two to meet him at the foot of the stairs.

"Going so soon?" she asked, placing her hands on the newel. "I thought you would stay for luncheon."

"Duty waits—impatiently," he answered, smiling, making as though to slip past her.

"Luis?"

"Yes, Eleanora?" He paused, alert to the seriousness of her tone.

"Why didn't you tell me about Jean-Paul?"

"I—judged that you had enough to worry you. Was I wrong?"

A frown between her eyes, she shook her head. "I might have done something, gone to him, explained."

"It troubles you that you and your brother are far apart in your hearts and minds? This is a natural thing,

161

a necessary thing. You cannot stay forever as when you were children."

"No, but I am all he has."

"This has been so, until now. Now he has Juanita—ah, I begin to see. This is what worries you?"

"She will use him."

"And he, her. It is the way of things."

Eleanora raised her lashes. "I don't need a lesson in worldliness. There must be something we can do."

Gently he reached out to take her hands in his. "Forgive me if I fail you, but there is nothing. He must make his mistakes, just as you, *pequeña,* must make yours." Lifting her hands, he pressed them to the warm smoothness of his lips, then released her. His smile held a tinge of sadness before he sketched a bow and strode easily away. The silver rowels of his spurs made a musical jangle long after he had disappeared from sight.

Picking up her skirts, Eleanora began to climb the stairs. Near the top, she glanced up. Grant stood in the doorway of his room, one arm braced on the frame. There was a black scowl between his brows that, against her will, sent a shaft of apprehension through her, until she realized he was staring past her, staring at the place where she and Luis had been standing. An instant's hesitation, and she started to move again. Grant shifted his gaze to watch her approach. Letting her slide past him, he turned into the room behind her.

The table was piled high with papers and the various books which it was Grant's responsibility to keep. He sat down once more to the paperwork that had accumulated during his absence. The sling of black muslin hung useless around his neck; he used it less and less as the days went by. As he leaned over his work, his hair, grown long, fell in a black wing over his forehead. Eleanora, stooping to pick up a sheaf of papers that had slid to the floor, removing the empty glasses from among the piles, resisted the impulse to reach out and push it back.

The scratching of Grant's pen slowed, stopped. He looked up. "Eleanora?"

162

His voice was soft, tentative, as if he were tasting the flavor of her name. "Yes," she answered, turning with the glasses, sticky with lemonade, in her hands.

"Why? Why did you come back?"

"You must know," she answered carefully.

He threw the pen down and swung around in his chair. "No. Tell me."

"I felt—bound."

"In what way?"

"You were injured because of me."

"I would have thought that would be a reason for gloating, not pity."

"Pity?" Eleanora said, her chin lifting. "I've never pitied you."

"No? Then if you're not Lady Bountiful on a charity case, what the hell are you doing here?"

Eleanora opened her lips to speak, but no words came. What could she answer? Certainly not the truth.

"Well?"

The blazing blue of his eyes was impossible to sustain. Staring past his shoulder, she said, "Perhaps for the same reason you stood and allowed my brother to put his bullet in you."

"You won't mind if I take leave to doubt it?"

"Think what you please. It makes no difference," she replied, stung by the irony of his tone.

The suspicion of a breeze stirred the muslin curtains that had been let down over the window to help keep out the flies. It smelled of the dust and the street refuse of the advancing dry season, and did little to alleviate the heat building in the small room.

"You'll be happy to learn," he said, the well-molded lines of his mouth drawing taut, "that I expect to return to the Government House tomorrow."

Her eyes widened. "Your shoulder is too tender. You'll open it again."

"Concerned, Eleanora?"

"Naturally," she said, her cheeks flooding with warmth. "I'm not unfeeling."

"I wonder," he muttered, his gaze sliding over the

smooth white skin of her shoulders revealed by the low neck of her blouse where her drawstring had loosened. Following the direction he was looking, she hastily tightened the string, tying it in a bow.

His movements were unnaturally stiff as he transferred his regard to the hazy view beyond the French door. "All that remains is for me to express my gratitude for the part you played in saving my life."

"It was nothing."

"I won't argue with you, beyond saying that I value it a little more highly."

"I didn't mean—" she began, then stopped, seeing the shadow of a dry humor at the back of his eyes. "I meant to say my part in it was small."

"That isn't the way Pedro tells it," he said, dismissing the subject with a casual gesture that held, once again, that subtle air of command. "I suppose you will now consider your duty completed?" he went on.

"I—expect so," Eleanora agreed quietly.

He pushed back his chair and moved around the bed to the washstand. From one of its drawers he took out a leather purse such as the Spaniards carried, and turning, held it out to Eleanora.

She made no move to take it. "Are you offering me money?"

"I want you to have it."

"To salve your conscience?" she demanded, her green eyes glittering in her pale face. "My services require no payment. They have never been for sale!"

"I have never offered to buy yours or any other woman's, and I'm not doing it now. All right. Call it conscience money, but take it, so you will never have to sell yourself!"

Eleanora did not stay to listen. She whirled, and with tears blinding her eyes, groped for the door handle. Finding it, she flung the panel wide and ran, seeking the sanctuary of the room she had made her own. Locking the door behind her, she threw herself on the bed and lay tense, listening. Unconsciously, she expected fury, a violent assault on the door. The silence without seemed to flow endlessly, to penetrate the room, crowding in where she lay, resting upon her chest with a great weight that, finally, forced the scalding tears from her eyes.

The nights of sleepless nursing, the days of anxious waiting, the emotional turmoil of the past weeks, swept in upon her. Exhausted from her bout of weeping, she slept, her wet, tangled lashes lying still as death upon her cheeks.

She opened throbbing eyes to darkness. Heaviness pressed her into the softness of the bed. It was difficult to move. Lying there, coming slowly awake, she knew she should be hungry, but her throat felt too swollen to eat. By degrees, she levered herself into a sitting position. This would not do. She had to gather her things together, to send a message to Mazie—no, it was too late. She must have been asleep for hours. Moonlight already silvered the rooftops beyond the French window. Tomorrow. It would have to wait until then. Perhaps she could keep still until morning, until Grant had gone. She need not see him again, nor he, her. It would be better that way.

Standing, lighting a candle, moving about, helped to clear her mind of the bitter dregs of sleep. Splashing water into the basin to wash her face made her feel more alert. On impulse, she removed her clothes, and setting the basin on the floor, stepped into it, then sluiced her entire body, letting the cool, soap-scented water run over her with a sensuous pleasure. Refreshed, she brushed her hair, standing naked before the mirror. When she had dried in the air, she slipped on the brocade dressing gown and set about clearing away the mess she had made. In the midst of mopping up the floor with a towel, she halted, her attention caught by a sound from the next room. It was the squeak of bed ropes as Grant turned in his bed. Had she disturbed him? She must be quieter.

For a time she sat on the side of the bed with her hands folded in her lap. The wail of a concertina, the monotonous barking of a dog came to her on the night air. It was no use returning to bed; she could not sleep now. Finding her clothes, making a bundle of them, except for the dress she would wear the next day, consumed a few more minutes. Placing it beside the door, she went back to the bed to sit and listen to Grant's restless tossing.

Was his wound paining him? Perhaps he had turned feverish again? It was foolish to trouble herself so over a grown man, but she had acquired the habit. She could not help it, any more than she could prevent herself from loving him. Of the two, which was more foolish?

The thudding sound of something falling on the other side of the wall made her jump. An instant later she sprang up and let herself out the door. Her bare feet made no sound on the galería. The position of the door and its knob were so well known to her she could have found them without the captured glow of moonlight in the well of the patio. By contrast, Grant's room appeared black-dark, alive with unseen dangers. Her skin prickled as she stood inside the door, then she began to move toward the bed.

Her foot touched a glass tumbler trailing water, no doubt this was what had fallen. It rolled with a deafening clatter across the floor. Still, there was no sound from the bed.

The sheets felt rumpled to her touch, and damp with night air. The pillow was easily located—the coarse silk of his hair—his forehead—

Suddenly her hand was caught and tugged. Off balance, she fell across the bed. An arm of tempered steel lifted her, gathering her close against the hard length of the man in the bed.

"You had your chance," Grant said, his breath warm upon her neck, his voice husky with desire. "You should have taken it. You'll never get another one from me."

"Grant—" she said weakly as she felt his hand caress her shoulder, brushing aside the lapel of the dressing gown. The belt gave to his quick tug, leaving her easy prey to his possessive touch.

"I'll never let you go again," he whispered, pushing the brocade robe from the bed, letting it slide to the floor. His mouth descended on hers, searching for, and

166

finding, the sweetness of willing surrender. He drew her soft nakedness to his lithe form, holding her close, ever closer, until her chest ached with the constriction of her breathing and the muscles of his arms trembled with the need to make her a part of him. He explored the corners of her mouth and the delicate curves of her ears, breathing deep of the warm, fresh fragrance of her hair. His hands, cherishing, sure upon the curves and hollows of her body, stirred the slumbering dragon-fire of yearning in her loins, and she clung to him with a fierce and sacrificial gentleness. He guided her beneath him, a tender shadow, guiding her also to the onslaught that filled her with such a shock of pleasure that she rose against him, his name a soft sound on her lips. Wide and far their ardor stretched, encompassing great reaches of mindless space, black, echoing with the pounding of their hearts, overflowing the narrow limits of world and time. Rapture and pain intermingled, subsiding slowly. It was several moments before Eleanora recognized the softness of a pillow beneath her head, or the sensation of Grant brushing her damp hair away from her face with his fingers, releasing the tangled strands from where they were pulled taut underneath him, and behind her shoulders. He framed her face with his hands and kissed her soft, faintly tremulous mouth, then with a sigh, settled back, turning her to him, pressing her head onto his uninjured shoulder.

Eleanora lay as he placed her for a time. The combined heat of their bodies burned along her hip and thigh. Still, she did not move until his chest began an even rise and fall. She inched away then, a fraction at a time, stopping only when a body width of cool linen sheet lay between them.

She was depraved. She must be, to find joy such as she had not known existed in the physical union with a man who offered her nothing but a whore's portion: money and passion.

Beside her he slept with the stillness of content while she lay wakeful. It was not a fair exchange, she thought with a seeping resentment. His shoulder must be more nearly healed than she had suspected to sustain the treatment it had received without paining him. Why, then, had he been so restless? Could she dare to hope it was for want of her beside him? But what did that count for, if it was no more than the result of his manhood's need? He had tried to send her away for the sake of honor, but finding her near him still, had weakened. *I will never let you go again,* he had said. Spoken in the flush of desire, the words were not binding, but she must take what comfort from them she could.

A cock crowed in the distance. The same dog she had heard earlier began to bark again. Her eyes burned, there was an aching pressure behind them, but she had no tears. They had vanished, leaving her with the brittle dryness of self-scorn.

She awoke to the confinement of a hard-muscled thigh across her legs, the dazzle of sunlight in her eyes, and a ravening hunger.

Breakfast was an omelette seasoned with cayenne, corn cakes dusted with panocha, brown Mexican sugar, plus hot coffee, and oranges. Grant peeled one of the golden-red globes for her, and when she had eaten it, leaned across to take a tart-sweet kiss from her lips. At the look in his eyes when he raised his head she said quickly, "It's getting late. They will be waiting for you at the Government House."

"Yesterday you thought it was too soon for me to go back," he told her, rising to stalk her as she got hastily to her feet. "I think you may be right. Would you suggest a few more days of bed rest?"

"Rest? I doubt you would get any!"

"Is that a threat? Then I know I'm staying, at least as long as my strength lasts."

His smile was laced with a free and unrestrained humor. His laughing eyes had lost their hard, feverish gleam. Within her, Eleanora felt her heart contract on seeing the difference it made to the pagan angularity of his features. His profile was not classically handsome— it was too strong, even predatory—and yet, it stirred her like no other. She would not have him different, even if she could.

168

His advance slowed, came to a halt. "Are you afraid of me, Eleanora?"

She shook her head. "Of course not."

"You watch me like a mouse watches a cat. You stay as much as possible out of reach, except when I take you by surprise and push inside your defenses."

"That may be—because I don't know what you intend—how you feel."

Frowning, he said, "I told you I want you with me, always. What more do you want?"

"Nothing you can't give freely," she answered, and found that it was true.

"But a set of marriage lines would satisfy you, wouldn't it? You may not give yourself the airs of a belle or a coquette, but you're like all the rest. You'll use any wile, any trick to tie a man down. And when he's shackled you'll make his life a living hell."

"Not all marriages are like that," she said, pride strengthening her voice, "but if that's the way you feel I should think you would make a bad husband. Then there is the question of security and your ability to provide a comfortable home—no, I don't believe you meet my requirements."

"That settles that, then," he said grimly.

"Not quite. I would like your promise to release me if I receive a better, and more honorable, proposal." When he did not answer, she went on. "You see? The knife cuts both ways. If you cannot be bound, neither can I, unless you intend to resort to locking me in again?"

"If you go," he said at last, "the choice will be yours."

It was a magnificent concession. Without the goad of anger it might never have been made, Eleanora knew. She accepted it with a quick inclination of her head before he could change his mind, and chided herself for wishing for something more.

"Are we quits now?" he inquired, coming closer.

"In a manner of speaking," she replied, her face calmer than she felt inside.

"Then—"

He held out his hand, a command backed by a promise in his eyes. What else could she do but go into his arms? It was, in any case, where she longed to be, held tight, uncaring of pride or the future.

Pedro was no longer needed. Dr. Jones was his immediate superior, but since he had not put in an appearance for several days, there had not been an opportunity to have the orderly dismissed. Pedro was in no hurry. His duties were light and he had a fine appreciation for the señora's efforts in the kitchen. The señora, however, did not appreciate Pedro, and she was not backward in making her displeasure known, once it became obvious that the colonel did not require his services. The best solution seemed to be to seek out the surgeon so that he might relieve both the orderly and the household at the same time.

Accordingly, later in the morning Grant returned to duty, Eleanora put together a basket containing a crock of the señora's strengthening beef broth, several dozen small cakes, and a number of back copies of *El Nicaraguense,* which had been sent to Grant by the general. Commandeering Pedro as her escort, she made her way through the streets to the enfermería.

The building selected by Dr. Jones was situated near the Church of Guadalupe, a long, low structure used originally as a hospital by the nuns. It was built of handmade adobe bricks which had the melted look of age associated with the buildings dating back nearly three hundred years, to the founding of the city. It had no glass in the casements of the long windows which lined both sides, using only batten blinds to keep out the wind and rain. Inside the dim room, the floor was of hard-beaten earth, the walls were plastered a dirty brown, and the hewed beams of the ceiling were exposed. From the beams hung huge water ollas suspended in slings made of coarse, raveling ropes. They lined the aisle between the double row of beds, turning slowly with their own damp weight and the warm air moving through the open blinds.

The free ventilation was necessary. Without it the smell of sickness, hot, unwashed bodies, and the death stench of gangrenous wounds would have been overpowering.

But with the fresh air came blue-bottle flies, bees, moths, and spiders. The floor crawled with ants, and each leg of the steel bed frames was sitting in a pan of rusty water, full of wiggle-tails, to keep the red, stinging insects from the patients.

"Miss Villars! So you came," Dr. Jones said, his voice cutting across the sound of buzzing flies, low voices, and the ceaseless moaning of the man he had been bending over.

"Don't let me take you from your patient," she said as he made his way around the end of the narrow bed and came toward her.

"It doesn't matter. There's not much I can do, poor lad. He needs morphia and that's one thing I can't give him."

"I have a little opium—that is, Colonel Farrell does."

"A drop in the bucket. Unless you have more than I've seen, it wouldn't provide an hour's sleep for half the cases that need it."

"I'm sure you would be welcome to it, all the same."

"So I imagine, but we are used to doing without. We couldn't get the stuff at all when we first got here, now they send us a few vials a month. We save it for the most desperate cases, those going under the knife. The rest make do with rot-gut whiskey—when they can get their friends to bring it to them."

Such an attitude was realistic under the circumstances. Still, Eleanora could not help but feel it was more than a little callous. She wondered if Dr. Jones had ever been in the place of the men who rolled on the single gray sheet and thin mattress allotted them, if he had ever had to guard an open wound against flies or try to sleep with a man muttering in delirium beside him. Perhaps he had become too familiar with such sights and sounds for them to excite his compassion.

Eleanora glanced down at the basket weighting her arm. "I brought a few things," she said, her color rising at the pitiful inadequacy of her offering.

"I'm sure they will be most welcome." Dr. Jones took the basket from her, directing Pedro to carry it to the kitchen.

Watching the orderly depart, she said, "Pedro has been a great help. I don't know what I would have done without him. I'm sure you have a greater need for him here, however, than we do at the palacio since Grant has returned to the Government House."

"Has he? I didn't know," the surgeon replied, inquiring into the particulars of the colonel's convalescence and listening closely to the answers. As they talked he stood with one hand thrust into the pocket of his white coat, the other slapping a sheaf of papers against his leg. Thinking the action might stem from impatience at being kept from his duties, Eleanora finished her report and began to make her excuses.

"Before you go, Miss Villars, I have a case I wish you would look at—if you don't mind?"

She would not have been human if she had not been susceptible to such flattery. She agreed, and it was her undoing. She was cajoled from one patient to the next, up one row and down the other. She visited the surgery, a bare room containing a narrow table and a battery of oil lamps. From there they proceeded to the isolation ward where the fever cases were kept. Looking at so much misery, staring into the eyes of men glazed with pain, and with self-disgust and embarrassment for the state in which she found them, proved more than she could bear. Before the morning was over she had organized the orderlies, and, using a combination of French, Creole Spanish culled from the Catalan dray-drivers around the French Market in New Orleans and from Grant, and also a bastardized English, had driven them to a frenzy of labor heretofore unknown. She saw to it that every slop pail under every bed was emptied and scoured, that every sheet was changed and the soiled ones boiled with lye, every mattress beaten and turned, and every man who could stand it bathed and shaved. In the process she used words she did not know she knew, and discovered the full weight of the position she held with Walker's forces in Nicaragua. There was not a man in the infirmary who did not know who and what she was, and yet, there was not one who spoke to her with anything less than the fullest measure of respect. As she

172

moved up and down the aisle they followed her with their eyes, and she thought they talked of her behind her back, but to her face they were unfailingly polite. And as the smell of lye soap began to replace the smell of death, they watched her progress with something akin to wonder.

In the afternoon Eleanora sent Pedro with a note to Mazie. By promising without fail to produce William Walker at their opening performance, she inveigled her friend into donating the services of the troupe. She did not know how she was to keep her part of the bargain, but she could not stand to leave the job before her half was done, and she could not see how it was to be accomplished without more help.

With the exception of John Barclay, who was out selling advance tickets, she set the actors to work washing down the walls with a solution of chloride of lime which she had found stacked in barrels in the storage room. They also added lime to the water they used to replace that in the pans in which the bedsteads were standing. The women she sent to ransack the shops of the town for the cheapest muslin curtain material they could find. Only enough for one panel per window could be had. Lacking the time to make them fancy, or the rods on which to hang them, they simply tacked these panels over the windows. They were so light, blowing into the room without discouraging the insects at all, that they tacked the sides also. The open weave of the cheap muslin let the air through while keeping the flies out. A few rounds with a piece of stiffened leather attached to a stick, and the infernal, nerve-shattering buzzing, the crawling and tickling, stopped.

The señora's beef broth provided the base for a nourishing soup for the evening meal. Using every means of persuasion and the last of her store of patience, Eleanora managed to prevent the cook from adding so much pepper it was unpalatable for the weak stomachs of sick men. She was still in the kitchen when she heard a familiar voice.

"Mazie!" the man called, obviously speaking to the actress down the length of the main ward. "I swore the

173

yahoo who told me he saw you come in here was drunk. What in the name of Satan do you think you're doing?"

"Imitating Miss Nightingale's exploits in the Crimea. Don't you read the journals? Nursing has become respectable."

The major laughed. "That still leaves you in something of a quandary, doesn't it?"

"You can be an ass at times, Neville," Mazie said caustically. "What do you want?"

"No offense intended," Major Neville Crawford said. "Where's your sense of humor? All right, all right. I just thought I'd see how you were doing. I haven't seen much of you lately."

"I've been busy, the theater and all."

"And good works?"

"And good works," Mazie agreed grimly, to the sound of a cloth being viciously wrung out. She was washing down the last of the bed frames and, tired from the unaccustomed labor and the irritation of keeping the other actresses working, was in no good temper.

"Who got you into this," the major asked. "Not Jones? He has about as much persuasive personality as a grizzly bear."

From the level of their voices Eleanora thought Major Crawford had sauntered down the aisle. Still, the renewed moaning of a man who had been quiet for several hours told her he was disturbing the patient. She stepped through the freshly hung curtain dividing the kitchen from the ward. "I persuaded her," she said cheerfully, "and I'm sure I can find a job for you too, if you intend to stay."

The hint was not lost on the major. His bow of greeting was brief, his smile twisted, as he answered. "Eleanora. I might have guessed, considering the barracks-room gossip I hear of how you pulled Farrell from the jaws of death. I'm afraid I must disappoint you, though. I'm on my way to dinner at the Government House."

"You are dining there often these days, they tell me," Mazic said with the lift of a thin brow.

"My charm of manner," he murmured deprecatingly.

174

"Take care you don't get in the general's bad books. He is a jealous man, and a dangerous enemy."

"I assure you my interest at the Government House is strictly of a business nature."

"Yes, but are you sure Niña Maria realizes it? Her vanity is colossal."

"You take care of your affairs and let me take care of mine," the tall, blond man told her, his smile perfectly pleasant.

Eleanora glanced from one to the other. She could sense an undercurrent of warning in their tones that she did not comprehend. The impression dissipated as Mazie turned to her. "Did you know it's getting dark? John has called a final dress rehearsal for nine o'clock this evening. I sent the others off a half hour ago. I'll have to hurry if I'm to get a bite to eat before we start, and I'll wager you'd like to get back before Grant does."

Eleanora had not realized it was so late. Whipping off the burlap bag she had fashioned into an apron, she went to tell Dr. Jones she was leaving, then joined Mazie and Major Crawford in the street outside. They walked along quickly in the gathering dusk. Eleanora, lost in her own thought, paid little attention to the other two until the major turned to her.

"Your brother was asking just yesterday if I had seen you."

"Oh? How was he?"

"That's just what he was wondering about you. It would be a tragedy if you let Walker's little sortie here in Nicaragua come between the two of you."

Eleanora smiled. "I don't think our estrangement can be blamed on General Walker."

"Don't you? Maybe not. Nonetheless, Jean-Paul seems to have soured on our little general. A lot of people have."

Seeing he was waiting for her comment, Eleanora said noncommittally, "I suppose so."

"You haven't? It's not as if this were the United States and we owed our loyalty to the man chosen to lead us."

"Rivas is the president of Nicaragua," she reminded him.

"Yes, but we all know who holds the power," the major said, shrugging.

That was too true for denial. "The men who signed as soldier-colonists took a loyalty oath," she said.

"That doesn't make them Nicaraguans."

"Doesn't it? I'm not sure of the legality of the question, but I thought that was certainly the idea, to own land here, to build a new and richer life."

"Central America, the new frontier? To be annexed to the United States eventually like Texas and California? Isn't that the goal of the concept of manifest destiny? Shouldn't our loyalty belong still to the country that will finally claim this one?"

"I somehow doubt the true citizens of Nicaragua would see it that way," Eleanora replied, stopping just beyond the guards outside the door of the palacio and turning with a smile that included Mazie, waiting quiet, almost passive, behind him.

"Oh, well," Neville said, taking her hand, a glint of wry amusement in his pale blue eyes, "fidelity is a fine thing—in a woman."

Twelve

Grant had not returned from the Government House, had not even, according to the señora, appeared at midday for the cold collation prepared for him. It was gratifying news. Eleanora could not think he would approve of her action, and it was a relief, in her weariness, to know she need not explain it to him tonight. Despite the heat, she boiled water for a scalding hot bath. She lingered in the cramped tin tub, soaping again and again, even washing her hair in an effort to remove the smell of the hospital. In the process she washed away some of her tiredness. When she was done and Grant still had not come, she sat down at the table with her hair drying upon her shoulders, and drawing a sheet of foolscap toward her, picked up a pen. It was necessary for her to frame her request to the general for his presence at the opening night of the *School for Scandal* as soon as possible. What could she say?

Frowning, she tapped the pen on her chin. Phrase it as an invitation and hope he would be moved to attend? She doubted he would be influenced to accede if she simply told him she had pledged his presence, without telling him why she had done so. A full explanation would be best, but it would serve no purpose to dwell on the horrors of the conditions at the hospital. It was no different from other military infirmaries, and was, perhaps, better, since Dr. Jones was not too immured in tradition and his own importance to recognize the need for change. No, it would not do to cast a slur upon the surgeon, even by inference. To speak to General Walker in person might be the best course, but she placed no confidence in his willingness to see her on the morrow. To judge by the number of hours Grant was spending with him, he was unlikely to appreciate being disturbed for such a small matter. Sighing, she began to write.

Grant advertised his arrival in the middle of the night by splashing noisily in the cold bathwater she had left. Eleanora eyed him with sleepy annoyance. He had the alert look of a man who had dined well in stimulating company and anticipates further entertainment before retiring. Setting her lips, she pulled the sheet up over her head to shut out the orange-yellow glow of the candle.

Smelling delectably of attar-of-roses soap, he sought her there, under the sheet. "Oh, Grant," she protested as he rolled her toward him, but diligent and tender patience required its reward, one it proved impossible not to share.

Finding Grant gone once more when she awoke at dawn, Eleanora sent one of Luis's guards to the Government House with her message to the general. His reply was made in person. He walked into the hospital with his quick, nervous stride while she was helping the surgeon on a morning round of the patients who needed attention to their dressings.

177

Dr. Jones stood long seconds in frozen immobility before he moved to greet Walker and express his not unnatural satisfaction that the general had seen fit to pay a visit to the men injured in his cause. Eleanora hesitated to put herself forward, especially when she saw the tall form of the colonel making his way down the center aisle with a half-dozen junior officers behind him. As he raked her with a frowning glance, she was made unhappily aware of his displeasure. Dropping her gaze, she went on with what she was doing.

The surgeon took his commanding officer on a slow and exhaustive circuit of the infirmary. Walker, with the thoroughness of a man on familiar professional ground, plied the doctor with innumerable questions concerning supplies, procedures, techniques, numbers of patients, types of wounds and their sites, and the rate of injured certified fit to return to their duties. By the time they were done, Dr. Jones was mopping perspiration from his brow with a sodden handkerchief, no longer certain he wanted Walker's interest in his province. He was still holding his own, however, as they passed into the isolation ward.

"Yes, I realize we have fewer mosquitoes here than near the coast," Dr. Jones's voice floated back. "But that doesn't mean there is a connection between them and yellow fever, General. We also are farther away from the miasma of the swamplands, considered to be the primary cause of infection by most modern, scientific thought on the problem—"

Deserting Walker's entourage, Grant found Eleanora where she was tipping water into a glass from one of the ollas for a man who had lost one hand and torn the other apart when his revolver exploded on a faulty shell.

"Why didn't you tell me you were coming here, risking your life?" he demanded.

"I would have if I had thought it mattered to you," she said, watching the rising level of trickling water with exaggerated caution.

With easy strength he took hold of the big pottery jar and tipped it. "Of course it does."

"Thank you," she murmured, indicating enough water

178

with an upraised hand. Reverting to his comment, she said, "I'm flattered."

He was quiet for the length of time it took for them to hold the tumbler to the injured man's lips.

"But you don't intend to stop. You may as well admit it, I read your note to Walker."

"No, I don't," she said evenly.

"Not even if I ask it?"

She raised her head. "If you really ask from concern for my safety, I would regret having to refuse you. Still, you have no right to ask anything of me."

As her meaning sank home his jaw hardened and his eyes went darker. "And if I made it an order, and stood ready to back it up?"

"Say, Colonel, you wouldn't do that, would you?" the man in the next bed asked, a beardless boy with a shock of cornsilk hair falling over the bandage wrapped about his head, and the soft sound of the southern back-country in his voice. "I had the first decent supper in a month of Sundays last night, and this morning I feel like a human being instead of a piece of buzzard bait. The good Lord knows I ain't no saint, so I reckon this lady here is about as close as I'm ever gonna get to an angel. You go taking her away, and I guess me and half the rest of the men here will just have to give up the ghost."

Grant's brows drew together as he allowed his measuring gaze to sweep over the young man and beyond him to the other interested faces turned on their white, fluffed pillows. Before he could answer there came the clatter of the general's party returning. Walker's voice, quietly incisive, cut across the stillness.

"A moving tribute, wouldn't you say, Colonel Farrell? They also serve who repair the ravages of war."

There was no one there who did not recognize the implication of General Walker's partisanship. Grant had no recourse but to signify his acquiescence and step aside.

The familiar twisted smile curving his mouth, Walker bowed to Eleanora. "The American Phalanx is in your debt, mademoiselle, how greatly only time will tell. I— have tickets to the opening performance in a theater

179

newly organized here in Granada. I would deem it a privilege if you, and Colonel Farrell, of course, would consent to be my guests for the evening."

Eleanora accepted with a dazzling smile and a suitable acknowledgment of the honor. She did not quite dare to look to where Grant waited on one side. It was to the highest degree improbable that he would wish her to decline the invitation, but she did not care to take the chance.

If General Walker considered it a pleasure to have her as a guest, Niña Maria did not. This was made plain at the outset of the evening when the woman barely extended a civil greeting, then nearly turned Eleanora completely around as she dragged her heavy skirts over Eleanora's lightweight muslin, sweeping past her on the way to the carriage without bothering to compress her enormous hoop. In the vehicle, a shiny black Victoria with sagging springs due to travel over bad roads but elegant gray upholstery, she insisted that Eleanora ride with her back to the horses between the two men, while she sat on the forward seat in solitary grandeur. In this manner she arrived at the theater with both her face and her gown unruffled. It became evident as the evening wore on that she bitterly resented attending the performance at any behest other than her own, but especially at Eleanora's. To sit through the play with the Nicaraguan woman became an act of endurance as Niña Maria complained in a perfectly audible voice of the hardness of her seat, the heat, the shoddy material of the costumes and the tedium of the intervals between scenery changes. Her point-by-point criticism of the acting effectively dampened the enjoyment of all but the most enthusiastic of those around her, while the glances of irritation cast her way left her unmoved.

In retaliation for the slight to her friends, Eleanora left her sitting in the carriage quite half an hour while she went backstage to congratulate Mazie and the rest of the troupe. This insubordination did nothing to endear her to Niña Maria, though Eleanora thought the general hid the twinkle in his gray eyes as he saw her coming half guiltily toward them.

180

Her work at the hospital continued. Grant did not attempt to interfere again. Insofar as it was possible, he ignored it, though she often thought that when he held her close with his cheek against her temple he was more intent on being certain she was not sickening for something, or losing too much weight, than he was on being affectionate. They had ceased to take the noon meal together, but at dinner he took an added interest in what she ate, placing an extra portion of meat, or another piece of fruit, on her plate.

It was true that she usually ate standing up while away from the palacio. The hours went so quickly, and she seemed to accomplish so little. She knew a frantic compulsion to make every moment of every hour productive.

Occasionally Dr. Jones was called on to attend a maternity case. It was not unusual for the midwife in charge, jealous of her prerogatives and reluctant to surrender her female patient to the coarse hands of a man and an American at that, to wait until it was too late to save the mother. In this manner, Eleanora was introduced to the orphanage run by the sisters of Guadalupe. Through lack of funds and a certain insular ignorance in the area of hygiene, it was in little better condition than the hospital. Bringing order to it was more difficult, however, because of the obstruction of the mother superior, who looked on Eleanora's attempts to help as impertinent meddling. Only the hard but inescapable fact that the orphanage could look for a substantial increase in its numbers within a few short months, Walker's men having been in Nicaragua since May of 1855, and in the city of Granada since October, reconciled her to the interference. The results of a group of virile fighting men coming together with the warm-blooded ladies of a hot country, and without the ties of official sanction, was inescapable. The justice of the Americans providing for their own offspring struck the mother superior forcefully when Eleanora pointed it out to her. A further breach in the religious's defenses was Mazie. She showed such honest delight in being allowed to care for the children and provide for them, such an

181

intimate knowledge of their most basic needs such as cuddling and loving, that she had not the heart to deny the actress. After a time Eleanora found she could leave the project in Mazie's capable hands.

One morning as she entered the main ward she was greeted by a double row of grinning faces. She had gradually taken the way the men waited each day for her to put in an appearance in stride, but for the most part they were more subtle than this. Feeling acutely self-conscious, she started down the aisle, putting on the long, bibbed apron she had made herself from a sheet, tying it behind her, as she went.

When she reached the boy who had called her an angel—still there because in addition to concussion they had discovered a blister on his heel so far advanced in gangrene they had had to amputate his foot—the mystery was solved. Holding up a copy of *El Nicaraguense*, he pointed to the headline, a suspicious sparkle in his eyes.

Angel of Phalanx—Eleanora read, and in her disbelief, could go no farther.

Turning the newsheet around, the boy read aloud the two columns of close print. There were no interruptions, no disturbance until his voice trailed away on the last laudatory paragraph.

It was ridiculous how near to tears she had stayed these few days, especially ridiculous now when she had a strong notion there was a political reason behind this tribute to her work with the wounded. Was it, perhaps, an underhanded way of pointing up the numbers of casualties stemming from the border disputes with Costa Rica, a way of showing that country's disregard of the proposals for peace sent out by the Republic of Nicaragua? If it became necessary to go to war with the Central American republics, it could be shown that the conflict was none of the general's choosing.

It was not, considering Eleanora's history, a long leap from the title the Angel of the Phalanx to the shorter and more pithy nickname the Colonel's Angel. Given the idle hours of the men in the narrow beds, with nothing to do but speculate on her relationship with the officer who either came each evening or sent an escort to walk with her through the dim streets, it was no distance at all.

The single benefit Eleanora could say she derived from the newspaper story concerned Jean-Paul. The day after it appeared he presented himself at the palacio. His arrival was so prompt upon Grant's departure that she could only suppose he had waited for him to leave before coming in. She did not comment; she was too happy he had come at all to question his manner. Gladness lighting her face, she rose from where she was having coffee on the patio and ran to meet him.

He caught her close, then held her at arm's length with his campaign hat clamped in his hand. Since she had last seen him, he had begun to grow a beard. It gave him a raffish look that was not becoming to her eyes. There were other, less easily recognizable changes. His hair was dull and badly in need of trimming, his eyes were more recessed in his head and his cheeks more hollow. The roundness and high color of youth were gone, but the hard lines of manhood still had not taken their place.

"I saw the piece in the paper," he said, his brown eyes earnest. "At first I was angry that they had the insolence to write about you—you remember how Grand-mère used to say that a lady's name appeared in print only three times in her lifetime—at birth, on her marriage, and at death? I reconsidered when I thought about it long enough. I think our father would have been proud of you for trying to help. It's better than sitting and whining over what can't be helped. I said some foolish things before, Eleanora, because I didn't understand. I hope you will believe me when I say how sorry I am."

"Jean-Paul, there is no need."

"I misjudged you," he went on doggedly, ignoring the appeal in her voice. "I hope I have a better understanding of your feelings now."

"You mean—"

"I mean my own situation is not so different from

183

yours. I've discovered it's not always possible to choose the right kind of person to fall in love with."

"You have come because—"

"Because of Juanita," he agreed simply.

He had made it impossible for her to condemn the woman he spoke of with such feeling. In any case, it was not her place to approve or disapprove of his choice. As Luis had said, they were no longer dependent solely on each other. They were two separate people, each with the right to find his own happiness, make his own mistakes.

"Come," she said, taking his arm and leading him to where she had been sitting in the shade of the orange trees. "Let me pour you some coffee, and you can tell me what you've been doing, what has been happening to you."

It was not a surprising recital. In response to a certain reserve on Eleanora's part, he did not mention Juanita again. He told her of his lodgings near the barracks, of a patrol or two he had been on, and an anecdote or two of army life, misunderstandings stemming, for the most part, from the polyglot nature of the men gathering to Walker's red star, and their language difficulties.

Speaking of a commendation he had received for marksmanship, Jean-Paul said suddenly, "I'm glad I— my aim was off when I shot Colonel Farrell. I—think I know what he—what you both went through. I hope I've gained a little more sense, a little more maturity since then."

There was in his tone a hint of patronizing that Eleanora could not like. She could not fault his intention, however. "I'm sure Grant would be delighted to hear it," she said. "Perhaps you will like to come to dinner one night?"

"I don't think so," he answered, rising to his feet and setting down his empty cup. "Understanding is one thing, facing him across the table is another. I expect it will be best if I remain just another enlisted man. But I would like to see you whenever I get the chance, that is, unless you object—"

"As if I would!" she said warmly.

"The situation is awkward, I know that. I wouldn't blame you if you decided the less you saw of me, the better."

Such humility was uncomfortable, in particular coming from Jean-Paul, who had always had such a fiery pride. Eleanora only shook her head. There were shattered petals of orange blossoms from the trees above them in his hair. She brushed them away with fingers that trembled a little.

His smile grew strained. Settling his hat on his head at an angle, he said, *"Au revoir, chéri,"* and turning, strode quickly away.

It was the first visit of many. It became his habit to arrive for morning coffee. If Eleanora had finished already, he would come upstairs and lounge in a chair at the table, talking to her while she pinned up her hair and found her apron. Sometimes he would push aside Grant's papers and have breakfast, since he rose too late for the regular army mess and Juanita's talents did not, apparently, include cooking. More often than not the inside of his mouth was thick with fur from the drink he had consumed the night before, and the most he could face was the traditional *petit noir,* literally "small cup of black coffee," of the aristocratic Creole gentleman. Afterward, he would walk with Eleanora to the hospital before continuing about his duties.

By the end of January, Vanderbilt, as Walker had predicted, was elected president of the Transit Company. On the twenty-third of February *El Nicaraguense* reported the official seizure of the property and records of the line by a decree signed, with undisguised pleasure, by President Rivas five days earlier. In less than a week President Juan Rafael Mora of Costa Rica, fearful of the strength Nicaragua might gain from control of the route, and also the direction Walker's ambition might take him if left unchecked, declared war on the filibuster government. Rumors abounded that Mora intended to assume command of his army, then resting at San José, for an invasion. Along the borders the clashes reached a new high. The stream of casualties increased hourly. By the eleventh of March the rumors were confirmed,

Nicaragua was under attack. President Rivas, bowing to the inevitable, retaliated with his own declaration of war.

The city buzzed with activity, with people besieging the Government House for news, with merchants closing their shops, and much of the Granadan populace closing up their houses preparing to take refuge with relatives outside the capital, which was certain to be a target for capture. They placed little faith in Mora's protests that he had nothing against the citizens of Nicaragua; artillery fire recognized no difference between citizens and filibusters. The latter, according to reliable reports, Mora had sworn to finish to the last man. He would take no prisoners, all would be killed. Some of the newest recruits, not yet signed up, discovered pressing business elsewhere, now that it had to come to a test. Women, especially wives with children who had come out in the last few weeks, swelled the list of those waiting for the next outbound steamer. The *Prometheus* had gone the morning of the eleventh, the day Rivas had made their involvement in the war official. There would not be another leaving for two weeks.

The furor could not last indefinitely. In a few days it began to die away as the countryside remained quiet. The Indians returned to the marketplace, though in small numbers. Cantinas opened their doors, the black habits of the nuns were seen on the streets once more. The angelus bell from the cathedral rang with a note that seemed to Eleanora, hurrying homeward with the escort Grant had sent for her, to be less doleful, less sharp with foreboding.

She entered the bedroom in a rush, meaning to wash her hands and face and tidy her hair before Grant came home. She halted in momentary confusion at finding him already there.

Straightening from where he leaned over the bed, he swung to face her with a shirt wadded in his hand. Her gaze moved to the pair of saddle bags lying open on the bed. Without meeting her eyes, Grant turned back to stuff the shirt inside, stow the waiting medical kit on top of it, and begin to close the flaps and tie them down.

"What is it?" she asked, her voice emerging in a

186

whisper as she came to stand beside him. She thought that unconsciously she had been waiting for this day, this moment, waiting ever since she had heard of Costa Rica's movements that made conflict between them and William Walker a certainty.

"We are taking to the field, a forced night march, the general's preferred way of maneuvering troops. Schlessinger and his men met a detachment of Costa Ricans at Santa Rosa. They were obviously expected. It was a rout. When Mora came up with the main army he ordered all prisoners, even the wounded left behind as too badly hurt to travel, before a dummy court-martial and sentenced them to be shot."

"No—" The protest was soundless as horror took her breath.

Grant made no answer. He checked his revolver, and that done, began loading ammunition into a cartridge belt.

"When do you leave?" she said finally.

"Within the hour, as soon as it's good dark."

"Is there anything I can do? Food—would you—"

"There's no time. You can do one thing though—" He stopped, his hands growing still on the metal shells.

"What is it?" she asked when he did not go on.

"If anything should happen—if things go wrong—I want you to take the money I left in the armoire and get out of Nicaragua whenever you can, however you can."

"Grant—"

"I mean it. This isn't war, it's annihilation. If Granada should fall you will be a prime target of Butcher Mora's men as a filibuster's woman, the Angel of the Phalanx. What they will do to you—it doesn't bear thinking."

"You will win, you will come back. You have to," she whispered, her face pale.

"But if I don't—"

The deep blue of his eyes mirrored the same anticipation of unbearable pain as the men being placed upon the surgeon's table. Gripping her arms, he entreated, "Promise me!"

She managed to nod, though she thought she would strangle on the knot of tears dissolving in her throat. Abruptly he pulled her against him, kissing her throat, the softness of her cheek, her eyes, searching with a passionate prayerfulness for the sweetness of her lips.

"Dear God," he said, and lifted her across the bed, taking her in a tangle of skirts and petticoats, and loosened coils of hair. And when it was done he dressed quickly, buckling his belt with a savage finality. He returned for a last, snatched kiss on lips and breasts, and then was gone without looking back, leaving her with dry eyes and the anguishing comfort of his husky groan, *"I should have loved you more—"*

The wounded from Santa Rosa began to arrive by morning, walking wounded, riding wounded, white with the narrowness of their escape. Some burned with rage and the lust for revenge, railing on of friends who had been slaughtered by Mora. Others were quieter, their enmity a cold and bitter thing, but there was little doubt that for the Falangistas the war had become a blood feud overnight.

As Eleanora worked with the surgeon, removing lead, cleaning and repairing the damage done by sword and bayonet, her thoughts were with Grant on the march south as she tried to picture what he was doing, whether resting beside some dusty trail, or eating some hastily concocted meal scrounged from the pole-and-thatch house of an Indian farmer. Late in the morning it began to rain, a sullen downpour that sluiced the dust from the houses and ran in rivers along streets that could not absorb it into their hard-baked surfaces. Inside the hospital the lamps had to be lit against the gloom as batten blinds were closed to keep out the wind-driven rain. Still the moisture penetrated, combining with the muggy heat of the low-ceiling rooms to turn them into steam baths. It would not make marching easier.

Opening a blind to throw a basin of red-stained water out into the rushing, open gutter, Eleanora stood a moment, breathing in the fresh air. She watched the rain stream from the red tiles of the roof, wondering for the dozenth time if Grant had thought to carry his slicker, wondering if the wetness would aggravate his shoulder.

The bullet hole had healed to a reddish purple scar, but there was still some deep stiffness.

With the sound of the falling rain in her ears, she did not hear Luis approaching until he was directly behind her. She swung around, startled, as he took the basin from her and handed it to a passing orderly.

"You didn't go with them," she said stupidly, after she had greeted him.

"I am left to defend Granada," he said with a grimace, "and to perform all the more unpleasant tasks."

"Oh?" She stopped in the process of wiping her hands, her fingers clenching involuntarily on her apron.

"Such as—telling you, Eleanora, that your brother was arrested at dawn this morning on charges of supplying information to the enemy."

She stared at him, the color draining from her face. Such an offense meant the firing squad.

"Why? How?"

"Information has been placed against him. He is accused of securing information from the palacio, of going through Grant's papers and selling what he found to Vanderbilt agents, who are supporting Costa Rica monetarily in an effort to oust the general."

"But—who accused him? Was it—" She could not go on. All too clearly she remembered Grant saying that Colonel Schlessinger and his men had been expected by the Costa Ricans. Had he known when he left her that Jean-Paul was to be arrested?

"It was not Grant, I promise you. The order came from the general's office, based on a complaint lodged by the woman your brother was living with, Juanita."

"It can't be true," she said, staring into the concerned brown eyes of the Spaniard. "Jean-Paul wouldn't— couldn't have done such a thing. He never once looked at the papers Grant left at the palacio. I was with him every moment."

"I knew you would say as much, *mi alma,* that is what worries me. This thing, it has the smell of betrayal to me. I am afraid for you."

"What?"

"Consider. The woman, Juanita, hates you. She be-

189

comes involved with your brother, who has access to the colonel's quarters. She informs on him. Why? I fear a plot—"

He broke off as a commotion began near the front entrance. Major Neville Crawford entered, followed by a detail of eight men with bayonets fixed, at the ready. He searched the room with his eyes until he spotted Eleanora. With a wave of his hand, he indicated that the men should follow him as he made his way down between the beds to where she was standing. His face sober, he came to attention.

"It is my duty to inform you, Miss Eleanora Colette Villars, that you are under arrest. You will come with me."

"What is the charge?" Luis rapped.

"Treason. Giving aid and comfort to the enemies of the Republic of Nicaragua."

"Who signed the orders?"

"The signature is that of General Walker, if you must know."

"When? He has left Granada," Luis pointed out through clenched teeth.

"I'm only following orders," Major Crawford said, the heat of an uneasy anger rising in his face.

"With quite a back-up force," Luis grated, glancing significantly at the men standing rigid behind him. "What did you expect her to do, attack you?"

Major Crawford had no ready answer. He flung a look around the hospital ward grown suddenly still as the men in the beds became aware of what was happening. The boy with the cornsilk hair, three beds along the line, threw back the sheet and made as if to get up. The major swallowed. "I am sorry, but if you will, Eleanora—Miss Villars?"

Another man wrenched over in bed, searching for his makeshift crutch that leaned against the wall. She could not allow a confrontation between sick, weaponless men and the soldiers standing with guns in their hands and the blank sheen of determined obedience in their eyes. In the dim light the bayonets had a deadly gleam.

"Very well," she said through the stiffness of her throat, "I'll go."

"Try not to worry, *pequeña*," Luis said, touching her arm in reassurance. "There must be something that can be done—and whatever it is, I will do it."

She had time to do no more than smile in gratitude. The detail fell into place about her. They began to move at a smart pace toward the door while the muttering of disapproval broke out from the four corners of the room.

Beyond the opening the rain came down like the silver lances of an ancient tilt-at-arms, smashing into the mud of the street. Without pausing, they stepped out into it.

PART TWO

193

Thirteen

The cell door closed with a clank and the rattling of keys. Eleanora took a hesitant step into the noisome dimness. As her eyes adjusted to the lack of light, she saw the scabrous walls with designs, messages, and doggerel scratched into their whitewash, the suffocatingly low ceiling, and rusty sleeping shelves with only a tangled rag of a blanket to add comfort to their hard planks. The air was dank with the rain falling past the small, high, barred window, and thick with the stench of the slop pail sitting in one corner. The one advantage was the fact that the barred cubicle was empty of other occupants.

"Eleanora—"

Stark, vibrant with horror, the whisper came from the next cell. Eleanora turned slowly, her skirts dragging wet around her ankles, to face her brother. He got to his feet like an old man, holding to the chain that supported the sleeping shelf on which he sat.

"Why?" he asked, a frown of bewildered anger between his eyes. "Why?"

"They—didn't tell you?" she ventured after a moment.

He looked away. "I can't believe it. After all, Juanita and I—I can't believe it."

"Then why else?" Despite herself, her voice had the flat timbre of weary defeat.

"I don't know. I don't know! That's what is driving me mad. Everything has gone wrong, everything, from the instant we left New Orleans. You were right, Eleanora. Does it please you to know you were right?"

"Hardly." To cry at this moment might relieve her feelings but it would do no real good. Looking away she began a cautious circuit of the tiny room. Four shelves, two per side, hinted at a capacity of four in the cell where there was barely room for two to stand with ease. It was a cage, no more, no less, a cage at the end of a row of cages. There were three such cells. Beyond her brother's cubicle was another occupied by a figure rolled in a blanket and snoring with the sodden monotony of the drunkard. The men who had locked her in had retreated out of sight. She could still hear them in the outer room however, hear the bark of orders, and then the good-natured murmur of men relieved of the presence of authority. Presently there came the slap of cards and the smell of coffee brewing.

The rain continued without letup, blowing in upon the unprotected sill of the high window and running in a thick, dark stream down the wall. As she paced, Eleanora had to avoid the growing puddle in the far corner near the slop pail.

"I didn't spy on the colonel, Eleanora. I don't care what they say. I wouldn't do a thing like that, on my sacred honor."

"I believe you," she answered in soft tones, fully alive to the undercurrent of desperation in her brother's voice.

"I—don't suppose you—"

Anger swept over her, then died away. "No," she replied as steadily as she could. "What scruples I still possess prevent me from stooping to that level also."

"Forgive me. I don't know what I am saying. It's just that—" He sank back down upon the shelf, burying his face in his hands.

The feeling of unbelief he was trying to convey was not lost on Eleanora. She would have liked to have believed Luis's assurances that Grant was not responsible for the imprisonment of Jean-Paul and herself. She could not quite. It was too convenient, his sudden departure followed by their arrest. Had he been so reluctant to face her, to listen to her pleas for Jean-Paul? Could it be that he did not trust himself to see his orders put in force if he had to watch her being carried away? The logic was inescapable —as inescapable as the fact that it was near impossible for such a momentous matter as the arrest of two spies to have been planned and carried out without the knowledge of the provost marshal, Colonel Grant Farrell.

Tiring, Eleanora sat down at last. A flea hopped from the dingy blanket to her skirt and she brushed at it in quick disgust, pushing the excuse for a coverlet to the floor before settling back. She pulled her knees up, leaning with her back to the wall. The drumming of the rain, the voices of the men, her brother's occasional outbursts provided a background for her thoughts.

One thing was obvious. Someone had betrayed Lieutenant Colonel Louis Schlessinger and his men, arranging for them to walk into a trap at Santa Rosa. If it was not Jean-Paul or herself, then who? Someone with access to the information concerning troop disbursements. Someone either at the Government House or the palacio, then. The general, Grant, Luis; none of them seemed remotely capable of treason. But at the palacio was Señora Paredes, and through her, Juanita. Eleanora could not feature the señora executing such a plan herself. It was always possible she had helped Juanita only by her failure to report the other woman's actions, but she could not be entirely innocent. The younger woman had both reason and opportunity, and she alone was responsible for the arrest which provided her own best protection. Anything she and Jean-Paul might say against Juanita would be weakened by their position, whereas she, by taking Jean-Paul as her new lover, had provided excellent camouflage for her own motives.

If William Walker had been there, Eleanora thought, he might have listened to her explanations despite his signature on the order for her arrest. It was possible a message might still reach him in time, if she could persuade someone to take it. For that she needed money. A dead end. Luis would go if she asked him. Perhaps he was already gone.

Failing that scheme, there was Niña Maria. She was certain to have some means of contacting the general. Surely she would not allow her personal dislike of Eleanora to weigh in the balance against two human lives, would she?

Eleanora clenched her hands together in her lap. She could not sit and wait, doing nothing until they came for Jean-Paul and herself. There had to be some way to escape this terrible coil. Against her will she thought of the deserted corner of the plaza where the executions were performed. Did they shoot women? She did not know. And if they did, who would give the order to fire with Grant gone? Who would perform the coup de grace?

She gave herself a shake, shivering a little in her wet clothes. Her hair felt plastered to her head and she loosened it with her fingers, taking a deep breath to steady her nerves. She had to think. Daydreams wherein Grant returned to release her, to hold her close and tell her it was all a mistake, were of no use to her. She must put such thoughts behind her. Forever.

Evening descended imperceptibly behind the dark curtain of rain. A bowl of watery chili con carne was brought with a tough flour tortilla. The smell of it was not appetizing even though Eleanora's stomach cramped with hunger. She had not eaten anything for breakfast nor at the early luncheon served to the patients. Apparently she and Jean-Paul arrived too late for the noon meal at the guardhouse. Nothing had been offered to them until now.

The man who brought their supper wore suspenders over his red shirt, suspenders of rattlesnake skin. His eyes were small and set close together, and his unshaven cheek bulged with an enormous cud of chewing tobacco. When he handed the warm bowl to Eleanora through the door his fingers touched hers. They were dry and scaly and covered on the backs with black curly hairs. Long after she had retreated to the sleeping shelf he stood watching her, tossing the key to her cell in his hand. Only the sound of his name called from the outer room drew him away. He went with reluctance and a last backward glance that made her flesh crawl.

Lamplight blossomed in the front room, shedding a faint glow into the back cell. Eleanora sat staring at the flickering shadows it cast as the men moved back and forth. After a time her clothing ceased to drip. The rain slackened. A horse trotted past outside, slowing to a walk. The card game broke up, leaving two men to stand the midnight watch. Their voices and the acrid smoke of their brown Mexican cigarillos drifted back to where Eleanora crouched against the wall. She would have liked to call out to them, to ask them to send for Luis or possibly take a message to Niña Maria at the Government House. Some instinct that went as deep as the desire for self-protection prevented her from drawing that much attention to her presence. Setting her teeth into her lip she remained silent.

In the next cell Jean-Paul stirred, calling her name.

It was a moment before she could force herself to answer him, and then her voice was a whisper of sound. "Yes?"

"What about your friend, the Spaniard? Do you think he will testify for us at the trial?"

"I'm sure he will if it comes to that." She was not at all certain, but it would not hurt to allow Jean-Paul this small hope.

"He has influence at the Government House. He might do us a lot of good."

Eleanora agreed. Luis also knew more than he had ever said of Juanita. It was just possible that he could discredit her story enough to win for them their freedom. She would not depend on it, however. The officers who served under William Walker were not known for their mercy. Arrest usually meant certain execution.

In her mind she pictured Grant and the general slogging through the mud and misting rain, uncaring of what was happening to her or her brother. A suffocating pain moved in her chest and for an instant she could not breathe. Her teeth began to chatter as she lifted her chin. Rubbing the chill, goosefleshed skin of her arms and shoulders beneath her damp clothing, she struggled to her feet. Moving might bring warmth to her body; nothing could thaw the frozen core of her heart.

As she passed the open side of Jean-Paul's cell, he loomed out of the shadows, his hands fastening on the bars. "What have I done?" he cried in a voice of self-loathing. "What have I done to deserve this? All I ever wanted was a new start, a place to begin to build back what we had lost. Is that so terrible?"

She could not bear the sight of his face contorted with the effort to hold back his tears. She moved closer, curling her fingers about his tight fists upon the bars. "Don't," she whispered. "Oh, don't."

"I can't stand it. Not Juanita, not my Juanita. God, but

198

she was sweet. She—she danced for me, laughing, daring me to—dear God!"

He leaned his forehead on his clenched hands, his eyes squeezed shut. Helplessly, Eleanora touched his hair, smoothing the curls tight with the dampness.

"I don't believe—I can't make myself believe she did this to me, used me, planned all the time, even when—when—"

He flung himself away across the cell landing on the sleeping shelf with a force that set the chain to creaking. He left Eleanora with a fresh, new pain. Had Grant, holding her in that farewell embrace, known what was to happen to her? *I should have loved you more*— She had hoarded those last words, seeing in them a promise. Now they had the ring of a death knell.

Quiet descended. The rain stopped except for an occasional drip from the eaves. In the front room a chair scraped and the lamplight swung in an arc and flowed toward the cells as one of the guards made a late round. He walked slowly down the narrow corridor, the lamp held high. Stopping, he peered at Jean-Paul, rolled in his blanket with his back to the door. The man was thin and tall with a graying walrus mustache, not the man with the rattlesnake suspenders. When he moved toward her Eleanora transferred her gaze to the dark corner of the far wall and kept it there the long moments he stood staring in at her.

The air left her lungs in a long sigh when he had gone, and she let her head fall back to rest on the wall behind her. Her eyes burned and her head throbbed, but she could not bring herself to stretch out on the hard board. The hours were too precious for sleeping.

It could not have been much later when she heard the horses. From the sound there were seven or eight at least, traveling at an unhurried walk. They halted outside the guardhouse, and through the open bars of the high window Eleanora caught the creak of saddle leather and jangle of bits as the men dismounted. A horse snorted through his nostrils, stamping. The soft tinkle of a spur had a musical sound in the humid quiet of the night.

A challenge was issued and answered in the outer room,

followed by the entry of a small group of men. Words were exchanged, followed by the sound of a scuffle. Voices rose in a confused babble that died away as quickly as it had begun. One voice alone stood out clear, and recognizing it Eleanora got slowly to her feet. That faint Spanish inflection brought mingled hope and dread. What was Luis thinking of?

"Back against the wall, you sons of Satan," she heard him shout. "Move, and I will give you a personal introduction to your father!"

Light slid along the wall. Luis appeared, striding along the corridor with a gun in one fist and the ring of jingling keys in the other. Another man followed, holding the lamp high, and in its light Eleanora could see the reckless smile that curled the Spaniard's lips, the excitement blazing in his eyes.

"What is this?" Jean-Paul asked in dazed tones, rolling to his feet.

"Deliverance," Luis replied, thrusting the key into the lock and opening it with a grating twist.

Eleanora moved to the door of her cell. "Luis, you can't do this. I can't let you—not for me."

"Too late, *pequeña*," he said with an infinitesimal movement of his shoulders. "It is done."

"Don't you realize—"

He threw the door wide. "Better than you, *cara*. It is the only way."

Was he right? In that moment she could not summon the strength or impartiality to judge, nor could she afford to endanger them all further by hesitating. With abrupt decision she stepped over the threshold and allowed herself to be hurried along behind Jean-Paul. In the main room she turned her eyes from the sight of the guards being trussed up like chickens in the market and she headed for the black rectangle of the open door.

The night air was fresh, scented only by the smell of warm horseflesh. Once, as a young girl, she had had riding lessons. As she moved instinctively toward the horse bearing the cumbersome, unbalanced weight of a sidesaddle, she prayed she would remember those lessons for this moment.

200

Luis gave her a leg up and handed her the reins. Around her the men, numbering six without counting Luis or her brother, were mounting. Eleanora pulled at her skirts, trying to settle her knee around the horn while staying on a horse even less used to carrying a sidesaddle than she was to sitting one. The sound of a distant shout sent such a jolt of apprehension along her nerves that she was nearly unseated. Flinging a glance down the street, Eleanora saw a uniformed officer running toward them, tugging at the revolver at his waist as he came.

Beside her a man drew, leveled his gun, and fired. The officer ducked behind the corner of the building beyond the guardhouse, and from its protecting wall began throwing shots at the milling group about the hitching rail.

A man cursed, spinning out of the saddle and scrabbling over the ground to avoid the prancing hooves all about him. Luis, just mounting, checked, hung for a moment from the pommel, then dragged himself upward. Before he had settled on leather he had kicked his horse into a run, slashing out at Eleanora's mount to carry it with him.

Bending low over their horse's necks, they streamed along the street, trying to get beyond the range of the booming navy revolver. That was accomplished in a few hundred yards of hard riding. As soon as the guardhouse was lost to sight they left the main street for the weaving back alleys haunted by huddled figures sleeping in doorways and by fleeing cats.

To the south of Granada lay Rivas, the transit line, and the armies of Walker and Mora. The direction Luis took when they left the town behind them at last was north. North toward Honduras, to the uncharted stretches of forest and jungle beyond Lake Managua, the province of the ancient Cookra and Toacas Indians, and to the beckoning heights of the Nueva Segovia Mountains.

From time to time Eleanora, remembering the sound of a shot striking so close beside her, glanced at Luis. She could see no more than his dark outline, but he sat erect in the saddle. If his quiet directions lacked his former insouciance, they were still strong.

The pursuit, disorganized, seemingly half-hearted at best, was soon outdistanced, though for good measure one of the men, a Nicaraguan, led them along a maze of twisting trails too faint to be called roads. They rode past silent fields of sugar cane and corn, past houses—haciendas—closed and tenantless, surrounded by bananas and breadfruits and avocados. The forest grew thicker, losing some of its jungle aspect in favor of large stands of oaks and an occasional pine tree. Still they did not stop, riding on and on through the predawn hours until the pounding of the horses' hooves became a rhythm in the blood, an endless thunder.

Daylight, gray with fog, caught them in a groove of ceiba trees. Throwing up a hand, Luis called a halt. They drew well off the track they were following and began to dismount. It was only as they gathered in a tight group beneath the trees that Eleanora took closer notice of the unwieldy bundle thrown across one of the horses. In the dark she had thought it provisions of some kind; now as it was unstrapped and dragged to the ground she saw it was a woman. Gagged and bound, her hair straggling in her flushed face, she was still recognizable as Juanita, still formidable in her venom.

Jean-Paul, reaching to help Eleanora down, made a strangled sound in his throat. His grip lost its strength so that she fell against him before regaining her feet.

Her eyes questioning, Eleanora swung to confront Luis. At that moment his right foot touched the ground as he left the saddle. He swayed, clinging to the pommel and cantle, his hat held on his back by a thong shielding his face. Blood, already turning black, overflowed the top of his boot, running in rivulets down the sides. His pant's leg glistened, crusting dark in the creases of the soft, smooth leather breeches.

The others, three Nicaraguans, a tall, thin sandy-haired man with the sun-dried look she had come to expect in a soldier from the Great Plains of the United States, and a blond man with saber scars on his face and a gutteral sound to his speech, were gathered around Juanita. Eleanora was the first to reach Luis's side.

At her touch on his arm, he turned his head. The smile that curved his mouth did not quite erase the pain in his

202

eyes. "So much for the heroic rescue," he said on a breathless, regretful laugh and slid into unconsciousness.

They stretched him out on a pile of horse blankets beneath a tree. The blond Prussian showed a tendency to take charge and Eleanora did not object, except when he tried to keep her away from Luis. At first she stood back while they stripped Luis of his breeches and wiped away the blood, but when the Prussian called for a knife to probe the wound she could contain herself no longer. She brushed under the arm thrust out to hold her back and dropped to her knees beside the man who had risked so much to help her.

It was an ugly gash. The bullet had torn across the top of his hard-muscled thigh at an angle to lodge in the groin. The injury did not appear dangerous. The fact that he was still alive seemed to argue that none of the main arteries in the area had been severed. Still, he had lost too much blood during the long ride and it appeared likely he would lose more before the bullet was out. A knife was a clumsy instrument; she would have given much for Dr. Jones's silver-handled forceps. In the end she had to introduce a second knife point into the wound before she could extract the lead slug nestled against his pelvic bone. Rye whiskey from the saddle bag of the plainsman was handed to her for the final cleansing. It was not carbolic but it was strong enough to have some of its properties. She used it before fashioning a bandage from strips of her apron and tying it into place with strings.

Luis regained consciousness within the hour, long before the sun had burned away the mist. He came awake in a rush, pushing himself into a sitting position against the tree trunk, his dark eyes alert. With a sweep of his arm he threw the corner of the blanket over his nakedness, then turned his gaze to Eleanora sitting on her heels beside him.

She was aware of the sudden silence behind her where the men stood about a small, smokeless fire that cradled a blackened coffee pot. The tension of their waiting filled the leaf-carpeted clearing under the trees so that the clattering of the leaves of the ceiba was loud above them. Eleanora thought, though with little foundation, that if

203

Luis should falter too badly here they would leave him to take his chances while they rode on. What her own fate would be in such a case she did not dare to imagine.

Rising, she filled a blue enamelware cup with steaming coffee, stirred in a generous splash of rye and several lumps of panocha with a twig, and brought it to Luis.

He thanked her, adding an endearment that made of his soft tone a caress instead of a weakness. The hand that grasped the cup was steady, conveying the hot liquid to his lips without spilling a drop. Eleanora relaxed, letting out her breath in soundless relief. Ignoring the quirk of humor at the corner of his mouth, she sat beside him until he had drained the cup.

"My breeches?" he asked when he was done. There was a faint sardonic inflection in his voice that seemed to reach beyond Eleanora toward the men behind her. As she took the empty cup he proffered and handed him the piece of clothing he had asked for, she was annoyed to find herself blushing. To cover it she turned on her heel and walked to where her horse was tied. She stood stroking it until Luis had pulled himself back on his horse and Jean-Paul approached to give her a leg up into her own saddle.

The noon meal came out of the saddle bags. No inducement to hunger, it was a collection of squashed tamales, tortillas rolled around slices of greasy pork, and bruised fruit. The heavy fare was lightened only by the addition of a dessert of oranges they had found growing wild as they rode.

Luis would not sit down. He leaned against a tree with one foot propped on the trunk behind him. Eleanora sat beside him on a log peeling an orange with a bowie knife and trying to keep the flies from crawling over her hands after the sticky juice. A frown between her eyes, she watched her brother. She did not like the brooding silence he had maintained during the morning. Jean-Paul had filled a cup with water from the canteen on his saddle and started across with it to where Juanita sat against a rotted stump with her hands tied before her. One of the Nicaraguans stepped in front of him as he passed their group near the horses and snatched the cup from his hand. Her brother protested but it did no good. The soldier poured the water out at his countrywoman's feet so that it spattered wet grit over her ankles. With a laugh he handed the cup back to Jean-Paul, but there was no humor in his eyes and no relenting. The younger man retreated to sit staring into space, neither eating nor drinking himself.

Eleanora glanced at Luis. His eyes, before he looked away, mirrored that same uncompromising hardness.

Carefully she finished peeling the orange, halved it, and passed the man beside her a portion. Stabbing her knife into the log, she asked quietly, "Who are these men?"

"Friends of mine, men from my regiment."

"Their names?"

"The Americano is Jasper Quitman, otherwise known as "Slim." The man with the scars is Kurt—his last name I find unpronounceable. The others are Sanchez, Molina, and Gonzalez. These last have, I think, a previous acquaintance with Juanita."

"I—doubt, somehow, that they are here for my sake."

"You mean you hope they are not," he said, smiling briefly. "No, they are here for mine, and for reasons of their own I did not question when they volunteered. Their fate will not be on your head."

Her acknowledgment was wry. "Since your insight is so accurate I must now wonder if what you say is the truth or only what you think I would like to hear."

"You need not worry about such men as these. For Sanchez, Molina, and Gonzalez it is the Democrático ideal that exacts their loyalty, not Walker or the Falangistas. They recognize no wrong in saving a pair of innocents from the firing squad if I ask it. As for the others, the gringos, danger is breath to them and treason only a word. Their loyalty is to themselves first and then to a multitude of other things that includes the red star of William Walker only to the extent that it can benefit them. They see that star as on the wane. Leaving it was only a matter of time."

"Do you think it is on the wane?"

His eyes narrowed slightly. "You are thinking that is why I came for you?"

"No," she answered, meeting his gaze squarely. "I believe I know why you did that." When he made no reply, she went on. "What I don't know is where we are going."

"To the mountains," he said with a gesture to the foothills rolling away to the northeast. "Hiding. It was not what I intended in the beginning. I thought to use my authority as commanding officer in the absence of Grant and the general to secure your release into my custody. I would then hold you under nominal house arrest until they returned to straighten out the situation. I was outmaneuvered. The guards had been given instructions to disregard my orders concerning prisoners, another of those orders signed by the general. It was necessary to use force."

"You must have suspected it would be necessary," she said with a nod at the other men.

"I could not be certain of things going as I wished. Niña Maria was even more thorough than I expected."

"Niña Maria? You think she was responsible?"

"Who else? She had easy access to the official documents and excellent opportunities to learn to copy the general's signature. She resented you and the popularity you were gaining both with the men and in the press. You made an excellent scapegoat."

"What do you mean?"

It was a moment before he answered. "Someone was feeding information to the Legitimista forces in Costa Rica. Juanita? Niña Maria herself? I'm not sure. In order for the damaging leaks to the other Central American countries to continue someone had to be blamed with the crime. Why not kill two birds with one stone? They could be rid of you and divert suspicion from themselves at the same time. With you out of the way there was an even chance Juanita could be reinstalled at the palacio and their sabatage of the Democrático regime could go on as originally planned—if Walker was lucky enough to return from Rivas."

"How do you know this?"

"I don't. I have only suspicions. It is possible, however, that our prisoner over there can be persuaded to corroborate them. With that knowledge in hand we can return to Granada, and all will be as before."

Would it? Eleanora found it hard to believe, found all

of it hard to believe. "How could Niña Maria hope to justify my death, and Jean-Paul's, to Walker?"

"If he returned by some misfortune there was Juanita's evidence, added to which would be the proof you and your brother could be expected to give—under torture."

Feeling more than a little ill, Eleanora looked away. "It seems I have much to thank you for. I am grateful, more grateful than I can tell you. I don't know how I can ever repay—"

He cut across her words with a fierce gesture. "Let there be no talk of payment between us. What was done was for myself, none other. How could I live if my soul were dead?"

Fourteen

In the scorching sun of midafternoon they crossed the narrow neck of water which ran between Lake Managua and Lake Nicaragua. They swam their horses, as much for coolness as to avoid the ferry further upstream. Soon afterward the land began to rise. The massed vegetation of the lowlands, the grassy savannas, were left behind for the stark green and brown and sandstone red of the pine and hardwood forest.

Eleanora rode with her teeth set in the effort of endurance. Her back ached as though a knife was stuck between her shoulder blades, and she saw the bobbing riders ahead of her through the wavering, dancing light of a heat shimmer. The single bearable moment of the past few hours had been the sighting of a Flame of the Forest tree, a tall, dark evergreen with huge, orange, tulip-shaped blossoms springing from among its leathery leaves. Always at the back of her mind lay the knowledge of what Luis had sacrificed for her. She would have liked to have had his faith in Walker; she could not quite find it within herself. She swung back and forth from hope to despair, from the joy of being free and alive to the depression of guilt.

Endlessly on they rode, circling small villages, now and then passing the stick-and-mud houses of isolated Indian farmers who stared after them with flat, incurious faces. The inside of her knee about the horn of her saddle was bruised and there was no feeling in her foot or calf. The glare of the sun spread into her eyes. Beneath the square of a neckerchief she had tied over her hair her skull felt on fire. Her face and arms, every inch of exposed skin was sunburned. Toward sundown she ceased to think or to notice her surroundings. She was a part of her horse. Was there a word for a creature half-woman, half-horse? The male counterpart was a centaur. Surely there was a female—

The sudden scream of a puma grated across her senses. Her horse shied, rearing. Only the quick grip of a strong hand on her bridle prevented her from being unseated. As the horse quieted she saw the cougar, a reddish-tawny streak disappearing over a rise ahead of them. Straightening, she turned to smile her gratitude and found herself staring into the eyes of the Prussian soldier-of-fortune. Thick lids hooded his expression, but she was aware of an intense, measuring quality in the stillness of his face that made her uncomfortable. Her nod was short and lacking in graciousness. Releasing her bridle, he fell back at once, but she was aware of him behind her from that moment until they made camp for the night.

Jean-Paul helped her from the saddle. Leaving him to tend to her horse and hobble it to keep it from wandering too far, she limped away into the trees, following the twists of the small, free-running stream they had elected to stop beside.

When she returned, a fire had been started and Juanita, watched carefully by the thin, long-faced man known as Sanchez, was making preparations for supper.

The meal promised no surprises. Having no real provisions for such a protracted journey, they had stopped to buy beans, meat, and ground corn, a couple of pans and a few other utensils, from the wife of a farmer. The woman had been no fool. They had paid dearly.

As Eleanora paused, wondering if she should offer her help, the black-haired woman looked up from the fire. Hate rose in her eyes and she raked Eleanora with a scathing stare before deliberately spitting on the ground. With the smallest lift of an eyebrow Eleanora turned and walked to where Luis sat against a rock with one foot stretched out before him. It was only as she took her place beside the lieutenant colonel that she recognized her uppermost feeling. It was relief bordering on gratitude that she did not have to force her aching muscles to perform the chores of the campfire.

Whether Juanita was a better cook than anyone had expected, was trying to placate them, or whether they were all simply starving, the meal was amazingly good. The men wolfed the beans and tortillas down with zest and looked around them for more. There was plenty. Juanita ladled it out with an expression of indifference, but once Eleanora saw her smile into the bean pot.

A vague fear they would all be ill did not materialize. The fire was extinguished as soon as possible; still, they lay around it, nursing the glowing coals while the men smoked a last cigarillo. The air cooled as the dusk deepened. Their clothing grew wet with dew instead of perspiration. A night bird called, a lonely sound. Juanita stirred, picked up the dirty dishes, and started in the direction of the stream.

Sanchez, loosening his revolver in its holster, sauntered after her. After a moment, Eleanora followed.

The woman walked fast. When Eleanora came upon her beside the brownish-green water she was already scrubbing a pot with sand. Eleanora knelt and picked up a plate. Sanchez squatted at a distance with his back against a tree, his cigarillo dangling between two fingers. Flicking a glance at them from the corner of her eyes, Juanita made a snorting sound through her nose, and sidled a few feet farther downstream.

The dishes were few; they did not take long. Juanita gave the pot in her hand a last sloshing rinse then rose to her feet with conscious grace. She dropped the rag she had been using and, with a sidelong glance and a defiant toss of her mane of dark hair, moved slowly toward a thick clump of scrub oaks and gum saplings.

Eyes narrowed, Eleanora looked after her. Something in the Nicaraguan woman's attitude struck her as peculiar. She was too fearless, too unwary for a prisoner. She exuded a sense of suppressed anticipation that put Eleanora in the mind of the mood she had seen in Luis as he dared to help her escape.

Sanchez, she thought, would not have hesitated to go with Juanita save for her presence. There was in the mind of Luis's men some doubt as to her exact position with their leader. For the time being they were treading warily.

Pushing to her feet, Eleanora started after the other woman.

The sharp smell of gum leaves lingered where Juanita had passed. Eleanora ducked under the branches, stepping over rotting logs crawling with termites. Ahead of her a bird whirred away in startled flight. She quickened her pace, jerking impatiently at her skirt as it caught on small thorn bushes and vines covered with briars along the stems. Rounding the trunk of a towering rosewood, she glanced ahead for some sign of Juanita. There was nothing, no flash of color, no unnatural movement. All was quiet, too quiet.

The whisper of an indrawn breath alerted her. She whirled, but not in time to avoid the swinging shadow of a pine limb. The blow crashed into her head just above her ear. She sagged, and felt the abrupt hardness of musty leaf-mold beneath her cheekbone.

She could not have been unconscious more than a moment. The noise of shots, three in succession in a signal for aid, penetrated the dimness of her mind. Sitting up, she was able to point out to Sanchez the direction she thought she had seen Juanita take as she was falling.

He did not wait. Before his footsteps had gone out of hearing the others came into view to be directed after him. Only Luis was not among them.

Eleanora touched the lump on the side of her head with careful fingers. That the skin was not broken was due more to the thickness of her hair than to Juanita's lack of strength. Bits of bark sifted to her shoulders as she brushed at the deep wave that covered the lump. Dusting them to the ground, she levered herself up, then stood still until her senses steadied and the throbbing behind her eyes had slowed to a gentle pound. Moving with caution, she turned in the direction of the camp.

Intent on keeping to the path that had been trampled in the grass and rocky earth, she flung her head up, startled, at a noise in the trees off to her left. The impulse to run gripped her, not wholly subsiding when the Prussian known as Kurt stepped from the oaks and came toward her.

"I circled back to see about you," he said, touching a hand to the brim of his hat. "I hope I did not give you a fright? You were so pale, so weak, sitting where we left you. I am glad to see you have made such a swift recovery."

"I—thank you."

He stepped closer, moving in front of her. "I am not certain you are recovered, after all. A woman of your sort needs a man to care for her. Permit me to go ahead and hold the branches for you."

"I am sure I can manage if you are needed in the search."

He smiled, a mechanical movement of too-firm lips. "I heard the woman running before them like a hare before the hounds. It is only a matter of time, and the Nicaraguans have more enthusiasm for the hunt than I—at least for that quarry."

She refused to ask him for his meaning. Slanting a glance from under her lashes at the heavy humor in his face, she picked up her skirts and walked on. He made no attempt to stop her, falling in at her side.

"You were lucky to have so faithful a cavalier as the lieutenant colonel, were you not? It is a greaty pity he was wounded."

Eleanora agreed soberly.

In the pretense of pushing aside a limb with his outstretched arm, Kurt barred the way. "You realize this hurt makes him of little use to you—as a man?"

"I don't think I understand you," she said, grimly certain she did but unwilling to have the man see it.

"In this kind of situation strength is needed," he explained, tightening the muscles in his forearm until they bulged. "A weak man, a man who is not whole, is a liability."

"I will trust Luis to be twice the man most are, whether he is injured or not." Her back stiff, she tried to slip past him.

Reaching out to grip her arm at the elbow, he held her just tightly enough to make her aware of the power in his hard, sturdy frame without hurting her. "Injured men cannot always protect what they hold," he told her, a suggestion of thickness in his voice as his eyes raked over the thin material of her blouse and the flare of her red skirt over her hips. His fingers began to knead her skin as he waited for her reply. There was a dragging tension in his grip and she knew that if she relaxed her resistance for so much as an instant she would be pulled against that burly chest.

"Sometimes," she replied with slow emphasis, her green eyes steady, "it is not necessary to hold something to keep it."

"That is only if there are no thieves around." Satisfaction with his own cleverness gleamed in his gray-blue eyes so that the scar near one crinkled lid was pulled like a bad seam.

There was no need for Eleanora to answer. Before she could find words Luis stepped into view before them, his revolver swinging from his hand. "I think it might be helpful," he said softly, "if I make it known that in my command the penalty for theft is death."

The eyes of the two men locked. For all the gentle quietness of Luis's tone, it was Kurt who shifted uneasily, dropping his gaze to the gun held so casually against the Spaniard's leg.

When the fingers about her arm loosened, Eleanora twisted free. She crossed to Luis, and sending him a small, flickering smile, slipped her hand inside his free arm. He pressed it to his side before inclining his head in the most ironical of half-bows and moving off with her toward the encampment.

By the time they reached the blankets Luis had indicated, placed well beyond those of the others, he was leaning on Eleanora for support. She was too involved with helping him to lie down comfortably and wondering where Kurt had gone, since he had not followed them in, to do more than register that her own saddle blankets lay beside those of the lieutenant colonel. Noticing at last, she took a step backward.

Hoisting himself up to rest his forearm on his saddle in place of a pillow, Luis reached out to draw her down beside him. His face was serious; there was nothing in his manner to alarm her. She did not resist, curling her feet under her and tucking her skirt over them.

When he was certain she was at ease, he turned from her to unbuckle a saddle pouch and take out what appeared to be a two-foot length of chain with a ring at each end. Shaking it out, he picked up her left wrist, and before she realized his intention, snapped one of the steel bracelets around it. With deliberate movements, he closed the other ring about the wrist of his own right arm. Only then did he meet her eyes.

"Forgive me," he said. "It is the only way I see to keep you safe beside me until we can return to Granada. Grant gave these manacles to me. They are like those used by the military marshals. The key to open them I have safely hidden—"

"You don't mean for us to wear these all the time, night and day?" She cut across his plea in stricken tones, the heat of mortification rising in her face as the implications of such enforced intimacy struck her.

"It must be this way."

"Why? I can fend for myself."

"As you did just now? What was to keep Kurt from taking you then and there among the leaves?"

"He wouldn't have—"

"Wouldn't he? Maybe not—yet. But there are long miles and days before us. We go deep into the jungle where the heat of the sun melts away the cool manners of the gentleman, and the strong prey on the weak as they choose. The nature of men like these who go with us is more nearly suited to the jungle."

"Must we go?"

213

"It is possible the general will relent. If he does not, we will have to work our way over the mountains and across an area where white men have never gone in order to reach the Mosquito Coast on the Atlantic shore. The British are patrolling that coast, since they claim the region of the Mosquito Indians as a protectorate of the Crown and are loath to relinquish the area to William Walker. We may be able to get a ship to pick us up."

Eleanora mulled this information in silence. An ant crawled across the hand on which she was leaning. Without thinking she reached to pick it off, only to be stopped by the short chain. Abruptly she clenched her fist, bringing it down on her knee.

"No!" she cried. "I can't, I won't put up with this. You don't know what you're asking."

Without replying, Luis lay back, folding his hands behind his head. The action of the chain unbalanced her so that if she had not caught herself on one elbow she would have fallen against his chest.

"I'm afraid," he said smiling, "that you must."

"Please," she began in a low voice.

"Are you going to try to persuade me?" he queried. "As much as I would enjoy it, I have to tell you in all honor that it will do no good."

She stared at his face so close to hers. Was the redness beneath his skin the effect of the sun, or was he flushed with fever? Was he less well than he wished her to know? Did that explain these desperate measures?

"This will be unbearable, you must know it."

His lips moved with a suggestion of bitterness. "I know it will not be easy, yes. But you, *pequeña*, have worked busily over my nakedness. Why should I cavil at revealing it again? As for you, nothing could lessen my feelings for you. Moreover, you have nothing to fear. I will not say I can stand your nearness unmoved, but I am incapable at the moment of taking full advantage of the opportunities you are so afraid will occur."

She heard him out without speaking. Searching his face, she asked at last, "And would you, if you could?"

"A thousand times yes, *mi alma*," he answered wryly. "Don't you know a man judges other men by himself?"

Night moved in, the moon rose, and still the men did not return with Juanita. Eleanora was too tired and over-wrought, and above all, too conscious of the limit on her free movement for sound sleep. She dozed fitfully, waking at every rustle and night cry. Even in slumber she was aware of minor discomforts, of each bruise and blister and strained muscle, of every twig and pebble on the ground under her blanket. When she had been still for a time she grew cool, and reaching down pulled the corner of the blanket over the lower part of her body.

The growl of voices roused her. Along her side the warmth was excessive. Had Luis moved closer in the night or had she? She did not know, but she eased away, being careful not to waken him. Only then did she turn her head.

She went still. Two men were helping her brother across the small clearing toward his bedroll. Jean-Paul stumbled along between them with his chin resting on his chest like a man who has had too much to drink. They let him fall on his blanket face down, and he rolled over, throwing his arm over his eyes.

Eleanora pushed at the blanket, trying to get up. Beside her, Luis reached across with his arm, stilling her movements. She flicked a look at him, then followed the direction of his intense gaze to the wood's edge where the rest of the men were emerging.

Sanchez, Molina, and Gonzalez stepped into the open, carrying with them the unclothed form of Juanita. Her flesh shone ivory in the moon's pale light, but though her eyes were tightly closed, she did not have the boneless look of death.

As Eleanora watched, Gonzalez, paunchy, with droop-ing mustaches, pointed at Jean-Paul's blanket with an obscene laugh rumbling in his belly. They threw the woman down beside him and flung a handful of clothes over her. She lay sprawled as she had fallen, unmoving.

Gonzalez fished with difficulty in the pocket of his breeches and brought out a coin. Molina, the youngest of the Nicaraguans, a broad-faced young man of Indian blood who had been their guide during the day, lost the toss. With a resigned shrug, he took his seat a short distance from the blanket on which the woman lay.

Jean-Paul gave no sign he knew the naked woman was beside him. After a time Juanita's eyelids moved and she stared with dark and baleful eyes into the dark about her. When she saw that all had settled for the night, she sat up and slowly drew on her blouse and skirt. Moving stiffly, she lay back down again.

Was her brother drunk, or hurt, Eleanora wondered? Had he tried to prevent the rape of his former mistress and met violence, or retreated from it into a bottle of rye? She could not tell. Watching, she saw the steady rise and fall of his chest. If he was hurt there was little she could do, and if drunk, there was nothing. In any case, there were times when the only thing that served was to be left alone.

Dawn met them riding once more. They were a silent cavalcade, sunk in weariness and resignation. Fever burned bright in Luis's eyes, making his temper uncertain with all except Eleanora. Clean-shaven despite the difficulties of using a sharp bowie knife and no soap, he did not look as villainous as the rest. Jean-Paul, with a purple welt spreading over the point of his jaw beneath his scanty beard, looked particularly bad. He was withdrawn, tailing the column for mile upon mile, not speaking unless he was spoken to. Often, when he thought no one was watching, his brooding gaze would fasten on Sanchez and the woman riding behind him with her bound hands gripping the cantle of the Nicaraguan's saddle. She too wore bruises, especially about the mouth and throat. Her eyes were dark-shadowed and sullen, but she did not lower them when one looked her way.

They climbed ever higher, winding among the rugged, blue-hazed hills, seeking always the passes and the downward slope leading northeast. Vultures, black grace in a hard blue sky, circled them with a worrying persistence, and flocks of ducks and geese passed, croaking, high overhead. A half-grown jaguar dogged their trail for several hours, though more in curiosity than with any intent of harm. They saw deer in numbers and an occasional peccary, the large wild animal with tusks like a boar used in

216

Central America as pork. Slim brought down one of these with his rifle toward dusk. Taking the best cuts and leaving the rest for the vultures might have been wasteful, but it was all they could do. They had to have meat.

Of humans they saw little. The Indian settlements they came across now were usually deserted. Not as civilized or domesticated as their lowland relatives, from long experience they had learned to avoid foreigners. The woven baskets of corn they left behind provided an agreeable addition to the larder, and the blankets woven to fit like a closed cape with an opening for the head were most welcome against the promised coolness of the night. Luis, his movements deliberate to disguise the trembling of his hands, had left Mexican dollars behind to pay for what they had taken. Looking back, Eleanora saw Gonzalez pocket the money but, pressing her lips tightly together, said nothing. This was not the time to point Luis toward a confrontation he might not be able to dominate. Just behind her Kurt was also aware of what had taken place. The expression in his eyes was unpleasant, and far too knowing.

The last rays of the sun were still bright on the tops of the mountains when they followed Molina into the twilight sanctuary of a long, narrow valley. The stillness of a small lake mirrored the surrounding peaks and provided water for the horses. Tracks of animals laced its muddy verge, but there were no human footprints among them despite the thatched adobe house that backed against the side of a sandstone crag as if trying to blend into it. A fence sagged across the small yard in front, held up only by the Spanish dagger planted behind it. The door was missing from the dark rectangle of the front opening beneath the shadowy overhang of a porch supported by rough, unpeeled poles. In places the thatch had harbored the windblown seeds of weeds and wild flowers so that they bloomed in the mildewed straw.

Molina, his young face anxious, looked to Luis for approval. Slowly the Spaniard nodded. "We rest here," he said, and the weakness of his voice seemed to confirm the necessity.

Juanita was not freed. They forced her down upon the

ground, tying her to one of the posts of the front porch. She sat up as straight as a ramrod, spitting defiance as long as they towered over her, but when they were gone she slumped back, her eyes closed.

It was Eleanora, restricted to the point of madness by the chain on her wrist, who cooked the corn cakes, mixing the ground meal with water, slapping it thin and browning it on an iron plate at the edge of the fire. Gonzalez took over the roasting of the chunks of peccary over the coals, there being no inside accommodation for cooking.

Seeing it killed, Eleanora had thought she could not eat the meat of the peccary. Still, watching as Gonzalez turned it on sticks with lip-smacking gusto, smelling the savory odor as it curled in smoke about the porch, she grew as hungry as any and sat waiting for the succulent, well-browned meat to be done with her tortilla in her hand.

The long ride had not only made her ravenous. As the stars came out she found her eyes, raw with sun-glare and the sting of woodsmoke, closing against her will. Luis, mindful of her comfort, had sent Molina to cut a mound of sweet grass for her bed. The blankets they had acquired during the day smelled less of horse than those they had used the night before. There was before her the cool, clear waters of the lake for a bathing place. She could, in fact, have looked forward to a night of sweet slumber, had it not been for the chain about her wrist.

Eleanora sighed. Luis glanced at her and, seeing the dissatisfaction in her eyes, his face lightened though he could not be said to smile. He got to his feet. Waiting until she had risen also, he picked up the blanket on which they had been seated, shook out the dirt, and turned from the fire.

Hanging back, Eleanora asked, "Where are we going?"

"You will see." He flung the blanket over his shoulder in the manner of a serape and stepped out into the darkness.

The night was made pleasantly cool by a soft wind blowing from the mountain tops. It lifted the tendrils of hair that had escaped from Eleanora's knot, brushing her senses with the soft pungence of pine and sage. Night birds called in melodic melancholy. The waving of the grass that carpeted the floor of the valley had a hypnotic quality that was soothingly sensuous.

The perfect stillness of the pool was disturbed only by a patch of reeds weaving in the wind. They stopped on the verge. Luis dragged the blanket from his shoulder and held it out to her. "Your dressing room and bathing machine, milady."

Eleanora made no move to take it. "What do you mean?" she asked.

"You wished to bathe?" He indicated the pool with a flick of his fingers.

She stared at him. "How did you know?"

"I know much of your habits. I am an observant man. As to my meaning, in Europe they have the wagons pulled out into the water by horses which offer a place of concealment for a lady from vulgar, prying eyes while she enjoys the sea."

"I will get the blanket wet," she warned, intrigued in spite of herself.

"No matter."

"But what of you?"

"What have I to hide from you? Ah, you blush, I think. It is cruel of me to tease you in this way again. Let us say, then, that I trust you to keep your eyes forward, regardless of how much I might prefer it otherwise. And I promise that on this occasion your trust also will be rewarded."

She stared at him, more concerned with the weakness of his voice than with what he was saying with such a labored attempt at lightness. But why should she object? Had they not shared the rest stops of the day, searching the most dense undergrowth to strain their chain between them? No, she had no reason to doubt him.

"Don't you believe me?" he demanded with that shade of hauteur that indicated damage to his fierce pride, that same pride that had kept her from inquiring more closely now into his well-being.

"Yes, of course," she murmured.

"Then?" He proffered the blanket once more.

The acrobatics of disrobing beneath the blanket with

one hand was soon done. Aware of Luis's struggles beside her, Eleanora realized how much more handicapped he was by the chain arrangement. It was his right hand that was inconvenienced. As she heard his soft curse she knew that it was irksome not only to her alone.

The water had the cold bite of a mountain spring, especially without the warmth of the sun to ward off its chill. They waded out, testing the bottom and depth with careful steps. After only a few feet Eleanora stopped abruptly. "What of your bandage?" she asked without turning her head.

"Stuck, and in need of loosening," he replied.

"Not this way," she protested, but he paid no attention, moving on so that the chain tugged her forward.

"Suppose—suppose there are sharks, and alligators, as in Lake Nicaragua?"

"Not at this altitude," he assured her.

"Are you certain?"

"No," he answered, "but neither am I certain that the sun will rise tomorrow. Will you be ruled by your fears?"

Wading on, she did not bother to reply.

To be clean when you have been dirty for a long time is one of life's chief pleasures, ranking with eating your fill after a fast and growing warm after freezing. Eleanora, splashing water over her limbs one final time beneath the blanket, acknowledged this truth without question, even when the bath consisted of cold water and the corner of a blanket. It was only as the sound of her ablution died away that she noticed the sound beside her. It was the rattling of the chain that connected her to Luis. Its links jangled together unceasingly.

Eleanora swung her head. Luis, with water to his waist, was shivering uncontrollably. A gust of wind blew across the expanse of the lake, fanning about his chest. He shuddered in the grip of convulsion, his eyes closed. Reaching out, she touched him. His skin burned with fever, and the feel of her cold fingers sent another racking shudder over him. His breath came fast through parted lips, and she knew without being told that his teeth were clenched to keep them from chattering.

"Dear God, Luis. Why didn't you tell me?" she said.

220

She whirled, taking a few steps toward the shore. When he did not immediately follow she grasped his arm, pulling him along.

"What have I done?" she asked herself, ignoring his feeble attempts to persuade her that her alarm was for nothing.

By the time they were out of the water her breath was rasping harsh in her throat. She whipped the blanket off over her head, and swinging it wide, pressed it down over the brown waves of his hair. It was not wet about the chest and shoulders; that should help a little.

Turning away, she stepped into her slippers and scooped up her petticoat. Pulling it on over her head, she tied the tapes with quick, impatient jerks, then reached for her blouse. As she searched for the armholes, she flung a look at Luis. He had not moved from where she had left him. His eyes dark shadows in the paleness of his face, he stared at her as she stood so close, at the soft sheen of starlight upon her shoulders and the fair, firm globes of her breasts with their tip-tilted nipples; so inviting, and within reach. He moved so slowly, winding the chain about his hand, that if she could have discovered some shred of indignation within herself, she might have avoided him. She could not. The sense of gratitude and helpless pity penetrated too deeply. She did not resist as he drew her to him, cupping her shoulders, smoothing his hands down her naked back. The sigh that shook him seemed to come from some empty depth within. His mouth was warm and gentle, tasting of panocha-sweetened coffee. It did not seek to consume her but merely to taste, but once, a forbidden pleasure. It was foolish, perhaps, but for an instant Eleanora responded, unable to deny that which cost her so little and seemed to mean so much. For a brief second he seemed warmed by her closeness, and then the trembling began once more.

Lifting a hand, she touched his face, then slowly, firmly, drew away. Little by little he released her. While she finished dressing he stared out across the lake with the unresponsive face of a blind man.

"Let us go," Eleanora said, picking up his shirt and breeches from where they lay. He started off, but in the

221

end she had to lead him in the right direction, back toward the adobe house and the fire flickering like a beacon before it.

For all the submersion in water, the bandage still clung to the jagged and torn edges of the wound. Staring at her bent head with eyes brilliant and heavy with fever, Luis endured her picking and gentle prizing until he could stand it no longer. Rising up, he ripped away the bandage, flooding the gash with blood once more.

It was Slim, watching over her shoulder as he held a torch of pitch-pine to supplement the light from the fire, who put her grim thoughts into words. "Cauterize it," he said.

Eleanora drew a deep breath. "It's such a long tear—the shock."

"Better than letting the poison get to it."

Eleanora had come to like the soft-spoken plainsman. In some indefinable way he reminded her of Grant. She trusted him as much as she was capable of trusting anyone in her present circumstances. Without further argument she nodded.

It was Slim who found the bowie knife that had carved their supper. He cleaned it as well as she could have done, scouring it with sand and rinsing it, much to the disgust of the others, in the water boiling for coffee over the fire. Thrusting it among the red embers with blue fire dancing above them, he left it to take on their heat while he poured out a generous measure of rye for both Luis and himself.

If she had been alone, if it had been a necessity, Eleanora might have found the strength to press that white-hot blade to the flesh of the man who had risked so much to save her. As it was, she delegated that task, gratefully, to Slim also, while she held Luis's hand and they endured together the sound and smell of searing meat. The grip of his fingers tightened cruelly, his body stiffened, but the expression in his eyes as they clung to hers did not change. He had placed himself in her keeping—his own words when she had asked his permission to seal the wound. It was frightening in a way she could not explain,

222

even to herself, as if he lived only through her and would have it no other way.

And when the thing was done and Luis's spare shirt had been sacrificed to cover Slim's handiwork, they carried him inside and lifted him upon the piled grass in the corner. They covered him with blankets, tucking them around him. Still, he was swept at intervals by bouts of shaking that left him spent. They did not go away entirely until Eleanora had slid beneath the blankets beside him and pressed close. For a time he hardly seemed to recognize that she was there, and then his arm tightened around her waist to draw her more firmly back against his chest. He kissed her hair, and slept.

Eleanora had thought to stay awake, and indeed she had not realized she had not done so until the thud of horses' hooves and shouts of warning invaded her dreams. She shook free of them with difficulty, staring bemused at the alien face of the man beside her, lying where Grant should have been. The memory of the possessive fire in his cobalt-blue eyes, the unrelenting enchantment of his mouth upon hers lingered, though she could not remember how they had been reunited.

Outside the clamor rose, waking Luis. He raised his head, shifting to his elbow in order to see over Eleanora to the open door. The lone rider had dismounted. The men had gathered around him, their voices falling to a low timbre that in its gravity sent a tremor of apprehension along Eleanora's spine.

Drawing in his breath, Luis called, "What is it? What goes?"

A man in the loose garments of a peon detached himself from the group and came with hat in hand to the dark doorway. "I beg pardon, Lieutenant Colonel," he said, his tone quietly respectful.

"Pablo!" Luis exclaimed. "You got away. I gave you up when you were unseated outside the guardhouse. I have been worried, my friend. It is good to see you."

"And you, Conde. But you need not have troubled your mind. It was agreed that every man would look to himself."

"Still, it was a hard thing to leave you. How do you come to be here?"

The soldier shrugged in his peon's costume. "My injuries were nothing, though I thought I was dead at the time. I was struck a glancing blow only, a ricochet off my saddle horn which struck the butt of the gun I had pushed into my waistband. My air, it go pouf and I fell, but I was lucky, was I not?" He seemed to take their agreement for granted, for he went on. "I ran very fast to the house of a friend and I stay there, hiding, afraid I would be recognized. And then I heard news I thought would be of great importance for you. I rode all day and all the night, for Molina is my cousin, and I guessed where he would bring you. Two horses, fine horses, I had when I started, and now I have only one. The other, she is winded and falls to break both knees."

"You will be repaid," Luis assured him. "Only tell me what is this news."

"It concerns the little general, Conde. He did not attack Rivas. Word of armies ready to strike at him from Honduras came to him just outside the city. Since he is afraid his capital will be captured, he turned his men around and began the march back to Granada. Perhaps he is in the city already, sending his orders from the Government House once more. Perhaps he already wonders what has become of the woman of the colonel, and would be interested in words in her favor. In a few days his aristocrática whore may have poisoned his mind, and the duties of war may make him forget. Now is the time to gain his attention."

"You are right," Luis said, a grim note entering his voice. "But first the information, the proof, must be secured."

"I—understand, Lieutenant Colonel. You may leave it to us."

It was a moment before Luis spoke, and then finality weighted his words. "It is well."

Outlined in the dying fire beyond him, the man in the doorway nodded once and swung away, disappearing into the dark. Luis sank back down upon their couch, the movement wafting the sweet smell of cut grass up through

224

the blanket on which they lay. Eleanora turned on her back.

"Luis?" she said tentatively. "What did you mean, the proof?"

The man lying so quietly at her side did not reply.

Fifteen

In the back of her mind, beyond the reach of conscious thought, Eleanora knew. Juanita had not been hauled along with them over the long miles for the sake of her convenience as a camp drudge, or even for her obvious usefulness in other areas important to men without their women. There had to be a purpose, and from the contemptuous and even brutal way in which they used the woman, Eleanora could not delude herself that their purpose boded any good for Juanita.

She would not allow her thoughts to go beyond this admission. With an effort she emptied her mind of all conjecture, straining after sleep. It was useless. Lying still, she endured the torment of aching muscles, needing to turn, but afraid of disturbing Luis. In disobedience to her will, her memory drifted back, curling with a passion of longing about the images of Grant as she remembered him best—in his scarlet uniform with its gold braiding and the epaulettes emphasizing the breadth of his shoulders which he had worn on the day they met; his vivid nearness, which magnified every brow and lash and seam of his skin as he carried her in his arms to the palacio; his bronzed form outlined in lightning like an ancient, haunted god on the night he had made her his; his pale face and bruised eyelids as he clutched her skirt in his hand while she tended his shoulder. So many memories, cruel and tender, gentle and strong, comic and filled with pain. Would it be enough to balance this terrible agony of doubt that she must carry as long as she lived?

As time passed and Luis did not move, she reached to

put her hand to his forehead, wishing distractedly that there was something she could do to relieve the fever that heated his blood. He did not respond to her touch; still she thought he was not sleeping either.

When the scream, faint with distance, came on the night wind, Eleanora's nerves leaped under her skin, but she could acknowledge no surprise. She swallowed, her muscles tense, and when the sound, with the shrill timbre of a woman's voice, came again, her hand went out to throw back the blanket that covered her.

Luis touched her arm, his fingers hot but strong. "No, Eleanora, you cannot help, nor will I allow you to interfere."

"I can't just lie here," she said in a taut voice.

"You must."

"It's barbaric."

"Like the firing squad, eh? No, *mi alma*, it is justice. Shall we ask this woman please to tell us what she has done and why? Should we have let her schemes prosper? Should we have let you, Eleanora, present your tender heart to the firing squad you so despise? No. This one will give up the information she holds. She will confess her sins and put her name to a paper that will make clear your innocence and restore you to your former place in the sun of the general's court."

Bitterness laced his tone, and with some right, Eleanora thought. The men were few who would risk so much to clear the name of a woman they cared for, especially when her exoneration might lead to her reinstatement as another man's mistress.

Beside her Luis spoke as another cry impaled the night. "In any case, a number of the men out there have a personal vendetta with Señorita Juanita. I doubt if you or I could stop them even if we tried."

A sick feeling moved through Eleanora. She clenched her hands. Despite the truth of his statement, despite what Juanita had tried to do to Jean-Paul and herself, it still seemed cowardice not to try to help another human being who was being hurt. To do nothing, and possibly to benefit from that inflicted pain, was infinitely worse. If it had been a man it would have been bad enough, but

226

that it was a woman, one of her own kind, seemed a special horror. Why it should be worse she could not tell, and yet it was.

"How——" she began, faltered, and then rushed on, afraid that he would misinterpret what she asked, and taking her literally, tell her exactly what he thought was occurring in the darkness. "How can they do it? How can they bring themselves to commit acts of such unspeakable evil?"

He sighed, shifting with the pain in his leg. "A man," he said slowly, "never knows the limits he can reach in degradation—when he feels he has just cause. An instant of time can change him into a devil for whom nothing is too vile. Even I—"

He stopped, his breath coming quickly in the quiet. "You need not explain to me," Eleanora said, masking her sudden apprehension with a tone of indifference, though her slim fingers plucked at the rough, homespun wool of the blanket.

"Even I," he repeated as if she had not spoken. "I told you once, did I not, that I had reason to seek the forgetfulness and danger of war. You are my soul, why should you not know the reason? It is a tale that begins in Spain. The house of my father is an old one, perched on the hillside among the olive groves above the Guadalquivir Valley. Pride, in my home and my family and in the Moorish blood that runs in my veins, was drilled into me in the nursery. My life was set before I was born; I would be educated as suited my station, I would be taught to revere Mother-Church, to wear always the attire of a gentleman, to acquit myself with a rapier, and to wear one on dress occasions without tripping over it. A marriage with a suitable *parti* would be arranged for me, I would be presented at the court of the young Queen Isabella II, where I would be expected to take my place among the conservatives. On the death of my father I would, of course, assume the responsibilities of the patron for the people who lived in the villages that belonged to me, people who had worked for my family for generations. I would look after the land and produce children to carry on after me. My portrait, with that of my wife, would be placed in the long gallery of my house, and with the march of the years my bones would lie in the cathedral with those of my ancestors. I was not dissatisfied with such a prospect. It was my destiny, and I don't recall entertaining the thought that it could be otherwise. Then I met Consuelo."

Eleanora glanced at him quickly through the darkness. He caught the movement, for he gave a short laugh. "You need not be jealous, my dove," he said with irony, "although she was very beautiful. I saw her one day on the steps of the cathedral as she came from mass, and I thought she was the loveliest thing I had ever seen. She wore a white mantilla over her midnight black hair, and her *dueña* hovered about her like a butterfly around an exquisite flower. I could not have been more awe-struck or more moved if one of the images of the sweet saints had stepped down from its niche. She smiled at me, the picture of shy innocence, and I was enraptured. I could not speak to her, of course, it was not allowed. But nothing could prevent me from learning her name or from conceiving for her such a sacred passion that I went at once to my father and demanded that he arrange a marriage. It was done. There was no bar to the union; she was of good family, the daughter of a neighbor of no more than fifteen miles' distance in fact, and only just out of convent school. Her father was a minor official at court, but a man of influence, since his wife was distantly related to the queen. She had also an uncle who was a general and a leader of one of the political factions. The betrothal was announced with much ceremony, and then, as is the custom, the courtship began."

His voice changed, becoming abrupt. "It is necessary for me to tell you that Consuelo, though she did not object to me as a husband, was not warm to the idea. I was not discouraged. With all the optimism of a youth barely of age, I felt that the warmth of my ardor must kindle an answering flame in her breast. I set siege to her heart with every ruse known to a lover, I wrote verses to the beauty of her eyes, arranged for serenades, escorted her with her crone of a *dueña* wherever she wished to go. I sent her gifts without number. Learning that she loved to ride and was an accomplished horsewoman, I sent men to the horse auctions of Spain, searching for a mount suited to my beloved. An Arabian mare of a whiteness and a purity of bloodline that could have been meant only for Consuelo was found. On the day that it was delivered I was the happiest of men, certain that at last I had found a gift that could not fail to please. With the mare on a lead-rein, I rode to the house of her father and presented myself at the door. Imagine my disappointment when I was told she was from home, riding out with her groom in attendance. So determined was I to see her pleasure, however, that I decided to await her return. Heated from exercise the mare could not be left standing, and I wanted to have the dust brushed from her coat before Consuelo saw her. There was a servant on the forecourt of the house, but I wished to see to it that the mare was walked and watered and rubbed down with the care I deemed necessary.

"Inside of the barn was dark and musty with the smell of old hay. The hot sun had searched out the cracks and holes in the structure, sending yellow shafts boring through the darkness in which dust motes turned, disturbed by my footsteps. I stood for a moment just inside the door, waiting for my eyes to adjust, and in that moment I heard voices coming from the tackroom that opened to my right. A woman laughed and I recognized Consuelo's voice. My suspicions were not aroused, my single thought was that my wait to see my betrothed was over.

"It is odd. For years what I saw that afternoon has been enough to make me feel that my eyes are bursting from my head and my heart exploding in my chest. Now it merely seems laughable in a bawdy kind of way. Consuelo, with her riding habit bunched about her waist, was seated on a saddle on a rest. Her groom stood between her legs with his breeches around his ankles, grunting under the whip she plied on his backside. There is no way to describe my shock then. My single coherent thought was that she had profaned my love for her. My pride, so carefully cultivated all my life, rose up in rage. I drew the dress sword at my side and cut the groom to ribbons with no more compunction than you would feel on killing a rat. That I did not kill him outright was due solely to his cowering, abject submission. If he had so much as looked about him for a weapon or raised a hand in his defense, I would have run him through. And then I turned to Consuelo. For her I chose the punishment of my Moorish ancestors for an unfaithful woman. I cornered her among the bridles thick with dust and spider webs, and grasping her chin in my hand, slit her nose. With my sword's edge I sliced it half off and stood and watched as her face dissolved in blood."

"Oh, Luis," Eleanora whispered, her voice an ache in her throat. She could think of nothing to say, no word of comfort or condemnation.

After a moment he went on. "A terrible waste; her beauty, her life—and my own. And beyond that, countless hours of remorse and self-disgust that did no one any good, least of all myself. To be cut off from friends and family, denied my country, may have been no more than I deserved, but it has, this decade and more, been a true punishment."

"I would have thought the courts would have been lenient to a young man who acted with the provocation that you had," Eleanora said.

"They might have if Consuelo's relatives had not been so firmly entrenched at court. Her father and her uncle swore to see me hanged, and they might have succeeded if my father had not also had his friends around the throne. As it was, I was banished. They thought to have a hired assassin complete their death sentence for them, but after I returned to them in a box the head of the third man they had sent, they stopped trying. During this time I was reduced to being always a guest in another country, wandering from London to Paris to Rome in winter, and in summer from one of the watering places of Europe to another, wagering nightly at the gaming table, returning the many entertainments I received, planning others in an attempt to find surcease from thinking. Such a life not only played havoc with the allowance paid to my bankers by a grieving and therefore indulgent father, but because it was not what I wished to be doing it grew tedious. Pitting my wits against the hired killers of Consuelo's relatives, I had felt more alive, and glad of it, than in months. Such a discovery, combined with such a talent for violent death, should not be wasted, I thought. I became a paid soldier."

"And had the misfortune to join William Walker?" Eleanora commented.

"There were other causes, other countries, first. But yes, eventually I came to California and Walker. A misfortune? I cannot agree with that, since the general led me to you."

Eleanora laughed, a husky sound. "That may have been the greatest misfortune of them all."

Reaching out, he touched her face with gentle fingers, turning her face to his. "Never say that, *pequeña*," he murmured against her mouth. "Never say that, ever."

His fingers trailed down the curve of her neck to the hollow of her throat, resting for a moment on the pulse that beat so steadily there. Then he moved lower, his palm smoothing over the soft mound of her breast.

Eleanora lay unmoving, neither accepting nor rejecting his caress until he lay still, his chest rising and falling evenly. Her sense of obligation warred with a feeling of disloyalty inside her. She had hardly dared to think that Luis might be right, that the order for her arrest had been forged by Niña Maria without the knowledge of the general, or more importantly, of Grant. To think of him returning to the palacio and finding it empty, learning that she was gone with Luis, sent a feeling of panic scurrying through her. What would he do? Would he believe Niña Maria's accusation? Would he think that rifling his papers and selling the information had been her retribution? There was, from his point of view, a certain logic in that explanation. Drawing a deep breath, she sighed. What was the use of torturing herself with these questions? Although it mattered desperately to her now whether he had left her behind to be arrested or learned of it only on his return, no doubt if she never saw him again it would, in time, lose its importance. If she never saw him again—

She was a fool. To let herself be drawn step by step

231

into such a trap of love and hate—there was no other word for it. It was useless to blame Jean-Paul. She did not have to go back to the palacio when Grant was shot. She had gone of her own free will, driven by an impulse she had no wish to resist.

Where was her brother? What was he doing while the other men persuaded the woman he had loved to incriminate herself? He would not join them surely? His conception of honor was too nice to permit him to hurt any woman, much less one he had held in something more than affection. Would he, then, have felt obliged once more to come to her defense? If so, he could not hope to prevail, of course. Would he, could he, allow that to make any difference? And if not, was he lying unconscious somewhere, beaten, bruised, growing chill in the cool night air of the mountains? He was getting so thin and haggard; it would not be surprising if he succumbed to pneumonia in such conditions. Another thought gripped her. These men had little respect for human life. If he annoyed them too much they might kill him. She had heard no gun shots, but they all wore knives thrust into their boots.

Moving with care she placed her right hand on the metal ring upon her left and pushed, trying for the hundredth time to slip it down over her hand with the fingers turned in to make it as slim as possible. She could not ask the sick man beside her to get up so that she could look for Jean-Paul, and she could not lie there, guessing his whereabouts, not knowing.

It was no use, the ring was too snug, so snug, in fact, that she was certain the bracelet on the other end of the chain must be cutting into Luis's larger wrist.

The key, where was it hidden? Was it, perhaps, in the clothes piled so unceremoniously beside the mound of the bed? By stretching a little she might reach them.

Luis stirred. His arms about her tightened, drawing her nearer to him. The movement shifted the blanket from his shoulder and his hold grew rigid as he endured a paroxysm of shivering.

"Cold," he whispered.

Eleanora subsided. It was cruel to disturb him for what might, after all, be nothing. Turning her head, she stared out through the door at the dark gray anonymity of the night, lit feebly by a late-rising sliver of moon. Unmoving, she watched with burning eyes as that moon waned, giving way without grace to a cloudy dawn. Long before then the screaming had stopped. There was no other sound of life to take its place.

At last Luis woke, and releasing her, rolled to stretch out flat on his back.

"Luis?" she said, loud enough for him to hear but low enough not to wake him if he was still asleep.

After a minute he turned his head toward her, listening.

"Do you think—she is dead?"

"They would not go that far," he answered, speaking slowly, as if concentration was an effort. "She is too valuable a witness."

"Valuable to me, to Jean-Paul, but not to them."

"But if you are lost, *pequeña,* so is their hope of reinstatement lost."

"I am not certain that will matter much to anyone else but you."

"Not so," he insisted, but he made no attempt to convince her, and his voice held no conviction.

Whether from the necessity of an early start or simply because the others had not gone to bed, the camp stirred not long afterward. The horses were rounded up with a great deal of noise, and the smell of smoke and coffee and frying peccary rose into the air heavy with damp.

Luis, drawing on some store of inner strength, dragged himself from their bed and moved outside, where he sat down with his back to one of the poles of the porch. Sitting on his haunches before the fire, in a strain which caused considerable danger to the seams of his tightly filled breeches, Gonzalez had taken over the making of breakfast. Mixing cornmeal, he slapped out tortillas to wrap around fried peccary with a quickness and economy of movement which put Eleanora's efforts to shame. Slim, Kurt, and their guide, Molina, were already eating, standing about with their breakfast in their hands, washing it down with hot coffee. Jean-Paul was nowhere to be seen, but the sound of voices rang from the grassy savanna where they had left the horses.

Beyond the radiance of the fire's warmth the valley was filled with a layer of mist. It hovered closest over the lake, made thicker by the sullen smoke of a second fire near the edge of the water. There was movement among the mist, and Eleanora went still, straining her eyes to penetrate the swirling vapor. It was only deer, a pair of does, and a fawn, coming to drink.

The clop of horses' hooves moving at a slow walk heralded the arrival of Sanchez and Pablo. They led four horses, a pack animal and three mounts, on one of which rode Juanita. She slumped over the horse's neck, a pitiable figure with her face battered and swollen beyond recognition. Someone had thrown a blanket over her, but it had slipped down, exposing her blouse hanging in tatters about her neck and sticking in shreds to the lacerated and bloody flesh of her back. A rawhide lariat was tied about her waist and then around the horse with several hitches to hold her in place. Her eyes were closed, she may even have been unconscious. If she felt the pain that was hers, she gave no outward sign.

Biting the inside of her lip, Eleanora averted her eyes. Slim, moving with his loping stride, approached with a plate and two cups of coffee. She took the cup of hot liquid, but shook her head decisively at the food. Luis, accepting his cup, nodded at Juanita.

"She has signed the confession?"

"She has," the plainsman said grimly.

"You had better give her something to drink if you intend to get her back down to Granada."

"Coffee is all there is." Slim gave a laconic shrug, glancing at Eleanora from the corner of his eye.

"That will have to do then," Luis told him.

"Slim?" Eleanora said as the man began to turn away.

"Yes, ma'am?"

"My brother. Have you seen him?"

"You'll find him around on the side of the house, ma'am, where he went to puke up his guts after finishing

234

off the last bottle of my supply of rye. But I wouldn't advise you going to look. He ain't a pretty sight. He fell down around there, and we just let him lay until he gets through sleeping it off. It seemed the best thing, all things considered."

Eleanora dropped her gaze from the man's far-seeing gray-blue eyes with their hidden contempt. "Yes, I suppose it was."

Pablo, his sombrero sitting at a jaunty angle on his head, led the small procession out of the valley, pulling the pack-horse behind him. Next came Juanita, with Sanchez, his hatchet face grim, bringing up the rear. At some council she had not been aware of they had decided only two should return with the woman to Granada. Though good strategy, no doubt, the tactic did not speak very highly of their confidence in the mission, Eleanora thought as she watched them go. Would William Walker listen to them, or was Niña Maria's sway over him too great to allow him to undo what she had done? There was nothing they could do except wait and see. Staring down into the muddy grounds in the bottom of her cup, she could find no hope to support the waiting.

The rising sun climbed to the level of the mountain tops that ringed the valley, peering over them with a red and bleary eye. Its rays plumbed the mist, striking copper gleams across the surface of the lake, catching a last glimpse of the figures on horseback grown small with distance. The sun had turned the pale face of Kurt, as he squatted on his saddle beside the fire and watched Eleanora through narrowed eyes, a bright and unbecoming shade of carmine.

Eleanora turned to Luis. "You may as well come back in and lie down. There is nothing else to do."

He did not argue.

The first week passed quickly and without serious incident. It was pleasant in the valley, with warm days and cool nights. In other circumstances they might have been able to relax, even to lose some of their weariness.

There was little chance of their starving. Slim, taking a

235

pack-horse, went hunting, returning with venison for a welcome change from the peccary. Molina introduced wild berries and roots into their diet, though they drew the line at the iguana lizard he surprised nosing around the hut and wrestled to the ground. Much disappointed, he withdrew to the lakeside to cook and eat his prize alone.

Jean-Paul had survived the night of Juanita's torture in his own way. The liquor to continue in that manner was not available, but it did not seem necessary. He sat around with his hands dangling between his legs, doing nothing, seeing nothing. He did not talk unless addressed directly, and he hardly ate. Sometimes a look of unleashed horror would spring into his eyes, and he would jump up to walk bareheaded out across the valley, even in the glare of the midday sun, striding, breaking into a run as if pursued.

It was Slim who usually went after him. Jean-Paul came docilely enough, and even looked shame-faced for his behavior, but he would never explain his actions. More than once Eleanora tried to talk to him, but when he attended to her he would only look at her as if she had lost her senses.

Gonzalez, the rumbling of his belly overcoming an inherent laziness, took over the cooking. It was better than waiting for the few times when Luis was awake and Eleanora could prepare something to eat, for she refused to wake him and she could not, of course, manage such tasks on a two-foot chain from the inside of the hut while he rested.

Luis did not improve. His fever continued, though not as high as before. He would not allow her to look at the wound, a megrim he developed as his convalescence proved slow, but she thought the wound was healing satisfactorily on the outside. Still, his lack of vitality, his gray color, the fever, worried her. Carrying his pallet out upon the porch in the fresh air and sunshine seemed to help, though he did not progress, and as the first week ended and another began, she stood often on the porch, shading her eyes with her hand, praying for good news that would allow Luis to obtain the care of the military surgeon, Dr. Jones.

Kurt was another worry. When she was out of the adobe hut he followed her with his eyes, and when she was not he often took up a position at an angle opposite the open door where he could see inside to where she lay with Luis. As the days slipped by she grew more resigned to her chain and inclined to look upon it as the protection Luis intended. Though sometimes, when the Prussian's gaze fell on Luis, she felt a throat-tightening tremor of fear that would not let her rest.

The days of the second week stretched longer, eons of time echoing with nothing but her thoughts. Her mind followed Sanchez and Pablo to Granada, dwelling on the benefits of civilization, baths, fine food, changes of clothing, hair ribbons and combs, scented soap and hairbrushes, all of which the two Nicaraguans were most unlikely to understand as advantages. She thought of them being ushered into Grant's presence, of seeing him, speaking to him, of giving him information of her if he should ask. At times like these jealousy gripped her, coupled with a vast impatience that made her want to saddle a horse and ride alone, if need be, through the countryside to Granada. Danger seemed to matter little against the desperation of her need to know what was happening.

In the effort to shake off such disturbing thoughts, she let her thoughts roam further afield, across the lake and down the river to San Juan del Norte and beyond the gulf to New Orleans. It would be basking now in the warm sun and marvelous fecundity of the semi-tropics, yet with a delicious wine-coolness in the air. Mardi Gras would be over. The flowers, the briar roses, winter jasmine, and Chinese camellias thrown down upon the marching, masked young gallants would have been long swept into the gutters. The austerity of Lent would be upon the city, perhaps, with much fasting and wearing of somber colors and visiting of the cemeteries. The ladies of the large houses along Royal Street, and in the Garden District where the Americans were building their mansions, would be thinking of shutting up their houses

237

for the summer and moving to their plantations in the country, to the resort at White Sulphur Springs, or even as far north as Saratoga. That life seemed so uncomplicated, so free of worry, that she wondered that she had ever been a part of it. It seemed impossible at the moment that she could ever be a part of it again.

Sometimes, as she felt the pressure of acting confident and certain of the outcome of Pablo's and Sanchez's mission, she would think of Mazie and the troupe of actors. What were they doing? Were they carrying on in their makeshift theater despite the almost certain advent of war, or had they gone, taking the steamer for New Orleans?

What had Mazie thought when she heard of her arrest? She could not have believed in her guilt. And hearing of her escape, did the actress ever wonder how she was and what had become of her?

How did the hospital fare? This thought also exercised her mind. Had the young, tow-headed Southerner been released? Was the standard of cleanliness she had established being maintained, or if it were possible for her to return, would what she had accomplished have to be done over again? Conceit, to think that they could not go on as well without her. She was not irreplaceable. She had, doubtless, contributed a certain amount of good, but Dr. Jones could and would go on healing the sick and maimed without her, sending them back as tools of greater or lesser strength for Walker's purpose.

Ambition, war, conquest. The importance of these things eluded her. At this time peace, safety, and solitude were much more ardently to be desired.

As the second week drew to a close without the reappearance of the two men, the situation began to look grave. It was decided that someone must go to Granada to discover, if he could, what had happened to Sanchez and Pablo. It was possible the bureaucratic workings of the Nicaraguan government had delayed their return, but if there was some other explanation it would be better if they knew.

The obvious choice for the journey was Molina. His

passage would be more swift and certain, and with his dark Indian face, he would be less apt to catch the eye of an officer on the lookout for deserters.

He made ready that same evening, using a saddle and horse stripped down for hard and fast riding. He saluted them with a raised hand, swung his horse around, and galloped from the valley. But despite such bravado there lurked at the back of his eyes the same uneasy fear which threatened them all.

Four days and three nights he was gone. He returned at a clattering run in the twilight of the fourth day. Dismounting before his horse had come to a full stop, he strode into the adobe hut while Eleanora was still getting to her feet.

Sweeping off his sombrero, he knelt beside Luis. A layer of dust caked his face and shoulders, sifting in a fine powder from the brim of his hat to the floor. It was caught on the tips of his lashes, and it turned to mud on his lips as he moistened them to speak.

"Lieutenant Colonel, we must ride. The woman, Juanita, is dead. Before they reached Granada she tried to take the gun of Sanchez while he slept. They struggled and she was shot. Walker and the main body of the Falangistas have marched once more on Rivas where a great battle rages at this moment. The *puta* of the little general now commands in his place in the city. This was what Pablo and Sanchez found when they presented themselves, Conde. The confession of Juanita was thrown into the fire unread, or so they say in the streets, and the men who brought it were put to the torture so that they might reveal the hiding place of the others who rode with them. I do not know if they did so, but few can withhold the knowledge they possess when presented to the pincers, the whip, the red-hot coal. Death would be allowed to release these men from their pain only after they had given up the information sought. Pablo and Sanchez were shot in the plaza three days ago."

In the sudden breathless silence, Eleanora stared at Molina. Stern-faced Sanchez and lucky Pablo. Tortured. Shot.

Luis put out his hand so that Molina could help him

239

sit up, and then a sound jarred upon their ears, cutting across the tense air with the jagged persistence of a dull knife. It was Jean-Paul, standing in the doorway, holding to the frame for support as he was racked by a harsh and hurtful laughter.

Sixteen

A month is a long time. Hours, days, weeks, it passes with exquisite slowness when spent in constant movement coupled with the effort of concealment. Tiredness and irritability do not make the time go faster, nor do the strain of worry and the monotony of eating the same things prepared in the same manner. It was not a pleasant group which Molina led from the valley. It was even less so when a month of days had come and gone.

The smell of woodsmoke had ceased to be appetizing, and the inevitable bits of trash, the feel of grit between the teeth, had long ago lost their novelty, becoming subjects of endless grumbling. The loss of one of the horses to bloat before they left the valley proved a major inconvenience, especially to the lightest in weight of their number, Eleanora, who had to ride double with Luis on the strongest mount. Uncertainty as to whether or not they were being pursued preyed on their nerves. Small accidents loomed as major disasters, reasons for blame and recriminations, while disaster was accepted with a hopeless calm. Minor indispositions were used as an excuse for a halt by some, in contrast to Luis who, though seriously ill, would permit nothing less than death to slow them. Both attitudes, carping or stoic, could not fail to irritate the sensibilities of some among them.

They continued north and east, winding among the hills and valleys, crossing countless small streams, sometimes following Indian and animal trails, at other times striking out to make their own. The terrain became less rugged, flowing into a series of rolling plateaus. They left the pine-scented coolness of the mountains behind them, descending once more into heat and rain. The hardwoods gave way to more tropical vegetation, to rubber trees and palms flaunting their greenness against the blue sky, and the fragile-looking toughness of tree ferns standing knee-deep in a lush carpet of some small, pink trailer without a name.

It was in the rain forest that a mysterious disease struck the rest of the horses. It caused their hooves to rot, falling away layer by layer until they could not walk for the pain. There was no remedy. Not even Molina with his animal lore and his faith in the curative powers of roots and Indian medicines could find an alternative to shooting them. The Indian, however, could see no valid reason for not benefiting by their misfortune to the extent of adding horsemeat to their larder. But like the iguana, he was left to eat his supper of horse's haunch alone. Not even Gonzalez could be persuaded to join him.

"So what do we do?" Slim asked, voicing the question that hovered unspoken in the warm, humid air. They sat around a fire lit to take the dampness from their clothes and hold at bay the swarms of gnats and mosquitoes that blackened the air. The sun had not yet gone down but it was already twilight beneath the canopy of tree limbs overhead. Shadows of giant moths moved ghostlike in the dimness, and among the leaves now and then there gleamed twin spots of light, the eyes of small, shy monkeys catching the light of the fire.

Luis, lying on the ground on a blanket-stretcher they had improvised with poles during the afternoon to carry him, looked up. "We go on, of course," he said sharply.

"Even I am smart enough to figure that out," the plainsman said in a mild tone. "We're not going to be able to go wandering in this kind of a jungle forever, though. Sooner or later we're all going to come down with some kind of swamp fever, and that will be the end of it. It looks to me like the sooner we get out of this, the sooner we get to some kind of town, the better off we'll be."

"A town is too risky," Kurt said, turning his broad face toward Slim from where he leaned against a tree.

"And this isn't?" Slim queried with a gesture toward the dark forest around them. "Tomorrow we will be tramping through snakes and scorpions and spiders. And if you think you have ticks and chigger bites now, just wait until you have waded through some of this greenery on foot. On top of that, most of these creeks we've been wading across are just swimming with blood-sucking leeches. Besides, if Walker is in as much trouble as I think he is with the Hondurans and the Costa Ricans, the phalanx is going to have its hands full without worrying about us, eh, Molina?"

"This may be true, señor," the Indian agreed, nodding.

Kurt threw up his hand. "Wait a minute. I've been giving this some thought too, and it looks to me like the best plan would be for some of us to go on ahead, get through as fast as possible, and send help back for the others."

"You mean leave Luis—and Eleanora—behind?"

Flicking a glance at Eleanora, the Prussian licked his lips. "Not precisely."

"The idea has merit," Luis intervened, his gaze focused somewhere beyond Slim's left shoulder.

"For one man, it does," Slim said, "that one man being Kurt. Forget it. You know splitting up is the worse thing we could do. It would weaken both parties."

Seated on the corner of Luis's blanket, Eleanora was, perhaps, more aware of the tension in his slender frame than any of the others. It was communicated through the chain that bound them like some metallic lifeline, a slight vibration perceptible through the nerves of the skin but not to the naked eye.

"I may prove something more of an impediment than you envision," the gaunt man, bearded now like the rest and who had once been their leader, pointed out.

"We will manage."

"But yes," Molina added, his eyes respectfully averted. Gonzalez, standing to one side, nodded. Kurt's face remained stiff with impassive disapproval. Looking to her brother, Eleanora saw he was not attending. With studious attention he was cleaning his fingernails with a knife point, removing the dirt from under them and around the cuticles with all the care he had once used as a New Orleans dandy.

When no more arguments were presented, Slim looked

at Molina. "Well, this is your country. How do you say we go?"

The Indian dropped to one knee on the ground, and with the flat of his hand, cleared a space, pushing aside the leaf mold and loose dirt. A few quick lines, and he had drawn a map that showed the funnel shape of Nicaragua with the double ovals of the two big lakes, Managua and Nicaragua, in place low on the left, and the snaking saw-teeth of the mountains they had crossed on a diagonal above them. Another crooked line represented the San Juan River, and then in the wide, open space of the un-explored territory between the mountains and the gulf, the Nicaraguan drew another line, tapping it with his finger-nail. "The Rio Escondido," he said. "She flows from far in the north, two hundred, maybe three hundred miles, to the lagoon called Bluefields on the gulf. If we follow it, sometimes on foot, sometimes on the raft we will build, we too must come to the gulf. It is not the Mosquito Coast, but the British ships patrol here also."

"And if we didn't spot a ship right off, we could always move up the coast toward Mosquito country," Slim said.

"That is true, señor."

"Luis?" the plainsman asked, deferring to the other man.

"It sounds well," he replied.

It did indeed sound well, but it was not that easy. They had first to reach the river, a march of several days attended by all the evils Slim had so carefully pointed out. Arriving, they had no tools other than knives with which to build a raft, and felling the trees by burning them about the bases proved a laborious process. Vines as a means of lashing the logs together were much less satisfactory than the cheapest rope. And the green wood, heavy with sap, floated low and sluggish in the water.

Eleanora, though she spelled Gonzalez as cook so that he might lend his strength to the project, could do little else. Luis would not hear of her foraging in the forest around them, much less release her to do so. She was forced to sit idle, watching the men work, though Luis would, on occasion, allow her to search for grubs to use for fish bait, hobbling to the river to watch her fish. He was able to do no more as yet, and watching his brooding discontent with his continuing weakness was worse for Eleanora than idleness. Or perhaps not. In idleness she had too much time to think of the phalanx engaging the Costa Ricans. That battle must be over now at Rivas. How had it gone? More importantly, how had it gone for Colonel Grant Farrell? It seemed that she must know, must feel instinctively, if he had been killed or injured, but she placed no confidence in such intuition.

Rapids, shallows, rocks, sand bars, broken and lost poles; everything seemed to have united to slow the progress of the raft. At one point it appeared best to abandon the idea in favor of walking along the riverbank, but the sighting of a raft of alligators and a black, yellow-speckled snake longer than a man scotched that idea in a hurry.

Still, they did not stay in one place for long. In fits and starts, they descended the long, treacherous, muddy Escondido. Day by day it grew ever more lush with vines and flowers, more alive with the raucous calls of parrots and the tiny trillings of small birds with the appearance of chickadees. And then in the middle of an afternoon when everyone dozed in exhaustion on the slimy, water-soaked logs, with the exception of the two whose turn it was to pole, the banks of the river receded and they floated gently into the salt-flavored waters of Bluefields Lagoon.

They had clams for supper, small, succulent mollusks, steamed in the yellow-brown sand of the beach. Lulled by the unceasing caress of the turquoise gulf upon the sand, they slept and did not wake until the sun was high, and the sea gulls, looking for carrion along the beach, found them.

The gulls could not be blamed for their mistake; they were not a prepossessing sight. Their hair was matted with dirt and perspiration. One by one Eleanora had lost her pins, and in an effort to control her long mane, had dragged it back to plait it into one long braid. That braid, not renewed in weeks, had taken on the packed and fuzzy appearance of wool. Dirt was ingrained in their hands and faces, a smudged, gray film that did not quite cover the red welts of mosquito bites or the myriad cuts and scratches they all carried in various stages of infection.

Beneath the dinginess, their skin was burned by the sun to the color of tanned leather, and with much the same texture. Upon their bodies they had other peculiar patches of reddened skin where the sun had reached through the tears and rents in their clothing. Shirts, blouses, skirts, and breeches, the colors were practically unrecognizable from the fading effects of the sun, the soiling, and the pervasive stenciling of gray mildew. The weakening effects of the latter had also caused the materials to tear more easily so that the hems of the men's breeches and Eleanora's skirt hung in tatters. Her slippers had long fallen apart as the stitching rotted, and she had constructed new footwear using layers of blanket tied about her feet and ankles with pieces of vine. These makeshift boots protected the bottom of her feet, but they had left her toes comically bare. The boots of the men, made for rough usage, had fared somewhat better, but these, like every other piece of leather they had with them, cartridge belts, suspender ends, and even Luis's leather breeches, had grown a thick, fuzzy layer of gray-green mildew.

The river trip had had one positive effect, however. The time it had taken and the relative ease compared to riding horseback had allowed Luis to gain strength. When the time came to break camp, he was now able to discard the stretcher and walk along the beach with the rest, as long as he had the aid of a long, crotched stick. As they trudged, they stared out over the heaving blue waves of the gulf, but the line of the horizon stretched without hindrance, meeting the sky cleanly, without the clutter of sails or the black plume of a smokestack.

One other problem plagued them. It was water. They had with them three filled canteens, and the problem was not immediate, but what little water they came across was either muddy or brackish. It was disheartening to think that they might be forced inland before a ship was sighted. As if every league they covered increased the chances of their being picked up, Slim, striding at the point quickened the pace. And seeing Luis still did not falter, he quickened it again.

As the second day of walking along the treacherous sands that dragged at their every footstep passed, Eleanora felt a creeping futility. In the rain forest she had been too frightened, too worried for apathy, but with rescue near, with Luis improving daily, she could feel her strength and her will leaving her, draining away into the hot, blistering sand. The silver glare of the sun, reflected from the dancing wavelets of the gulf, pierced her eyes, shafting into her skull. She had to watch her steps with exaggerated care, compensating for an increasing tendency to stagger. Nor did she want to fall behind, becoming a drag on Luis. He had enough to do just holding himself erect without adding her weight. Good intentions were not enough, however, to keep her on her feet. Toward evening her knees began to sag, and sinking down upon the sand, she held her head in her hands.

"Eleanora," Luis said urgently. "Are you ill?"

"I don't think so," she answered, and was surprised at the weakness of her voice. "I just can't take another step."

"You are sure that is all, you are certain?" he insisted, scanning her face with an anxious gaze, noting the shadows like bruises beneath her eyes, the too-prominent cheekbones, and the pulse pounding in the golden-smooth fragility of her throat.

"I will be fine when I have rested," she said, and hearing the trace of coolness in her tone, he did not press her further.

She lay with her forearm over her eyes, trying to blot out the all-too-familiar voices of the men around her. For an instant she was so tired of them, of their constant presence, of the lack of privacy, and most of all, of the jangling chain that marked her arm with an almost uneradicable reddish-brown stain from its crusting of rust. When Luis handed her supper of baked turtle eggs to her, she turned away, moving the utmost length of the chain from him. Such a revulsion of feeling would not last long, but for the moment she felt if he pressed her, if he touched her, she would scream.

After a time the wash of the waves soothed her, and scooping a hollow in the sand for her body, she slept.

A whispering scuffle of sound brought her awake. She lay still with her eyes closed for a moment, waiting for it

246

to be repeated, then little by little she lifted her lids, peering through the slits.

The surf had fallen to a soft murmur. The blue-black waters spread as nearly still as they ever came. Upon their surface lay a phosphorescent path, and at the far end of it stood the fleeing moon, looking over its shoulder. In that light, the brown sand of the beach had taken on the glitter of gold dust. It lay heaped and piled, massed riches waiting to be plundered. The quiet was tense, echoing with that careful stealthiness which had awakened her.

Abruptly she opened her eyes wide. A man was crawling over the sand toward her, his face less than a yard from hers. The light of the moon turned his hair to silver-gilt and winked along the honed edge of the knife he clutched in his hand, leaving the sockets of his eyes in darkness. It was Kurt. In the instant of time in which they stared at each other across the space of golden sand, Eleanora realized his purpose; to kill the man sleeping behind her.

Without waiting for her reaction the Prussian levered himself to his hands and knees with bared teeth, preparing to lunge across her. She drew in her breath to scream.

A shot exploded at her shoulder. The knife slithered from Kurt's grasp as with a strangled yell he grabbed at the spouting hole in his throat. The impact of the lead flung him back. He collapsed, shuddered once, and was still.

Before Eleanora could move the night was alive with gunfire, with shouts and orders and the sound of running feet. From the scrubby and twisted trees beyond the line of dunes that marked high tide, soldiers ran with bayonets fixed on guns held at the ready. There was no time to decide whether to fight their way free or declare themselves noncombatants. They were surrounded, staring up at their captors.

When nothing moved, and quiet had fallen, an officer, a zambo of mixed Indian and Negro blood, dressed in white with gold epaulettes, stepped from among the trees and walked gingerly across the sand with his breeches legs held high. He flicked a glance over their dishevelment, smothered a yawn, and then said in a clipped British accent, "You are under arrest, in the name of the ruler of the sovereign kingdom of Mosquito."

"This woman," Luis said with a trace of Castilian arrogance in his tone, "is my prisoner. She is the mistress, and a much-beloved one, to the second in command—second only to General Walker—of the army of Nicaragua. It was my intention to hold her for ransom. Colonel Farrell will reward handsomely the man who can return her to him—unharmed." He shrugged. "Unfortunately, my men and I lost our way. That is the way of it, is it not?"

The commandant of the outpost to which they had been taken leaned back in his chair, the stare he turned in Eleanora's direction frankly skeptical. She could not blame him. After being marched at bayonet point for what had seemed like at least a hundred miles, they had reached this slattern collection of thatched shacks which had the look of a barracoon, a place where slaves might have been held in other days, the slaves that had eventually become absorbed into the community of the Indian kingdom of Mosquito. They had been thrown into a hut which had all the size and fetid smell of a privy. Inside were no accommodations for sleeping, not even space for them all to lie down, and barely room to sit. They had not been fed since lunch the day before, and before sunup the interrogations had begun. One by one they were taken away until only Luis and Eleanora were left. Now it was their turn.

"The man you killed," the zambo commandant said, playing with the pen on his desk, "attacked you for the sake of this reward?"

"He did."

"And what do you say?" he asked Eleanora, rounding on her unexpectedly.

It would not do to uphold Luis too strictly she thought, aware of the doubt that still lingered in the commandant's eyes. "I am not certain," she said, her tone soft. "He—may have had other plans."

He nodded briefly, letting his eyes run disparagingly down her slender frame. They rested for a moment on the slimness of her waist and the chain about her wrist before he swung abruptly back to Luis. "You were a Falangista, were you not?"

"I was."

"But you decided taking the colonel's woman was better than taking the general's shilling?"

Luis allowed himself a smile. "It seemed a more promising way of mending my fortunes."

Picking up a palm-leaf fan, the commandant waved it languidly. To Eleanora he said, "What is your name?"

"Eleanora Colette Villars," she told him, unconsciously raising her chin.

"Oh, yes. One has heard of you. The newspapers, you know? One must keep up with the enemy. It is possible," he continued reflectively, "that you might make a valuable hostage. It just might be possible."

"I do assure—" Luis began.

The commandant, his voice suddenly brisk, cut across his words. "You realize that the kingdom of Mosquito does not recognize the Democrático regime in Nicaragua?"

"Yes, but—"

"We are allied with the Legitimistas. You will, therefore, consider yourselves political prisoners. That is all."

It would have been unwise to argue with the bayonets of the guards. Luis stepped back, and with a stiff, somewhat awkward bow, allowed himself to be led away, with Eleanora, of necessity, at his side.

"Thank you for what you tried to do," she said as the door of the hut was closed upon them once more.

Though Luis did not look at her, he caught her hand, gripping it tightly in his own. "Let us hope it is enough to buy for us a little time, and let us pray that it was not too much."

They received an indication that his effort might be bearing fruit that evening. Two men, bearing an anvil, a hammer, and a chisel, entered their prison. Their intention was plain, and giving way to the inevitable, Luis took the key from a chain about his neck and unlocked the rusty manacles. Watching his bent head as he worked over her wrist, Eleanora wondered at his foresight. The key had not been around his neck before. All the chain

249

had held was a gold religious medallion which she had seen often. Where had it been hidden?—not that it mattered. It was only that it was less painful to worry about a key than about the future.

A further hint of the impression they had made on the commandant was the quality of the food served to them at dinner that evening. But the greatest evidence was manifested early the next morning. Toward dawn there was a commotion in the town. A ship had dropped anchor offshore, they learned from the guard, and a short while later they saw through the cracks of the hut the arrival of a detachment of men in the uniforms of the British Navy, including an officer of high rank. The commandant of the small post greeted the visitors beneath the Mosquito flag in the center of the clearing, and escorted them with much deference and ceremony into his quarters.

The British conclave left within the hour, none of them so much as glancing at the hut where Eleanora and the men were imprisoned. Whether as a result of this meeting, as they suspected, or simply because they had been with the Democrático party, a short time later Eleanora and the former Falangistas were led from their hut, loaded into a bullock cart, and driven north under a mounted and armed guard numbering twenty or more toward the Honduran border.

They were not told where they were going. They could speculate, of course, but no more. Even that did not serve for long to beguile the tedium of the jolting journey.

After a time Eleanora turned to Luis. "Why do you suppose the British came this morning? What is their stake in all this?"

"Their reasoning is based on distrust," Luis replied with a slight smile. "Like two strong men facing a weakling with a cake in his possession, neither trusts the other to keep hands off. Britain doesn't want to see the United States add Central America to its territory, and the United States has no stomach for seeing this valuable isthmus fall into British control. According to the treaty signed a couple of years ago, neither is supposed to interfere with Nicaragua and the workings of free enterprise. Nothing is ever that simple. The British see an American gaining sway in a Central American country, and as a counterbalance they support his enemies, in this case, the Hondurans. Then, you can't discount Vanderbilt's influence in England. He wants Walker toppled—and money makes a very good lever if you know where to place it. He has spent a great deal of time, and money, in England in the last few years. Then, money means little when revenge drives a man of wealth."

"And so the British, for purely political reasons, have advised the Mosquito commandant to turn us over to the enemy," she said bitterly.

"That's only a guess," he reminded her. "And even if it's so, when we explain who we are we may find the Hondurans most hospitable."

Eleanora sent him a wan smile, but her fears were by no means stilled.

The Honduran prison had once been a Spanish fortress with projecting conical lookout towers that faced the sea. Its thick stone walls crumbling now, it was still impressive, dominating the small town behind it.

They saw no official before being admitted. They were met by a detail of Legitimista soldiers in blue tunics with red facings. Despite the smell of stale *aguardiente* about them, the Lebel rifles and cartridge belts they carried were most menacing. At bayonet point, they were marched through heavy, iron-studded wooden doors, and without stopping, pushed down a dark corridor, musty with the smell of old limestone and uncleaned drains, to a common room.

Though large, with a high ceiling rising to darkness unreached by the light from small windows far above the floor, the room was overcrowded. People, men and women numbering perhaps two hundred, lay everywhere, their sharp faces, avid with curiosity, turned toward the door. Seeing the numbers of healthy men among the new arrivals, they turned away with their talonlike fingers clenching and unclenching in feral disappointment. Eleanora glanced at Luis, seeing in the flaring of his nostrils and the tightness of his lips an echo of what she suspected. They would not be attacked now, while they presented a united front with such small prospect of reward, but what little of value they possessed would be stripped from them bit by bit as soon as they could be separated.

These were not ordinary prisoners. From the length of the men's beards and the state of the clothes they wore, she guessed that they had been incarcerated here for many years. Their faces mirrored only the most primitive of emotions; hate, fear, jealousy, and in the men, something that was even more disturbing, naked lust.

As the door clanged shut behind them, Slim leaned toward Luis. "What do you say we take ourselves one of those little rooms?"

Eleanora saw at once what he meant. Along one wall there were several doorless cubicles. Though small, they represented the only possible security. For the moment, they were a comparatively strong group. There could be no better time than now for what Slim proposed. This was not an occasion for sentiment or the recognition of rights. Such emotions were a liability here. They must take what they could while they had the strength.

With Luis limping in front, they moved in a body toward the last cell on the end at the far side of the common room. The skirmish with the occupants, a pair of ferociously bearded men and their paramours, was brief.

Nursing his hand where one of the women had bitten him, Molina looked around. "Very nice," he said. "Better than our last—"

"—Our last accommodation?" Luis finished. "Yes, I must agree. We will have to remember to thank them for their—hospitality."

Though they could not all sleep on the bare stone shelf across the back, they could at least all be seated. This proved a definite advantage, since there was nothing to do but sit. By standing on the sleeping shelf they could peer out of the tiny, barred window set high in the wall, but there was nothing to be seen. The view was of a large, empty square enclosed by a stone wall. The light from the window was welcome during the day, making a pleasant dimness within the cell, but at night, because the torches could not reach their closed-in space, it was terrifyingly dark. And by some odd quirk of acoustics, the screams and cries, the grunts and moans and other

252

bestial sounds of the natural and unnatural acts being committed outside in the common room, were funneled through their cell multiplied ten times over.

Before they had been in the prison a week they had learned to live with other sounds and their meanings, such as the clatter that heralded the coming of the two meals they were served a day. They knew when to stand back out of range of the guard's bayonets, and when to surge forward to get their fair share of the food. They discovered who was considered to be the leader among the other prisoners, and what the rules, such as they were, consisted of. They came to the conclusion that as long as the four weakest members of their group remained in or near the cubicle, letting the two strongest, Slim and Gonzalez, bring their food, they were safe. This arrangement was made with so little discussion that it was several days before Eleanora, the person most benefited, was aware of it. It was done so quietly and matter-of-factly that it was difficult for her to comment on it, much less voice her gratitude.

"Don't try," Luis said in one of their rare moments of conversation while they took their exercise walking up and down outside their cell. "Not one of them will admit why they are taking such care not to leave you alone. Oh, they know, of course, but they will not admit it. Molina will say it is because you did not laugh when he ate the iguana, Gonzalez because you praised his cooking, and Slim perhaps because you remind him of his sister who died long ago. They will say it is because you cooked for them, smiled at them without teasing, did not scream at snakes and leeches, and took the splinters and thorns from their fingers with your long nails. All that will not be lies, and yet there is more. It may be that which the young soldier felt in you who called you an angel—a thing enhanced by your beauty though it does not depend upon it, a bright steadfastness that in a man might be called shining courage."

"You flatter me, as always," she said huskily, trying to smile.

"That is not possible," he replied, and taking her arm, turned her gently back toward the safety of their cubicle.

More than all else, they learned to watch for the gray-haired priest, Father Sebastian, and to dread his arrival of an evening, for his prayers and his blessing unerringly marked the man he chose to give to them for death at dawn. For that, they discovered, was the use of the square which their cell overlooked. It was there, in its hot emptiness, that those whom Father Sebastian blessed were executed.

Time, in that place of constant torchlight, had no meaning. After so many calendarless days, they had little idea whether April was on the wane or May had already begun. Asking the other prisoners proved futile; they had even less idea. Money might have extracted the information from the guards, but of the few pesos they held between them there was none to spare for such luxurious knowledge. It may have been two weeks or three that they had been guests of the Hondurans, when a disturbance at the main door of the common room caught their attention. It was not mealtime, being only midafternoon, nor was it time for Father Sebastian. Glancing at Luis and Slim with a raised eyebrow, Molina sauntered to the doorway to take a look, his hands on his hips. Suddenly he was still.

"What is it?" Luis called. "New arrivals?"

"You might say so," Molina answered cryptically, swinging back into the room to stand with his back to the wall, arms akimbo.

Gonzalez, in a corner, was matching Jean-Paul in an endless game of odds-and-evens with their share of the food for stakes. Eleanora had been playing a form of tic-tac-toe in the gritty sand on the floor with Luis. She glanced at him to see resignation come into his face, and then she turned toward the door.

Two men, backed by a pair of armed guards, shouldered into the tiny room. One wore the white-corded epaulettes of an officer in the Legitimista army, an older man whose grizzled mutton-chop whiskers grew to meet his mustache. The other man towered above him, a broad-shouldered giant in civilian clothes with sandy blond hair and pale blue eyes.

"Major Crawford!" Eleanora exclaimed, getting to her feet.

The other man did not answer. He turned to the Honduran. "That is the Villars woman and her brother, and one of Walker's officers. These others I don't know."

"Very good," the officer replied. Without another word they turned and left, leaving the silence of dismay behind them.

Seventeen

Major Neville Crawford. Traitor, spy, and Vanderbilt agent. Why had she never guessed? It seemed so obvious now. There had been Mazie's surprise aboard the *Daniel Webster* at his becoming a soldier, and his indiscreet admission of money as the motive. She must have realized that to a man who spoke as he did, the few hundred acres of land he might expect to gain would not mean wealth. Mazie's guarded attitude should have warned her. The actress, a woman of experience, must have had her suspicions, though she could not have been certain or she would have mentioned them to someone. On second thought, this was not necessarily true. Mazie had little reason to love the Walker regime. Eleanora thought that she knew Mazie well enough to suppose that she would have come forward for her sake—if there had been time. There had not, and so speculation was useless.

Dimly, Eleanora remembered another conversation she had overheard between the actress and the major. Mazie had warned him to take care in his dealings with Niña Maria. Had the meetings between him and Walker's mistress been something more than social occasions? Had they, perhaps, been trysts between fellow conspirators? Who better than the aristocratic Niña Maria to filch information from the papers of the American Phalanx? Such a valuable position as hers must be protected at all cost, of course. Juanita, Jean-Paul, herself, even Grant and his career, could be sacrificed with impunity. There was a certain rightness in discovering a more valid reason than

255

petty jealousy for her own implication in this mess. What seemed suddenly monstrous was the use to which Juanita had been put, and the lack of protection she had received for her service.

The urge to prove her theories was irresistible. "Slim?" Eleanora spoke in a voice she thought low enough to escape attention. "Juanita's confession. What did she say? How was it worded?"

Slim, sitting some small distance along the sleeping shelf with his head tilted back against the stone wall, turned slowly in her direction. "Why?"

"It isn't idle curiosity," she said quickly, and outlined her reasons.

Slim shook his head. "There was nothing like that. She confessed to being the sister of a young boy who was killed at the battle of Virgin Bay. She said that she first took up with your brother because she thought she could persuade him to bring her papers and reports from the colonel's desk. She urged him to get close to you again for that reason. But she decided later that he had too many principles to do what she wanted, and so she never asked him; she just did it herself."

"She didn't mention Niña Maria at all?"

"Nope. She cleared your name, made it sound like she was working by herself, getting even on account of her brother being killed by the phalanx. That was all."

Niña Maria did not deserve such loyalty, for despite the lack of evidence Eleanora could see no other explanation for the facts as she perceived them. She looked away, her gaze falling by accident upon her brother's pale face. Something in his stillness dragged at her attention. Looking closer, she saw in the light of afternoon falling clear through the window the tears of silent pain.

The day wore on. The men dropped their games, their banter and drawling anecdotes. They sat quietly talking, and when by chance their eyes would meet, they would each let their gaze slip away, afraid of what the other would see hidden there. Occasionally Slim would get up and lounge to the door. Ignoring the obscenities hurled at him, he would stand, quartering the common room with his far-seeing eyes. Sometimes he would take a few steps beyond the door, standing with his head up, like a deer scenting danger. But after all his prowling he always returned to join the others in their inescapable, interminable waiting.

Father Sebastian, his shoulders bent beneath the black linen of his cassock, came at sunset. His sandals made a soft scuffing sound on the floor as he made his way across the room. The prisoners gave way in the gladness of reprieve before him as his rheumy old eyes failed to seek theirs. Louder and louder the scuffing grew until it seemed to reverberate through the cell. The pulse of the room quickened. Slim, standing straight, turned slowly toward the door. Jean-Paul raised his head, while Molina and Gonzalez shared a searching glance. Luis put aside Eleanora's hand, which he had been toying with, and got slowly to his feet. As the old man appeared in the opening, he bowed. "Good evening, Father," he said quietly. "We have been expecting you."

Confession, absolution, their sins were heard with compassion, and absolved with a trembling dignity that was much more comforting than the hurried and pompous grace of a cathedral prelate.

"Not you, my daughter," Father Sebastian said whenever Eleanora stepped forward, but at her softly murmured pleas he acquiesed.

And when he was done at last, Luis touched his arm. "One thing more, Father, if I may trespass upon your goodness?"

"Yes, my son?"

"I wish you to perform the rites of marriage between myself and this lady."

As he spoke, Luis reached for Eleanora's hand, drawing her close against his side. She stared at him with wide eyes, her mind curiously blank.

"The lady wishes to be wed?" the old priest asked.

Luis turned to her, catching both her hands in his. "Do not refuse me this, Eleanora, I implore. It is a small thing that will mean so much. Allow me to know for this short time that you belong to me, and to offer you what protection there may be in my name. I know I should have broached it earlier, but you might have refused me from

257

pride or from reasons of the heart that mean little to me. But now I ask it without shame as my final request of you, my soul. Woll you be my wife for this night?"

How could she deny him? Even if she could have found the words, the will was not there. "You do me great honor," she whispered, meeting the tenderness of his brown eyes without subterfuge. "Yes, I will marry you."

The ceremony was, perforce, a simple one. Their combined names echoed around the stone chamber. Luis's signet, bearing the coat-of-arms of his family, slid heavy and warm from the heat of his body over her finger. Their responses were low, and glazed with a seriousness that was unavoidable. Eleanora knelt to receive the blessing of Father Sebastian with her senses steeped in unreality. Her mind refused to grapple with what she was doing and the reasons for it. Tomorrow was a distant time without meaning. For now the present was enough. The sand on the floor grated beneath her knees, the feel of Luis's hand was firm on hers, the torchlight through the doorway flickered as it shone on the white hair of the priest, the shuffling of their audience both inside the cell and beyond it made a quiet background to the solemnity of the moment.

And then it was over. There was a moment of awkwardness after Father Sebastian had gone. Jean-Paul stepped forward to banish it with a grave smile. "Happiness," he said and embraced her, kissing her ceremoniously on each cheek.

"And you," she said, clinging to his arm a moment longer than was necessary, her eyes on his face, knowing all the while that he too had received Father Sebastian's blessing. Slim shook Luis's hand and claimed a hug from Eleanora. Gonzalez and Molina contented themselves with a bow, and a salute upon her fingers. Then, as by some prearrangement, they filed with exaggerated casualness from the cubicle.

Frowning, Eleanora stared after them. Aware, as always, of her feelings, Luis took her arm, leading her toward the sleeping shelf. "Don't worry, *pequeña*. They will guard the door, and then, perhaps, if the women of the common room are kind and the omens are favorable, they may seek for themselves that which comes closer to immortality than anything found in war by warriors."

She had grown used to lying beside Luis, used to the feel of his hands upon her body. For the sake of the safety of sleeping next to him, she had gladly endured the bruising force of his frustration at his inability to possess her. This night was different only in that she surrendered to his will, withholding nothing of herself from him. His kiss did not warm and excite her, did not, as Grant's did, command a response she was powerless to withhold, but it was so sweetly tender that she longed to give him surcease. She followed his guiding, holding him, moving in accommodation in an agony of tension. He drew her closer, ever closer, the circle of his arms tightening until the breath was crushed from her lungs. Her face was rasped and her mouth scorched from his bearded lips. His fingers, cruel with desperation, held her to him, until she could not help the small moan of pain that escaped her.

He released her at once. Burying his face in the hollow of her throat he lay still until their breathing quieted. At last he murmured, "I burn for you, Eleanora. In my mind I taste the rapture of your giving. I want you beyond my dearest hope of heaven."

"Oh, Luis," she whispered, pressing her hand to his bare shoulder. "I wish—"

"No. Don't." He raised his head, his eyes shadowed in the dimness. "It may be that it was wrong of me to expect the good Lord to grant all my prayers. It is sacrilege to press desire upon an angel."

"Please, not that." Eleanora forced the words through the constriction in her throat.

"You are so beautiful," he went on, gently drawing his fingers down across her shoulder to the swell of her breast. "It may be that it is best, for the good of my soul, that I do not profane what I feel for you. Kiss me, then, sweet angel, and tell me that you care for me, even if it is a lie."

She reached up to still that last word upon his lips. "I do love you," she said, her voice breaking a little. "Please believe me." And it was not an untruth. There was a part of her that, in the purity of her compassion, responded to him. It was a gentle emotion, not that powerful, carnal passion of belonging that she felt when she thought of Grant—still it was no less real.

Slowly Luis lowered his lips to hers in a kiss that carried within the depths of its gentle forbearance a benediction. He held her fitted against his heart, a long, unceasing caress, through the night. And when the first fingers of light began to steal into the room, he helped her to don her clothing and rebraid her hair.

Fastening the end of her braid with a scrap of cloth, he laid it gently over her shoulder, smoothing the silk of it with his rough fingers. Without looking at her, he said, "I fear for you when I am gone."

"Please don't worry," she said, trying to smile, not succeeding very well.

"I may have made a trap for you with my fool's tongue."

"There was nothing else to be done. I am grateful for the thought you took for my safety."

Glancing toward the common room where in the gray light the men and women lay like lumps upon the floor, he said, "I may have done no more than postpone the ravishment. Dear God! How can I leave you?" He caught her close, pressing her against him. "How can I ever leave you?"

They stood for a long moment, clinging to each other, and then beyond the main door of the common room they heard the soft thud of marching feet. Luis went rigid before he slowly relaxed. Smoothing his hands over her back to the roundness of her shoulders, he put her from him.

"Listen carefully," he said. "Your best hope is Major Crawford. Trust to his mercy. It can be no less than that of the canaille in there." He nodded beyond the door.

The door in the outer room swung open. There was a general outcry of those disturbed by the firing-squad detail. A shadow appeared in the doorway of the cell, a shadow that resolved into the shape of the plainsman. Seeing them, he nodded and turned away, taking up a stance facing into the common room.

Hastily, Luis reached inisde his shirt, and taking the

260

chain he wore, lifted it off. He slipped it with care over her head, settling it into the valley between her breasts, then raised his brown eyes, aching with sorrow, to hers. "St. Michael will protect you now, for I have failed you, Eleanora. Forgive me," he said.

"No, no," she tried to tell him. "I'll be all right." But even those words, inadequate as they were, would not come from her throat.

A last kiss, flavored with the salt of her tears, and then the others were with them. She embraced Jean-Paul, clinging to his arm with icy fingers, searching the calm of his features with something like disbelief. She could not remember what she said to the others, what good-byes, what words of appreciation. They kissed her hands, speaking to her in voices deep with sincerity. They had a moment to speak among themselves, and then they were marching away, their backs straight, between the double file of soldiers.

Clutching the gold medallion Luis had given her, Eleanora stared after them until the great outer door had clanged shut. She stood a moment longer, then she ran to the sleeping shelf and climbed upon it, standing on tiptoe to see from the tiny barred window above. By gripping with her hands she could pull herself a little higher, though the stone ledge of the window cut into her wrists and the wall was cold and clammy against her breast.

The parade ground below was empty except for the old padre and an officer in his uniform of red and blue and white, holding an open watch in his hand. The pair stood as they were for long minutes. Finally, as if alerted by some sound, they turned toward a wide gate set in one wall.

The gate swung open to admit the firing-squad detail. They marched across the square toward where Eleanora stood. Luis was first, followed by Slim and Molina; with Gonzalez, sagging between two men, his face twisted with horror, bringing up the rear. There was no one else.

Eleanora ran her gaze over the men once more. She had been right. Jean-Paul was not among them. What had they done with him? Her scalp crawled with horror as she thought of him being held somewhere, being tortured, though for what reason she could not imagine.

Now the soldiers were tying their hands behind them. Father Sebastian moved down the line with painful slowness, his low voice intoning, his hand making the sign of the cross again and again, his gnarled and quivering fingers holding out the wooden crucifix to receive their kiss. From somewhere Slim had found a cigarillo, and while those of the faith received their rites, he drew upon it, letting the smoke drift from his lungs with a quiet, almost reflective courage.

The blindfolds were dirty white handkerchiefs folded inexpertly to go about their eyes. With a definite shake of his head, Luis refused his, the only one to do so. A heavy hand on their shoulders forced the men to their knees with their backs to the firing squad, lined at thirty paces behind them.

The officer snapped the case of his watch shut and put it away. With a rattling clatter, he drew his sword. Imperceptibly, the day grew brighter. A cool morning breeze floated across the open square, stirring the soft, brown waves of Luis's hair and lifting small puffs of dust from the ground.

A command rang out. The soldiers raised their rifles, steadied them. The sword of the officer flashed as it began its descent.

Below her, not ten yards away, Luis lifted his head. Seeing her face outlined in the window, a glad light sprang into his eyes. His lips moved as they formed her name. But the sound was lost in the roaring crash of the volley of the firing squad.

The blue smoke of gunpowder hazed the square. Strong, acrid, the smell of it drifted into the cell. Still Eleanora did not move. Her gaze fastened on those four figures sprawled across the sand, she hardly breathed. The Lebel rifles had done their job. Not a single shot had struck the wall at her feet. There was no need for a coup de grace. And yet it did seem callous for the detail to stand in the first rays of the rising sun, alive, reloading. It was a relief when, at a series of barked orders, they shouldered their weapons of death and left the square to Father Sebastian and the fallen.

Even sounds behind her did not quite penetrate Eleanora's concentration. It was as though as long as she refused to accept the knowledge of her eyes it could not hurt her. Her muscles were stiff from cramp, but she could not release them, and more than all else, she could not permit the onslaught of tears that burned behind her eyes. To cry would be to admit a cause for grief, something to be held at bay at all cost.

The feel of hands dragging at her skirts, ripping away the rotten material, broke her perilous absorption. She was aware, suddenly, of a foul-smelling, pot-bellied man at her side, tearing at her hands upon the bars with dirty fingers ending in long, horny, yellow nails.

Pain burst into her mind, bringing uncontrolled fury. Releasing the bars, she slashed out at the grinning, snaggle-toothed face, so that three bloody streaks scored the dirt that coated it. More hands reached up for her, grabbing for the gold chain at her neck. She caught the disk in her hand, cradling it protectively as she backed along the shelf to the corner. Her stomach knotted with hate and disgust, but she did not dare kick at at the horde around her for fear they would catch her foot and pull her down among them.

Her blouse was torn, hanging halfway down one shoulder. Her skirt dangled in shreds over her tattered petticoat. She had removed her makeshift slipper-boots for the night, so that she stood in her bare feet, cornered, at bay.

"St. Michael protect you. Luis had invoked the aid of the archangel, patron saint of warriors, to her cause, and now, surrounded by the sea of grinning, brutal faces, she found a prayer heard once in some distant, childhood year running through her mind. *St. Michael the Archangel, defend us in the day of battle . . . and do thou, O Prince of the Heavenly Host, by the power of God, cast into hell Satan and all the evil spirits who prowl the world seeking the ruin of souls—*

The answer, if answer it was, came with shocking unexpectedness. The sound of a shot exploded in the room, hushing the babble of obscenities and shouts of encouragement to silence. Across that sea of vacant, startled faces she saw the broad-shouldered form of Major Crawford. The smoking pistol in his hand still pointed toward the ceiling as he searched the crowd for any sign of an inclination to argue with his authority. There was none. Totally cowed, the men backed away and let him come forward.

As he approached, he extended his hand, his face grave and his pale blue eyes somber with concern. Eleanora's first inclination was to draw back, to stand on her dignity, refusing to traffic with a man she considered her enemy. But she was in no position to stand on pride. Moreover, the advice Luis had given came back to her, the remembrance of his hauntingly soft tone carrying a greater authority than any order could have done.

Moving like a sleepwalker, she gave the major her hand. His fingers closed large, warm, and supportive around it, as she stepped down. Feeling the trembling that shook her, he reached to scoop her into his arms. Making nothing of her weight, he bore her out of the cubicle, through the darkness of the common room and the corridor, and into the hot and precious sunlight.

Eleanora lay in the long copper tub, her face tight-lipped and cold. Major Neville Crawford had been all concern, ordering a deep, hot bath for her with a supply of linen towels and pure Castile soap. He had even borrowed a wrapper of white lawn lined with silk for her from the wardrobe of the wife of the fort's commandant, a circumstance Eleanora viewed warily. These courtesies, the luxury in which the major was living here in Honduras, the room allotted him in one corner of the official palacio, his ordering of its servants, the tub fit for a royal governor, the niceties he could command at will, indicated that he was someone of importance. It tended also to confirm what she suspected. She frowned. There had been as yet no indication of his intent toward her. If it was his purpose to carry her back to stand trial in Granada there was no occasion for this attention to her comfort. She could have gone back in her dirt and rags as easily as not.

On the other hand, if his interest was personal there had been no suggestion of that either. He puzzled her, but in her present malaise she had no energy to expend on riddles.

Easing deeper into the water, she soaped herself with precision. When the water began to cool, she washed her hair, lathering it again and again in the effort to remove the prison stench. She rinsed one final time with the can of clear water provided, and then to avoid the gray scum forming as the water grew cold, she struggled to her feet and stepped out.

Despite the gathering heat of the morning, she felt chilled, so that she dried hurriedly, wound the towel about her hair, and slipped into the wrapper which lay across the bed. The only comb in sight on the heavy dark-oak dressing table belonged to the major, and with a faint flicker of a smile she picked it up. If he had not intended that she should avail herself of it, he should not have left it there.

Lifting the tortoiseshell comb to her hair, she paused, stabbed by a memory of Luis, combing her tangled curls with his fingers, braiding it, such a short time before. For an instant she could not breathe, then, with an effort, she pushed the image from her, closing her mind against it.

When at last her hair hung wet and sleek down her back, she walked out onto the small, stone-balustrade balcony attached to the room. The sun shining down upon it felt good upon her face, and combined with a trade wind from the gulf washing blue in the distance, it soon dried her hair.

She was still standing there when the major returned. Hearing the door close behind him and his quick footsteps, she swung slowly around, taking the two short steps to the doorway.

He was not alone. A young maid with shy brown eyes, hair severely dressed, covered by a cap, and wearing the fine materials of a superior ladies maid, entered behind him. She set a tray down upon the dressing table, and bobbing a curtsy in Eleanora's direction, took from over her arm a full red skirt with deep ruffles cascading from

265

the knees, a petticoat and matching camisole of eyelet shot with black ribbons, and a white blouse with sleeves of ruffled eyelet. A black mantilla and black kid slippers with satin ties completed the ensemble. Setting the slippers on the floor, taking up Eleanora's discarded rags, the maid curtsied once more and moved with delicate dignity from the room.

The major had not spoken. He stood with an arrested look on his features, staring at Eleanora. In the bright rays of the sun she had a gilded look. Her hair, bleached by the elements, rioted around her with a look of gold-tipped flames. Her skin, after the long weeks of imprisonment, had faded to a soft gold perfection that gave her eyes the look of emeralds shining with inner fire in the head of some ancient Mayan idol. After weeks of privation, her form was so slender as to appear ethereal, and there was about her the appearance of such fine-honed suffering that a look of extreme doubt came into his eyes.

A muscle in his face moved as his jaw tightened. "How are you?" he asked.

"Very well," she replied in her coolest tones. "I must thank you for seeing to my comfort."

"It was the least I could do," he answered shortly. "Won't you come in and sit down?"

She obeyed, taking the seat he indicated, one of a pair of brocaded armchairs with a small table between them. Relaxing was impossible, however, and she sat straight on the edge with her hands folded in her lap.

The major took the opposite chair. Seemingly at a loss for words, he searched in his frockcoat pocket for a panatela, and receiving her permission to smoke, lit it with a sulfur match. The scent of the smoke invaded the room, gradually overcoming the smell of soap. When the red coal on the end of the cigar was glowing to his satisfaction, he glanced at her through thick, sandy lashes.

"The first thing I expect you will want to know," he said abruptly, "is that the charges against you have been dropped. Juanita Santamaria, the woman who accused you, is, as you may know, dead. Her story has been discredited. General Walker, on his return last month from Rivas, made a thorough investigation of the matter, and you have been exonerated."

Eleanora lifted her head. "The general—and the phalanx—have returned safely?"

He gave a short nod. "One more time."

"They were victorious?"

"After the general's peculiar fashion," he admitted. "I don't know if you are aware that he retreated from Rivas without directly engaging the Costa Ricans on his first attempt in early March because of rumors of a Honduran invasion. When the rumors proved to be without foundation, he marched on Rivas again. He forced his way through the Costa Rican line to capture the center of the town, but the Costa Ricans far outnumbered Walker's men, and he was surrounded. The position was untenable, and he had no recourse but to retreat under cover of darkness, leaving his wounded behind in a church near the plaza."

"That was a victory?" Eleanora said in bewilderment.

"It proved to be. The fools of Costa Ricans entered the church and butchered the wounded, then threw their bodies out with the rest of the fallen on the edge of town. Afterward, they proceeded to go on a week-long celebration of their defeat of the Immortals. As was entirely natural under the circumstances, cholera broke out, and the pestilence did a far more effective job of eradicating the Costa Rican army than Walker could have dreamed. The stupid idiots died like flies, and then, instead of quarantining themselves and containing the disease, they fled in a rout back to Costa Rica, carrying it with them. They say ten thousand have died down there, with more to come. It will be a miracle if they are able to put another army into the field within the next two years."

"You are very hard on them," she suggested, her eyes narrowing.

He barely looked at her. "I hate bungling."

"You would have preferred that the Costa Ricans had showed more judgment, even enough to defeat General Walker?"

A sardonic look entered his pale blue eyes. "Perceptive

of you to guess," he said. "However, I had every intention of making you familiar with the secret of my sympathies. It is, you see, necessary for my plans."

Eleanora regarded him with care. She must not allow herself to be intimidated. She said nothing, waiting for him to continue.

The major drew on his panatela, letting the blue smoke shield his expression. Then, as if finding the cigar distasteful, he got to his feet, walked to the window, and tossed it out. With one arm propped on the frame, he said over his shoulder, "From what I have told you, you should realize that you are free to return to Granada. It should not be hard, once you are there, to regain your former position with Colonel Farrell—and even your place in the affections of Uncle Billy. They will be anxious to make up to you for what you have suffered."

"I don't—" she began, but he cut across her words.

"It isn't a question of what you want. What I have suggested is exactly what you will do. Once entrenched again, you will keep your eyes and ears open, and every bit of information you discover concerning the plans of the Democrático government you will report to me personally."

"You are asking me to—spy for you?"

"Not asking, telling you."

"And what makes you think I will agree?" she demanded, her voice rising.

"You have excellent reason for a grudge. You have been falsely accused, hounded, subjected to hardship, imprisoned, seen your friends killed. And then there is the question of reimbursement. You will be paid, paid well, for this service."

"No doubt. By Vanderbilt."

"Indirectly, yes," he agreed, a wary look appearing in his eyes as he turned to face her.

"I am sorry to disappoint you, but I feel no malice against William Walker. He, I am convinced, had no part in what happened to me. It is his mistress who has earned my hate."

"Niña Maria?" he asked with a pretense of doubt.

"The same. Tell me, if you can, that it wasn't she who arranged for you to come to Honduras."

He was silent, his face revealing nothing as he held her jewel-green gaze. In sudden decision, he nodded. "You are right. We received an offer to exchange you and your brother for a Honduran officer, the son of a rich planter who was captured in a raid across the border and is now being held prisoner in Granada. For some reason the officials here seemed to think Walker would value you at least as highly as one of their officers. They were right. The decision was made to agree to their terms. Niña Maria suggested at the last moment that I be sent to identify you, and, if the offer was legitimate, effect the exchange."

Eleanora's eyelids flicked down as she wondered why Grant could not have volunteered to come—if he was interested in her return. "It—must have been an excellent opportunity to meet with Vanderbilt's representatives," she managed to say.

"Excellent," he agreed with candor.

"It is too bad then that the secondary part of your mission is doomed to failure. Niña Maria will not, I sincerely hope, be pleased with you."

"I understand your sentiments," he said unexpectedly, his expression troubled. "But I am afraid I cannot risk displeasing any of my employers. If you will not accept my suggestion willingly, you will only force me to find a way of persuading you."

"Simper and flirt my way back into Colonel Farrell's bed just so I can rifle his correspondence and eavesdrop on his conversations?" she said tensely. "No amount of money, nothing you can possibly say, will persuade me."

Pushing away from the door, he walked to the luncheon tray sitting on the dressing table. Beneath the linen cloth that covered it he discovered breast of chicken, yeasty white bread, peaches, grapes, and a bottle of cool white wine between a pair of crystal goblets. Uncorking the wine, he filled the goblets and brought one to her, pushing it into her hands. Automatically she raised it to her lips.

A little sour, but good enough, she thought abstractedly, and watched while Neville Crawford drained his glass.

With his back to her, he filled it once more. "You haven't asked about your brother," he said quietly.

Eleanora went still. "You—know where Jean-Paul is? You know what they have done to him?"

"They haven't done anything—yet. He is here in this house in a room much like this."

"You know it for certain?"

"As I stand here. I give you my word."

Eleanora looked down into her glass. The liquid within it trembled, and she was aware, suddenly, of the pounding of her heart. Carefully, she set the wine glass on the table at her elbow. "It was kind of you to tell me," she said in a colorless tone.

"Not at all. I have to tell you that when you return to Granada your brother will not be leaving here. For all purposes, he will have died before the firing squad. He will remain behind, a prisoner, a—what is the phrase?—hostage to your good conduct."

"Meaning?"

"Meaning that if you do not follow my instructions to the letter your brother will be executed, like the others, as an enemy of Honduras."

Eleanora could feel her face going blank with shock. Clenching her teeth, she raised an eyebrow. "Charming people you have aligned yourself with, Major Crawford. People who kill the wounded and prisoners of war."

"I find a most positive charm in winning," he replied without rancor. "Make no mistake about it, eventually these people will win."

She held his sober regard as the slow poison of her plight sank into her mind. She must do this thing; there was no other choice. Luis had feared she would be ravished—and so she would be, though not, perhaps, in the way he had envisioned. Was it really so unusual? Hadn't they all, Luis, Grant, Jean-Paul, Mazie, even Neville Crawford, been ravished by life? And in an ever-widening circle, Grant's mother, Consuelo, and many, so many others. They were born with confidence, self-respect, idealism, a dream of happiness. And the very

270

act of living stripped these things away, leaving their souls naked and shivering with pain.

Taking a breath so deep it struck like a knife through her chest, she sighed, shaking back her hair. "All right," she said, her voice dull with resignation. "First I would like to see Jean-Paul. Then you can tell me when, and how, I must return to Nicaragua."

Eighteen

Eleanora stepped down from the pony cart. The instant her feet touched the ground she drew her hand from Major Neville Crawford's supporting arm, and squaring her shoulders, stood waiting until her guard detail had formed around her. A barked order, and they began to move, keeping to the stately pace the officer in charge considered suited to the occasion. The glare of the morning sun was in her eyes, making it hard to see the group of men advancing toward her. A gulf breeze, warm, heavy with the smell of salt, caressed her face and tugged at her mantilla, swirling it around her. It lifted the ruffles of her tiered skirt, and catching the sand disturbed by her footsteps, sent it flying. High in the blue sky a pair of gulls swooped, their cries sounding in her ears with an underlying note of desperation. The soft wet roar of the incoming tide throbbed on her left, while far out on the purple-green waves a ship rose and fell at anchor. It was the Nicaraguan sloop-of-war *Granada*.

The Mosquito Coast, neutral ground to a degree, had been chosen as the place to exchange Eleanora for the Honduran officer. To return alone to that stretch of hot, brown sand where she and the others had been captured was an ordeal for her. She tried not to think, to remember, but was only partially successful. The heat waves rising from the rumpled sand unreached by the sea were peopled with wavering figures drawn from her imagination, sunburned, tattered figures with anguished eyes.

271

Blinking quickly, Eleanora stared hard at the approaching men in their red shirts. There was a tall man in the tunic of an officer in the lead. Her breath caught in her throat for a moment and her heart began to pound. Then she recognized the craggy features of one of Grant's good friends and fellow officers, another of the Immortals, Colonel Thomas Henry. He walked with a decided limp, leaning on a cane; a memento perhaps of the victory at Rivas.

Eleanora stumbled, weak, suddenly, with relief. Major Crawford reached for her arm to steady her, keeping his hand under her elbow. She did not resist. Her knees, after her fright, felt like jelly, and her fingers trembled so that she clasped them together in front of her. She was not ready to face Grant. The terrible necessity of offering herself to him once more paralyzed every feeling of joy or anticipation at the prospect. What was she to do, what was she to say, to persuade him to take her back into his bed? Should she seduce him, or should she appeal to his sympathies by a pathetic recital of what she had suffered? Either was loathsome to contemplate, either would demean the love she had nurtured, holding it tightly within her, in the months just past. Yet, somehow, some way, she must return to a position of intimacy with Colonel Grant Farrell inside the palacio. Jean-Paul's life depended on it.

She had not liked the way her brother had looked when she had left him. He had heard her explanations through without interruption. Then staring at her with dull eyes, he had said, "I should have died with the others." When she had looked at him speechlessly, he had continued. "That would have been right and fitting. I would not have to endure this living death, knowing how little I deserve to live, knowing my existence forces you to prostitute yourself, even put yourself in danger."

"Don't say that," she begged him, shaken by his despair, but unable to find the words to combat it.

"Why not? It's true. The thought of your dishonor for my sake weighs more heavily on my conscience than my own."

"Nonsense. This is not our war," she tried to tell him.

272

"We made it ours," he replied with uncompromising exactitude, and Eleanora did not argue. She could not, for she knew he was right. Kissing him gently, she had left him standing, staring out the grille-barred window of his pleasant prison.

Colonel Thomas Henry drew closer. She could see the seams of old scars on his face and his narrowed, intent stare, caused only partially by the sun. He was a man who seemed particularly prone to collecting injuries; the first time she had seen him his arm was in a sling. Because of his many hurts, including everyday accidents, he had been a frequent visitor to the hospital. Based, perhaps, on their earlier meeting, an unlikely friendship had grown between them, and the beginning of a smile began to show white now in his weatherbeaten face. Nearer and nearer the detail came. Behind them, the long boat which had transported them to shore was drawn up upon the sand, and the sailors who had manned it took a seat on its gunwale, watching.

When the Falangistas were no more than ten feet away, Major Henry raised his hand and removed his hat in a salute that was copied by the men he led. Stumping to a halt, he held his hat over his heart and leaned forward in a deep bow, supporting himself on his malacca cane.

"Eleanora—beg pardon—Señora de Laredo, I can't begin to tell you how thankful I am to see you. Bear with us and we will soon have you safely home."

"Thank you," Eleanora replied, but there was a wan quality in her smile. For her there was no such place.

Still, Major Henry was as good as his word. Within minutes the formalities were over and the long boat was skimming the waves toward the sloop. The run down the coast to San Juan del Norte was accomplished in a matter of hours—a cool, clean passage compared to the trip by river steamer over the winding San Juan with its muddy banks baking in the sun of early summer. The burned-out transit offices and wharf at Virgin Bay, only recently completed at a cost to the company of over a hundred thousand dollars, were a grim reminder of war. It had been a casualty of the Costa Rican offensive. The office had been ransacked and the workmen killed, many of them slaughtered in cold blood as they lay wounded on the ground.

Eleanora had been entertained with all the ceremony due a heroine during the trip, fêted at the captain's table, given the best in the way of accommodations, escorted everywhere by either Colonel Henry, Major Crawford, or one or more of the men who had comprised the exchange party. She was grateful, since their constant presence kept her from thinking, but she assigned such singular attention to their sympathetic appreciation for her experience, not to policy. She certainly did not expect it to continue once they had reached Granada. Her surprise was genuine then, when, as the lake steamer pulled into Granada, she beheld a large delegation on the wharf fenced around by Falangistas with rifles casually held at the ready.

Her searching gaze picked out the figure of William Walker with his dark frockcoat trimly tailored to his slight frame and his fine blond hair shining like cornsilk in the sun. Then, striding through the crowd that had collected, she saw another man in a red tunic. She could not see his face for his hat was worn low on his brow, but still she knew. She could not mistake that hard-muscled frame and lithe, Indian stride. It was Grant. He joined General Walker and they spoke quietly for a moment, then together they raised their heads to scan the people lining the rail of the steamer.

Instantly Eleanora started back. Beside her, Major Crawford touched her arm. "Don't run away," he said softly. "Think of this as an opportunity, one that can mean a great deal—to Jean-Paul. Smile. Wave. That's it, gently. We must remember too that you are the bereaved widow."

There was little chance of her forgetting, still Eleanora said nothing. It was necessary to concentrate to keep her smile from turning into a grimace and her hand from clutching the railing under the onslaught of panic. Schooling herself to a calm she was far from feeling, she looked away out over the noisy, boisterous crowd.

Granada, miles from the fighting, had changed little. A dust pall hung over the streets due to the hot, dry weather. The smells of animal dung and street refuse were stronger. But the pigeons still wheeled above the tall palms and red-tiled roofs, the buildings stuccoed white and coral or built of golden stone still shielded blue shadows against the glare of the late afternoon sun. The people still laughed and talked as if they had never heard of war.

So peaceful. It was an effort to drag her harried senses away as the gangplank was lowered at last and, on receiving a signal, Major Crawford indicated that it was time to disembark. At the head of the shaky collection of wooden planks she paused. Taking a deep breath, she put her foot forward in the first of the half dozen or more steps that would take her back into the town of Granada, back to jurisdiction of William Walker and, she hoped, back to Grant.

"On behalf of the Republic of Nicaragua, President Rivas, and myself, may I make you welcome once more in Granada, Señora de Laredo. Accept also my sincere condolences on your recent bereavement. The tragic loss of both Lieutenant Colonel Luis de Laredo and Private Jean-Paul Villars will be keenly felt. Accept also our most abject apologies for the misunderstanding which led to your unfortunate experiences, and my humble offer of renewed, and constant, friendship."

The general's gray eyes were steady, the tone of his voice warmly sympathetic. Eleanora's mouth curved in a hesitant smile, and then, forgetting her suspicions, she gave William Walker her hand.

"We realize nothing could possibly compensate for the hardship you have endured or the horror you have had to face, but we would deem it an honor if you would allow us to present to you this medal of valor from the state of Nicaragua as a gesture of our remorse and good will."

A sick feeling moved through her as she thought of Luis, who had forfeited his life because of the power wielded by this man's mistress; but at a touch of Major Crawford's hand on her elbow, she inclined her head with a soft word of gratitude and stood still while the gold star on a ribbon of red and black was pinned in place. William Walker bowed over her hand, the uniformed men straightened in a salute, and the ceremonies were over. There was a greeting and handshake for Colonel Henry and the men of the exchange detail who had disembarked behind her, jamming the end of the gangplank. But the people waiting to land after them were growing impatient at the delay.

"My carriage is waiting," General Walker said to Eleanora. "I would be proud to take you wherever you wish to go. Also, I believe Colonel Farrell has offered to see you settled into suitable quarters."

Through the ritual of the reception Eleanora had not been able to bring herself to look at Grant, nor did she do so now. She turned to Major Crawford. "I must thank you for arranging my release," she began, only to have him cut across the speech so carefully committed to memory on his instruction.

"There is no need. I was only following orders."

"You have been more than kind. I wish there was some way I could repay you."

"If you will pledge not to deny yourself if I should chance to call on you, I will consider myself amply rewarded," he replied with meaningful gallantry.

"I—will always be happy to receive you," she said, though her smile faded and she turned away as soon as possible. Passively, she allowed the general to direct her toward his carriage, the same dilapidated victoria she had ridden in before.

As they settled into the seats, Walker said, "One thing more, señora. You need not feel under any obligation to stay in Nicaragua. We will all understand perfectly if you should decide that you would prefer to leave us, and will gladly defray your expenses to the destination of your choice. It is the least we can do."

Was that a hint that they—meaning he and Niña Maria—would prefer her to go? It would not be surprising. She could not help but be a reminder of an episode they would like to forget. No doubt Niña Maria would think differently, however, after she had spoken to Neville Crawford. She would not be astonished, Eleanora told herself with a shade of cynicism, if she became a close friend of the general's mistress before all was said and done.

The general was waiting for her answer. "I appreciate

your concern, sir, and your kind offer, but I have yet to decide what I want to do. It may take a little time."

"I—quite understand," he answered, slanting a glance at the set face of Colonel Farrell, seated across from them with his back to the horses. "There is no hurry. In fact, if you feel it is compatible with your mourning, I would like you to come to a small dinner party we are having in three days' time, on Thursday next. We are—as always, anxious to have the beauteous element among us represented at Governement House."

It seemed politic to accept both the compliment and the invitation, regardless of any other arrangements she might make. It was a formality, however, for the general seemed to expect nothing less than compliance.

"Someday, Eleanora—if I may revert to a more familiar title in private—I would like to hear your story of what happened to you in the past three months. We had the bones, of course, from the message sent by the Hondurans, still I am sure there is more, much more, which we can't begin to guess. I don't mean to press you, or to suggest anything in the nature of an interrogation, but I would like to hear what you feel you can tell me, later, when time has had a chance to dull the edges a bit."

Eleanora gripped her fingers in her lap, an agonizing ache beginning in her throat at the mere thought. She swallowed hard, her gaze moving to a point just above the general's head. "With all due respect, General," she said in a voice that trembled, "I'm not certain that I will ever be able to speak of it."

Street noises, the calls of vendors, the continuous murmur of soft voices, the squeal of a family of pigs disturbed in the mud of the gutter, invaded the carriage as silence descended. Eleanora flicked a glance at Grant to find his hard blue stare resting on the signet ring that gleamed on her finger, held in place by a thick wrapping of cloth through its circle. Slowly he lifted his eyes to her gold-flecked green gaze.

She could not tell what he was thinking or feeling. His emotions were under such tight rein that the bronzed planes of his face were rigid.

The humid heat was intense. Perspiration trickled down

her spine where it rested against the velvet squabs. The general had turned his attention to a sheaf of papers with the look of a report which Colonel Thomas Henry had thrust into his hand at the moment of meeting. Frowning, he looked up from them to stare fixedly into the middle distance.

Eleanora would have preferred to remain silent. It would not do, however, to appear sullen and ungracious, or to advertise her disinclination for making polite conversation with Colonel Grant Farrell. Clearing her throat, she said, "I must congratulate you, General, on your victory at Rivas."

"The plaudits belong to my great ally, the cholera, my dear," he replied, turning a wintry smile upon her, "but I accept the sentiment."

"Still, I understand your men fought bravely for you, and you have secured your position here."

His chest expanded and fell beneath the black broadcloth of his coat in what would have been a sigh in any other man. "For the time being," he agreed, then his light brows drew together as he went on. "I meant what I said earlier about your brother. He had the makings of a good soldier and a fine, upstanding man. I don't mean to distress you by reminding you of your loss and the manner of it, but I want you to know that the phalanx is neither so big or so impersonal that it can't regret the passing of a promising young member. You must not think we value him the less—but no, I won't say anymore on that head. We will speak of it another time, when you are rested."

A conventional answer rose to Eleanora's lips as she realized with bitterness that nothing she had said earlier had really penetrated William Walker's basic self-absorption. He wanted to be informed and he expected her to overcome her scruples, however painful. Recognizing that did not help her to understand why he had singled out Jean-Paul for special praise, and not Luis, surely the more valuable, militarily speaking, of the two. She had no intention of questioning him. She accepted that he had a reason, just as she had learned to accept so much else in these last few months.

The carriage braked to a halt before the Government

House. The instant the general stepped out, he was surrounded by his guards, who had been following on horseback.

"Until Thursday," he said with his slow smile, and turned away.

As the carriage jerked into movement once more, Grant's voice, coldly, polite, grated in the quiet. "Where do you want to go?"

"I—don't know," she said, distractedly aware of the necessity of returning to this man's protection, and yet unable to make herself say the words which might bring it about. "Perhaps a hotel?"

"You stayed at the Alhambra once before, I think?"

At her nod he put his head out the window to give the necessary order. She watched closely as he settled back, but he seemed to have no new battle scars, no visible wounds. To her eyes inside the dimness of the carriage, he appeared as fit and as strong as when they had first met. Following the trend of her own thoughts, she said on impulse, "Your shoulder healed? It doesn't pain you anymore?"

Turning to stare at her through thick, dark lashes, he answered brusquely. "It healed."

"Were you with Walker on the second march to Rivas?"

"I was."

She managed a light laugh. "I can't believe you were injured there. You certainly look healthy enough."

"What the hell is this?" he demanded, his voice vibrating with something between scorn and passion. "Coming from someone who spent weeks in the jungle with another man, and came back wearing his name and his ring, I find this pretended concern hard to stomach!"

"I don't know what you mean," Eleanora said unsteadily, the suddenness of his attack throwing her into confusion.

"I think you do," he countered, and waited, watching her with an intentness that was unnerving.

Without compunction, Eleanora abandoned her feeble attempt to return their relationship to a more familiar footing. Her concern had not been spurious. It would not do, however, for her to tell him so, and so she fell silent, studying with an interest completely assumed the scene unrolling past the carriage windows.

Grant subsided also for the remainder of the short journey, though Eleanora thought he glanced at her once or twice with a puzzled frown between his brows.

The Alhambra was much as she remembered it from the time when, with Mazie, she had enjoyed its hospitality. It might have been a little quieter, with fewer comings and goings, but the atmosphere of unostentatious comfort was the same. There was no difficulty in securing a room, especially when it was made known that she would be the guest of General William Walker.

Following on the heels of the scurrying manager, Grant saw her to her room, though he came no further than the door. The manager hurried here and there, throwing windows wide and pulling back the drapes. He checked the water in the pitcher and carafe, and saw that the washstand was supplied with towels and a small cake of soap before coming to stand, awaiting anxiously the approval of the man in the uniform of the American Phalanx. Grant gave him a nod that was both the approval he sought and a dismissal, then stood with his hat in his hand until the man's footsteps had ceased to scuff upon the worn runner in the long outside hallway.

"Thank you—" Eleanora began.

"You have everything you need?" Grant started to say.

They both stopped. Eleanora glanced up in time to catch an odd softness allied to a quirk of humor in Grant's face as he watched her. It vanished so quickly that she was not certain she had not imagined it. An instant later he was saying, "I will see to your baggage when it comes off the steamer."

"There isn't much, only a small valise."

"I will see to it," he repeated.

"I—may need some of the things I left at the palacio."

He nodded. "They are still there. Nothing has been moved. I'll have Señora Paredes pack them and send them to you."

The harsh tone was back in his voice. Eleanora gave him a small, self-possessed smile, and inclining her head in a regal gesture she had learned from her grandmother, who claimed to be descended from French aristocracy, she closed the door upon him.

She was kept busy in the days that followed. The editor of *El Nicaraguense,* a young man with ink-stained fingers, a harassed expression, and boundless enthusiasm, came. His interest in her ordeal was so artlessly genuine that she found herself telling him far more than she had intended.

She received also a visitor from the military surgeon, Dr. Jones. Citing orders from someone high in the command of the phalanx, he waved aside her objections and examined her thoroughly. He gave her a salve to soften the calluses on her hands, recommended lemon juice and buttermilk for what he persisted in calling the discoloration of her skin due to the sun, and pronounced her fit, though too slim for his taste. To remedy this he prescribed a diet rich in red meat and fresh vegetables, and gave her leave to eat all the rich desserts he denied himself. Their conversation naturally turned to the hospital and the wounded from the recent conflict, scarce though they were due to the tactics of the enemy. Before he finally took his leave, Eleanora found herself promising to look in again upon the infirmary for the purpose of viewing one or two improvements he was anxious to have her opinion upon. An afternoon was devoted to fulfilling this promise. The situation there was vastly improved, allowing her to refrain from committing herself to returning to her former position with a free heart, though she was not sure how long she could withstand the sincere entreaties of the surgeon and the orderlies who remembered her.

Grant was as good as his word. Her baggage and the clothing from the palacio arrived in due course. The latter was so neatly packed that she suspected Grant of boxing her gown and Thompson crinoline personally, and was troubled for several hours by the pleasure the thought gave her.

Shaking them out, seeing that they were pressed and hung away, Eleanora could not make up her mind which of the three ensembles that made up her limited wardrobe to wear for the general's fête. The skirt and blouse procured for her by Major Crawford were not in keeping with the formality of the occasion, and neither of the gowns—the one strewn with pink cabbage roses or the green muslin—seemed to suit her mood or changed circumstances. It might be possible to take the black ribbons woven through the eyelet of her petticoat, plus her black mantilla, and add them somehow to the green muslin to create a costume subdued enough to pass, but she was by no means satisfied with the compromise.

To open the door, then, to a grinning soldier bearing a dress box on the afternoon of the third day was more in the nature of having her innermost wishes fulfilled than a surprise.

"The colonel's compliments, ma'am, and he hopes you will wear this tonight," the young man said, holding the box out to her.

Eleanora hesitated. Only the reflection that this was probably another example of the Republic of Nicaragua's "defraying her expenses" allowed her to accept the box with a smile and an expression of gratitude worded as graciously as she was able. It would be less than generous to refuse William Walker this opportunity to make amends.

The gown was of black lace over ecru satin, and it seemed on examination to have been made using the green muslin as a pattern. The measurements were the same as well as the style, with the layers of flounces falling from the pointed waist and the wide lace bertha covering the shoulders. The fit, after she had struggled with the row of tiny jet buttons down the back for a good half hour, was quite good; perhaps a trifle loose in the waist, but so, no doubt, was the green just now. It was a good choice, she thought, turning this way and that before the mirror in the wardrobe door. Somber without being falsely deep mourning, the cream-colored satin, glimpsed through the lace, was a foil for her hair without giving the gold of her skin a sallow cast as deep black alone might have done. There did seem to be the need of something to break the open expanse of the line from her chin to the low dip of the neckline, and on impulse, she stripped the medallion of St. Michael from its chain and strung it on a length of black ribbon, tying it so that it lay in the hollow of her throat.

She was dressed and waiting when the general's carriage

came for her, and if she felt disappointment that Major Neville Crawford was to be her escort, she was careful not to let him see it.

He had no such reticence about her feelings, however. The instant they were seated in the carriage, he crossed his legs, bending a pleasant smile upon her strained face. "No luck, so far, eh? If he won't come to you, you'll have to go to him."

"What do you mean?" she asked tightly.

"I mean that we no longer have the time to wait for the colonel to get over his jealousy and stiff-necked pride."

"Jealousy?"

"Naturally. Think how Farrell must have felt when he found out what Luis de Laredo had done for your sake. Now that the man is dead he will get over it eventually, but as I said, we don't have time to wait."

It was an instant before Eleanora could bring her mind to bear on what the major was saying. When she did so, she realized he was waiting for her comment. "Why this sudden urgency?"

"We hear rumors that Walker intends to arrest President Rivas and his cabinet as traitors to the Republic because Rivas has been corresponding with the leaders of San Salvador and Guatemala. There have been some street disturbances in the capital at León that are anti-American in feeling. To be perfectly frank, I suspect Rivas of planting the rumors himself. *El Presidente* got his nose put out of joint earlier this month when Walker was given a savior's welcome in León, because of the retreat of the Costa Rican Army. It's my bet Rivas wants to test his popularity against Walker. Also, now that the little general has taken care of the threat of invasion for the time being, he would like to stir up enough feeling against him to push the American Phalanx out of the country before Walker gets too big for his britches—and maybe casts his eye on the president's job."

"Another betrayal," Eleanora murmured.

Neville Crawford shook his head. "That may be, but it doesn't make any difference to us where the rumors start. We want the same thing as Rivas, the ouster of William Walker."

"And what is it that—we—are supposed to do?"

Overlooking the sarcasm, Neville explained, "It is obvious that Walker can't afford to ignore the situation. It may turn out that he will be forced to do exactly as the rumors suggest, if he can arrange the support for such a move. We need to know exactly what he does intend to do, and when."

"Why must I be involved? Why can't Niña Maria discover this for you?"

"Because," he said after a moment of deliberation, "General Walker no longer confides in her since the incient with Juanita, and he has taken to holding his most important meetings in his officers' quarters, usually Farrell's."

"I begin to see," she said expressionlessly.

"Good. I think we can be certain that Walker will not make this decision without consulting Farrell—whether he follows his advice or not."

"And what if this conference has already taken place?" she asked.

"My sources of information are somewhat faster than Walker's. It may be that he has yet to learn what I have just told you, but if he knows, he can only have known for a few hours at best. I think you will be in time, if you act swiftly. Tonight, for instance."

"I am sure you have a suggestion as to how I am to go about it." She looked away from him out the window. They had entered the plaza. Within seconds they would be arriving at the door of the Government House.

"Few men can resist a direct appeal," he said, his voice quiet in the darkness beside her. "If it came from you, Eleanora, I am quite sure I couldn't."

Neville Crawford's declaration left her shaken. She had thought him too intent on the pursuit of his fortune to find her attractive. There had been an odd kind of security in the knowledge that he was impervious to her charms. She had no reason to believe that he would capitalize on the hold he had upon her, and yet, she was left newly vulnerable.

The Government House blazed with light and hummed with the sound of confident voices and laughter, the indi-

284

cators of prosperity. To Eleanora there seemed to be more candles burning in the chandeliers than when she had last danced beneath them, more women present in the long reception room wearing more glittering jewels. The supper table was provided with more sumptuous viands, the wine glasses were passed with greater frequency, the music was louder, the waltzes faster. It was possible that this was only her impression because she had been so long isolated from such affairs, but she did not think so. There was a hectic feeling in the air, and standing back, watching the men and women eating and drinking, it appeared to her that their movements held a grasping greed for this moment, coupled with a pervasive fear of the next.

Despite Niña Maria glowering beside him, William Walker made Eleanora a pleasant speech of welcome, but as she went down the receiving line, she was not singled out for any greater attention on this occasion. She was not surprised. The general was much busier with foreign dignitaries and guests of obvious importance, including a man with the richly satisfied appearance and the accent of a New York business tycoon.

Despite the lilting music of a waltz, Eleanora's Creole conscience made her reluctant to take the floor while wearing black for Luis. Major Crawford, obligingly, strolled with her around the edges of the floor until summoned as a dance partner by Niña Maria while the general was occupied. For a time she was entertained by Dr. Jones. Later Colonel Thomas Henry took the air with her, teetering back and forth beside her on his cane. They were followed by first one and then another of Luis's fellow officers who remembered her, until she began to feel as if she were holding audience. She was not sorry when they began to disperse. Answering the many expressions of condolence had not been the easiest of tasks, and avoiding the questions prompted by their natural curiosity was even harder.

She was standing alone in a window embrasure when a slight sound made her turn. Grant stood beside her, and as her chin came up in something like alarm, he pushed one of the two glasses of champagne he held into her hand.

"Drink this," he said without preamble. "You look as if you could use it."

Hurt that had little to do with vanity moved through her. Her voice had a caustic edge as she murmured, "So thoughtful of you."

He made no reply, and after a moment, for something to do, Eleanora raised the glass to her lips to take a sip. At the same instant, Grant reached out to pick up the medal of St. Michael at her throat.

Startled, Eleanora swallowed the bubbling wine the wrong way. It burned into her windpipe and she made a choking sound, her hand going to her mouth.

Looking around, Grant hastily took her glass from her, setting it with his own on a nearby table. He pushed wide the half-open French window behind them and swept her out onto one of the small balconies that jutted out from the back wall of the Government House. He raised his hand to thump her on the back, but by then she was recovered enough to shake her head vigorously, saying in a husky tone, "I'm all right, thank you."

"Certain?"

She nodded, the ridiculousness of it curving her mouth into a smile before she glanced down. "I hope I didn't get champagne on this gown. It might spoil it, and I would hate that. Will you remember to thank General Walker for me for sending it this afternoon?"

Something in the stillness of the man beside her made her look up. She was in time to glimpse the self-derision that flitted across his features.

"It—wasn't the general, was it?" she said slowly. "It was you. The soldier said— But I thought—"

"Don't make a tragedy of it," he said shortly. "I thought you could use a gown and I bought one for you. Forget it."

There was more to it than that, she knew. Before she could put her feeling into words he swung on his booted heel and left her. Moving a little to one side, Eleanora watched him go with a trembling feeling in her heart, as if she had just lost an important opportunity. Standing

286

there, she saw Niña Maria glide forward with her snake-like tread and place a predatory hand on Grant's arm. It was at that moment that the desperate gamble she must take occurred to her.

Nineteen

There was no difficulty in leaving the Government House unnoticed. Even the soldiers on guard at the front doors appeared not to see her as she drifted past them.

It was not late by tropical standards. The plaza was filled with the mellow glow of the lamplight falling from the open doors in the square that surrounded it on three sides. People—couples, families, and older men and women—sat and stood about, enjoying the coolness of the night air and the music coming from the windows of the house she had just left. But even in pitch darkness Eleanora could have found her way from the plaza down the Calle Santa Celia to the palacio. She had trod these gray cobblestones so many times; it could not be held surprising that they had the feel of the homeward path beneath her slippers.

She hesitated for a moment under the overhang of the galería, her gaze going to the thick, woody trunk of the bougainvillea that grew at the end of the house. With a slight shiver, she shook the intrusion of memory from her, and turning to the bell, set it to jangling on its wrought-iron support.

It could not have been more than a moment or two before there was a rattle of a key in the lock and Señora Paredes's thin visage appeared in the crack of the opening door, but to Eleanora, it seemed like an hour. Nerves, allied with purest fright, froze her face into a mask as she pushed past the old woman.

"Good evening," she said over her shoulder as, removing the black mantilla she wore over her hair, she continued along the cool tiles of the entranceway.

287

Behind her, the señora hurriedly fastened the door. "The señor colonel, he is expecting you?" she called after Eleanora.

Eleanora turned back at the foot of the stairs. "I believe he will be glad to see me," she said gently.

Nothing had changed in the bedchamber she had once shared with Grant. Eleanora did not need the light of a candle to show her that. The moonlight flooding in at the open French window was sufficient. The wardrobe, the washstand, the table they had taken their meals upon, the *cuadro* in the corner, the bed draped in virginal white; all were the same. Even the rugs scattered on the floor were in their same places. The only difference that she could see was that the grille was open, its halves resting back against the outside wall. Grant's belongings were just as they had been before he left for Rivas. His extra shirts and breeches were stacked in the wardrobe, his shaving equipment and silver-back hairbrushes reposing on the washstand. Dropping her mantilla beside them, she touched the back of one brush with a tentative finger. It was purple with tarnish, sadly in need of polishing. After a moment, she wandered away again.

Few men can resist a direct appeal, Neville had said. What he meant was, few men will bother to resist a woman who throws herself at them. The only trouble with that was, she had good reason to know that Grant not only could, but would. He had wasted no time in resisting Juanita's appeal on that memorable morning. He had, in fact, dealt with it with great directness. Suppose he rejected her in the same way? Despite the bravado of her statement to the señora, it was not impossible. She would die of the humiliation if he did.

Taking a step out onto the galería, she surveyed the long fall from the railing with a sinking sensation in the pit of her stomach. Grant had had ample reason for what he had done, she told herself. Juanita had been wild, clawing, attacking both her and Grant. It did not help. The prospect that she might not be welcome had to be faced.

It might make it more difficult for him if she was not

288

dressed for the street. It should make it harder still, then, if she was not dressed at all.

She caught her lower lip between her teeth, staring over the railing, and then slowly raising her hands to the back of her neck, she turned into the room, freeing the tiny jet buttons from their holes as far as she could reach. She dropped her arms to her sides to rest them, then twisted them behind her back trying to reach the rest.

Intent on what she was doing, she did not see the shadowy movement in the doorway which led to the inner galería until Grant stepped into the room. As she froze, he tossed his hat at the top of the wardrobe, caught her elbow, and turned her slowly around with her back to him, encircling her waist with a strong, muscular forearm. The touch of the fingers of his right hand tingled against the bare skin of her back, and his voice, warm and deep, whispered at her ear. "Let me help you," he said.

Relief sapped her strength and she leaned against him. Her pulse throbbed and her breast rose and fell with the quickness of her breathing in the aftermath of fear and the foretaste of excitement. A trace of guilt surfaced in the tumult of her mind, dying away before the rush of an uncontrollable yearning.

Grant's hand moved from the last of the buttons to the nape of her neck. His probing fingers found the few pins which held the heavy chignon of her hair, and he drew them out one by one, letting it fall in a rippling cascade down her back. When it hung free, he turned her in the circle of his arms, and slipping his hands beneath the red-gold waves, tilted her head back, seeking the tender shape of her mouth. His lips moved on hers with a slow insistence that grew steadily more demanding. Her arms, freed, lifted to his neck, and her fingers grasped the tightened broadcloth of his tunic where it stretched across his shoulders. She felt the burgeoning heat of his desire, and knew a quickening response deep inside that spread with the sting of acid along her veins. His lips slid from the corner of her mouth, along the softness of her cheek, to the curve of her neck just below her ear. She made no protest as he pushed the lace from her shoulder, while his mouth burned its way to the hollow of her throat, displacing the cool disk of the medallion with a searing kiss.

Her eyes closed, she felt herself lifted and swung dizzyingly onto the bed. In a few swift moves she was freed of the restricting folds of her clothing. The pores of her skin seemed to breathe in the warm night air, expanding in a voluptuous nakedness that welcomed joyously the slide of warm skin against her own, the roughness of the coverlet beneath her, and the feel of pressing caresses. With her lashes lowered, she smoothed the open palm of her hand over his chest with its faint dew of perspiration, trailing her nails down the lean hardness of his belly. The fresh smells of sun-dried clothing, cornstarch, and bay rum was in her nostrils, mixed with the scent of heated bodies closely held. Grant's hand, rough at the fingertips, cupped her breast, and then, as his mouth closed on hers once more, she knew the tart-sweet rise of passion on her tongue. His hands moved lower, over the slim indention of her waist to her hips, and she accepted in swift, mounting pleasure the full weight of his body as he pressed her to her back.

A certain knowledge, communicated by touch and taste and intuition, that this man would not leave her aroused and unsatisfied, acted like an aphrodisiac to banish inhibition. Her ardor welled, fed by the burning touch of his lips. The faint quivering of his arms betrayed the depths of his longing and his need. The beat of her heart increased, roaring in her ears. His panting breath fanned her cheek, mingling with her own, and her sides ached from the vise of his arms. There was a painful fullness in her loins, a fullness that grew, stretching beyond containment. Like a long-held dam the paroxysm flooded over her in a wash of molten silver, spreading liquid fire along the length of her body, invading her brain with a pulsing, metallic glow.

She opened her eyes, and as her vision cleared, she smiled into the deep, dark ocean-blue eyes of the man above her. He kissed her trembling mouth, and she sighed softly, feeling the gentle ebb of her being dissolving into the pure stillness of love.

"Eleanora?"

The urgency of his voice drew her back from a darkness

so deep it had the feel of unconsciousness. She lay for a moment, collecting her senses before turning toward the sound, and in that instant shame, black and blighting, struck at her.

How much of the abandon she had shown had been of her own free will, how much for the sake of the vile purpose she had been recruited for? To do what she wished, pretending she must, or to do what she must, pretending it was her desire—which was the more degrading? Behind her shoulder, where it had been twisted on its ribbon, the medallion of St. Michael burned into her skin like a brand. The vows she had exchanged with Luis might not have been compelling or binding, but surely her mourning for his death could have been more closely and lengthily observed. More humiliating than these things, however, was the realization that they did not matter beside the single, overriding question: What must Grant think of her?

Her face flaming, she levered herself on one elbow and reached out, drawing her petticoat toward her. Grant put his hand on her arm, but she pulled away, sliding from the bed.

A swift lunge, and he stripped the petticoat from her, dragging her back down beside him, holding her still until her struggles ceased.

"Where were you going?" he asked lazily, wiping at the strand of her hair that tickled his lips.

Eleanora swallowed on the hard knot growing in her throat. "I—back to the Alhambra."

Her answer obviously disconcerted him. When he spoke at last there was a tone in his voice that sent a quake of fear along her nerves. "I think not—not until you tell me what you meant by coming here if you didn't intend to stay, and while you're at it, what in God's name happened to you to make you look like a wide-eyed, breakable china doll!"

"Grant—"

"From the beginning," he said, his tone implacable for all its softness.

She caught her breath. "If you knew what you are asking—"

"I do know. But it won't help to pretend it didn't happen. Or would you rather tell the general? I can spare you that."

"I don't think I can find the words," she said. The thought of compressing so many events, so many feelings, into short, cool sentences filled her with despair. It would be so fatally easy to make a mistake, to tell him more than it was wise for him to know.

"Try," he recommended, and there was nothing else to do but comply as best she could.

She began, haltingly, with her arrest at the hospital, the words coming with less difficulty than she had imagined. As she spoke of the escape and the early days in the mountain valley when she had tended Luis and he had been so attentive of her comfort and safety, her voice grew stronger. She recounted in vivid phrases their lack of hope on learning of Juanita's death and the execution of the men who had returned to Granada with her. The jungle trek, the sighting of the gulf, the death of Kurt, their arrest and transfer to Honduras; these things were told with comparative ease. She faltered, however, as she came to the arrival of Major Crawford, followed by the blessing of Father Sebastian, the eleventh-hour wedding.

"You are saying that Luis and the others were still alive when Crawford reached you?" he said, breaking into her narrative.

"That's right. Why?" The sudden rigidity of his muscles made her aware that she had been in danger of succumbing to the languor stealing over her from being held firmly against his side.

"The major was empowered to negotiate the release of all the prisoners," he said grimly. "I will be interested in reading his report. Still, don't stop now. I was just beginning to be fascinated. Tell me about this marriage. A love match, no doubt, overcoming all obstacles, consummated in the glorious filth of a prison cell?"

"No—no," she said on an indrawn breath, taking care to keep the tears rising in the back of her throat from seeping into her voice. "It was not like that at all. It was—a splendid gesture, no more than that. Luis gave me the protection of his name in a chivalrous union that

292

was—never consummated. Not, I assure you," she added hardily, "from a lack of willingness on my part, but because he was unable to do so. And the next morning I watched him walk toward death with my name on his lips —and I think that, except for leaving me behind, he was glad to die—"

Her voice broke with a strangled sound on the last word, and the bitter tears, so long restrained, welled into her eyes, running in scalding tracks down her face and into her hair. In an effort at self-control she tried to break away from Grant's arms, but he would not release her. The sense of sheltering protection breached her last defense, and she no longer tried to stop the aching, hopeless flow.

Grant was silent for long minutes, and then his soft curse rent the moonlit darkness. As if what he felt demanded the release of action, he thrust himself up in the bed, found her eyelet petticoat, and pressed it into her hand to use to wipe away the tears. Then, sitting there with his arms resting on his knees, he stared through the bright dimness at the shape of the wardrobe in the corner.

His concern was a potent force, both balm and salt to the lacerations that had been inflicted upon her spirit. It also reinforced her guilt, so that the urge to confess everything became unbearable.

Drawing a deep breath, she began, "Jean-Paul—"

"You don't have to say anymore. The rest I know," he told her, the strength of his tone overwhelming her weak voice without effort. His next words effectively banished what she was trying to say from her mind. "I know everything—except why you came here tonight."

"It must be obvious," she countered after a moment's silence.

"Not to me." He lay down beside her again, resting on his elbow. He did not touch her, but she was aware, abruptly, of the tight leash he held on his emotions.

"I came because—I was sorry that I misunderstood about the gown—"

"You were going to give it back to me?" he asked in dry disbelief.

Eleanora's cheeks grew hot. Tears persisted in oozing

from her eyes and she scrubbed at them abstractedly. "No," she answered, determined to speak the half-truth though she could not look at him. "I wanted to stay, and I thought it would be harder for you to throw me out if I—undressed."

His breathing stopped, then reaching out to smooth the wet curve of her cheek with the back of one finger, he said, "Very wise. I would like to show you how wise once more, but I think it would be better for you if you tried to sleep."

He believed her. He had questioned nothing she had told him. It was more than she had expected from a man with such a jaundiced view of life, more than she deserved. In the face of the kind of suspicions, the kind of questions, she knew Grant to be capable of, she might have weakened. His attitude made her ashamed, but it could not help but loosen also the straining grip of apprehension on her nerves. Her green eyes faintly luminous in the dark, she turned to him. "I may look breakable," she said softly, "but I am stronger than you know, much stronger."

The moon had set before they finally closed their eyes. Eleanora slept deep, more exhausted than she would have liked to admit. Still, toward dawn she woke herself crying loud with anguished sobs in some nightmare she could not remember. Grant, awakened, held her until she was calm. Though she tried, lying in the reassuring comfort of his arms, she could not tell him what she had dreamed. The details had slipped beyond her grasp, leaving only an incalculable sense of loss.

"What did you think when you came back from Rivas and found me gone?"

They were seated at the breakfast table. Flies were blowing the orange peelings and bacon rinds left lying on their plates, and heat rose already like a wall beyond the overhang of the galería. Grant's coffee cup was empty, and Eleanora refilled it from the blue enamelware pot so she would not have to look at him while he answered.

"At first," he said, taking up his cup, "I was angry that the charges had been made, though I thought Luis had acted like an idiot, riding off with you in that melodramatic way before Walker could come back and settle everything. That was before I realized what they were trying to do to you. I recognized, after a while, that a major part of Juanita's plan depended on the fact that I wasn't on hand. Still, it hurt that Luis was there, and I wasn't, when you needed me—that he knew where you were when I didn't—and was with you at night when I wasn't. If I had found you then, in that mood, I might have tried to kill him. I cooled off under house arrest. I even learned to be grateful to him for taking care of you."

"Under house arrest?" she asked quickly.

The corner of his mouth tugged in a smile without humor. "For my own protection. At least, that's what Walker called it. It wasn't long in actual time, less than two weeks, but it was long enough for you to get far beyond my reach, beyond my help. Long enough for Walker to save an officer for the phalanx, a fighting tool he knew he would need when he returned, as he had to, to Rivas. And long enough for him to lose a loyal follower."

Had he cared so much? The words she might use to draw from him how much he cared pressed hurtfully against her throat, but she had forfeited the right to ask them. She said instead, "I don't suppose it would have made any difference if you had caught up with us, or even if you could have come to Honduras instead of Major Crawford."

"Honduras? I wasn't informed of that mission until after Crawford had left. I guess I gave Uncle Billy good reason to doubt my cooperation, even my good faith, but that's another thing I hold against him. That whole affair smells as high as the San Juan in the dry season to me. The information that you had been captured didn't come through regular channels, I'd stake my epaulettes on it. Nor did it come through our regular Democrático contacts like Walker says; I would have known about it if it had. No, there's something funny about that situation. I'm still not sure that the general has his information leak plugged."

It would be normal for her to take an interest in such matters. "Luis and I talked of that possibility," she said. "We wondered if Señora Paredes wasn't involved?"

"Maybe. She is a cautious old woman, though, and too frightened of losing what she has for it to have been anything but against her will."

"That makes a difference?" Eleanora asked with care.

It was a long moment before he answered. "I suppose not."

Swallowing hard on her disappointment, waving at a fly which buzzed persistently around her face, Eleanora made herself question him further. "You have someone else in mind then?"

Shaking his head, he downed his warm coffee and reached for his hat. "Only a feeling." Coming around the table, he drew her to her feet. "You had better shut the doors. It gets infernally hot in here these days if they are left open—or even if they're not, for that matter. I don't think you will be able to stay in here during the day, and as much as I like that costume you are wearing," he added, glancing down at the red shirt which hung upon her in the most enticing fashion, "I don't think I want you receiving patio visitors in it. I suppose I had better do something about clothes for you again."

"Do you mind?" she asked anxiously.

"I might even learn to like it," he answered. "A little knowledge of women's buttons comes in handy, now and again."

"So long as you make a study of only mine," she said with mock tartness. Accepting his farewell kiss, she watched him stride from the room with an ache in the region of her heart.

Her boxes arrived from the Alhambra by handcart an hour before luncheon—a marvelous example of organization and forceful persuasion in this country of *mañana*, and a positive indication of Grant's personal supervision. Eleanora was smiling to herself over his comments on the subject, and getting into the skirt and blouse she had come to think of as her Honduran costume, when the bell clanged below.

Eleanora stepped out onto the galería in time to see the señora escorting a buxom female with an unlikely bonnet on her head, covered with fresh magenta hibiscus, into the patio. At the sight of the brassy curls fringing the forehead, Eleanora found her tongue.

"Mazie!" she cried, hurrying down the stairs. The actress opened her arms wide, and Eleanora flung herself into them.

"I'm welcome, am I?" Mazie asked when they drew apart.

"You know you are," Eleanora said, smiling with an odd mistiness before her eyes.

"I had my doubts. You've been home for days and I've not seen hide nor hair of you."

"I know," Eleanora said contritely. "I asked Dr. Jones about you. He said you were doing well, happy with your John and the theater and your orphans. It sounded so idyllic I didn't want to intrude with my problems."

"Don't be silly. If you know me at all, you should know I'm dying to hear from your own lips how you are and what happened to you. I had no idea it was such an ordeal until I read the paper this morning. I thought it was just a case of Laredo taking you away into hiding. Romantic, but scarcely the dangerous and trying time the *El Nicaraguense* hinted at. All the rest has been kept quiet here in town, very quiet."

"Oh—the papers," Eleanora said, wondering, suddenly, what Grant would make of her having talked to the editor. Not that it mattered. Still, she preferred to avoid any strain between them. "Come and sit down," she went on. "And I will see what I can do about a cup of coffee."

The orange blossoms were gone from the trees at the end of the patio now, leaving only a few fruit here and there and the cool shade of the polished green leaves. The sun's glare was brilliant on the stones of the patio floor, and puddles of water, draining from the pots of the señora's flowers which she had just finished watering, evaporated before their eyes.

"I have a curious message for you from Neville," Mazie said when Eleanora had set the coffee tray before them on the wrought-iron table.

"Oh?" Eleanora handed Mazie a cup, leaning back with her own.

"He said to tell you 'Congratulations,' and warn you he will call sometime tomorrow."

Eleanora lifted a brow in an attempt at wry amusement. "Does everyone know I'm with Grant again?"

"You are something of a celebrity. Naturally people are interested. Correct me if I'm wrong, but I believe Neville was more interested than most. It was he who told me you were here."

The thought of Neville Crawford watching her movements, perhaps even watching the palacio during the night to see if she was sent away, filled her with repugnance.

Her hazel eyes on Eleanora's expressive face, Mazie said, "If you find him so distasteful, you don't have to see him—or do you?"

"I don't know what you mean," Eleanora answered, flicking a glance at the other woman through her lashes.

"My dear, I have known Neville for a long time. He has his good points. He has the instincts and breeding of a gentleman, and he can be good for a woman's ego, but he has few principles when it comes to money. I know enough of his past dealings to guess that he is up to his neck in the tug-of-war between Walker and his backers, and Vanderbilt and his money. And I have a shrewd idea which faction is most attractive to Neville. You can pretend, if you like, that you have nothing to do with all that, but I'm warning you, I won't believe you."

To be relieved of her intolerable secret, to pour out the whole story to Mazie, including all the details she had not been able to speak aloud to Grant, much less expect him to understand, all the difficulties and embarrassments only another woman could appreciate—what harm could there be? Mazie was not likely to warn William Walker, even if it had not meant betraying both of her friends, Neville and Eleanora. In addition, the other woman had genuinely liked Jean-Paul. To lodge information that would bring all three before firing squads was a malicious act Eleanora judged Mazie incapable of committing. Neville, himself, with his cryptic message, had given Mazie her first clue that all was not as it should be. If Eleanora supplied the missing facts, he had only himself to blame.

She could not do it. The risk was too great. Raising her head, she said, "I'm sorry, Mazie, really I am, but I just don't understand what you are talking about."

Mazie stared at her. In the pitiless daylight there was a coating of rice powder on the actress's face, and traces of lip salve on her mouth. It gave her a dissolute look that in no way detracted from her appearance of greater-than-average worldly wisdom. The petals of the flowers on her bonnet fluttered as she nodded. "It's worse than I thought then. All right. We won't talk about it. Just remember this: if you need a place to go, you are always welcome wherever I am."

"Mazie, you—"

"Don't worry about me. I can't see much ahead except trouble for you, honey. I'd like to help with it if I can. If I can't, then the last thing I want is to add to it."

As Mazie got to her feet, Eleanora touched her arm. "There is something you can do, if you will?"

"What is it?"

"Tell Neville I don't want him here. I'll meet him anywhere else but here."

"That's all?"

"That is all." Eleanora's voice was firm. It might be harder for her to meet Neville elsewhere, still it would be worth it. She could not bear the thought of him penetrating to the fastness of this patio, of having to make him welcome here within the palacio where she had once known a fleeting happiness. It might be impossible to bar the effects of his machinations, but she could bar his presence, and she would.

Although Grant returned to take the noon meal with her, his manner was preoccupied and he did not tarry. When he had gone, and Señora Paredes, after clearing the table, had disappeared into the lower regions of the house for her siesta, Eleanora wandered about the patio. Her nerves were as tight as stay strings. Under the circumstances, it was impossible for her not to speculate on the reasons for Grant's distraction. Had the news of the disturbance at León reached Granada? Was Walker even now holding council to outline his strategy to counter the move of President Rivas?

Doubtless she should be doing something, but what? She could look through the papers left in the bedchamber; there had been a stack of them in the wardrobe. Not that she supposed there was anything of value among them. If Neville was correct, there would have been little time for Grant, or anyone else, to put anything in writing.

The bedchamber was stifling with afternoon heat. Eleanora pulled back the drapes to let in light enough to see, then as perspiration began to trickle along her hairline, she threw the window wide. The sun had moved to the other side of the house now. The street-side galería was in the shade; it had to be cooler. Even if it was not, anything was better than this close airlessness.

Or was it? There was something disconcerting in rifling a man's papers in an open room. Her heart beat higher and her fingers trembled as she turned over the guard book, the horse books, and the registration book with its hundreds of recruits listed in her own painstaking copperplate. The sheaf of papers underneath these journals seemed to be concerned with supplies and their storage and movement during the days of conflict just past. There was nothing else.

She had looked. It was a relief to be done with that disagreeable task, to stack the books and papers neatly away and know that she need not touch them again.

Intent on putting everything back exactly as she had found it, Eleanora failed to notice the opening and closing of the door below. Her first warning was the sound of masculine voices in the patio, followed by the tread of footsteps on the stairs.

It could only be Grant. No one else would walk into the palacio without ringing the bell, or seeking out the señora to rouse her from her nap.

With quiet haste, Eleanora replaced the last of the papers in the wardrobe, closed the door, and stepped out onto the galería. If she had the time she would whip out of sight; if not, she could pretend to be taking the air. It did not, in her guilt, occur to her to stay where she was and brazen it out with the natural excuse of the siesta hour.

In any case, she was able to stroll along the galería to the end with reasonable dignity. Taking a seat on the railing beneath the waving, untrimmed branches of the bougainvillea, she waited to see if she would be discovered.

She was not. Grant appeared to have forgotten her presence in the house. He ushered his guests into the bedchamber with apologies for its heat, and amid the disclaimers there came the scrape of chairs as the men were seated about the table.

Eleanora recognized the voice of William Walker without difficulty. One of the other men was Colonel Thomas Henry, she thought, while the fourth man she could not quite place, though he sounded vaguely familiar.

In the agitation of her discovery, it was a moment before she realized the implications of the meeting. What other than a need for secrecy would make these men choose a hot, cramped bedchamber for their conference instead of the large, open rooms of the Government House? And what other than the crisis at León could make such a conference necessary at this time?

From her present vantage point she could hear the rumble of the men's voices, but she could catch only a word now and then of what they were saying. Casually, for the sake of anyone who might be watching from the street, she moved back against the wall of the house. Avoiding the iron grilles between the windows of the other rooms along the wall, she picked her post and leaned with her shoulders to the warm, golden stone of the building. In her concentration, she shredded the petals of the bougainvillea she had plucked, dropping them to the floor without noticing, as she listened.

"Seems to me," Colonel Henry was saying in his slow drawl, "that it was just a matter of time before Rivas started acting up. It couldn't help but go against the grain, being a figurehead president, what with him being an aristocrat, and all that. This trick of his of starting false rumors seems about what we ought to have expected. Wouldn't surprise me if you didn't have some plan in mind already for dealing with him, General."

That Walker was pleased could be heard in his voice. "Maybe. I want to hear what the rest of you have to say first."

"I say get rid of him!" the stranger in the group said,

his tone grim. "Arrest him and his colleagues, try them, and execute them as traitors just as the man has accused you of planning. You can't afford internal disputes right now. Not only would it look bad to any of the more powerful countries who might be disposed to lend you their support, it would be an invitation for an attack from San Salvador or Guatemala. Costa Rica may be crippled, but the others aren't. All of them, even the Hondurans with their pretense of neutrality, are just waiting for you to turn your back."

"That may be," Grant said slowly. "But it looks to me like moving against Rivas would be more likely to start a civil war instead of quelling the disturbance."

Colonel Henry slapped the table. "Grant's right. On the other hand, we can't let this Rivas keep stirring things up. We have to be practical. Nobody takes kindly to having strangers move into their country and set leaders up over them. What we ought to do is call an election in the good old American way. Ten to one, you'd beat Rivas to a standstill, the way most of these people feel about you right now, General."

"You have a point," Walker admitted.

"Think of how much more convenient it would be if you were president," Colonel Henry went on, warming to his subject.

"First we have to do something about the riot the current president has started," Walker reminded him gently.

"The easiest thing to do would be to assassinate him," the stranger muttered, an observation no one appeared to take seriously.

Grant spoke next, his voice slow, as if he were forming his thoughts aloud. "What would you think, General, of letting Rivas understand that we intend to do exactly as his rumors suggest, arrest him and his associates? His reaction, if I'm any judge, should be to get out of the country as fast as he can, taking the main opposition in León with him."

"That way, we are rid of him without touching a hair on his head," Colonel Henry exclaimed.

"Exactly," Grant agreed. "With him gone, you, General Walker, could appoint a provisional president, someone with few political ambitions, and, after a suitable period, this man could call a new election."

"Ferrer," Walker said thoughtfully.

"What was that?" the strange man queried.

"Fermin Ferrer, a good man and a fine Democrático. He should be an excellent choice as provisional president."

"And the election?" Colonel Henry asked.

"By all means, though I believe it should be called as soon as possible."

"The rioting in León will need time to quiet down," Grant objected.

"León is a stronghold of the *aristocráticos* and the Legitimista party," Walker told him quietly. "They are used to electing one of their own to power. If they are in an uproar it may be difficult for them to organize the voting in that district—which would be most unfortunate, wouldn't it?"

She had heard enough. The longer she stood there, the more dangerous her position became. Waiting until one of the men was speaking once more, she moved to the French window of the next bedroom, eased it open, and stepped inside. She crossed the room with exquisite care to its inner door which stood open upon the galería. Moving a little farther along it, she turned and started back with normal footsteps, letting her hand slide along the railing. It would be unnatural for her not to put in an appearance while there were guests in the house. She might plead that she had stayed hidden from embarrassment, of course, but it was a little late for her to even pretend to blush for her reputation.

Arranging a smile of artless welcome on her face, she pushed open the bedchamber door, coming to a stop holding to the knob. "Grant," she began, "I thought I heard your voice—I'm sorry! I didn't mean to intrude. But, as long as I'm here, could I get something for you gentlemen? Coffee? Or I believe there is lemonade?"

An instant later her gaze was drawn irresistibly to the man who sat on Walker's right, the man whose voice she had not been able to identify. It was the American minister to Nicaragua, John Wheeler.

Twenty

"How is Jean-Paul? Is he all right?"

"He's doing fine." Neville Crawford answered Eleanora's anxious questions with something near irritation, returning at once to his foremost interest. "Are you sure that's all they said?"

"I'm sure," Eleanora replied. That made the fourth time Neville had repeated his same query, and she was not immune to annoyance herself. It was bad enough to have to connive with Mazie to meet him without having him act as if he suspected her of withholding information from him. Which, in point of fact, she was. She had kept to herself the knowledge that the planned arrest of Rivas was no more than a ruse. It was unlikely that Neville would find out otherwise, and without that small piece of information the rest became no more than what Grant and the general wanted the Legitimista faction to know anyway. She had also told Neville of the decision to appoint a provisional president, but she had been deliberately vague about his name, distorting it in several ways. It was the best compromise she could make with her conscience.

Now she said in her most subdued manner, "I'm sorry I couldn't be more helpful."

"I'm sorry too, for Jean-Paul's sake," Neville said.

Alarm coursed through her veins, though her expression did not change. "What do you mean? You said he was all right."

"So he is, for now. But we are dealing with impatient men. They want solid, accurate information; times, dates, the number of men expected to be in the arresting party, this sort of thing."

"What am I supposed to do? Ask General Walker to satisfy my curiosity? I did the best I could."

"Believe me, I sympathize, Eleanora, but I have to answer to these men too."

She wanted to throw his falseness back into his broad, handsome face. She held her tongue instead. It would not be very intelligent to antagonize this man. Moreover, there might be a grain of truth in what he said. In any case, she was grateful to Mazie for choosing that moment to come into the room.

"This is the most unloverlike clandestine meeting I have ever witnessed!" the actress teased. "A person would think the two of you were married, to hear you bickering with each other. Give it up and come give me your advice, both of you, on the new set I'm designing. I might even be able to find a drink for you, Neville, to calm your liver. You are looking decidedly bilious to me."

"I'm not one of your orphans," Neville growled, "so don't try mothering me." Still, his words lacked the force of real anger and he put his arm around Mazie's ample waist as she half-led, half-cajoled him from the theater loft where he and Eleanora had been talking.

"You, too, come along," Mazie said, looking back over Neville's shoulder at Eleanora, and, seeing the gratitude shining in her green eyes, the actress winked reassuringly.

The news of President Rivas's hurried departure from León with his cabinet was soon being discussed on every street corner. Ferrer took office within hours of official confirmation of the vacating of the capital. One of his first acts as president was to order a new election. The plan discussed in Eleanora's bedchamber had, so far, succeeded admirably.

At that moment in time there were three men in Central America calling themselves the president of Nicaragua. There was the original leader of the country, a man named Estrada, who had fled Granada on the day Walker captured the town nine months before. There was Rivas, the moderate legitimist who had been appointed as provisional president to take Estrada's place in a joint action by the defeated Legitimista army and Walker's Falangistas, and there was the new appointee, Ferrer. The reign of the latter was short. Within days, Nicaragua had its fourth president in less than a year, the man accredited with the majority of the votes cast in the duly held election. His name was William Walker.

The Granadans celebrated the election victory of their deliverer with fervor and fiesta. They ate, they drank, they danced in the streets. Lanterns were lit early and hung from brackets outside the houses, or from ropes slung over patio walls, and from the limbs of trees. Particular attention was given the plaza before the Government House. It was decked with dozens of lamps and torches illuminating the red-and-white bunting which decorated the government building, Walker's red-starred flag, and the group of musicians which would later move inside for the official fête.

The music and laughter came faintly to Eleanora as she stood at the window of the bedchamber. The warm evening breeze brought also the smells of dust and smoke and lantern fuel, of spicy food and the sweet, milky fragrance of the candy which was being consumed in rich, thick chunks, a part of every celebration. From the cathedral came the melancholy toll of the angelus. As always it stirred the pigeons, throwing them into flight. They swept across the sky in formation, a wheel of dark grace.

There was a chance the festivities would be spoiled. Out over the lake, beyond the cones of Ometepe, lightning flickered sullenly. It might be no more than heat lightning, but it gave the wine-dark sky a portentous look as it arched over the glowing town.

She should be getting dressed, donning the things laid out on the bed behind her, her party finery. Somehow, she could not summon the energy. Depression weighted her limbs, making it seem too much of an effort to put up her hair and struggle into the heavy petticoat, crinoline, and gown for celebration she had no desire to attend. She thought of making an excuse, but staying at the palacio alone while everyone else made merry had even less appeal than going to the Government House.

She had been alone so much in the last few days. In ways, the time reminded Eleanora of her first week with Grant. When he was with her he was passionately possessive, but he was so seldom with her. Walker, as always, commanded his first loyalty.

It had been a busy time, a time of decision for Uncle Billy, true enough. There had been days of traveling during the campaign for election. Also, from a few things she had heard at various times, she thought the plans for the transfer of the transit line were still going forward. Regardless, she found herself resenting Grant's duties more and more. She would have liked to have been completely alone with him somewhere, free of duty, free of entanglement or outside interference; a simple place where they need heed no desire other than their own.

Sometimes, catching an odd look in his deep-sea eyes as they rested on her, she was moved to wonder if Grant regretted taking her back. At others, she questioned if she meant anything more than a convenience to him—a woman always near to mend his clothes, see to his laundry and his meals, to slake his lust and send him comfortable into dreamless slumber. Was she foolish to expect more than this superficial intimacy? Was there anything more?

At a sound behind her, she half-turned to see Grant enter the doorway of the dusk-filled room. Finding her in the dark, he paused, then sauntered toward her. Coming near, he reached above her head to close the window and pull the drapes together. After dropping a light kiss on her mouth, he moved to the washstand where the lamp blossomed into light under his hard, brown fingers.

"Why aren't you getting dressed?" he asked with his back to her. "Don't you feel well?"

Here was her opportunity. She let it pass with no more than a flash of recognition. "I'm fine. I was just waiting for you."

"Good. You can do something with this pelt of mine. I look as shaggy as a bear."

Swinging to the wardrobe, he took out the case of medical supplies, picked the scissors from among the clutter, and threw them on the bed.

"Cut your hair?" Eleanora, watching him, asked doubtfully.

"Before I take my bath," he answered, stripping his shirt from his breeches.

The fault was her own. She had made the mistake of telling him that she had cut Luis's hair, and Slim's and Jean-Paul's, during their days together. That had been

307

different. In their situation, they had expected no more of her and the rusty knife she was forced to use than that she get the hair out of their eyes so they could see, and off their necks for coolness.

"I couldn't," she told Grant plainly.

"You have to. There's no one else."

"You would be better off wearing your hair long than going bald-headed."

Dropping onto the bed, lying back on his elbows, and lifting a booted foot for assistance, he said, "I don't plan on doing either one."

Automatically, she went to his aid, dropping the boots one after the other onto the floor. "You will if I get hold of you. I mean it. I can't. I've never done anything more than trim around the edges."

"That's all I want," he said, putting the scissors into her hand and sliding from the bed to take a seat in one of the straight-back chairs at the table.

His calm air of waiting for her to do as he asked set her teeth on edge, coming, as it did, so soon after her doubts. "Very well," she said. "Don't say I didn't warn you."

His thick black hair looked nearly straight, hard to cut without leaving it gapped or jagged. When she began to clip it, however, she found that it curved down the back of his head with a crisp vitality of its own. No matter how she cut the strands she picked up in her fingers, they sprang back to blend without difficulty with the rest of his hair. Grant did not fidget, offer her advice, or try to watch what she was doing as Jean-Paul, and even Luis, had done. He sat perfectly still, totally relaxed. After a few minutes, it reached her that his attitude was one of trust, not arrogance. Her hands steadied and she was able to do a creditable job, so creditable that it was impossible to resist taking his brushes and smoothing it into place, when she was done.

"Satisfied?" he asked, his hands closing about her waist as she stood between his legs, slipping under the worn army-issue shirt which she wore as a dressing gown.

"Yes," she answered without looking at him, giving his thick sideburns a last touch, and brushing at the dark mantle of clipped hair that lay across his naked shoulders.

"I'm not," he said, his voice muffled against the front of her shirt as his arms tightened, drawing her closer against him.

"Too bad," she told him, her hands gripping his shoulders to hold herself away. "I've already had my bath, and the hair—"

"We can take another one."

"We will be late for Uncle Billy's *levée*. Besides, you'll get hair in the bed."

Slipping the buttons out of their holes so that her shirt hung open, he asked, "Who said anything about the bed?"

"You don't mean—"

"Don't I? I seem to recall one of these rugs making you a fine pallet. The big one by the window, wasn't it?"

Scooping her into his arms, he kicked the rug nearer and lowered her upon it. His breath warm against her neck, he said, "It's one of my favorite memories."

The soft strumming of a guitar drifted over the assemblage. It grew gradually louder as the player, an attractive young man with proud, laughing eyes and flashing teeth, strolled through the doors and into the long reception room of the Government House. In appreciation of the spattering of applause and murmur of delighted compliments, he inclined his head, then began to sing as he continued in his slow circuit of the room.

He was good, very good. His guitar throbbed in perfect accompaniment to the love song he poured forth in a deep, caressing timbre. The fact that he was aware of his own excellence did not in any way detract from his raffish charm. The ladies looked at each other with small smiles. The gentlemen assumed expressions of boredom. Only Eleanora stood unmoved, as if turned to stone.

The young man, a Spaniard, was so like Luis. The song he was singing, a lover's serenade, was the same haunting madrigal that Luis had played for her once in private concert upon the galería. At least, she had thought it was private.

A sibilant hiss of silk skirts behind her put Eleanora on her guard. Marshaling her defenses was effective, to a degree, in banishing remembrance, and it was with tolerable composure that she turned as Niña Maria stopped beside her.

"How do you like our troubadour?" Walker's mistress inquired archly. "I was assured by Major Crawford that you would find him quite—devastating."

"Major Crawford is too observant," Eleanora replied after a moment, "and you are too kind." The falsity of it made the last word hard to force from her throat. Abandoning pretense, she raised her green eyes, dark with pain, to Niña Maria's coldly malicious face. "Why do you dislike me so? What have I ever done to you?"

The woman unfolded a fan of flesh-colored silk decorated with line drawings of Rubensesque nudes. "The answer to that is simple. You have done nothing but cause difficulty and embarrassment for me since the day you arrived. You supplanted Juanita, spoiling plans that had taken months to bring to fruition. You wormed your way into my William's affections so that he spoke of you with more genuine fondness in his voice than he has used with any woman, no doubt since that milk-and-water mademoiselle who captured his heart in New Orleans died."

"That can't be so," Eleanora protested, her brows knit in a frown of dismay. "There has never been the least indication—"

"Well, no, not in the way you are thinking. But the contrast between his genial, gentlemanly attitude toward you and his manner with me was marked—until the episode with Luis. That served to convince him you were not the innocent you looked. Nonetheless, your mere presence has made my task more difficult than it need have been."

Eleanora glanced involuntarily at the general standing some distance away. There was no danger of him, or anyone else, hearing their conversation over the music, especially in the alcove filled with potted plants where Eleanora had stopped to rest. It was ridiculous of her to think there might be, Eleanora realized. Niña Maria would never take such a chance.

"More than these things," Niña Maria went on, "you brought the invincible Iron Warrior to his knees so that he mooned after you like the most fatuous of suitors. My

310

friends had, at the time you came on the scene, been waiting with some amusement for me to pierce his armor as I had promised them I would. You made me look a fool. Under the circumstances, you can see that I have little reason to love you."

"You mean you intended to—?"

"Seduce is the word you are searching for," the woman supplied with a brittle laugh before Eleanora could complete her sentence. "Certainly. Who better than the intriguing Colonel Farrell?"

"What of you and the general?"

Niña Maria shrugged, an elaborate gesture which drew attention to the whiteness of her shoulders barely covered by her gown of maroon-and-black brocade. "The general is a man of power, and I find that exciting, but as you must have guessed by now, my association with him is a matter of politics, not choice. I see nothing wrong in entertaining myself elsewhere when he is not at hand, or is too busy to notice." As she spoke she had been watching the strolling singer, her eyes narrowed and a smile playing at the corner of her mouth. Now her smile widened and she turned to Eleanora. "Never mind that. A quarrel is meaningless between us as we are presently circumstanced. We are, I suppose, quits—as the Falangistas would say—since the Honduras episode. Let me congratulate you on your decision to join the party which will eventually rule in Nicaragua, and, incidentally, on your efforts in our behalf. It will interest you, I'm sure, to know that President Rivas escaped and is now in Chinandega, where he has set up an absentee government. He is in communication with the heads of state of San Salvador and Guatemala in an effort to gather aid in expelling the American invaders."

"So long as we are being honest," Eleanora broke in, "let me tell you that I have no interest whatever in President Rivas."

"I see. You are happy, then, that the general has been elected?"

Eleanora smiled. "That's right."

"With such sincerity in your favor, it should not be difficult for you to discover the date set for the inauguration."

311

"Surely that can be no problem?" Eleanora asked, turning to stare at her. "It should be posted on every wall, and half the tree trunks, in the city within a day or two."

"You are mistaken," Niña Maria said coolly. "There has been a threat on the general's life. It was one of those silly notes thrown through a window that comes to most public figures, but he has chosen to take it seriously."

"He wouldn't include you in his suspicions, I'm sure," Eleanora said, lowering her lashes in a gesture that did not so much conceal the irony of her question as reveal it.

Frowning, Niña Maria said. "Of course not! The general will trust no one except colonels Farrell and Henry with the information. I would have been included as a matter of course but for this stupid threat. William has not forgotten the cousin of my maid who entered our apartments unannounced. It was nothing more than a misunderstanding, but he refuses to believe it or to chance a repetition."

"Foolish of him," Eleanora murmured.

"We can defeat this man without resorting to cold-blooded murder," the other woman said in the cold tones of offended pride. "My main concern with discovering the date is convenience; my own. I have a tremendous amount of work to do to get ready for the inauguration, and it would be helpful to know how many days I have in which to arrange for the ball. It would be nice to be certain the pyrotechnics I ordered will be here in time. If you are reluctant to find this out for me, you can, naturally, apply to Major Crawford. I believe you will find that he will request—no, compel—you to do as I ask."

"I am aware of the collaboration between you and Neville," Eleanora said, "and so I am sure of it."

"Then, as you say, there can be no problem," Niña Maria returned with finality.

Eleanora ignored the dismissal. "Except that Grant may not feel compelled to tell me what you need to know."

"I'm sure you will find a way around that difficulty," the woman said, turning away. Then, as if on impulse, she swung back. "That is a charming gown you are wearing. Most becoming, but then it could be nothing else. My seamstress always outdoes herself."

Her seamstress? Eleanora felt a smothering sensation in her chest. If Niña Maria had had a hand in choosing the gown she wore, she would never wear it again. She would like to tear it to shreds and throw it in Grant's face. How dare he reveal the deficiencies of her wardrobe to that witch of a woman? How dare he expose her to Niña Maria's pity and condescension?

Her hands clasped tightly together before her, she searched the room with her eyes for Grant's wide-shouldered figure. Her heart ached a little as she saw him bending to catch the words of some blond nonentity in pale pink satin, the daughter, she thought, of an under-secretary in the office of the American minister. The lamplight gleamed blue-black on the sculptured cap of his hair, and was caught shimmering in the gold fringe of his epaulettes. Despite her intimate knowledge of his body, he was, from this distance, no more than a bar-barically handsome stranger, and she was struck anew by how little she knew of what he thought or felt.

Glancing up, he saw her and smiled in reassurance. His attention was diverted at that moment by the Spanish guitarist just letting the last notes of his song die away. In the following burst of applause, he spoke what was apparently an excuse to the girl beside him, and began to make his way through the crowd toward her.

Wanting to have him near her, Eleanora, perversely, did not want him to find her alone. When Major Neville Crawford passed near her, she beckoned to him with a surreptitious movement. Neville moved to her side with easy, big-boned grace, though he too watched Grant's approach from the corner of his eye. Leaning close, he said, with more perspicacity than she had credited to him, "What are you playing at, dear Eleanora?"

There was no time to answer. Grant, nodding coldly at Neville, stopped before them. "Ready to go?" he asked, placing a hand under her elbow.

"Yes," she answered with a show of readiness. "As soon as I give Major Crawford the waltz I promised him."

His grip tightened. "Another time," he said evenly. "I'm sure Major Crawford will understand."

Neville stepped back at once, though his gaze, as it

moved from Grant to Eleanora, held a tightly controlled envy.

They made their adieus with the utmost grace and harmony, Grant good-humoredly refusing the offer from his fellow officers to extend the evening by going on to a cantina, accepting the sly innuendos directed after him without rancor.

As they passed out the front doors, Grant returned the salute of the guards with mechanical precision. His voice was just as mechanical, just as precise, as he said to her, "You seem to have gotten very friendly with Crawford."

"He was kind to me in Honduras when I came out of prison, and we were together on the ship as I came home," she answered coolly.

"But you knew him before that?"

She did not at all care for his manner. "We arrived here on the boat from New Orleans, if that is what you mean?"

"You have been seen walking with him in town, both before you left, and since."

"Before I—left, as you call it, he was good enough to escort me to the hospital once or twice. We were usually in company with Mazie, since he is a friend of hers."

"Oh, yes, Mazie," he said with a slow nod.

Eleanora came to a halt at the turn into the Calle Santa Celia. "I must ask you not to speak of Mazie in that tone," she told him, her voice trembling with the anger building inside her. "She has her faults, but she is a better person, kinder, less immoral, than many of your so-called friends."

"Such as?" he asked, his voice hard.

"Such as Niña Maria," she declared, and turned swiftly away, afraid she had said too much.

He caught up with her in a single stride. "I suppose you mean something by that."

"Nothing I need explain to you," she answered.

"That's what you think," he grated, thrusting open the door of the palacio, slamming it behind them when they had passed through.

Take care—a part of Eleanora's mind whispered, but she did not heed it. "Your Niña Maria," she said, her eyes glittering in the dimness of the patio, "was good

314

enough to tell me this evening that until I arrived in Granada you were all set to succumb to her Spanish charms!"

It was a pleasure, in her present frame of mind, to see him taken aback, but it seemed unwise to stay around to enjoy the spectacle. She was halfway up the stairs before he found his voice.

"The hell she did! It's a bare-faced lie! But even if it were so, what is it to you? You weren't here."

There was no answer to that. She tried another tack. "And I suppose I am to overlook the fact that that woman is responsible for the gown I am wearing?"

"That's not so," he said, following her into the bedchamber.

"Deny, then," she said, swinging on him, "that it was made by her seamstress! Hurried through for the sake of the patronage of the mistress of William Walker."

"I can't deny that," he told her, a black scowl drawing his brows together. "It was made by her seamstress because I had been there before with Walker, and she was the only one I knew. But I chose the goods, and I told the woman the style I wanted, and it was paid for with my money. The extra premium that got the thing rushed through so you could wear it when you needed it was paid for by me too. Niña Maria had nothing to do with it. How she found out about it, I couldn't say, except she makes a point of knowing everybody's business. She is a Nicaraguan bitch I would like to see kicked out of the Government House on her backside. She has led a fine man a merry dance, maybe even jeopardized what we have been trying to do here, but as long as she holds Uncle Billy in the palm of her hand, I have to put up with her."

His blue eyes, dark with anger, raked her face left pale by the receding of her rage. "Of course," he said, taking a step toward her that had in its smooth strength a touch of menace, "if you don't like the gown, you don't have to wear it. You don't have to wear anything at all!"

Reaching out, he hooked his fingers into the low neckline.

"No!" she cried, her hands closing over his as she realized his intention. "I do like it," she went on contritely, her eyes searching his face as she felt the tension leaving him. "Really I do. It is the most beautiful thing I have ever owned."

For the space of several heartbeats they stared at each other. Slowly, the grip of Grant's hands slackened. They slid over her shoulders and down her back, to clasp behind her waist. Eleanora made no attempt to draw away.

"Would you like to swear," Grant queried slowly, his gaze on the sensitive curves of her mouth, "that you weren't a little jealous just now?"

Though she tried, Eleanora could not raise her eyes above the level of the gold buttons on his tunic. "I might," she answered, "if you will swear the same?"

"Never a straight answer," he said pensively. "I wonder who you are afraid of—me, or yourself?"

Such insight could be dangerous. Throwing back her head, she asked, "Does it matter?"

"No. Nothing matters as long as you are here, in my arms," he said, and lowered his mouth to hers.

Twenty-one

Eleanora hurried along the streets, her basket swinging empty on her arm. On the outward trip it had been filled with carbolic and ointments, baby napkins and shirts carefully hemmed by hand, plus candy and cakes provided by Señora Paredes. Mazie, in answer to a note from Eleanora, had suggested that she meet Neville on this occasion at the orphanage of the Church of Guadelupe, and, on consideration, it had seemed like a good idea. An extra measure of care had appeared reasonable in view of the way her every action was reported to Grant. What could be more innocuous than visiting the children of the orphanage? At the same time she had had the pleasure of seeing to their inevitable small injuries, of adding to the

316

supplies of the sisters in charge, and watching the pleasure of the dark-eyed children as they devoured the treats she had brought.

There was, in her opinion, little other value to the journey. She had had absolutely no difficulty in learning the date of the inauguration. She had mentioned it to Grant in a casual manner at the breakfast table, and, just as casually, he had informed her it would be held on the tenth day of July, six days hence. Why Niña Maria had made such an issue of it, Eleanora could not imagine, though there was a vague suspicion in her mind that the woman had given her a fool's errand merely to cause her agitation. Neville's attitude on receiving the information had been noncommittal. She had not been able to tell if he had expected or even wanted it. He had asked for further details on when and where the ceremonies would be held, but when she had been unable to tell him, he had not pressed her.

As Eleanora neared the palacio, her footsteps slowed. There was an odd equipage standing before the building. It had the look, she thought in amazement, of a traveling carriage. Beneath the coating of dust, its body was painted a hard, shining black. Its fittings were of polished brass which gleamed like gold in the sun. On the side panel, in red and blue and gold, was emblazoned a crest. Under the haze of dust, she could not see the insignia with any clarity until she was opposite the carriage. Then she stopped, the flush of heat and hurrying draining from her face to leave it pale. The design on the panel was the same as that cut into the signet ring she wore on her finger, the arms of Luis's family.

Señora Paredes was waiting for her in the entrance hall. Her eyes glittered beneath her best lace cap and there was a hint of color in the waxen paleness of her cheeks. "You have a visitor," she informed Eleanora in a voice which trembled with hushed excitement. "I gave him coffee and some of my cakes in the *sala*. He has been waiting this hour and is growing impatient, I'm sure."

The *sala?* The man must be a personage indeed. No one was allowed in this room except the most distinguished of visitors on the most stately of occasions. Of good family herself, it took someone extraordinary to impress the señora.

"Thank you," Eleanora murmured. Smoothing her hair, she put her hand on the handle of the tall, carved door leading from the hall with a distinct feeling of trepidation.

The man who rose to his feet at her entry was tall and thin with white hair and a silver beard trimmed to a small point. His bow was an exquisite model of grace, though he did not offer to take her hand. Straightening to his full height, he stared down at her with cool and distant courtesy. No expression crossed his aquiline face, but Eleanora knew he was both surprised and displeased at her appearance.

"You are Señora de Laredo, the wife of Luis Andres Charles Emmanuel de Laredo y Pacquero?"

"His widow, yes."

"Of course, my apologies," he said, lowering his eyelids in a gesture which did not quite conceal the lashlike flick of his eyes over her skirt and blouse.

Eleanora might have been excused for resenting his attitude. She did not. In a quiet voice she said, "There is no need for apologies. If you know I was wed to Luis, you must know the marriage was of only a few hours' duration. You cannot know, however, that I was sincerely attached to him and would be wearing black if such a thing were economically possible."

He stared at her while she returned his gaze with calm green eyes. After a moment, he inclined his head once more in an obeisance that was far deeper. "I must beg your pardon, señora, for underestimating the depth of your sensitivity. Permit me to present myself. I am Esteban de Laredo, the uncle of the man you married."

Acknowledging the introduction, Eleanora indicated that they should be seated. "When I saw your carriage outside I suspected you might be related to Luis," she said with simplicity. And removing the signet, she held it out to him.

He took it with fingers that trembled slightly, holding it to the light which filtered through the curtains and the grille over the windows. He wiped at his eyes as if a film

318

had covered them, and Eleanora looked away, aware suddenly that the Spaniard was an old man, and grieved.

It was stuffy in the room but not uncomfortably warm. White walls stretching to the dark beams of the high ceiling gave an impression of coolness. This was aided by the stone floor which was polished to a sheen and laid with a single rug of oriental design positioned before the plain-fronted fireplace. On each side of the rug was a settee of carved walnut fitted with velvet cushions, and walnut framed the paintings, crude copies of Spanish and Flemish masters, which hung on every wall.

"There can be no doubt that you had this of my nephew," the Spaniard said, returning the ring to Eleanora at last. "I was present when my brother, his father, gave it to him on his twenty-first birthday. He was very proud of it. I cannot imagine him parting with it unless he cared for you very much."

Closing her hand tightly over the ring, Eleanora returned no answer. She sat on the edge of her seat, unable to relax, conscious of the dirt on the hem of her skirts from walking through the filthy streets, and her generally grubby appearance from handling and hugging the children at the orphanage. Looking up, she said, "Was there something you wanted of me, some way I could help you?"

"I hope, señora, that I will be able to help *you*. It seems to the highest degree likely. I have the honor, you see, to serve in the capacity of *abogado*—you would say in English the attorney—of the Conde de Laredo and the estates belonging to him and his family. Six months ago my brother, Don Carlos, was killed in a fall from his horse. It was clearly necessary for Luis to return home for the purpose of assuming the title and his duties as the Conde. I made the proper arrangements, including an application to the court of Isabella to intervene in a private matter, a dispute between Luis and a family of our acquaintance, should the occasion arise. This done, I had only to find Luis. Our last communication with him came from California in the United States of America. Receiving no answer to my letters sent to the last address given, I set out to find him. Unfamiliar with the state of the roads in this new world, I brought, among other things, the family carriage you saw in the expectation that having it would expedite the search. A mistake, not the first on this endless quest which, for the most part, has been by water. Arriving in California, I discovered that Luis had involved himself with this William Walker. I will not bore you with a recital of my wanderings since that day. Suffice it to say that when I came to San Juan del Norte on the Atlantic coast, it was to be met with the intelligence that my nephew was a fugitive. I am not without influence, even in this country forsaken of God. I learned finally that he was imprisoned in Honduras. But when I landed at that place it was to receive the terrible message that Luis, my nephew, the heir to the title, was dead. The Conde de Laredo had been shot before a firing squad like a common felon."

Eleanora made an involuntary movement with her hand, as if to stop him, but she could not speak. The Conde. The Falangistas had called Luis by that name in jest. How could they have known? The answer was, they could not. Such a story would have been given full circulation. Perhaps there was something to be said for breeding and bloodlines?

That was certainly true of the elderly man before her. Conquering the feelings which threatened to overcome him, he lifted his head.

"Forgive me," he said quietly. "Being reminded of that time cannot but be painful for you. I was telling you why I am here, wasn't I? You had been taken from Honduras by the time I arrived. Your existence was revealed to me by the priest who heard my nephew's last confession, one Father Sebastian. I believe you, señora—or perhaps I should say *Condesa*—have cause to remember him? He told me of Luis's last days and of his marriage. He showed me the official record of the bond, duly entered in the register of his church, and he gave me also a document which Luis had entrusted to him. It was a will, scrawled on the flyleaf of the priest's Bible. Irregular, certainly, but entirely legal. Luis had instructed the priest to send it to me, as the *abogado,* and no doubt he would have done so when he could be assured it would arrive safely. He

320

was quite relieved to hand it to me in person. This will named you, Eleanora Colette de Laredo nee Villars, as the beneficiary. The estates, the castle and land, the olive orchards, exporting firm, and a number of other enterprises, are all entailed. Luis was, however, the possessor of a handsome fortune in unentailed property, an inheritance from his maternal grandmother. This is yours."

Allow me—to offer you what protection there may be in my name—Eleanora shook her head dazedly, those words running like a soft refrain through her mind.

"It is quite true," the older man assured her in response to the negative. "The arrangements may take a little time, but these monies will be paid into the bank of your choice." He hesitated, then went on, "Naturally, if there is any issue from the marriage the situation will change drastically. The son of Luis, born posthumously within nine months of his death, would become the new Conde, acceding to the honors of his father. He will, of course, be reared in Spain, and you, as the dowager Condesa and his mother, would have a place there."

Eleanora found she could not bear to quench the hopefulness in the Spaniard's eyes entirely. In suffocating tones she replied, "There is little chance of that coming to pass, señor."

He nodded as if he had expected no less, saying only, "You will inform me in such an event," before going on. "At the end of nine months the title will revert to the next male heir, in this case, though it is painful for me to say it, myself. You, of course, will be entitled to be known as the Condesa de Laredo until your death—or remarriage."

When he paused, obviously waiting for her comment, Eleanora said slowly, "What if I were to refuse this legacy?"

"Refuse—You can't be serious?"

"But if I did?" she persisted.

A frown knitting his silver brows, the Spaniard said, "It would not be at all the thing for a Laredo to leave a woman he cared for without funds, much less his wife. Even if Luis had not made provisions for you, I would have felt bound to make you an allowance from the estate at the very least. No, what my nephew intended for you to have shall be yours. What you do with it afterward is your affair, but I would hope you would use it for your future security, as Luis wanted. The world is not always kind to women alone."

It was plain that this aristocratic old gentleman knew more of her than he had said. The trace of censure hidden behind the understanding in his eyes brought her position home to her as few other things had done since she had come to Nicaragua. A bleak feeling settled in her chest and would not be dislodged. She was, despite the reasons for it, living with a man out of wedlock, a fallen woman, a Magdalene. Something in the austere face of the old man seemed to hint that the least penalty she could expect would be, eventually, to find herself alone.

There was little more to be discussed. With grave gallantry, Don Esteban de Laredo gave her his direction and took his leave, pausing only to collect his hat and cane from Señora Paredes and cast her into a dither by complimenting her on the cakes she had given him. When the door had closed behind him, Eleanora stood almost as bemused at the señora. It would, however, have been cruel to leave the older woman's palpitating curiosity entirely unsatisfied. "The gentleman," Eleanora told her as the woman made to pass her to tidy the *sala*, "was a relative of Lieutenant Colonel de Laredo. He only wanted to speak to me of him."

The glibness of the half-truth troubled her for some time. Lying, treason, fornication—she seemed capable of anything with the proper justification.

The preparations for the inauguration continued apace, despite the fact that, contrary to Eleanora's expectations, no notice of the date had been posted. From the plaza came the constant ring of hammers as the grandstand was nailed together. Here and there bunting was being draped across the windows of houses, in defiance of the lightning which still flickered nightly above the lake. There were reports of rain from the south, but not a drop fell on Granada.

She had not told Grant of the visit of Don Esteban or of the legacy. He might not go so far as to forbid her to accept it, but he would not like her to use it while she was with him. On the other hand, he had offered her no lasting security, and there might come a time when she—and Jean-Paul—would be glad of the stability and freedom from care embodied in Luis's name. The Condesa. Did Grant know she had the right to that title? Could he begin to guess what a hollow sound the syllables had in her ears?

It was not a time, in any case, for confidences of a personal nature. Grant grew more withdrawn with each passing day, and his manner more irritable. Eleanora ascribed it to the heat and long hours he was on duty with the general. She had little right to complain. Her own temper was none too stable. Prey to a terrible uncertainty, her moods varied from snappish, to pensive, to a forced cheerfulness. During the nights she lay for long hours beside Grant, watching with wide, sleepless eyes the intermittent glow of lightning as it lit the dark walls of the room.

The morning of the tenth dawned sulfurous and breathlessly warm. Only the need of a stimulant to put life into her leaden limbs made it possible for Eleanora to endure the heat of her coffee. She could not bear the thought of eating anything. She sat at the table, watching Grant, trying not to think of what it would be like on the grandstand in the full glare of the sun with everyone dressed in full regalia.

"What time does the inauguration begin?" she asked presently.

Grant slid his plate to one side, leaving half the food upon it untouched. He wore only his breeches, and as he stretched the muscles rippled under the skin. Pushing back his chair, he moved to the washstand and picked up the pitcher, bringing it back to fill his empty coffee cup with water. Watching him, Eleanora felt her stomach muscles tighten. It was a moment before she realized he was taking his time about answering her, but before she could decide whether it was deliberate or just slowness caused by the hour and the temperature, he spoke.

"It will be after the siesta hour, when it's cooler and the grandstand is in the shade of the buildings. The church bells are supposed to ring to announce it. Don't worry about it. I'll come for you when it's time."

323

She nodded, mentally chiding herself for her suspicions. He had only been thinking of how to make it easier for her to be with him.

In contrition, her kiss, as later he made ready to leave her, might have been more lingering than usual. He raised his head, his arm tightening around her so that the tail of the shirt she wore rode up high on her hips. Her breasts and the lower part of her body were pressed against him. Twin flames of desire burned in the depths of his eyes as he stared down at her, but they were nearly obscured by an odd and inscrutable severity. A pulse throbbed in his throat and his jaws were rigid. Abruptly he kissed her hard and put her from him. Settling his hat on his head, he stepped through the door. He did not slam it, but Eleanora thought he only just prevented himself from doing so.

Alone, Eleanora dressed, cleared the breakfast dishes, and made the bed. With that much concession to order out of the way, she spent quite some time before her mirror dressing her hair for the inauguration. Doing it now would pass the morning as well as saving precious time later when Grant might be waiting for her to make herself ready. She was patting a last pin into place when the bell jangled through the palacio. She stood listening, but had almost decided it was nothing to do with her when the señora, out of breath from struggling up the stairs, tapped on the door.

It was inquisitiveness, Eleanora thought, which brought her. The dress box she carried was heavy and bulky, and she could just as easily have either sent it up with whoever had brought it or called to Eleanora to come and get it. Instead, she stood panting in the doorway. "This came for you," she said, her lashless eyes hopeful, yet shadowed with doubt.

In the days since her return, Eleanora, dismissing her suspicions, had come to an unspoken understanding with the old woman. They were both lonely at times, both felt some dependency on Grant and, therefore, were concerned with his comfort and well-being. These were powerful forces, within the enclosing walls of the palacio, to bring them together. They had fallen into the habit of discussing

324

the menus for the day each morning, a ritual which had come to include the drinking of coffee or lemonade in the patio. Their discussions had gradually gone beyond food to a range of uneasy communication which could be classified as passing the time of day. By no means a friend, the señora was still a woman with a woman's craving for something new and different to enliven the dullness of her days.

"Thank you for bringing it up," Eleanora said. "Let's put it on the bed, and perhaps you will help me open it."

Removing layers of tissue paper from the top of the box revealed a day gown of pale yellow dimity sprigged with clusters of cool green leaves. To be worn with it was a bonnet of white chip-straw lined under the brim with yellow and decorated around the crown with a wreath of green leaves made of silk. Under still more layers of tissue was a ballgown constructed of layer upon layer of white tulle edged with rosepoint lace and featuring a bertha of lace held in place over the shoulders by a breast corsage of pink silk roses surrounded by green leaves. Included was a pair of combs for the hair supporting sprays of the same pink roses.

The señora exclaimed, clasping her hands before her, as each new item was lifted from the box and spread out upon the bed, though toward the last she ceased to exclaim, only standing staring at the beautiful things with ravaged eyes.

"Once I had such things," she said unsteadily, when it was plain there was no more. "It was before Señor Paredes, my husband, died; when we were young together, and he hoped to find favor in my eyes. The colonel—if you will forgive my saying so—must love you exceedingly."

The gowns, even the thoughtfulness behind them, were not, to Eleanora's thinking, proof of love. Still, remembering her ungraciousness and the accusations she had thrown at Grant concerning the other gown he had had made for her, she could not help but feel an echo of the señora's wonder in her own heart. Recalling also his strictures on the greedy and grasping ways of women when they had first met, she was inclined to succumb to a hope that the older woman was right.

They were interrupted by the clanging once more of the bell. Before the señora could get halfway down the stairs, they heard Mazie's raised voice from the entrance hall. Stepping to the galería, Eleanora called down to her to come up, then stood smiling as she watched her climb the stairs, thinking that the heat had finally had its effect on her friend, for Mazie wore a man's shirt open at the neck and with the sleeves rolled high above her plump elbows. She had left off her crinoline, and an apron made of sacking was draped over the fullness of her skirt of worn purple taffeta. Over her hair, she had tied a discarded scarf with fringed ends.

Rallying words rose to Eleanora's lips, but as she saw the face of the actress they died unspoken. She was grateful then to the señora, whose relenting did not include Mazie, for continuing on down the stairs after the nod of greeting, making her way back to the kitchen region.

When the door had closed behind them, Mazie swung around. "There is something I have to tell you. What you do with it is up to you, but I couldn't just do nothing, knowing you might be going into danger."

"What do you mean?" Eleanora asked, standing still with her hand on the handle of the door.

"I mean there is a plot to assassinate William Walker, today, at the inauguration!"

Eleanora let her breath out slowly. "I know there was a threat against him, but he is aware of it, and I'm sure he is taking preventive measures."

"This is no threat! This is solid, stone-hard fact."

"You had better tell me about it," Eleanora said, moving into the room. There was a hard knot forming just under her ribs, but she disregarded it, her eyes never leaving Mazie's face.

Looking around her, Mazie found one of the straight-back chairs near the dining table and sat down upon it. Her elbow resting on the table, she put her hand to her head. "Two days ago Neville came to the theater. He talked to me awhile, then he asked to see John, alone. They went outside, and in a little bit, I thought I heard raised voices. Before I could look out to see, John came on back in. He was so quiet I thought I had been mistaken, that

326

the noise had come from down the street. I should tell you, I guess, that before John turned actor back home in his native England, he was a miner. He worked with black powder in the coal mines, using it to blast the coal loose so it could be mined. He got the beginning of lung sickness and quit several years ago. Acting seemed a profession that would not require much in the way of hard labor, so he took it up. At some time I must have mentioned this to Neville and he remembered it. At any rate, John woke me early this morning to tell me that what Neville had wanted of him was to set a charge of black powder, get it all ready—or at the very least tell him how to get it ready—so that it would go off after a certain period of time, say as long as five minutes. Neville wanted an explosion guaranteed large enough to blow scaffolding to splinters, and he was willing to pay what amounted to a small fortune to get it.

"It wasn't too hard, knowing Neville's leanings, the amount of money involved, and the secret nature of the project, to guess what was in the air. John told Neville he wanted no part of it. He told him to get somebody else, but then he got to thinking about it, and he began to be afraid Neville *would* find somebody who could do what he wanted. John has no liking for Walker—or any kind of authority, for that matter. Hasn't had since he was in the thick of the fight between the mine owners and the miners attempting to band together in unions for better conditions. But it went against the grain to stand by and see a man murdered when he could prevent it. He got to thinking too about who else beside William Walker might be on that grandstand today, maybe even you and Grant, and he decided he had to tell somebody what was going to happen."

Slowly Eleanora moved to take the chair across from Mazie. "Neville is going to—blow up the grandstand this afternoon—with the general on it?" The general and Grant, certainly Grant.

"Is it to be this afternoon? Thank God I'm not too late. I was afraid they might try to get it over in the morning cool," Mazie said.

"No, it will be toward evening. There is still time,"

Eleanora answered, though she was hardly aware of what she was saying. What should she do? Tell Grant, of course, but how was she to convey the warning without letting it be known that she was responsible for the assassins knowing the date scheduled for the ceremony?

"I am so relieved. I was afraid I might find you gone already when I got here. I swear I aged ten years," Mazie declared, inclined to laugh now that the urgency was passed and she had shifted the responsibility to other shoulders.

"I can't tell you how grateful I am," Eleanora, recalled to her manners, told her. "I am sure Walker will wish to thank you, also."

"No, no," Mazie said, alarm sounding in her voice. "I don't want thanks. In fact, I would rather not have my name, or John's either, mentioned in it. The less I have to do with the high-ups, the better I like it."

Eleanora could not blame her. She felt much the same way, but she could see little chance of keeping aloof from it. There was a single possibility.

No dispatch riders kicked their heels outside the Government House; no sutlers or tradesmen waited, no petty municipal officials strode about big with their complaints. All was quiet, a certain sign that the general was not in. In her gratitude for the mercy, Eleanora did not stop to question his whereabouts. She asked at once for Niña Maria. A junior officer in a red tunic without epaulettes took her name and asked her to wait in an antechamber. She entered the room he indicated with the greatest reluctance, afraid Grant would appear at any moment and demand that she account for her presence there.

A small mirror hung over a table on one wall. Eleanora, walking about the room, caught sight of herself in it. She had thrown a mantilla over her hair. Now she pushed the triangle of black lace down upon her shoulders as a fichu, smoothing the carefully arranged waves and curls, thinking with distraction of how unlikely it was now that she would have need of such an elaborate coiffure. Her eyes were dark green with apprehension, and lavender shadows smudged the skin beneath them, giving her a look of fragility that was not unappealing, though she could not appreciate it. Turning from the mirror, she began to pace the small room. She had just forced herself to be seated in an uncomfortable armchair, striving for at least the appearance of composure, when the young officer returned to lead her upstairs.

The apartments occupied by William Walker and Niña Maria were opulent, hung with brocade and velvet in rich colors and furnished with heavy, ornately embellished furniture which, Eleanora suspected, had been confiscated from the homes of some of the aristocrats who had quit Granada when Walker captured the town. The bedchamber was done in black and gold with an almost oriental attention to comfort in the profusion of cushions and pillows and the velvetlike softness of the Persian rug that lay upon the floor. Niña Maria sat before an enormous dressing table built with several levels, inset boxes for jewelry and cosmetics, and a towering mirror which reflected the entire room, including the brocade-and-satin-draped four-poster bed.

That bed was covered with gowns and petticoats, chemises, and pantaloons and bonnets. Trunks and boxes sat about on the floor, and tissue paper lay in drifts over everything. With a hairbrush in her hand, Niña Maria was scolding her maid, a stolid, middle-age Nicaraguan woman, instructing her in how to fold a silk petticoat. She did not acknowledge Eleanora until she had finished her tirade. Then she waved her to a small slipper chair, saying without ceremony, "I hope this isn't merely a social call. As you can see, I am busy. I must get this packing done and out of the way before the general returns."

"You are leaving?" Eleanora asked, momentarily diverted from the reason for her visit.

"There is a possibility. That can't interest you, however. Tell me what I can do—no, you stupid cow! Put the slippers in a box by themselves, not on that velvet mantle."

As Niña Maria turned back to her, Eleanora said, "I would like to speak to you alone. It is most urgent."

"There's no need, I'm sure, to be melodramatic. My woman has been with me for years. Whatever you have to say can be said in front of her."

"I would rather not," Eleanora insisted.

"I assure you, she enters into my every sympathy; my thoughts are hers. Furthermore, I have no intention of delaying my departure from here for your sake. If you wish to speak to me, speak. If not—" She shrugged.

Eleanora lifted a brow at the tone of the woman's voice, her face hardening. "Very well," she said. "I have learned of a plot to assassinate William Walker, and who-ever might be with him on the grandstand, during the in-auguration this afternoon."

"What do you mean? What is this plot?" Walker's mis-tress demanded.

"There is a possibility the grandstand will be blown up with explosives," Eleanora told her, explaining briefly how she had gained the knowledge.

"Madre de Dios! Why wasn't I warned? I might have been killed, the imbeciles!"

"Precisely," Eleanora said in her driest tone.

The maid had stopped what she was doing to stand listening. With an irritable gesture, Niña Maria waved at her to continue with her work. "This may change my plans," she said, half to herself.

"We must do something to stop this thing," Eleanora said, her patience growing thin.

"We? You mean I must, don't you? But what? Tell me that?"

"Warn the general. Tell him what has been planned so he can be on his guard, so he can set his men to watch for those who will set the explosive charge and stop them."

"Why?" Niña Maria asked, turning cool black eyes on Eleanora.

"Why?" she repeated blankly. "To save the man's life, that's why! His, and that of all the others who will be on the grandstand."

"It is a matter of indifference to me," the other woman said with a careless gesture. "I had nothing to do with this plot, but if the arrangements have been made I have no fault to find with them."

"I thought you said you could defeat the general with-out resorting to cold-blooded murder?" Eleanora reminded her.

"That is still my belief, but if the others are not in agreement, what can I do?"

Her helpless attitude grated on Eleanora's nerves worse than her refusal to act. "You could go to Neville if you object to exposing the people you are working with to danger. Go to him and threaten to tell Walker if he doesn't call the plan off."

"Now there is a thought," Niña Maria said as if much impressed. "I congratulate you on it, and recommend that you act on it at once. Not that he will listen to you. He will be hard to convince that you would lay yourself open to a charge of conspiring with the enemy. The general will want to know how you came by your information, you understand, and what are you going to tell him? Do you think you can explain without implicating Major Crawford? It will not be easy. Think of the consequences, too. Major Crawford, if he were arrested, would feel little compunction in revealing the part you have played since returning from Honduras. The people he is working for might not look on his arrest with favor either. That could be tragic for your brother, could it not?"

"That is a chance I will have to take. I can't just do nothing," Eleanora said with deadly quiet. "Though perhaps it would be better if I went to Grant and the general directly."

"By all means, if you are determined to ruin yourself. I would hurry about it, if I were you. It may be nearly time for the ceremony before those two return. The general received a message this morning that General Ramon Belloso of Honduras was marching south within striking distance of León. It is too late to put an army in the field in time to save León, but William and Colonel Farrell are out now inspecting the fortifications of Granada with a view toward reinforcing them. I wish you much luck in running them to earth."

Undecided, Eleanora sat without speaking. Niña Maria watched her with narrowed eyes, her fingers gripping the hairbrush going white at the knuckles. Becoming aware of the other woman's tension, Eleanora searched her mind for the reason. Niña Maria seemed confident that she would be ruled by self-preservation and the force of circumstances, but was she in truth that sanguine? If not, what could the woman do about it? She might call the guard, have her arrested on some trumped-up charge. There would be repercussions, of course, but with any luck, not until it was too late. She must take care, Eleanora thought, not to fall into that trap. "That settles it then," she said aloud, adding for good measure a movement of her shoulders which might have passed for a shrug. "I suppose General Walker will have to take his chances."

"There," Niña Maria exclaimed, relaxing visibly. "I knew you could not be so stupid. We must both of us have our excuses ready as to why we refuse to mount to the grandstand. What shall it be? Modesty, for you, I think; you have the face to get away with such a tale. I, perhaps, have sprained my ankle and cannot stir a step more than is necessary to have a good view of the proceedings. It might be wisest to postpone my departure until tomorrow. And I must have mourning clothes. It will be expected." Already oblivious to Eleanora's presence, the woman turned to her maid, instructing her to search for a gown of black lawn, describing it in minute detail while abusing the woman for her slowness in unearthing it. She did not notice when Eleanora got to her feet and slipped from the room.

As she left the Government House and crossed the plaza, Eleanora noticed that the work had stopped on the scaffolding of the grandstand and the carpenters were resting under the dusty-leaved trees near the market place. It was still unfinished, and to her untrained eye it looked as if there was too much to be done before evening for lying in the shade, however hot it might be. Someone would have to drape bunting to cover the bare wooden railings that surrounded it also, but no doubt a detail of soldiers had been assigned that duty. It was not like William Walker to leave this sort of thing to the last minute. Still, perhaps he had his reasons, even something to do with his fear of an attempt on his life. That fear had proven to be well grounded. He was entitled to take whatever precaution he pleased.

What was she to do? The question was pulling her

apart. She had thought that Niña Maria might like to take full credit for discovering the danger to the general, allowing her to keep out of it. That was not to be. She must choose, then, between sacrificing Jean-Paul, or watching William Walker and Grant and, perhaps, Colonel Thomas Henry and a score of other men, mount the steps of the grandstand to their deaths. Her brother, or the man she loved? It could be put as simply as that.

Was there another solution? There was still her first impulse, to tell Grant. Surely if she explained everything to him, he could prevent the assassination attempt and do it in such a way that no one could guess that she was involved, thereby preserving Jean-Paul from danger. He had to. There was no other way she could take and still live with herself.

First, she had to find Grant, no easy task. As a beginning, she retraced her footsteps to leave a message for him with the riflemen on guard at the door of the Government House, then she walked away with a quick, half-running stride. She would quarter the town. Someone, somewhere, must have seen him.

She visited the guardhouse, the barracks, and the hospital first, on the chance that Niña Maria had tried to direct her to a false scent. She did not find him, but she left word with everyone to whom she spoke. Making her way down to the wharf, she ran into Colonel Henry on horseback, and when she explained, mendaciously, that her urgent need to see Grant was connected with some unsatisfactory arrangements for the inauguration, he offered to make a circuit of such fortifications around the city as were in existence. Failing that, he told her, laughing, he would be glad to make a round of a few of the cantinas on her behalf. That was where he would expect to find any sensible man on a day as hot as the one they were having—

Eleanora, grateful to him both for his help and for lightening her mood, gave him her leave to visit as many as he chose. She stood for a time after he had gone, enjoying the suggestion of a breeze off the lake on her heated face, wishing she dared submerge herself, clothes and all, into the cool gray-green water. After a while the comments and importuning of the loafers around the pier grew too bold, and she made her way tiredly back toward the palacio.

As she turned into the Calle Santa Celia from the street which ran along the lake, she saw a man on horseback in an officer's tunic making his way from the far end through the street vendors and the crowd of other men and women who had decided, unanimously it seemed, to make the quiet street a thoroughfare. Eleanora began to hurry, taking that uniformed figure with a campaign hat pulled low on his forehead for Colonel Henry coming already to report to her. Then as the man drew nearer, she paled, her footsteps slowing once more. It was Grant, and as he looked up and saw her making her way toward him, she fancied she could see already the condemnation in his stern-lipped face.

Dismounting, he turned to walk back toward the palacio with her, leading his horse. "They told me when I reached the Government House just now that you wanted to see me," he said. "What in heaven's name is so important you have to wander about the streets in this kind of weather, and alone?"

"I—I have to talk to you," she said, glancing at him, then looking quickly away again.

He studied her averted face for a moment, then said more quietly, "All right."

The distance to the palacio seemed incredibly short. They tied Grant's mount to the hitching ring set into one of the posts on the lower galería and stepped inside. Eleanora led the way into the patio, deliberately turning away from the stairs to the bedchamber. She needed no reminders of past ecstasy to weaken her resolve. Moreover, in the shade of the orange trees was seclusion enough for her to say what needed saying without it being so isolated that she need fear the full release of his anger.

These thoughts skimming the surface of her mind, Eleanora turned to face him, and was nearly demoralized by the look of concern which clouded his eyes. With one hand, he gestured toward one of the wrought-iron chairs, waiting until she had seated herself upon it before taking the one beside it. "Tell me," he commanded.

334

Simple words, plain, fatal sentences that must be spoken. She dragged them one by one from her unwilling tongue. "Please don't ask me how I know," she begged when she was done. "Just accept that I do, and do something to stop this terrible crime before it is too late!"

His concern was gone, seeping slowly away to be replaced by a brooding anger, edged with regret. Running his fingers back through his hair, he lifted his hat from where he had placed it on his knee, and got to his feet. The blue of his eyes had the metallic hardness of steel as he looked down at her. "I'll do that, for now," he said slowly, "because I'll have to move fast if I want to catch these men in the act, and put a stop to their game. But I'll be back, and I'm going to want to know a lot more than I do now. If you are going to make up a story to tell me," he ended with soft bitterness, "make sure it's a good one!"

Twenty-two

A hot gust of wind billowed the curtain which had been hanging so straight at the windows. From where she lay on the bed with her hands behind her head, Eleanora looked in the direction of the movement. She had been lying for hours without feeling the slightest draft between the open door onto the inner galería and the window. A rumble like distant thunder came to her ears, and she went still. No, the sound was too soft to have been an explosion. It must be thunder. Was the rain coming at last? Straining her eyes, she watched for the flash of lightning in the evening sky. She saw nothing, perhaps because it was still too early, the storm too far away. Wind swirled the curtains again, drawing them in and out of the long opening of the window in a tired kind of dance, a dance which ended abruptly as the bedchamber door was closed.

Eleanora felt the nerves tighten over her body before she turned her head to see Grant. Her supine posture on the bed was both suggestive and vulnerable, and she refused to shelter behind either attitude against what was to come. She pushed herself to a sitting position and slid from the high mattress, searching for her slippers with her toes, ignoring the sardonic look on Grant's face as, watching her, he tossed his hat to one side and began to unbutton his tunic.

"Is—is it over?" she asked, her head bent as she retrieved a slipper from under the bed.

"It never began," he answered.

She looked up briefly. "I was speaking of the inauguration ceremony."

"So was I."

"You don't mean—" she began, then stopped, unable to go on.

A hard, almost impatient tone in his voice, he said, "No, I don't. The general is in perfect health. The would-be assassins, a couple of unfortunate Nicaraguan workmen looking for a little extra money, were picked up with the keg of powder before they got halfway across the plaza. They were persuaded to describe the man who had hired them, and I have a detail searching for him now."

She took a deep breath and let it out slowly. "I'm glad the general is safe," she said quietly. "Though I would feel better if the ceremony was over and done with. I suppose with the excitement and the spectacle of having the men caught beneath their noses the workmen couldn't finish the grandstand in time?"

"Not at all. The date set for the inauguration is the twelfth, day after tomorrow."

"But you said—"

His eyes were dark and unreadable, and his voice bleak as he answered. "I did, didn't I? I said the tenth. And you, Eleanora, were the only one I told."

It made sense of a great deal she had not understood. His withdrawn silences, the look in his eyes when they rested on her, the feeling that he was exerting greater-than-usual control over what he said to her and how he said it, indeed over his every reaction to her. "You knew—what I was doing, then?" she whispered.

Reaching into the wardrobe, he took something from

336

a pair of his breeches. Holding it in his fist, he reached for her hand and placed what he held on her palm. It was the shredded magenta petals of a spray of bougainvillea—bougainvillea exactly like that which grew at the end of the galería, exactly like that which she had been holding in her hand as she listened to Grant and the others outside the window that day. "Let's say I guessed," Grant told her, and dropped her hand, letting the dried petals float to the floor.

"And telling me the date of the inauguration, the wrong date, was in the nature of a test?" she queried on a sigh. "One I failed?"

"That's right," he answered in abrupt tones, then took a step toward her, leaning over her as he rested one hand on the bedpost. "What I don't understand is, why? What made you do it? Was it the money? Or for the sake of that two-faced bastard, Crawford? Or was it because you hate me and what I did to you?"

"No—nothing like that!" she exclaimed, flinging him a startled glance. "It was for Jean-Paul."

"For Jean-Paul?" he repeated without comprehension.

"Yes. He—he wasn't executed with the others before the firing squad. He is being kept a prisoner in Honduras as a hostage for my actions. If they find out what I have done today, they will kill him!"

Grant drew back, a flint hardness coming into his eyes. "Try again," he grated. "You know as well as I do that your brother hanged himself with his dressing-gown cord on the day you left Honduras."

Eleanora stared at him, the color slowly draining from her face. It could not be true, it could not. But there was no relenting in Grant's face. His words and his manner were inexorable. Jean-Paul would not do such a thing, she tried to tell herself. Still, she kept remembering his despair, remembering him crying that he should have died with the others. She seemed to be swaying a little on her feet, and to hide it from Grant, she turned away, catching her lip between her teeth.

"So you didn't know," Grant said, the harshness gone, leaving his voice tired.

She shook her head numbly. "They let me think he was

still alive, and when I asked about him, I was told he—he was fine." All these weeks of tension and anxiety, of worrying about Jean-Paul chafing in his prison room, for nothing. For no one. Her brother, cold and lifeless, unable to feel pain or sorrow, could no longer care what sacrifices she made for his sake. He had tried to make them unnecessary with a greater sacrifice of his own. It was no fault of his that she had been duped. The anguish of loss and self-blame moved through her. She thought of his grave, unsanctified, unmarked, unmourned these many weeks. If flowers there had been to make sweet his passing, their petals would be as dry and brittle as those lying about her feet.

"They kept it from you so you would do as they asked." It was a statement with the sound of relief as well as regret in it.

Eleanora nodded her head in a movement which caused the tears to spill over her eyelids, though she quickly raised her chin in an effort to stop them.

"I should not have thrown the truth at you like that, but I had to see how you would take it," he said. He made a gesture, as though he would touch her shoulder, then drew back.

Eleanora knew an almost overwhelming need to seek the comforting circle of his arms. That was impossible now. She would meet no response except, perhaps, an insupportable pity. She needed no such weakness. She must summon strength, the strength to learn what she needed to know, and to tell him what she felt it was necessary, for her peace of mind, for him to hear. Her voice a thread of sound, she asked, "How did you learn of it?"

"We have our sympathizers and our sources of information too. Among them, in the area where you were, is an old priest. He sent a dispatch to the leader of the exchange party, Colonel Henry. The news about your brother—and your friendship with Crawford—was in it."

"I see," she said. Until that moment she had not been certain Grant realized to whom she had been reporting. Carefully, she went on, "I promise you that I told Neville nothing I thought would damage the phalanx. I did tell him what I overheard the general say he intended to do about President—ex-President—Rivas. But only as much as you were going to make known anyway for the sake of your plan—or what it seemed Neville must learn soon himself. Later, I thought there could be no harm in telling him the date of the inauguration, that it would be posted everywhere in a matter of days. I had no idea he planned to harm the general. I would never have told him if I had. That is all the information I gave him, I give you my word."

"I believe you," Grant said, "since I went to great lengths to make certain that was all you knew to tell him."

The satisfied sound of his voice, after her difficult confession, stirred anger as well as shame in Eleanora's breast. "Was I that transparent?"

"Only to me," he admitted, acknowledging the stringency of her tone and the flashing light in her tear-drenched eyes with an odd smile. "Then, I have the advantage of living with you."

She eyed him doubtfully. It was not a satisfactory answer; she might even suspect him of deliberately trying to change the direction of her thoughts. She was not in a position to argue, however. "There is something else I must tell you. You may discover that I met Neville at Mazie's arrangement. It was not because she had anything to do with what I was involved in. She had a good idea of what it was, but no more than that. Knowing she and Neville were old friends, I asked her as a special favor to let me see him at her place because I didn't want him to come here. I swear to you that is the truth. In fact, it was Mazie who set off the events this morning," she continued, telling him of John's part in exposing the abortive plot against the general.

"That's interesting to know," Grant said when she had finished, "but why are you so anxious to tell me? No, let me guess. You want to be sure I don't take Mazie and her John and stand them up before a firing squad and shoot them. That's it, isn't it? Without going into what I might like to do, let me remind you that I could hardly arrest them without incriminating you."

"I don't see that that matters," she answered without

looking at him. "When Neville is caught, he is certain to draw me into it."

"Strange though it may seem," Grant mused, "I appear to have a better opinion of Major Crawford's sense of honor than you. I don't think he will mention your name unless he has to. In any case, we haven't caught him yet."

Slowly Eleanora turned to face him, a frown between her brows. "But you said you were looking for him."

He let his gaze slip past her shoulder. "The men arrested this afternoon were in some doubt as to his name. They described him well enough; tall, American, light hair, but it was a description which could have applied to any number of the men in the phalanx if they were out of uniform. The officer I put in charge of the search detail will do his best, I expect. Still, he doesn't have my sources of information. If Crawford is half as smart as I think he is, he will be far away from here by morning."

"It doesn't make sense," she said slowly. "I would have thought you would have wanted to tear him apart for what he was trying to do."

"So I would, but that doesn't mean I want a public inquiry."

"But—why?" Her face mirrored her bewilderment, and yet she felt a waiting stillness within.

"I think you can guess, Eleanora, but if you want me to say it, I will. I don't want your name drawn into it. Nobody is going to take you from me again."

Lightning flashed beyond the window with an odd yellow light. In the stillness they heard the ominous rumble of thunder coming closer. Eleanora swallowed hard on the constriction in her throat. "Grant, I—"

She had not been certain she could put what she felt into words. He did not give her the chance. "Oh, I know you had your reasons for coming back to me after Honduras, reasons that had little to do with what you felt or wanted. It makes no difference. You did come, and now you will stay, regardless, for my reasons. You are in my blood and my brain. The scent and feel and taste of you are with me always. You are as necessary to me as food and water. I can't sleep away from you or work without knowing you are somewhere waiting for my return. Resign yourself, if I have to keep you under lock and key the rest of your life, you will never leave me. I won't let you go."

His face was drawn, as if the course he was taking gave him no joy. And as he caught her to him and lowered his mouth to hers she thought she saw pain vying with a muted self-disgust in the shadowed blue of his eyes.

His kiss was savage, branding her his, taking her with him headlong into wild rapture as the rising wind buffeted the building outside. Freed of the constraint of guilt, Eleanora gave herself to him, matching his craving for her with her own pain-driven ecstasy, molding herself to him with bittersweet pleasure in a deep, intolerable need that he would not assuage because he could not. She wanted a gentle, endless surcease for her yearning and he gave her the fury of his passion. She wanted his love and he gave her nothing but desire. She wanted, in the secret recesses of her heart, to be his wife, and he made her his obsession. It was not enough.

The rain darkened the gray of the sky to the charcoal dimness of early night. It fell from the roof tiles in steady streams like the silver tears of grief, washing away the accumulated dust and dirt, just as grudges and resentment are dissolved by the sorrow of parting. Eleanora could find no release for the hard pressure of tears closed away within herself, but still she must go. Grant must not compromise his strong sense of duty or betray his commanding officer for her sake. If he did, he would come to despise both her and himself. She could not ask that of him. Nor had she any right to ask him to love her. She had used her love for him, bartering it for value in the form of information like the most wanton of whores.

More, she would not be held in loveless bondage against her will. Not again. Not ever again. If he had asked her to stay in the soft words and tender manner he was capable of using, she would not have been able to resist. He had not. And because he had not, pride and an aversion to captivity in any form, coupled with the shaming certainty that if she did not get away she would make a fool of herself by confessing her own love, forced leaving upon her.

Beside her Grant stirred, drawing her nearer. He pressed his lips to the top of her shoulder, smoothing her hair back away from her face. Eleanora closed her eyes tight against the rush of tears, breathing in the warmth of his skin in slow, uneven breaths. Still, even in her nearness she was apart from him, gathering to herself the courage to make the severance final, and to sustain her afterward.

The oars dipped and splashed, the sound echoing over the still surface of the lake, spreading like the ripples made by the boat's passage. Eleanora, sitting in the stern of the small native craft, little more than a canoe with a sail, wished fervently that she could tell the two men bending to the oars to be quieter. The night was dark and their chances of being discovered slight with the attention of Granada centered on the inauguration proceedings. Still, she had no inclination to tempt Providence. Not that she actually thought the soldiers who had been lining the wharf and guarding the ticket office for the lake steamer these past two days were watching specifically for her. At the same time, to be caught in the net spread for Neville Crawford and brought up with him before the provost marshal, Colonel Grant Farrell, could cause nothing but embarrassment for both Grant and herself.

It was strange, after all that had happened, for her to be leaving Nicaragua in the company of Neville Crawford. She recognized the strangeness, but accepted its fatality. She could have refused to share either his place of refuge with Mazie, or his boat, but where would that have got her? She had no one else to turn to except Mazie, and no idea how to go about arranging alternate transport that would be half as swift or as discreet.

Dear Mazie, she had not even looked surprised to find Eleanora standing on her doorstep in the early-morning light. She had pulled her inside, heard her out, and then exclaiming about the meagerness of Eleanora's belongings for an ocean voyage, set about finding something to wear. Eleanora had protested that it did not matter how she looked, but Mazie would not listen. Watching the vigor with which she attacked the problem, listening to her strictures on the cheese-paring ways of the military, Eleanora had not the heart to tell Mazie of the two gowns she had left hanging in the wardrobe at the palacio. She had not been able to make herself bring them away with her. It had seemed, in her keyed-up state, too much like accepting a bribe with no intention of carrying through on her part of the bargain. It may have been ridiculous, for Grant had no use for them, and her need was great. Still, an aching pride was all she had to support her, and she would do nothing to lessen it.

She had needed that support when Grant left her that morning. Taking her surrender the night before for acquiesence, he had made no move to lock her in. She almost wished that he had, that there had been that obstacle to overcome to gain her freedom. Instead, he had kissed her, then turned and walked away, like any other day. Standing at the window, Eleanora had watched him out of sight with her hand twisted in the curtain. She had not lingered long behind him.

That was not the end of it. Grant had gone to Mazie, pounding on her door in such a blazing, tight-lipped rage, that the actress readily admitted he had her in a positive quake. But by then Eleanora was not in the house. Mazie had found a place for her with a Nicaraguan woman, the mother of one of the children they had helped the sisters of Guadalupe nurse through typhoid. Mazie had not made the mistake of telling Grant she had not seen Eleanora. With as much force as she could summon, she had rung a peal over him for his treatment of her friend, then told him with every expression of enjoyment that Eleanora had already left Granada, going overland on horseback to reach the transit road for a connection to California. Her acting experience must have stood her in good stead, for Grant had left in a hurry without stopping to thank her for the information.

Mazie, with an air of giving the devil his due, told Eleanora that Grant had not so much as mentioned Neville's name. She confessed she had half expected the colonel to demand Eleanora on pain of being arrested as an accessory to the assassination attempt. Whether because in his concern for Eleanora's disappearance he had forgotten the major, whether he believed Mazie's tale without question, or whether in honor of his pledge not to draw Mazie and John in the assassination plot, he did not so much as question Neville's whereabouts. Not that Mazie would have been intimidated if he had. She had Neville well hidden also, and though she was not about to condone what he had tried to do, she had some small understanding of how Neville's mind worked. She could not bring herself to turn him over to the firing squad, for friendship's sake, if nothing else.

It was Mazie also, who insisted that Eleanora sit down to pen a note to Don Esteban de Laredo. She was as excited as a child at Eleanora's good fortune and went around calling her the Condesa at every opportunity. She had no sympathy with Eleanora's reluctance to put herself forward or appear anxious to receive her legacy. Searching out writing paper and a pen with a good nib, she had pushed them into Eleanora's hands with the dire threat of writing the note herself if Eleanora did not feel able. Wincing a little at the color of the ink, a bright Irish green, Eleanora had complied, writing hurriedly, sealing the missive with green wax and sending it around to the address Don Esteban had given her by another of the widow's children, before she could change her mind.

The result, delivered by a messenger in the livery of a private servant, was a bank draft described as a small advance against her inheritance which made her open her eyes in shock, and a needlepoint purse of pin money for the journey that in her days as a keeper of lodgings would have fed her household for six months.

Though the money was comforting, Eleanora was apprehensive about traveling with such an amount jingling at her side. As they stood beside the lake, ready to climb into the boat drawn up on shore, she tried to make Mazie accept some of it as payment for the gowns she had altered for her for the journey. The actress had refused, pushing her toward the boat with a laugh which had a catch in it. "*Vaya con Dios!*" she called, the Spanish admonition to go with God as comical, coming from her lips, as it was touching.

Safely out of hailing or firing distance of the town, the boatmen shipped their oars and began to raise the sail of thin, flapping canvas. Their progress was faster after that as they ran before a nice breeze. The lights of Granada, ringing the shore like a semicircle of fallen stars, receded. There was nothing but the sound of the soft voices of the men, the creaming of the water against the hull, and the creaking of rigging.

Abruptly one of the men gave an exclamation, pointing toward the town. Looking back, Eleanora saw a ball of fire soar toward the heavens, showering downward again in orange sparks. Another followed, and another, in bright burning blue and red and green, fountains of fire splashing golden embers, lighting the night, for an instant, with magic.

It was the pyrotechnics Niña Maria had ordered for the ceremony installing President William Walker of Nicaragua. Was that woman there, or had someone else found them and set them off? It didn't matter. The deed was done, the inauguration over. The little general had triumphed. His *coup de main* was crowned with success. It was time to celebrate the victory, to retire to the Government House to eat and drink and dance, time for the Falangistas to laugh and slap each other on the back in congratulations and an excess of high spirits.

None of it meant anything to her. She was no longer a part of that madness. Resolutely, she turned her back, staring straight ahead. It was odd how black the night and the surface of the lake appeared, stretching endlessly before her, and how blurred was the outline of the looming peaks of the volcanic island of Ometepe.

New Orleans under the sun of late July was as hot and as pestilential as the country from which Eleanora had come. The air was more sluggish than at Granada, the glare on the rooftops was hurtful to the eyes, and black-banded placards on every post proclaimed the victims of yellow fever. Still, there were no red-shirted soldiers walking the streets, no sound of drilling or marching, no rumbling of ammunition carts. The language in the streets was not Spanish; and the people, the shopkeepers and street vendors and the servants with their masters and mistresses, all smiled.

Eleanora said good-bye to ex-Major Neville Crawford

at the dock on the levee. If she were honest, she would have to admit he had made the voyage easier for her. During the boat trip across the lake to San Carlos, he had kept to himself, unwilling, as he put it, to intrude on her preoccupation and grief for her brother, to risk the vicious snub he knew he deserved. But at San Carlos they had landed on the bank of the lake. Seeing her hesitating as it came her turn to disembark, trying to decide if she could jump the stretch of lapping water and mud which lay between her and dry land, he had scooped her into his arms and carried her ashore. He had released her the instant her feet touched the ground, turning away after receiving her frigid expression of gratitude, but the ice had been broken.

On the journey by river steamer down the San Juan to the Atlantic, it was not surprising that they were thrown into each other's company. Being together was a defense against the attempts of the other passengers to strike up a conversation. They were both traveling under false names, and had no wish to be put to the effort of elaborating on a background to go with them. The situation was much the same aboard the ocean steamer out of San Juan del Norte, complicated by the greater number of passengers and the necessity of taking meals at the long tables in the dining saloon. Much of the problem Eleanora solved by keeping to her private cabin, a luxury she paid for gladly from her pin money. On her first night at sea she sought her bunk in the middle of the afternoon and slept the clock around without moving. Caused, no doubt, by the release of the intolerable tension which she had been under for weeks, her drowsiness continued. She could not seem to wake before noon or hold her eyes open after the moon had risen.

Nevertheless, there were the afternoons, and it was not unpleasant to have a gallant and attentive escort to stroll with her around the decks, or to shield her at dinner by explaining to those who were too insistent on becoming acquainted that she was recently bereaved and not up to making polite conversation.

She was not so pleased with him when their fellow travelers began to address her as the Condesa. Challenged,

Neville admitted to letting her cabin steward in on the secret of her incognito. There was no longer any danger from having it known, and he had thought it might prompt the man to better service. He was most contrite that the steward had seen fit to spread the tale and apologized handsomely. And yet, Eleanora had seen him in that mood so often during the voyage, as he tried to excuse his perfidy in Honduras, that she was unmoved. She could not, in fact, rid herself of the notion that his action was deliberate, though she could find no reason for it. Until that incident, she had been on the verge of warming to Neville, and disposed to believe that he had been little more than a pawn on Vanderbilt's chess board, as he explained—caught up in forces stronger and more dangerous than he had expected, from which he was unable to escape. She found it reasonable enough that he was not sorry the plan to kill Walker had failed, though she was skeptical that he was actually glad to be exposed. Still, there were advantages in having someone who, even if they did not often speak of it, had common memories of Granada and of how things had been there. For this reason, she pretended to accept what Neville was at such pains to have her understand.

Other than a meticulous attention to her well-being, and constant companionship which she could take or leave, Neville did not put himself forward. He made no attempt to gain entry to her cabin or to capitalize on the balmy hours of the evening they spent on deck. Such consideration was unlooked for. He was aware of her position as Grant's mistress and must have joined with the rest of Granada in speculating on her relationship with Luis while they were together. But he did not betray by word or deed any expectation that she might be free with her favors. Nor was it that he was immune to her attraction. There was a certain look in his eye, a way he had of touching her to guide her, a note in his voice, which told her this was not so. No, she suspected, without vanity, that he had determined on a course of making himself indispensable to her. He was playing a game of patience, waiting for her to ready herself to turn to him. If she was right, she could not but respect his intelligence. Nor could she help nourishing doubts about the strength of his emotions.

Eleanora went from the dock to the Hotel St. Louis, where, under the supercilious and somewhat doubtful stare of the clerk, she signed the register with her full name and title. The results were all she could have hoped for in the way of deference and instant service. Neville had been correct in that, at least. From that base, she sallied forth the next day to the dressmaker and milliner. She ordered gowns in black and gray and lavender, as was right and fitting and in harmony with her mood. To go with them, she bought bonnets and scarves and shawls and gloves and lace mittens and a dozen other items, though she turned down without hesitation a mantilla touted to her as the latest rage in fashion. She purchased a new crinoline and a single set of lace-adorned petticoats, camisole, and pantaloons to be worn for the present. The rest of her undergarments and nightwear she ordered from the convent— lingerie of silk and lawn exquisitely embroidered by the nuns, such as her mother and her grandmother had worn next to their skin, including a set in black embroidered with gray satin stitch.

The first of her new finery to be delivered was a day gown of gray lawn, embellished with yard upon yard of white lace, with a matching coal-scuttle bonnet and lace-edged parasol. Attired in this ravishing outfit and carrying a new reticule of silver mesh in which reposed her purse, fan, and calling card case, she set out in a hired hack to visit her Uncle Narciso and his son, Cousin Bernard, at her old home on Royal Street.

The butler who opened the door to her ring asked her to wait in the library and took away on a silver salver her card, engraved with her name and the arms of the Conde de Laredo. Her uncle himself came to greet her with hands outstretched, drawing her into the salon. Bernard rose to make her his bow, a rather strained smile on his face as if the effort of being cordial was too much for him, but he did second his wife's invitation to have a glass of ratafia with them. His wife's parents, a rather stout and benign couple, were ensconced upon the settee, and by their presence kept the interrogation to which she was subjected from becoming too severe or acrimonious. Eleanora bore it with fortitude, telling them what she pleased and smilingly turning away those questions she did not wish to answer, wondering all the while why she had ever allowed herself to be made to feel inferior to these singularly dull people so full of their own consequence they could not tell when they were being gently ridiculed or maneuvered. At the end of the visit she was pressed to come to a supper party, a small gathering which could not be thought too gay for one in mourning. She accepted with every expression of gratification and went away grimly pleased that the first shot in the battle to regain her grandmother's house had been fired.

Though New Orleans appeared quiet and peaceful on the surface, the enthusiasm for the war efforts of William Walker was higher than ever. It was inevitable, then, that once Eleanora's identity became known the news sheets would make much of her. The tale of a New Orleans beauty of prominent family who had traveled very nearly to the front of battle, become known as the Angel of Mercy to the wounded Americans in Nicaragua, and then returned to the city the wife of a Spanish nobleman, had too much the scent of romance about it to be ignored. That she had been widowed by the war in that foreign country added pathos to the story, just as the hint of wealth gave it a certain indescribable, and irresistible, luster.

Eleanora's room at the St. Louis was besieged by merchants bent on capturing her interest in everything from health tonics to perfume, jewelry to carriage horses. She was pointed out each time she left the hotel, and followed along the street at a distance by a crowd of young boys squabbling among themselves for the honor of carrying her purchases.

After the first incident of this nature, Eleanora decided that, despite her married state, it was unwise for her to go about unattended. She sent, therefore, a message to her uncle begging for the services of her old nursemaid. Her uncle released the elderly woman without argument, doubtless anxious to be free of the expense of feeding her, Eleanora told herself cynically. Eleanora was tearfully glad to see her nurse's gnarled brown face, however, and took delight in dressing her in black silk with ivory lace, and a turban of ivory satin trimmed with jet beads. With her features set in a mask of ancient dignity and her silk skirts and petticoats rustling along beside Eleanora, she was enough to daunt the most intrepid busybody.

Eleanora strolled about the city, visiting old scenes such as the convent and Cabildo, and new ones like the statue of Andrew Jackson set up that spring in the recently landscaped old Place d'Armes which had then been renamed Jackson Square. She visited also the newly completed apartments built by the Baroness Pontalba, the first of their kind, with the idea of moving into a suite of the elegant rooms if she did not achieve her ambition concerning her grand-mère's house.

Some who stared and nudged each other as she passed were more than curious. It was not reasonable to expect that none of the men who had known her as the colonel's woman in Granada would have returned to New Orleans, or, that recognizing her, they would be able to refrain from circulating such a juicy tidbit of gossip. When she began to see the sly leers in the eyes of the men who leaned against the walls of the coffee houses and cafés and the shop clerks who bowed her out the door of their premises, when the courtesies extended to her grew fewer and the charges higher, she was forewarned.

Without delay, she increased her attentions to her relatives. She entertained them at quiet dinners and even a theater party behind the *loge grille,* putting on such an air of gracefully borne heartache that they could not but feel for her loss and wish to do what was in their power to make her burden easier to bear. The instant she was notified of the draft received from a Spanish firm in her name, she went to Uncle Narciso with an offer for the house on Royal at what she knew to be a considerable profit over what he and Cousin Bernard had paid Jean-Paul less than seven months before. As she had hoped, Uncle Narciso could not refuse an appeal to sentiment, nor Cousin Bernard an addition to his purse. Within hours the key was in her hand. A few days later she was able to take possession, to walk through the empty rooms and the vine-hung back courtyard, and feel, at last, that she had come home.

Twenty-three

"I demand an explanation!"

Eleanora looked at Bernard, her green eyes cold. Her hands were clasped at her waist as she stood before him in her widow's weeds, but it was more in anger than in fear. "By what right?" she asked.

"The right of kinship! Your actions reflect all those known to be of your family. I demand to know the truth of this scandal I hear concerning your conduct while in Nicaragua."

"Why?" she asked bluntly.

Bernard drew his head back to stare at her, his thin, aristocratic face frozen in disbelief. "Why?" he echoed.

"Exactly. A lady does not rush to defend her good name. Her friends will not believe what they hear of her, and her enemies will believe the worst whatever she may say. What will it profit you to know whether I am falsely accused? Did you have in mind taking the matter to the field of honor? I beg you will not. It will only prolong the chatter."

"You refuse, in short, to tell me."

"The long *and* short of it," she told him, meeting his gaze without a tremor, "is that I refuse you the right to meddle in my affairs."

"I should have known this would be your attitude," he threw at her.

"Most certainly you should, if you had ever taken the time to study my character."

"A profitless enterprise, cousin. You have changed since you left New Orleans."

"I should hope so."

"You have let your new position and affluence go to your head," he said with a hint of querulousness. "What you need is a man to curb your excesses. It is a great pity Jean-Paul isn't here to perform that duty."

Eleanora felt herself go cold with rage. "I couldn't agree with you more," she said with deliberation. "That he is not I place directly at your door. You encouraged an impetuous boy to throw away his inheritance and his future to go to his death. If you had not been so ready to take this house off his hands—at a lesser price, of course—he might have listened to reason and stayed away from William Walker!"

"Jean-Paul had already signed up when I bought this house."

"Yes, he had. But you needn't think you can convince me you hadn't discussed the transaction with my brother beforehand."

"That may be, though I contend he would have joined regardless. He was wild, and I've always said that was your doing, letting him come and go as he pleased, with whomever he pleased, instead of living up to his responsibilities."

"I see. Now it is I who should have curbed his excesses," she said.

"That wasn't my meaning at all. I realize that was an impossibility for a fond member of the weaker sex, but I was there for you to lean on. I could have handled Jean-Paul."

"By putting him in a counting house?" she asked scornfully.

"At least he would have been alive," Bernard flashed.

"In a living death, like yours!" she answered.

The sound of clapping broke the strain between them. Neville stepped from the house out into the courtyard, applauding as he came. "Bravo," he said, a laugh in his eyes as he came toward Eleanora. "Forgive the informality. Your butler let me in. I heard voices out here and I was afraid you might be in need of a champion. I should have known better."

Eleanora's smile was stiff and very nearly as ungracious as the introduction she performed.

"Shall I go away again?" Neville asked after the briefest of nods in Bernard's direction. "I can always return later. We have some catching up to do since we last saw each other."

"By no means," Eleanora said. "Cousin Bernard was just leaving."

"Yes indeed. I will leave you with your—friend. Concerning your obstinate attitude, however, I must tell you that I regret ever welcoming you back into the family or allowing you to regain possession of what I consider to be the family home. I cannot speak for my father, but as for me, you will not be surprised if I inform you that I hereby sever the connection."

"Thank you," Eleanora said in accents of heartfelt gratitude. "I'm sure that if you are unable to find your way out someone will show you the way."

When they were alone Neville lifted a blond eyebrow. "What was that all about?"

"Nothing," Eleanora said, leading the way to a vine-covered arbor against a brick wall at one end of the courtyard. A small fountain in the shape of an iron lion's head set into the brick at the back made a cool trickling sound. In the dampness moss had grown over everything, its soft green adding to the impression of a gladelike retreat. Eleanora sat down on a wooden bench and swept her skirts aside to make room for Neville. Summoning a smile, she asked, to change the subject, "Where have you been? What have you been doing?"

"I've been in the East, Washington and New York," he said, crossing his knees, watching the sheen on his boots.

"Oh." Eleanora made no effort to say more.

"I felt I owed Vanderbilt a personal report," he said defensively. When Eleanora said nothing, sitting with lashes lowered, straightening the frill of her gown, Neville said, "A man has to get by the best way he can. I was raised to expect a carefree life on inherited money. I can't help it if I still have a tendency to look for the easy way."

"Can't you?" Eleanora asked quietly.

"Maybe I could, if I had a woman like you behind me," he told her with a disarming smile. "Now don't go all stiff and cold on me. Anyway, it was a wasted trip. Commodore Vanderbilt refused to see me. Said he had no time for failures. A low blow, that, but I suppose the man with victory in his fist can say what he pleases."

"Victory?" Eleanora asked, her head coming up.

"The nearest thing to it. Minister Wheeler, who rashly took it upon himself to recognize Walker's regime after the election, has been recalled to Washington by the secretary of state for a reprimand, and asked to turn in his resignation. Hard on old Wheeler, considering that until the last few weeks he had every reason to believe the U.S. Government would applaud his move. The wings of the American Eagle have been spread over the former Mexican territories of Texas and California; why not Nicaragua—or Central America, for that matter? I'll tell you why not; because Spain and France have both announced they are sending sloops-of-war to watch the shores of Central America. Chile and Peru have pledged monetary support for the states allied against Walker, and England has on the high seas at this moment a squadron of thirteen ships manned by twenty-five hundred men pledged to protect British interests in the area. The climate for expansion, you perceive, is not right. Walker has been abandoned by his country."

"But—he has not been defeated on the field?" Eleanora asked, a worried look in her emerald eyes.

"Not yet. I'll have to say—if you'll pardon the cock-fighting parlance—that Walker shows as game as a bantam rooster. There is a rumor that he has declared slavery legal in Nicaragua, an obvious attempt to court the favor of the Southern contingent in Congress so they will sway the government in his behalf—or failing that, secede, as they have been threatening for years, and join him. I think he will find that was a mistake. Slavery has been illegal down there for thirty years. Britain and France, to say nothing of Washington, won't stand for a return to it. No, I'd say we got out of Nicaragua in the—pardon—nick of time. Something besides the temperature is about to get hot down there!"

Neville went on to talk of other things, but Eleanora gave him only a small portion of her attention. When, realizing her self-absorption, he finally took himself off, she sat for a long time staring at nothing, thinking of Grant and Mazie and John and the troupe, of Walker and Colonel Henry and Doctor Jones and all of the others still in Granada. She wondered what they were doing and what they felt and if they ever thought of her. And she longed with an almost frightening intensity to be with them.

It would not have been the best place for her. A day or two before, while standing on a stool trying to match a scrap of material for new wall hangings in her boudoir to the drapes, she had turned faint. Her old nurse had been near to steady her and lead her to a chair.

"Sit still, Mam'zelle Eleanora," she had said, giving her the title she had used since childhood. "It will pass away soon."

"I feel so silly," Eleanora had laughed with a shaky sound, "I don't know what's the matter with me."

"It's a common complaint among women who are married, *chère*. Like I suspect these weeks, me. You going to have a *bébé*."

A baby, Grant's child. Thinking back, she knew her nurse was right. In the haste and turmoil of leaving Granada, and the determined busyness of the the last few weeks, she had not stopped to consider.

Alone, Eleanora had slowly removed Luis's ring from her finger and unclasped the medal of St. Michael from her neck. She had often thought, when a bleak mood was upon her, that she had more to remember Luis by than she had the man she loved. That was true no longer.

After that morning, Neville was a frequent visitor. With his connections and mobility, he often had details of the progress of the war in Central America which were not mentioned in the press. As the summer turned to fall he kept her informed on the movement of the armies of Guatemala, Honduras, and San Salvador. For a time it looked as though internal disputes would prevent a concerted attack, and then in early November Costa Rica was able once more to enter the fray.

Within days had come the word that Walker, in a move to protect the Transit Line over which would come his reinforcement in the way of new recruits, had evacuated Granada. Unwilling to leave the town as a stronghold of the allied forces, he had left behind his second in command and a detachment of three hundred men with orders to destroy it.

The allies had attacked the burning town as soon as possible in an effort to halt the destruction. They were thrown back once with heavy losses, then the Guatemalan army had advanced to take possession of Guadalupe Church. The colonel in command had stormed the church, routing the defenders, but his men, with over a hundred women, children, sick and injured, had been besieged in the church by the superior forces of the enemy. For nineteen days they held out, subsisting on horse and mule meat and a dwindling ration of flour and coffee. The dead from the fighting in and around the church were left unburied. With the terrible stench of putrefaction came cholera. Yellow fever, sunstroke, smoke inhalation—it began to look as if disease and exposure would carry off the defenders before they could be relieved. Then on December 12, approximately two hundred and fifty new recruits plus those seasoned veterans who wanted to volunteer for the job landed the lake steamer *Virgin* above Granada during the night. They stormed the barricades and joined the others within the church. The allies, convinced they were under assault by Walker's entire field force, withdrew. Within twenty-four hours everyone left alive in the church was loaded on the *Virgin* and taken to safety. Behind them lay the smoldering ruins of the town and a tattered rawhide banner fluttering in the wind bearing the words *Agui fue Granada:* "Here was Granada."

For several days there was no word of the dead. People lined up outside the office of the *Crescent,* waiting to hear of sons, husbands, fathers, uncles, and cousins who had gone as "colonists" to Nicaragua. Eleanora waited with the rest. When the news sheet was in her trembling hands she quickly scanned the list of more than two hundred names. Grant's name was not among the men. She sighed, reading lower, and then her eyes blurred with tears. Among the women was printed the name of Mazie Brentwood Barclay, dead of yellow fever while heroically nursing the wounded and the children caught within the Church of Guadalupe.

The months which followed were a time of waiting for Eleanora; waiting for news from Nicaragua, waiting for her child to be born. As the weeks slipped away the

356

sensation concerning her identity faded, replaced by other, more exciting, scandal. The fact that after Christmas she ceased to go out and about due to her advancing pregnancy was, no doubt, a contributing factor. She spent her time refurbishing the old town house, making it livable, sewing for her child, and listening for the sound of the newsboys in the streets so that she could send a servant hurrying out to purchase a news sheet while the ink was still damp upon it.

There was no good news to be found. In early January the San Juan River was successfully blockaded, cutting off supplies and men for Walker. While the young gallants of New Orleans cavorted in the streets in Mardi Gras costumes under a banner declaring themselves as the newly organized Mystic Krewe of Comus, Walker and his men were left with short rations and dwindling ammunition to face the combined armies of Costa Rica, Guatemala, Honduras, and San Salvador. Walker's army consisted of less than a thousand men at this point. They were opposed by twenty times that number. In the face of such odds, desertion began to bleed the strength of the phalanx.

According to Neville, Vanderbilt was responsible for much of Walker's woes. He had hired and equipped a team of professional soldiers to lead the Central American forces, giving direct payment and the promise of loans totaling millions to make the men acceptable to the proud and hot-tempered Central Americans. That leadership was responsible for the river blockade and molding the different armies into a single cohesive force. In addition, Vanderbilt had convinced the leaders of the allies of the lack of wisdom in their policy of a war to the death. Thereafter, prisoners and deserters were offered free passage home on Vanderbilt ships.

It was a wearing spring with endless alarms as the filibusters engaged in a series of small battles, repulsing the enemy again and again. In April those American women and children still at Rivas with Walker were taken out under the protection of a guard of Marines from the United States sloop-of-war *St. Mary* which had been hovering off the coast for two months. The end, all conceded, was very near.

For Eleanora, the end of a part of her waiting was even nearer. On the evening of the ninth of April she dragged herself up to bed. She was awakened before midnight by the first pangs of birth. Before dawn, long before the doctor finally arrived, she was delivered by her nurse of a beautiful, healthy, perfectly formed son.

The world narrowed immediately to the walls of her bedchamber and the cradle that sat beside her bed. She received no guests and little news. Her time and thoughts and cares were taken up by the lusty appetite, the cries of her child, and the rituals involved in keeping him clean, sweet smelling, and comfortably asleep. He was so infinitely vulnerable. The only thing which mattered was to keep him safe and content. Sometimes, lying with his small warm body against her own, she would feel a wash of love so strong it had the feel of an agonizing fear.

A month later, on May 12, the baby was quietly baptized in a private ceremony held at home. The name chosen, after much soul-searching, was Charles Michael de Laredo y Villars. As Eleanora smilingly wiped away the water from her indignant son's face, she touched the medallion of St. Michael she had placed around his neck. Luis would not mind the using of his name as a protective gesture this one last time. The child had been born nine months, two and a half weeks after his death, not an impossibility from a physical standpoint; babies were often born a little later than expected. The legal limit for a posthumous child did not concern her since she had no intention of making any such claim. This resolve she held despite Neville's representation of the advantages to be achieved for her son in representing Michael to the de Laredo family as the rightful Conde.

Neville, though uninvited, had put in an appearance at the baptism. Bearing the traditional silver cup and priest's fee in the bottom of a cone of sugared almonds, he had played the part of godfather to her child. It was impossible, after that, to keep from asking him to participate in the small family dinner which she had arranged afterward. Uncle Narciso, braving his son's censure, was to come in for the gala meal, though he had declined to be godfather on the excuse, weak to her ears, that he could not afford it. As it turned out, her uncle never put in an appearance. She was grateful to Neville, then, for keeping the small celebration from falling flat.

He did not stay long. Eleanora's duties as a mother interrupted their after-dinner coffee as her nurse, now heart and soul Michael's nursemaid, came to tell her he was crying for her.

She tarried long enough to see Neville to the door. His hand was on the knob when he asked, "I suppose you have already heard the news?"

"No, what?" she said absently, her mind attuned to the faint cries issuing from the upstairs bedroom.

"About the surrender?"

He had her full attention now. "Tell me," she said, a sudden strain in her voice.

"After negotiations by Commander Davis of the *St. Mary*, Walker and his men laid down their guns."

"When?"

"The first day of May. He and his officers were taken to Panama aboard the American ship. They are expected to arrive here in New Orleans any day now."

The steamship bearing William Walker home docked in New Orleans on May 27, 1857. People thronged the levee and the streets leading to it. There was such a crowd of jostling spectators that Eleanora's carriage could not move, and only by the use of the most shocking language and ear-splitting cracks of his whip was her coachman able to force a passage to a vantage point where she could see without leaving the hooded victoria.

The sight of red uniform tunics, numbering perhaps sixteen, their gold buttons and fringe bright in the warm sun, brought a tightness to her throat. She had to blink several times before she could make out the slight figure of the general, a blackbird among cardinals in his dark frockcoat. And then behind him she saw Grant, standing straight and stern-visaged, looking as gaunt as when he had been ill with the wound in his shoulder. Dazzled by the sunlight, he looked out over the crowd. As his gaze passed over her carriage, Eleanora drew back, though she was almost certain he could not penetrate the shadow beneath the hood.

At the sight of Walker, a great roar went up from the crowd, a sound of welcome, admiration, and approbation, as though he had returned as the conquering hero rather than in defeat. There were shouts of hurrah and hats thrown into the air. Small boys yelled and screamed and ladies applauded with gloved hands. A dozen men surged forward as, after smiling and waving to the crowd, the president of Nicaragua moved toward the gangplank. They lifted Walker on their shoulders and bore him through the crowd the short distance to where a carriage waited. Several of his officers pushed after them to join him. The rest crowded into a second vehicle. Trailed by the main body of his enthusiastic well-wishers, the carriage moved off in the direction of the St. Charles Hotel.

Even then, Walker was not allowed to rest after his weary journey. The people stood outside the hotel cheering and chanting for his appearance. He was forced to make not one but two speeches before they were finally satisfied and began to disperse.

Those who were not privileged to hear him on that occasion were given the opportunity two days later. At a great mass meeting on Canal Street, Walker, flanked by the American flag on one side and his own red-starred flag on the other, spoke for two hours. His face shining with perspiration in the light of the gas lamps, he praised the courage and strength of his men and the warmth and hospitality of the common people of Nicaragua whose benefactor he considered himself to be. From there he plunged into a wholesale denunciation of the people he considered to be the cause of his downfall. He railed against the tyrannical might of Vanderbilt, the short-sightedness of President Buchanan in not coming to his aid, with a hint of graft in public office in official Washington's preference for the commodore's viewpoint in the affair. He was critical of Commander Charles H. Davis, chief officer on the sloop-of-war *St. Mary*, claiming he sold the phalanx out during the negotiations with the Central American allies and blaming the commander for refusing to transport the remainder of his men to Panama, leaving them to make their own way. Lastly, he attacked Morgan and Garrison, the two men he had been at such pains to favor in the takeover of the Transit Line, for not forcing their way through the blockade to bring troops and supplies to relieve the phalanx.

Standing among the crowd with her nursemaid pulling anxiously at her sleeve, urging her to come away, Eleanora could not hear all of William Walker's impassioned speech. Still, what she heard disturbed her. It would be too much to expect the man to be unaffected by his experiences. At the same time, the shrillness of his voice, the uncontrolled nature of his diatribe seemed to smack of a man at the edge of his reason. It is never pleasant to lose when victory is almost within one's grasp, and Walker must, she thought, be extremely weary, but he would have been better served if someone had represented to him the wisdom of a long period of reflection before he began to try to justify his defeat. His last words reinforced her views as nothing else could. William Walker concluded his speech with a personal promise to return to the fight in Nicaragua as soon as the men and resources could be raised.

While she was standing, stupefied by this announcement, Eleanora's nurse caught her arm and drew her away, muttering under her breath. Her mistress was crazed for uniforms, she said with some force. She could not stop Mam'zelle—her, she was too old—but she could see that young M'sieur Michael was given his proper care and nourishment before his mother who had forgotten him went running off to the ball for the military gentlemen.

The event to which her nurse referred, a reception for Walker with a ball to follow, was to be held in the public ballroom of the St. Charles Hotel. It was to be the event of the spring season with a guest list numbering several hundred, including the governor of the state, Robert Wickliffe, the Baroness Pontalba, and representatives from the best of the Creole as well as American families in the city.

For the occasion Eleanora had ordered a new gown of

white tulle banded about the deep scoop of the neckline, sleeves, and at intervals down the enormous skirt with wide white satin ribbon. Between her breasts she wore a corsage of fresh red roses backed by silver leaves, and just beneath it, reaching from her shoulder to her left side, a wide sash of red-edged white ribbon to which was pinned her medal of valor, Walker's gold star on a black-and-red ribbon. Her hair she wore parted in the center and drawn back into a chignon of ringlets. Tucked into the side of it, just below her ear, she had pinned another, smaller, nosegay of rosebuds. The red roses, worn for Walker, should have been a terrible clash with her hair. Instead, they seemed somehow to drain away the fiery sheen, leaving it the burnished color of newly minted gold coins. And if her gown was deliberately reminiscent of the one she had left hanging in the wardrobe of the palacio, who was to know except herself—and one other; the man who had bought it?

"The Condesa de Laredo!"

To Eleanora's ears, the sound of her name as she was announced echoed over the quiet hiss of the gas from the chandeliers and the polite murmur of voices like a clarion call. She was aware of the turning of heads as she gave William Walker her hand, but she ignored them, greeting him with the deference that was his due.

A faint tremor ran through his fingers, though his face betrayed no surprise as his gray eyes rested upon her, dropping to the medal she wore and then lifting to meet her clear green gaze. "You are looking well, Eleanora," he said in calm accents. "It is a pleasure to see you again."

"And you, sir. You—all of you—have been in my thoughts these last months."

"As you have been in ours," he replied.

There was no time for more. The line behind her pressed Eleanora forward. As she moved away, she took a deep breath, letting it out slowly. He had not denounced her. There had been nothing in his manner to indicate that he knew of any blot upon her name. The idea had crossed her mind that he was trying to convey a message to her with his last words, until she remembered

362

his habit on ceremonial occasions of speaking in the royal plural.

She wandered about at something of a loss, inspecting the arrangements of flowers, huge bouquets of roses and jasmine in urns on stands, and the streamers of ribbon in red and black draped from the chandeliers fastened to the walls in loops with ribbon rosettes. The supper tables were already laid with the hotel's famous gold service, and centerpieces of nougat were in place, formed in the shape of a cannon, a flag, and a five-pointed star. There were several dowagers present, friends of her grand-mère with whom she had a nodding acquaintance. She saw one or two friends from convent school who plied her with eager questions, for the most part concerning not William Walker but the family of her titled husband. If they had heard of the birth of her child they did not ask after him, and Eleanora found she was not anxious to expose so private a matter as his birth—and with it the question of his succession to Luis's honors—to their curiosity.

By contrast, the gruff and hearty good wishes of Colonel Thomas Henry were like a breath of fresh air. Standing talking to him, she was aware of the way his uniform had faded, of the darned places on it and the tarnished, verdigris look of the fringe on his epaulettes.

He was favoring his left hand, keeping that bandaged member behind his back. The end of his forefinger had been shot away just below the first knuckle and had not healed as it should. Eleanora rallied him on his accident-prone ways, accusing him of shooting himself; but she agreed to look at it as he insisted, if he would come to her home. She had then to listen to a recital of all the things he had learned to do one-handed. When he included carrying two punch cups in one hand, she accepted with gratitude his offer to prove it.

It was hot in the room from the growing press of people and the light of the gas lamps. She would have liked to have withdrawn to an open window but thought it best to stay where she was so Colonel Henry could find her when he returned. She was opening the fan of handpainted parchment which hung by a silk cord from her wrist, when she saw Grant. He stood straight and tall just inside the door. He wore no hat and his hair, in the wavering light, was as shining and blue-black as a crow's wing. There were new lines engraved at the corners of his eyes, and, though she would have thought it impossible, a leaner, tougher set to his shoulders.

As if drawn by the intensity of her regard, he turned his gaze toward her. His eyes narrowed slightly and she was certain he lost a shade of color under the mahogany darkness of his skin.

Her lips curved in the faintest possible trace of a smile, she slowly raised her chin. No breath disturbed the roses at her breast until he moved in a slow step toward her.

And then, without the least change of expression, he stiffened and the black fire of his stare seemed to pass through her. He halted, turned as if at a command, and made his way against the tide of people out of the ballroom.

Eleanora stood still, the carved ivory sticks of her fan bending under the grip of her hand. The sound of one of them cracking broke the tension that held her. Then she swung around, her cheeks flaming, as a man spoke from where he had moved, unnoticed, to her side.

"Look what you've done," Neville Crawford drawled, reaching out, taking up the fan that dangled at her wrist to spread the fragile parchment open. "It's broken."

Twenty-four

Eleanora received Neville formally in the salon. She had considered refusing him admittance, but discarded the idea. There might be a certain cold satisfaction in it, but there was greater satisfaction in making the weight of her displeasure over his conduct at the ball personally felt.

Neville was no fool. He was fully alive to the nuances of social conduct. Glancing around at the elegant room as he walked down it, at the pale-green striped silk walls, white brocade settees, Aubusson carpet in a design of cream and green and rose, and rose velvet drapes, he lifted a brow. "I am suitably impressed by your new grandeur, my dear, but I prefer the simple comforts of the courtyard—unless, of course, you have something of a private nature to say to me?"

His smile was calculated to charm but it left her unmoved. She did not come forward from where she stood stiffly in a morning dress of orchid-flowered white lawn beside the marble mantle. Neville, perforce, had to remain standing also.

"You know what I wish to speak to you about," Eleanora said challengingly. "There can have been no doubt in your mind, after our discussions on the subject, of Grant's reaction to seeing you standing beside me. It could not help but look as if we were the conspirators he suspected, if not more. Why? Why did you interfere?"

"Shall I be honest?" he asked, tilting his head to one side. "I think yes, since I doubt anything less will serve. I have noticed in you, my dear, a lamentable preoccupation with our Colonel Farrell. I saw signs that you had come to regret the impulsive way you left him, signs that you might be inclined to use young Michael to further a return to your old relationship, now that Walker is finished. I couldn't allow that."

"A man has the right to know he has a son!" she defended herself.

"You could have written him a note," Neville said dryly. "But that would have had none of the force of a personal confrontation, would it? It would be harder for a man to ignore the natural duty of caring for the child, and perhaps its mother, if he was face to face with them?"

"I find your suggestion contemptible," she declared. "I have no need for a man to care for me."

"That may be. Deny, if you can, however, that you have no need for a man—"

Eleanora lifted her chin, aware of the flare of lust in Neville's eyes. "You are being deliberately offensive."

"Am I? It's no more than the truth. I thought these last few months that you were beginning to see me as a fair substitute for your precious colonel. I thought, until

Colonel Grant Farrell came back, that you and I might throw in our lot together. We would make a good team. With your beauty and my brains we could turn that pittance you got from Luis into a fortune. We could live like royalty, move in the first circles in the East and in Europe. If you would let yourself, you could learn to care for me, I think. In the meantime, what I feel for you will be more than enough to carry us through."

"I don't—"

"No, wait! I'm not suggesting anything in the least underhanded. I want to take care of you, to marry you. I'm asking you to be my wife."

Eleanora stared at him, her green gaze level; her tone when she spoke at last was scathing in its contempt. "You are the most arrogant, conceited, viciously immoral man I have ever met! You contrived to have my brother and me arrested on charges that could have led to death; you allowed men who had been your friends to go to the firing squad when you could have saved them; you lied to me, blackmailed me; kept the knowledge of my brother's suicide from me in order to arrange a political murder, and yet you expect me to entrust my fortune and myself to your tender care? You must think me the most stupid woman alive! I thought more of your intelligence. I thought you realized that all I wanted of you was the information you could give me about Walker and the Phalanx. If you thought anything else, if you have been staving off your creditors with the expectation of having my fortune at your disposal, then I am sorry for you. I recommend that you leave town before you are found out. There is nothing to be gained by lingering, I promise you!"

He smiled, a cynical twist of the lips that left his eyes cold. "That is your pride speaking. Women, in our society, have an awkward time of it alone, especially a woman like you. In time you will reconsider, and when you do, I will be waiting—impatiently."

He had moved gradually nearer as he spoke. With the last word he reached for her, grasping her shoulders to drag her against his chest. His fingers caught the back of her neck, forcing her face up, and his lips came down, devouring hers. He wrapped one arm about her waist, and with his free hand explored the curves beneath the softness of her lawn gown.

Shuddering in disgust, Eleanora brought her hand up with the fingers curled, ripping at his face with her nails. As his hold loosened, she tore herself away and grasping at the mantle, tugged hard at the tasseled bell pull which hung beside it.

Neville drew himself up. Taking out a handkerchief, he put it to his face. "If it wasn't for your houseful of servants, I would teach you a few things about yourself."

"Would you?" Eleanora asked, looking up from straightening the frill at the neck of her gown, and running a hand over her hair. "Pretty behavior for a gentleman. I wonder who taught you, unless it was Niña Maria? I'm persuaded the two of you were well suited.

"She at least had sense enough to know how to pick a winner. I expect she is queening it in León at this very moment."

"I wish her joy of her victory," Eleanora said, her lip curling, "and of you, if you should decide to join her."

"Maybe I will," he told her, adjusting the cuffs of his shirt below his coat sleeves, "if I don't hear from you within the week. It may help you to make up your mind once and for all if I tell you that your colonel has followed his gallant leader to Memphis, so there's little chance of him coming to heel."

The opening of the door prevented Eleanora from replying, though the glacial look in her green eyes was sufficient to blast the hopes of a less egotistic man.

The butler had Neville's beaver hat in his hand. Taking it, Neville threw a last look at Eleanora, a look of hate and frustration and whetted desire. "I can see myself out," he said shortly, and slapping his hat on his head, strode from the room.

Memphis, Louisville, Cincinnati, Washington, New York; it was possible to trace Grant's whereabouts with Walker through the news sheets. Uncle Billy was greeted everywhere with acclamation. At Wallack's Theater in New York his arrival was marked by the band playing "Hail Columbia," and he was forced to make a speech from his box. He was in that city for the touching reunion with the remnants of his army as his men straggled in from Panama.

Not everyone looked on him with favor, however. His complaints about Commander Davis were ill-received in some quarters. In addition, Vanderbilt had no time to exchange either compliments or recriminations with him, and his pleas for a meeting with President Buchanan were ignored. Before long he turned toward the more receptive climate of the South again, moving his entourage to Charleston.

Eleanora, for her own self-respect, did not sit around and mope. This was due largely to the effort of Colonel Thomas Henry to get himself killed. Deep in drink and boredom, he had entered into a bet with Major Joe Howell, a sometime friend, sometime enemy, sometime opponent in fisticuffs, sometime drinking companion. The bet over the fighting prowess of a couple of newsboys had ended unsatisfactorily and the ensuing argument had turned into a duel in which Colonel Henry was the injured party. Laid on his bed with a hole in his arm and another in his abdomen, he had cursed the doctor chosen to minister to him and sent for Eleanora. When he was able to be moved, she had had him brought to her house and put into one of the best bedchambers.

A great favorite with his men, the colonel drew visitors like flies, many of them men of the phalanx who had chosen to land at New Orleans from Panama. Eleanora's house became a mecca for the men who, by and large, rightly or wrongly, considered themselves legal citizens of the Republic of Nicaragua. A few of them had small hurts which they brought to her, but for the most part they needed only feeding, a place to sleep for a day or two, a small stake on which to return to their homes. Eleanora, with some understanding of what it meant to be tired in body and soul with no money, no food, and nowhere to go, was glad to do what she could. She was treated at all times with the greatest of respect, perhaps because of the presence of her servants and the bull-like Colonel Henry, perhaps because of something within herself. She could not begin to think what tales must be going around the city concerning the constant stream of men passing in and out of her house, and she could not bring herself to care. Let them think what they would.

Toward the last days of August, the number of men who came began to drop off. One by one the familiar faces disappeared; one of the last ones to go was a tow-headed boy with a soft country accent, the boy who had defended her the day she was arrested in the hospital. He came to say thank you, to wish her happiness and tell her he was going home to a small farm in the back-hill country of northern Louisiana, a farm he hoped he would never have to leave again. By the middle of September they were all gone except for Colonel Henry. Soon she would be alone again.

Not quite, of course. She had Michael. Michael, with his fine black hair, skin which looked to be permanently sunburned, and eyes as brown and shining as chestnuts. At five months he was a good child, seldom crying except when he was hungry or wet, though he was just the least bit spoiled from all the attention he had received from the men who could not resist picking him up from his pallet in the courtyard when they found him there.

Eleanora, kneeling on the pallet in a billow of skirts, told him so in fond accents as she changed him one mellow September afternoon. There was a feeling of autumn in the air. The leaves were falling from the trees around the city. A drift of pin oak leaves from a nearby court-yard had landed on the pallet, and she removed one of them from the baby's determinedly clenched fist before propping him back upon his pillows. He was learning to sit alone, and could do so by himself for several minutes at a time, holding the position by sheer will power exercised with the most humorous look of total concentra-tion. She had sat him up, holding both hands out to catch him if he fell, her lips curved in a fond maternal smile, when a sound caught her attention.

She had heard no bell. Looking up, she half expected to see Colonel Henry or perhaps her old nurse coming to take Michael for his nap. The man she saw instead was Grant, and beside him, a white-haired gentleman of noble bearing whom she recognized immediately as Don Esteban, the Conde de Laredo.

Something grim in the features of the two men sent alarm coursing along her veins. Her first reaction was instinctive. With a swooping reach, she picked Michael up and held him against her. The child in her arms, she struggled to her feet, hampered by his weight and the treacherous width of her full skirt. In the surprise and unreasoning agitation of the moment she abandoned preliminaries. "How did you get in?" she demanded. "And what do you want?"

It was Don Esteban who answered. "As to how we got in, a gentleman who was just leaving informed us where we could find you and assured us of a welcome. What do I want? You must know, señora, that I have come for my grandnephew, the new Conde."

Eleanora glanced at Grant. His face betrayed no expression, he seemed not to have heard as he studied the face of his son with every appearance of no more than dispassionate interest. Steadying her voice with an effort, she said, "You have been misinformed."

"I think not, señora. I have in my possession a copy of the baptismal record of this child. I have been in correspondence with your paramour, a man named Crawford. He dared to send the copy to me along with the threat of exposing the birth if I did not pay him blackmail money. The pair of you mistook your man, I fear. I would never usurp the place of the rightful heir to the title. I am convinced, however, that you are not a fit person to have the custody of a child of such importance, if you would consent to let him be used in such a manner. Therefore, I have come to take him with me back to Spain. You can fight it, of course—I would not expect otherwise considering the fortune at stake—but that fortune can and will be used against you—"

"One moment," Eleanora interrupted, her voice hard in her efforts to keep it from trembling. "I know nothing of such a threat. I deny completely ever having a part in it. Why should I blackmail you if I have such proof of my child's birth? Why not claim the title with the money, the exalted position of dowager Condesa, and

370

the guardianship of the estates which goes with it? Why would I settle for less—unless this child was not your grandnephew?"

"The baptismal certificate—?"

"A subterfuge, to keep from branding my child a bastard," she said, uncaring of her choice of words as long as they had the required effect.

"You are saying your child is illegitimate, fathered after the death of my nephew? This I cannot believe of you. My reading of your character—"

"I am sorry that you have traveled so far on a useless errand. I am sorry that I cannot gratify you by claiming a relationship with you for my son, but my child was not fathered by Luis de Laredo."

The old man shook his head. "I think perhaps you were afraid the child would be taken out of your hands if you claimed the title. I think you thought, you and this Señor Crawford, that you could keep the child and bleed the estate, having your cake and eating it too, as the English say."

"You must make up your mind, Don Esteban, whether you consider me an overprotective mother or a monster who would let her child be used as the pawn of a blackmailer. You can't have it both ways."

"Perhaps not," the old man said with dignity, "but I must ask you to reveal to me the father of this child, the man to whom you turned so soon after wedding and being widowed. I feel you owe me this much proof of good faith."

Involuntarily Eleanora looked at Grant, half expecting him to claim parentage. He gazed back at her, his face still. She could not tell what he was thinking behind the deep, fathomless blue of his eyes, anymore than she ever could. It was odd that he was content to let Don Esteban be her inquisitor, but then, it would not have been like him to hurl accusations at her in company with any man. Alone perhaps, but not with another. The baby held close against her, sensing the tension around him, began to fret.

It was a third man who answered the request hanging in the breathless silence. "I don't like the question," Colonel Thomas Henry said with grating deliberation, "and I'm of the mind that the lady don't like it either. Furthermore, I'm plumb staggered that either one of you yahoos could stand up there and put it to an angel like our Miss Eleanora here. I've a good mind to take exception to you both, call you out, that's the ticket! 'Cept I'm sorta given to think maybe I have a few things to say that might shed a little lamplight on this subject. Yes, sir, I'm mighty glad I decided to come back here and find out whether Miss Eleanora wanted to see you two buzzards, instead of ambling down to Halfway House for a drink, cause I got me something I want the both of you to give a real good listen to."

Colonel Henry moved into the courtyard as he spoke, choosing the stone wall near the vine-shaded arbor in which the baby's pallet had lain for his support. His left arm he held close to his body and he walked with a slightly bent-over posture, but he was beginning to regain a healthy color. With his great stamina he would be able to return to whatever duty called him within a fortnight at most.

Settled, he began. "It's like this. I been going down to Halfway House about this time every evening for the last week or so; sorta to give Miss Eleanora a spell of relief from my ugly face. I saw this fellow Crawford in the place several times. Couple of days ago I heard him mention Miss Eleanora's name. We got to talking and drinking, and drinking and talking, and the more Crawford drank the bigger brag he made and the worse threats. He said he was either going to make a haul big enough to live high as a lord on, or else he was going to get even with Miss Eleanora for throwing him out of her house. Fuming mad he was because she wouldn't have anything to do with 'im anyway he asked, including parson's noose, and because he had wasted months on end hanging about her, waiting for her to come around. Said as how she was mighty fond of that brat of hers, beg pardon, ma'am, and she'd be sorry when she lost him to his rich relatives in Spain. He said a lot more, laid his tongue to more cuss words than an uneducated man like me ever heard, but I figured I could still teach him a lesson in manners. Did too, out back. Only thing, I'm 'feared he was so drunk it might not have took. He was back again last night. I expect he'll be back this evening, too—if a man was to want to find him."

As Colonel Henry finished his tale, he stared hard at Grant, an obvious message in his eyes.

Grant turned to Eleanora, the lines about his mouth stern. "That's the way it was?"

The resonance of his voice vibrated through her body. She nodded, unable to speak, willing him to believe her.

He said not a word. His gaze dropped to the child in her arms. Turning, he went from the courtyard with a long, determined stride. What remained with Eleanora was the look of furious concentration in his eyes. It should have; it was the same expression she had seen so often on her son's face.

Colonel Henry did not tarry. "Excuse me, ma'am," he said, hurrying after Grant.

"Where are you going?" she cried in exasperation.

"To the fight, of course. I wouldn't miss it for a Morgan horse and a new pair of Navy Colts!"

"Señora?" Don Esteban asked in bewilderment.

"I'm afraid," Eleanora replied, a wan smile on her lips, "that Colonel Farrell has gone to meet Mr. Crawford on that bloody battleground, littered with pride, they call the field of honor."

"Ah, a duel, I apprehend?" he inquired.

"More on the order, I think, of a chastisement," she replied, such a distant look in her eye that he bowed and said no more on the subject.

Michael chose that moment to register a vehement protest to the tightness with which he was being clasped. Recalled to her duties, Eleanora looked about, and seeing her nursemaid hovering near the bedchamber door, motioned for her, and gave the baby into her keeping. Turning to Don Esteban, she invited him to join her for coffee. Not that she cared for anything in the way of refreshment. She had the idea, looking at the elderly man's face, that he had something he wished to say to her. Listening to it over coffee or ratafia would pass the time until she might learn what had occurred between Grant and Neville.

"I thank you, no," Don Esteban surprised her by saying. "You are most kind to ask, after my conduct—or want of it. Your friend was quite right, I am in need of a lesson in manners. I feel justly rebuked for letting my sense of responsibility to the estate overcome my feeling for what is proper, especially when the person concerned is a lady."

It was a handsome apology. Eleanora could be no less generous. "I am certain that if my son had indeed been the heir, I would be most appreciative of your zeal and the selfless spirit which led you to seek him out. There are not many men who would not have kept the crest for themselves, regardless of the cost. It is good to know Luis has such a worthy successor."

"You flatter me, señora. My one hope is that I may have repaid some of the harm I have done by bringing Colonel Farrell with me today. You see, I am staying at the St. Charles, where former President Walker and the colonel checked in only a few hours ago. Naturally, I made inquiries of Señor Walker, since this Crawford had been one of his men and I wished to know the scoundrel with whom I was dealing. In the ensuing conversation, the nature of my business was made plain, and the colonel became greatly interested." Don Esteban glanced at her diffidently. "I seem to recall that in Granada I found you in the palacio belonging to this man, Farrell. Now he goes angrily away to punish this Crawford for his perfidy." He touched a hand to his small, pointed beard. "The thing explains itself."

A few more compliments, a final apology and expression of regret, a wish for good fortune, a last bow, and the man who was the rightful and only true Conde de Laredo was gone.

Eleanora could not help thinking that she might have been more gracious, more attentive to his farewells. He had traveled a long and weary way for nothing. She knew he was already staying at the St. Charles from what he said, but she still might have offered him the hospitality of the house, for Luis's sake, if for no other reason.

It was no use repining. The opportunity was past, and

in any case, she knew that such considerations were no more than a defense against thinking, against picturing Grant dead on the sawdust floor of a barroom. She had few illusions about Neville. Survival was his specialty. He would not be a bad shot with a pistol, given a fair chance, and if there was a way to take an unfair advantage, he would not hesitate.

Waiting, waiting, pacing in thought-racked fear, sweeping the dust from the gray ballast-stone flooring of the court, seemed her fate. It had been the only recourse of women for countless generations, stretching back to the beginning of wars, and of hate and revenge.

Or was it? She had defied convention in all else, why should this be an exception?

In sudden determination she swung about, calling across to the servant quarters, which opened onto the courtyard, to have her carriage made ready. Hurrying upstairs, she cut short her nurse's exclamations and instinctive protests, merely telling her where she was going. Gloves, bonnet, lightweight cloak to cover her gown, and she was ready. Her coachman was unconscionably slow, but at last the victoria was brought out. She climbed in without waiting for assistance, and they were off, swinging into the quiet and sunlit streets.

Halfway House was so named because it lay at the end of Canal Street, halfway between the Mississippi River and Lake Pontchartrain. A popular saloon and hostelry with the rougher American element in New Orleans, it boasted a stretch of field in the back bounded only by woods on either side that was perfect for engagements of a sanguinary nature. It was here that Colonel Henry and Major Howell had met. Eleanora had heard of the place in detail during the convalescence of Colonel Henry.

She arrived before the unprepossessing building of a uniform gray hue in time to see men streaming toward the rear of the saloon. They were laughing and shouting at each other with all the gleeful anticipation of children at a circus. She did not need to hear their cries of "Fight!" and "Shootout!" to guess their destination. Alighting from her carriage, she followed them, aware only vaguely of her coachman wrapping the reins around the brake and climbing down to trail protectively behind her.

She saw them the instant she rounded the corner, two tall men, Grant in his uniform, the buttons like flashing targets, Neville in white shirt, white breeches, and a black alpaca coat. They stood facing each other at ten paces, their revolvers held loosely at their sides. To one side, distinct from the crowd of nearly a hundred spectators, stood Colonel Henry and another man she did not know, obviously acting as seconds, and a young gentleman with a drink in his hand and a doctor's kit at his feet, the surgeon in attendance. As she approached, Colonel Henry was saying, "Your guns are fully loaded. You may fire at will when the signal is given, understood?"

Both men nodded. Quiet descended.

"Ready!"

"Fire!"

With an indrawn breath, Eleanora closed her eyes as the guns exploded simultaneously. When she opened them Grant stood unscathed. Neville was holding his left forearm.

"That," Grant said quietly, "is for Luis, for letting him go to the firing squad when you had been sent to save him."

Neville, his face contorted, lifted his gun. Shots rang out again. A rapidly widening red spot appeared on the white of Neville's breeches.

"That was for Jean-Paul, the boy you left to kill himself," Grant explained, his voice implacable. Blood was trickling from his ear lobe, but he seemed not to feel it.

An extraordinary hush held the crowd now as they realized they were watching no common meeting. Neville, giving a little to his hurts, stared at Grant. At the back of his eyes lurked a primitive fear, a fear that made him lift his gun again, saying through gritted teeth, "Be damned to you, Farrell!"

His shot kicked up dirt at Grant's feet. Grant's bullet took him in the fleshy part of the other thigh, sending him staggering back several steps.

His voice expressionless, Grant said, "For Walker, and your coward's attempt on his life."

"Bastard!" Neville screamed, wavering. Whether from a reflex action or another try at killing his opponent, his fingers squeezed off a shot.

"And this one," Grant said, raising his gun, "is for trying to sell my son's birthright."

Neville dropped his gun, as the last bullet passed through his right arm, falling forward to measure his length on the green, clover-strewn grass. Grant stared down at him, his face grim, then slowly he turned his back and started to walk away.

The man on the ground was alive, thrashing, it appeared, in pain. The doctor, his face white, made a move to go to him, waving forward one of two others with a suggestion that they carry Neville into the house.

And then a man hollered, "Look out! He's going to shoot!"

Neville, writhing on the ground, had retrieved his gun. Holding it with both shaking hands, he had it pointed at Grant's broad back.

Colonel Henry, who had fallen into step with Grant, gave him a push, tearing the revolver from his hand. Thumbing back the hammer, the veteran soldier fired.

Men scattered in all directions, uncertain in the confusion of who was firing and where. When Eleanora could see again, Neville lay still upon the ground. The gun had fallen from his lax fingers, his eyes were open, staring. He would have no need for the services of the doctor.

Eleanora sat in her darkened bedchamber. The last rays of the setting sun poured orange light into the courtyard but it did not penetrate this shuttered room. That was the way she wanted it. When she had returned the baby was crying for her. Now he slept, replete, against her breast as she rocked in a high-back chair ordered especially for that purpose from Boston. She should lay Michael in his cradle and think of dressing for dinner, but she could not bring herself to do it. There was such sweet consolation in sitting with her cheek resting on Michael's head, not thinking. No, not thinking.

She had no wish to remember Grant standing, oblivious to Neville's firing, placing his shots with a marksman's care, no wish to recall the words with which he had claimed his son, or to bring to mind that harrowing moment when she thought he would be killed. How she had arrived home she did not know, except she had an uncertain memory of being led back to the victoria, probably by her coachman. She was not sorry she had gone. It would have been unendurable to be still waiting here, unknowing, after all this time. But if she had never known how close Grant had come to death, she would not have this trembling deep inside, or the press against her eyes of incipient tears.

A commotion in the courtyard below drew her attention. It sounded like a domestic upheaval of some kind, one of the stable cats caught sneaking into the kitchen no doubt, or something similar. At the sound of footsteps, more than one set, on the stairs, she looked toward the door, annoyed that anyone should come for her to settle a crisis at this time, or that they would be so noisy about it. Then, making out the voice of her nurse from the babble, she began to be alarmed.

"Here, you can't go in there, m'sieur," the old woman said. Hard on her words the bedchamber door swung open and Grant walked in.

Behind him was ranged the butler, caught in his shirt sleeves, the coachman, the scullery maid, and the nurse.

"I'm sorry, madame," the old woman said, speaking for all of them. "This one, he came through the servants' door in the back of the court. We could not stop him. Shall I send for the *gendarmes?*"

"No, no, thank you," Eleanora said, finding her tongue. "It will be all right. You can go, all of you."

They did not like it. The nurse, with the liberty of an old family servant, lingered after the others had moved off. "He's a heathen, mam'zelle. I will stay, me, until I can see him out of the house."

"That won't be necessary," Eleanora said gently. "You see, this man is Michael's father."

It was not possible for the old woman to have cared for Eleanora through childbirth, and the long months that preceded and followed it, without learning what had happened to her. She understood at once. With a softly

378

murmured, "Pardon, mam'zelle," she reached out to catch the door, closing it carefully before she shuffled away.

There were some grounds for her nurse thinking Grant a heathen, Eleanora admitted as she regarded him. His uniform was gone. In its place he wore buckskin breeches, a leather shirt with fringed seams, and about the crown of his campaign hat, instead of the regulation band, the skin of a rattlesnake. His Navy revolver was in a holster at his waist and he carried a rifle in his hand.

"I didn't mean to disturb you," he said, standing stiffly erect by the door. "I thought I would slip in while you were at dinner. I see I should have come to the front door. You're well protected."

"Yes. Would you—mind lighting a lamp?" she asked, irritated with herself for the nervous tremor in her voice.

The outline of a lamp was visible on the dressing table. He crossed to it, propping his rifle against the bed, snatching his hat off as an afterthought, to hang on the barrel. As he replaced the globe over the flame, he surveyed the room quietly with his eyes, noting the four-poster with its canopy and hangings in sea-green brocade looped with pale-green mosquito netting, the rosewood washstand and dressing table with silver-back mirrors, the soft oriental rug underfoot.

"Not much like Nicaragua," he commented, a wry smile moving over his face.

"No," she answered bluntly, adding, "If you didn't want to see me, why did you come?"

"Not for the reason you think," he answered, his ironic gaze on her arms, which had unconsciously tightened around the sleeping baby. "I came to say good-bye to my son."

"Good-bye? Where are you going?"

"To Texas. There's a place out there with my name on it in the Rio Grande Valley. It was bought with my mother's money with the understanding that it would revert to her children, that is to me, when the man she married died. I found news of his death waiting for me when I reached New Orleans this morning. There's nothing to keep me from going back now."

"Not even William Walker?" she asked quietly.

Grant shook his head. "Uncle Billy lost his hold on me over a year ago. I think you know the circumstances. I served this past year of hell as the price of loyalty, served until the dream was over. Nicaragua is lost now, over and done with. It's time to start over somewhere else, only Walker won't admit it. He'll never admit it until he kneels before a firing squad. That's how strong his vision is within him."

"I'm sorry I could not be there for the end of it," Eleanora said, dropping her gaze to the tops of Grant's boots.

"I'm not," he told her, his voice harsh. "I didn't know where you were, but that was better, a thousand times better, than worrying about you getting hit by a shell at Granada or working with the sick and wounded during the siege. You heard about Mazie—"

Eleanora nodded her head quickly. After a moment, she asked, smoothing her cheek over the fine hair on the top of Michael's head, "Would it have mattered so much, if it had been me, instead of Mazie?"

"Mattered?" he said in a strange voice, his dark eyes resting on the rose flush of her cheeks. "No more than losing my heart and soul. You are the beat of my blood and the air I breathe. You are my greatest strength and most feared weakness; the only joy I have found, and the only pain. I love you, Eleanora."

She had left Grant so many months before out of pride and fear and shame. She had no need for pride as long as he loved her. Her fear had been that he would grow to hate her for forcing him to choose between her and his loyalty to William Walker and the phalanx. That specter need trouble her no longer. The shame of her betrayal she had paid for with the anguish of leaving the man she loved, of bearing his child in solitude, expecting daily to hear that he had been killed in the hot and brutal country she had left. Wasn't that enough?

The gold flecks were bright in her green eyes as she raised them to Grant's. "Would you consider—taking me and Michael with you—wherever you go?"

"Take you with me? What about all this?" he asked

slowly, indicating the house and its furnishings, "and what of the damnable money Luis left to you?"

"The house I would like to keep as my own, a place to come to when we are in need of civilization. The servants are free men and women of color hired for a wage—except for Michael's nurse, who will have to come with us, I'm afraid."

"The three of you?"

She nodded meekly. "As for the money, I seem to have squandered it in a remarkably short time—"

"You needn't think you can fool me," he said, lifting one eyebrow. "Henry told me what you have been doing for the men coming home from Nicaragua."

"They were all so hungry—"

"I know," he answered shortly. "Are you certain that's all? No walking, wounded, or stray cats or—"

"I forgot Colonel Henry!" she exclaimed.

"To the devil with Henry. He can find himself another nurse—and another bivouac, for that matter."

"Oh, Grant," she said, her eyes unaccountably filling with tears.

Coming toward her, he dropped to one knee beside her chair. "All right, if it means so much to you, Henry can come too," he said.

"It's not that," she said, smiling, "It's just that I've loved you so long, and I was so afraid."

"Of what?" he asked, gently touching the tears that stood like jewels on her cheeks.

"That you wouldn't want me—that you wouldn't believe that my child was your son."

"I will always want you," he said, his eyes steady upon hers. "I will keep you near me all the days of my life if you will let me—and if you can bear to be wed to a man of Indian blood."

"I can think of nothing I would like more," she answered, pronouncing the words with grave emphasis.

The expression in his eyes held the warmth of a caress before he glanced down at Michael in her arms, awakened by their voices, staring at Grant with solemn curiosity. Tucking his forefinger into the baby's small hand, he said, "As for this being my child, you never had the

381

honor of meeting the Apache chief, Running Wild Horse. If you had, you would know I could never deny his great-grandson."

The baby, unimpressed by his illustrious ancestor, unerringly carried the finger in his grasp to his mouth. Tasting the salt of his mother's tears upon the calloused tip, he gnawed hungrily at it with the two teeth just breaking the surface of his gums.

Grant winced, though he made no move to retrieve his finger. Looking up at Eleanora, he said with a crooked smile, "For such a fierce little warrior, I think the only place is Texas."

Afterword

Although *The Notorious Angel* is fiction, William Walker was a real historical personality, one of the most fascinating, if little known, in the era in which he lived. His campaign in Nicaragua, along with his early life and his attempt to annex Lower California, occurred substantially as given. His determination to fulfill what he conceived to be his destiny in Nicaragua did not end with his initial defeat by the Central American coalition. He mounted four additional expeditions to Nicaragua between 1857 and 1860. On his second try, he was stopped and turned back by Commodore Hiram Paulding of the American steam frigate *Wabash,* who was acting on the orders of President Buchanan. On his third and fourth attempts, he failed to make a landing due to storms at sea and other adverse circumstances. The fifth try in August of 1860 was more successful. He landed in Honduras and proceeded to capture the fortress of Truxillo, the first step in a plan to make the Honduran island of Roatan a base from which to launch his attack on Nicaragua. This was a mistake. Truxillo, being mortgaged to the British government due to a debt, came under the protection of Great Britain. On August 19 the British sloop-of-war *Icarus,* under Naval Commander Norvell Salmon, entered the harbor. Training the ship's guns upon the fortress, Commander Salmon ordered Walker to surrender.

Walker, playing for time, put off his answer until nightfall. Under cover of darkness, he abandoned the fort and his wounded, including Colonel Thomas Henry, who died a few days later of his injuries. Walker marched overland, driving off his Honduran pursuers, and turned toward the coast. His escape was cut off, however, at the Rio Negro by the *Icarus* and a schooner bearing two hundred and fifty Honduran reinforcements. In the face of overwhelming odds, Walker surrendered once more on being assured of safe conduct for his men and himself. They returned to Truxillo where Commander Salmon, violating his given word, gave Walker into the hands of the Hondurans. After a fiasco of a trial, held on September 11, 1860, William Walker was sentenced to be shot. The sentence was carried out at daybreak of the following morning.

In the decade after Walker's death, the Nicaraguan transit route was owned by a series of different companies. The continuing political upheaval within the country made profitable operation of the route impossible. The route, as the single asset of value in the country, was seized and resold at each change of government. Due to the constant interruption of service and resulting lack of reliability, the route never regained its competitive position with the Panama passage. The completion of the transcontinental railroad, assuring fast and inexpensive transportation from the Atlantic coast to the Pacific, effectively sealed the doom of the Nicaraguan transit route. It ceased official operation in 1868. Fifty years later there was some revival of interest in the transit route at the time of the discussion of the best location for the construction of an interoceanic canal. In the end Panama was selected and the Nicaraguan route sank back into obscurity.

For those who are interested in such details, the real people other than William Walker in *The Notorious Angel* were the New Orleans recruiting agent, Thomas Fisher; Colonel Thomas Henry; his opponent in the duel in New Orleans, Major Joe Howell (the brother of Varina Howell Davis, second wife of Jefferson Davis) and, of course, Cornelius Vanderbilt. All others are fictional. The characters of Mazie Brentwood and, to some extent, Eleanora, were based on a passing reference found in my research to a true heroine of the Nicaraguan campaign, Mrs. Edward Bingham. The wife of an invalid actor, she came with her husband and children to take up one of the land grants issued by Walker to American settlers. She won the deepest gratitude of the soldiers of the Phalanx for her services in the military hospital at Granada. During the siege of Guadaloupe Church, she ministered unceasingly to the sick and injured until, tired and weak, she succumbed to cholera.

Patricia Maxwell